Prais

'Unabashedly romantic ... no
infused with Mediterra

'I loved this wonderful ... and mysterious
family secrets . . . completely beguiling and beautifully told'
Kate Furnivall

'This wonderful family saga has it all: the irresistible tempta-
tions of a love long-denied, burgeoning secrets from the past.
The gorgeous background of the Italian Riviera. A perfect
summer read' Rachel Hore

'A beautifully crafted slice of escapist fiction' *Heat*

'The ultimate feel-good read, perfect for fans of Santa Mon-
tefiore, Victoria Hislop and Leah Fleming' *Candis*

'Impeccably researched and deftly written' Kathryn Hughes

'A great page-turner' Lucinda Riley

'I loved the sultry sensuous feeling . . . a fascinating story with
engaging themes' Dinah Jefferies

'Romantic, escapist and mouth-watering . . . everything you
could wish for in a summer read' Veronica Henry

'Holiday Romance at its most evocative and escapist' *The Lady*

'A gorgeous, mouth-watering dream of a holiday read!' *Red*

'A glorious read that feels like a summer holiday in a book'
People's Friend

'A wonderfully relaxing sun lounger read' *Sunday Express*

Rosanna Ley works as a creative tutor and has written many articles and stories for national magazines. Her writing holidays and retreats take place in stunning locations in Spain and Italy. When she is not travelling, Rosanna lives in West Dorset by the sea.

Also by Rosanna Ley

The Villa

Bay of Secrets

Return to Mandalay

The Saffron Trail

Last Dance in Havana

The Little Theatre by the Sea

Her Mother's Secret

The Lemon Tree Hotel

ROSANNA LEY

From Venice with Love

Quercus

First published in Great Britain in 2020 by Quercus
This paperback edition published in 2020 by

Quercus Editions Ltd
Carmelite House
50 Victoria Embankment
London EC4Y 0DZ

An Hachette UK company

A CIP catalogue record for this book is available
from the British Library

PB ISBN 978 1 78747 629 5
EB ISBN 978 1 78747 630 1

10 9 8 7 6 5 4 3 2 1

Typeset by CC Book Production
Printed and bound in Great Britain by Clays Ltd, Elcograf S.p.A.

MIX
Paper from
responsible sources
FSC® C104740

Papers used by Quercus are from well-managed forests and other responsible sources.

For Grey: research photographer extraordinaire

The First Bridge

CHAPTER I

Joanna

London

Joanna was hardly aware of the train leaving Waterloo station. She supposed she was in shock – if shock was the right word for what she was feeling. She'd known as soon as she walked in the door of their Victorian terrace in Crouch End that something was wrong. It was in the atmosphere, lying in wait, and although it was only four in the afternoon, Martin was home.

'Do you want a cup of tea?' he'd asked her from the kitchen. His voice had sounded different from usual too – and not in a good way.

Joanna had felt the first shiver of foreboding.

Now, sitting in the train carriage, she let out a small noise that sounded a bit like a choked sob and the man at the table seat opposite her inched slightly away. Joanna couldn't blame him. No one needed to be landed with a hysterical woman at their table when all they wanted to do was read the evening paper on the train.

'Or maybe a drink?' Martin had called through to her. Which was even more worrying.

Joanna had put her bag down in the hall. 'It's a bit early, isn't it?' she'd said. And then he'd come to stand in the kitchen doorway and she'd caught his expression; noted the evasiveness in his pale blue eyes, a hint of guilt or regret, and . . .

She stared out of the train window at the tall office blocks and cranes as they passed by. More building, always more building. Where she was going, there would be no tall office blocks or tenement buildings. Where she was going, there would be green fields with grazing sheep and the acid yellow of rapeseed lined with dark blackthorn bushes.

'I've got something I need to tell you, Jo,' Martin had said.

She took a deep and steadying breath. 'Go on then.'

They had been married for ten years. They hadn't had children because of Joanna's career as a freelance journalist, because Martin had kept saying they should wait a bit longer, and because . . . it had never happened. They lived together in this skinny terraced house bought before house prices in the city rocketed and they had always been happy enough. Well, hadn't they? And what did it mean, 'happy enough'? she pondered. It definitely seemed to suggest something lacking.

There were more houses now that they were pulling into Clapham Junction and also more trees, already touched with the reds and yellows of early autumn. Joanna sniffed loudly and the man opposite glanced at her briefly over the top of his newspaper. Checking she was still keeping it together, probably. And she was – just.

'The thing is . . . I've been seeing someone else,' Martin told her.

Joanna stared at him, waiting for more information, waiting

4

for this, the only piece of information that really mattered, to sink in.

'I feel terrible,' he said. He tore his fingers through his fair hair in a familiar gesture. 'So guilty. So angry with myself. I can't sleep, you've got no idea.'

Was she supposed to feel sorry for him? The anger flooded through her, a release. 'Why?' she managed to say. Wasn't she enough for him, was that it? Didn't he love her anymore? But the word emerged strangely devoid of emotion. He was right – she'd had no idea.

'I couldn't help myself,' Martin muttered. 'She was just there, throwing herself at me and you . . .'

Ah, she thought. *Here we go then. The double-pronged defence.* She (whoever she might be) had thrown herself at Martin, poor defenceless lamb that he was, while Joanna . . . Joanna was always too busy, too tired, too distant to give him what he wanted. He was a man, wasn't he? Who could blame him for succumbing?

Joanna could. 'Who?' Perhaps from now on, she would only be capable of one-syllable questions.

He took a step towards her and she took a step back. A dance of betrayal, she found herself thinking.

'It's come to a head.' Martin was answering a different question. 'Oh, God, now that Brian—'

'Hilary,' said Joanna. Her thoughts flitted back to that awful dinner party with Martin's colleague Brian and Hilary, his wife, whose breathy voice set Joanna's nerves jangling with irritation. And now she knew why. 'Jesus, Martin.'

He looked offended. Only Martin could look offended at a time like this, she thought. 'Brian knows,' he said.

Which explained why Martin was now telling Joanna. She

5

turned away, unable to look at him anymore. 'You absolute bastard,' she said.

'Jo . . .'

The train didn't stop at Wimbledon. Opposite Joanna, the man took slurps of his coffee and when his mobile rang loudly, she didn't point out that they were sitting in the quiet zone. She felt unshed tears blocking her throat and she pushed them back down. She wouldn't cry. At least, not yet.

'How long?' Joanna asked Martin. She kept her voice strong although she was shaking inside.

'Hardly any time.' He looked away when he said this and then straight back at her so that she knew he was lying. 'I told you, it just happened, and now . . .'

'Now?' What was he saying? Was he leaving her? Did she want him to leave?

He grabbed her arm. 'Admit it, Jo. It's been a while since you and I . . . We have to face it. Maybe we've just grown apart.'

She shook him off. That stung. He was right, it had been a while. But had they grown that far apart?

It was leafier when the train passed through Weybridge and then stopped at Woking, although some of the leaves were already falling, horse chestnuts on the ground wrapped in green spiky jackets. Joanna glanced at her watch. They had been travelling for less than half an hour. There were more people milling on the platform here and the coffee shop was full. The man opposite had finished his phone conversation and when the refreshment trolley passed by, he ordered a packet of crisps in an authoritative voice that made Joanna wish she'd sat somewhere else. She'd never been good with authority – or so Martin had always told her.

But Martin had a point when it came to growing apart.

Hadn't she been thinking the same thing – in the rare moments when she wasn't researching a story, talking to people about a story or writing up a story? She was fortunate to have work – and Toby, her editor, who had become a good friend over the years, sometimes reminded her about this, but with a wink so that she didn't have to take it too seriously. But had her work taken her away from Martin? Was Joanna guilty too – of not giving her husband the attention he needed?

She snorted loudly – as if this justified his behaviour, for goodness' sake! – and the man opposite offered her a steady look from dark brown eyes and opened his crisp packet. *Crunch. Rustle. Crunch.* She looked away.

But Martin was right, even though neither of them had openly acknowledged it before now. There was distance between them, more distance than there should be between a married couple. She had even been thinking that she should stay at home more – she'd said as much to Toby. She'd half decided to cut down on the travelling blogs, maybe even find a permanent position in-house on some magazine or newspaper that would also offer her more financial security. After all, if she could earn a bit more, then maybe she could give some to Mother and Harriet to help with the farm. It would give her more time for her marriage, it would give Joanna and Martin more time to reconnect.

Oh, she had noticed the distance all right. She and Martin were hardly still in the first heady throes of romance. But when had they stopped talking about everything? When had they stopped sharing their dreams? She couldn't even remember.

So yes, maybe she was partly to blame. Only it still stung. Because while she'd been thinking of ways to save her marriage, Martin had been breaking it into little pieces.

7

'What do you want to do, Martin?' she'd asked him.

'It's up to you,' he said.

Was it? They stared at one another. *Impasse*, she thought. *His hands on Hilary's body. Her hands on his*. She felt sick. 'Have you stopped seeing her?'

He looked away and then back at her once more. 'Yes,' he said. 'I don't want you and me to break up. I'm sorry, Jo.'

'Perhaps you should have thought about that before.' If Brian knew, then half the company where Martin worked as an accounts manager also knew. Martin had told Joanna simply because he didn't want to risk her finding out from someone else.

The knowledge filled her head. This was what was happening to her marriage. This cliché. This was how it was. The distance between Joanna and Martin had grown because someone had slipped between them. And Joanna had never even guessed.

She glanced up at the case she'd heaved onto the luggage rack of the train. She'd packed swiftly and carelessly, just wanting to get out. It was all she could think of to do. And doing might stop her from thinking, from feeling. She could have just walked straight out of the door again, but something practical and instinctive had kicked in. It was autumn. She might be away for a while. She needed different clothes, something warm to wear.

'Jo . . .' He'd followed her up to their bedroom, spread his hands. 'You won't leave me?'

'I need time to think,' she said. She looked at the bed, looked at Martin.

'No,' he said. 'No, of course not. Not here.' Once again, he came closer, reaching out, wanting some sort of instant forgiveness, she supposed. Well, instant forgiveness didn't grow on trees.

'Don't touch me,' she warned.

'But where are you going?' He was wearing the yellow shirt that she'd always thought too young for him. He wasn't quite manly enough, either, to pull off that particular shade.

'I don't know yet.'

'But you'll come back?'

She shot him a look. Did he really want her to? 'I need to think about things,' she repeated. Like, where did they go from here? She felt brittle enough to crack neatly into small squares. And Martin . . . Martin suddenly looked so helpless.

They were travelling through open countryside now. The sky was a cool grey with that pinkish shade of autumn. There were fields, a solar panel farm, dappled brown cows. Bracken cloaked the high banks above the railway line and behind this came the odd farm building and yet more fields, a tractor, some sheep.

The familiar strains of 'Daydream Believer' by The Monkees cut into her thoughts. She groped in her bag for her mobile, saw the man opposite flinch with disapproval, so allowed it to play a few more bars. She glanced at the name on the screen. 'Harriet,' she said.

'Jo?' Harriet's voice was blurred, as if she'd been crying.

'What is it, Harriet? Are you OK?' *What now?* Determinedly, she pushed the thought of Martin aside. Her sister had never been the emotional one. Was it something serious then?

'Oh, I'm busy, that's all.'

Clearly that wasn't all. But despite everything, Joanna felt a dip of nostalgia. *Busy* . . . She ignored the man sitting opposite her as he rustled his newspaper meaningfully and turned the

9

page. She thought of her father in the old days at Mulberry Farm Cottage – feeding the pigs, organising the sheep-shearing, flat cap, shirtsleeves rolled to the elbow; waltzing their mother over the flagstones of the kitchen floor. Harriet and Father shaking the branches of the spreading mulberry tree. *You're too young, Joanna. Harriet can do it*. Mother gathering mulberries from the nets with stained fingers, making sweet-sharp jam so dark red it was almost black. Joanna remembered one, two, three, alive, the hide-and-seek game she'd played with Harriet. And all the times she could never find her. Joanna's first kiss in Big Barn with Pete Painton from the year above her in school, Harriet's face when she told her . . .

She blinked away a tear. Was she thinking about the old childhood days or was she thinking about her marriage falling apart? 'Harriet . . .' *Terrible timing, Harriet.*

Of course, autumn was a busy time at Mulberry Farm Cottage with all the fruit to pick from the orchard, bottling, jam-making and all. But Harriet wasn't talking about that – didn't her sister always cope with all the work that needed to be done on the farm? So much of their land had now been sold to the neighbours. She must then be talking about their mother. Harriet sounded as if she'd just about had enough and Joanna knew exactly how she felt.

'Yes?'

'I'm on a train.'

'Oh, I see. Sorry.' Her sister's voice changed.

'And . . .' But she couldn't tell Harriet what had happened – not here on the train with this awful man sitting opposite and besides . . . She sighed. She and Harriet had never been close.

'Anyway, it's a long story,' Harriet was saying. 'But we do need to talk, Jo. We need to discuss it properly – what to do about Mother. So, whenever you get to wherever you're going, perhaps you can—'

'Yes, of course.' Joanna hadn't known where to go. She could have gone to Lucy's or maybe Steph's. She could have stayed at the house and told Martin to leave – after all, he was the one who'd done the deed. But . . .

Mulberry Farm Cottage had always nestled in a corner of her mind, never forgotten, her haven, just as the cottage itself nestled deep in the protective folds of the hills and valleys of Warren Down in West Dorset – as tatty and ramshackle now as it had once been pristine. It was a long time since it had been home in reality, but now, she felt catapulted back. She didn't want to be in London, she wanted to be sitting under the mulberry tree.

'We can talk about it when I get there,' she told Harriet.

'Get there?' Joanna could almost hear Harriet's frown.

'Can you pick me up from the station?' Joanna asked her. 'I'm on my way home.'

CHAPTER 2

Harriet

Dorset

So, Joanna was coming home. It was a bit sudden – why on earth hadn't she said? And why was she coming by train? Joanna almost always came to Dorset by car. Living in London, it was probably the only time they used the thing. Harriet sighed. Her younger sister was so selfish. It didn't occur to her that a visitor descending out of the blue meant food to prepare, a bed to make, a room to dust. Harriet peeled another potato and dropped it in the saucepan. Fortunately, beef casserole could always be stretched with more vegetables from the kitchen garden and some extra mash. But if she hadn't phoned Joanna when she did – when had her sister intended to tell her she was on her way?

Harriet heaved the saucepan onto the hob and turned her attention to the onions. Joanna would be at Axminster station in an hour, so she just had time to get the casserole into the oven and have a quick whisk round upstairs. She'd only phoned because it had all got too much for her today. She'd intended to tell her sister – at length – what had been going on with Mother. She'd meant to insist – forcibly – that something had to change. She'd wanted to knock on the door of Joanna's perfectly ordered life, she supposed, even perhaps break into it, and demand that her younger sister took some of the responsibility that weighed so heavily on her own shoulders. Instead, though, Joanna had sounded so . . . Harriet frowned as she tried to locate the word . . . vulnerable, that she stopped before she began. Plus, of course, Joanna was on the train.

Harriet peeled and sliced the onions in seconds – no crying for her – took the broom from the cupboard and gave the kitchen a quick sweep. She didn't have the time or energy to be house-proud and Joanna was family, but she owed it to her father's memory not to let things slide – things that, she supposed, included Mother. She grimaced. As for Joanna, she had always been unpredictable, but she'd never been quite this spontaneous when it came to visits home. No matter. It would be a chance for Harriet to tell her how bad things really were.

She put away the broom and shoved the ironing pile – dark, misshapen T-shirts, jeans and sweaters (Harriet's) and a paler more slippery pile of silk blouses, chiffony dresses and angora cardigans (Mother's) – into a cupboard. Out of sight, out of mind, she hoped, at least for a day or two. Mother had never been exactly a jeans and wellies sort of person, but when Father was alive, she had at least been practical – Harriet could recall her in thick winter tights and a wrap-around pinny, in cotton summer dresses and sandals, a scarf tied around her hair. Laughing.

Armed with a cloth and cleaning spray for Joanna's room, Harriet glanced into the living room as she passed by. Her mother,

13

dressed today in a voluminous white skirt and ruffled blouse of pale pink, was draped across the threadbare green sofa, eyes closed. When she woke up, Harriet would tell her that Joanna was on her way home. That should bring a smile to her face, at least.

Harriet went upstairs. Looking back over the past seven years, she couldn't pick a defining moment when their mother had changed. After Father's death she had seemed bereft, as she gradually relinquished all the household chores. At the same time, she became more eccentric, more needy, more desperate for attention. And she seemed to be getting worse, not better, as yesterday's events had proved . . .

At the top of the stairs, Harriet stuck her head round the door of Father's study. The two of them had sat here together so often: reading, talking, putting the world outside Mulberry Farm Cottage to rights. The room continued to hold his presence – Harriet would swear she could still smell his pipe tobacco, feel the rough wool of his favourite brown crew-neck sweater. She swallowed hard. How she missed him . . . The study was now Harriet's sanctuary, filled no longer by her father but by her computer. Thank God she'd bought that when there had been a bit of money spare, taught herself how to use it, arranged to get the Internet.

'What do you do on that computer?' Mother sometimes asked her. 'I really can't imagine.'

Which was a good thing. What she did was for Harriet to know and her mother never to find out. It was her secret. She'd die of embarrassment if Mother ever discovered the truth – or Joanna come to that. Or anyone.

It had become her lifeline now. She allowed herself a small smile of pleasure. *Later*, Harriet promised herself. When everyone else was safely tucked up in bed . . .

14

Next to the study were a small guest room and Joanna's bedroom; they still called it this though it was fourteen years since her sister had lived with them. Harriet went in and gave it a quick going over. The room, with its small double bed, wardrobe and old-fashioned dressing table, seemed poised, as if waiting for Joanna's return. 'She's on her way,' she told it. On the far wall, the painting of a wooden bridge in a gilt frame was in shadow. Venice. Joanna and Martin had gone there when they were first together. Harriet had never had the chance — when did she get to go away anywhere? There was always far too much to do at home.

Harriet put clean sheets on the bed and a towel on top of the covers. Of course, it would be good to see her sister, and if Joanna spent some time with their mother, it would certainly give Harriet a break, but . . . Oh, well, it was complicated. It was just that Joanna seemed to have it so easy. While Harriet . . .

On the other side of the cottage, overlooking the farmyard, were the bathroom, Harriet's bedroom and her mother's room. Harriet went in here, wrinkling her nose at the familiar smell of musty lavender cologne. She avoided looking into her mother's dressing table mirror as she passed. She knew already that she looked angry and tired, that her hair was frizzing and had premature strands of grey. She should take more care with her appearance, she supposed. But somehow everything else took over and she never quite found the time.

She crossed to the window, pulled on the sash, desperate to let some fresh air into the room. It creaked and gave under her fingers, the paintwork cracked and splintering. Below, the farmyard rested, damp and silent, but for the rooting of the pigs, the rustle of the hens bobbing in and out of Little Barn, scratching at the dusty ground. There had only been five eggs in the nesting boxes when she looked before breakfast. What was wrong with the Rhode Island Reds? OK, so the light was getting low – it was September after all – but they should go on laying well for longer. Maybe they were stressed? Why not? Everyone else was. Maybe that damn fox was hanging around again. Whatever, five eggs a day wouldn't keep them going – even with 'organic, free range' stamped on the box.

She leant out. The mulberry tree was a shroud of jagged green below, the bank of grass wet, sparse, muddy; the pond water dimmed by plant life. Harriet breathed in deeply. Fresh farmyard air. Lovely. She turned back to the room. The wardrobe door had been left open to reveal Mother's collection of dresses, a rack of elegant, old-fashioned shoes and a pair of pink fluffy mules. Harriet felt an unexpected lump in her throat. Mother never got rid of anything. She sighed as she closed the door. But if it made her happy . . .

There were some stockings on the bed. She touched them. Filmy and full of static, the nylons clung and snagged on her rough skin. Working hands. But it had been her choice – hadn't it?

Next to the nylons was her mother's cavernous black bag, which she seemed to have owned forever. Harriet remembered Mother taking it to Torquay when she and Joanna were children. Inside, it held everything they could ever need on a day out: hankies, eau de cologne, Germolene, even a flask of tea. She remembered Mother opening it with a snap, producing a precious bar of chocolate for them to share as they sat in deck-chairs on the beach. Father, his newspaper on his lap; Mother's contented smile; Harriet and Joanna with their skinny legs dangling, eager to run off to the sand, the sea.

Poking out of the bag was a slip of paper, tucked between two glossy catalogues. Harriet plucked it out. It was an invoice for servicing the boiler. She clicked her tongue. But it wasn't too bad, and after all, that old thing hadn't been serviced for years – she always just vacuumed inside and crossed her fingers. She glanced at the brochures. One was advertising neat, wall-mounted boilers and the other, luxury bathroom suites. Inside this was an estimate for central heating that took her breath away. *Ye Gods. In your dreams, Mother* . . . Harriet had missed the plumber's visit completely – she'd have to be more on the ball.

In her bid for attention, Mother had taken to phoning tradesmen, asking them to come round to give her a quote for work that needed to be done. And yes, work did need to be done, but as Harriet kept reminding her, they couldn't afford for work to be done. Mother liked to dress the part, make them tea, give them cake, have a little chat, as if she were the lady of the manor. She drew them into her web with promises, leaving Harriet to disentangle them with apologies. It might sound amusing to some. But it was becoming more of a problem with every day that went by.

Harriet shoved everything back in the bag. She'd told her mother before, *You shouldn't waste people's time. I don't like tradesmen coming to the house when I'm not around. We don't have the money* . . . But––

'What are you doing, Harriet?'

Harriet spun round. Her mother was standing in the doorway. Her fine grey hair was swept into a chignon and with her almond-shaped eyes and high cheekbones, she had an almost aristocratic air as if she were of some exotic heritage and had been dropped here on the farm accidentally. She looked as if she'd never done a day's work in her life. But she had. Harriet remembered.

'Nothing.' May as well try her mother's tactics – they worked for her. Harriet felt about twelve.

'Are you going through my things?' Sometimes, just sometimes, Audrey Shepherd at seventy-six could become the mother she had been before. The mother Harriet had respected, had tried to understand and longed to love. Now was one of those times.

'Of course not,' she said. 'I was only clearing up.'

'I would like to think,' her mother said, 'that I still have some privacy in this house.'

Even though I'm old and useless, Harriet thought.

'Even though I'm old and useless,' her mother said. 'At least in your eyes.'

Where had Harriet gone wrong with Mother? How could she tell? Harriet hadn't gone to university – unlike Joanna. She had stayed here on the farm looking after things – not only Mother, but also the hens, the pigs, the small orchard, the organic veg she sold to Bloomers restaurant and the pub, making jam and chutney for the local post office and general store, running the café she'd set up in Big Barn doing cream teas and cakes in the summer.

Why had she ever, in those far-off days, assumed it was temporary? Had she really imagined that Joanna – lucky Joanna – was going to come back to Warren Down and take over the responsibility of the place? Of course not. Her sister had always been shielded from responsibility. She had a different life to live – a working life in the city. Although it was the place in which she had grown up, Joanna knew very little about what needed to be done on a farm. Her sister hadn't made any promises, as Harriet had. She was free to do as she liked.

'Come on now, Mother,' she said. She must stay calm. What was the point in bitterness?

'Look after your mother,' he had said. 'Promise me you'll do that.'

'Yes, Father,' she had told him. 'I will.'

And she had tried. She worked hard to keep everything going, she hardly stopped.

'If you wanted to see anything in my room,' her mother said sadly, 'you only had to ask.'

Harriet crossed again to the window. Outside, the sky was pale grey, layered with silver. Were they in for more rain? She pulled the window shut and the room wrapped itself around her once more. How had it got to be this way?

Her mother was sitting on the bed looking at one of the plumber's brochures.

'Don't get upset, Mother.' Harriet sat down beside her. After Father died, so many things had changed – not just Mother. That's when Harriet had started having the dream too – the dream that haunted so many of her nights. But she wouldn't think about that now. 'I've got a nice surprise for you. Joanna's on her way.'

Her mother's eyes lit up. 'Really? Joanna's coming home?'

Harriet pushed away the demons. 'Yes, she is. Now, let's go downstairs and I'll make us a nice cup of tea before I go and pick her up from the station.'

And then Harriet would try to work out where the money for the boiler service was going to come from, she thought. How she could stop herself from feeling so trapped. How she could go on. And how much, exactly, she was going to tell Joanna.

19

CHAPTER 3

Harriet

Dorset

When Harriet pulled up outside Axminster station, she spotted her sister immediately – a lonely-looking figure with a small suitcase at her feet. And as she watched, Joanna put her hand to her hair in that gesture Harriet remembered from childhood. Nervy. So, she'd been right – something had happened.

Harriet waved at her but she seemed lost in thought. Why didn't she come over? She blasted the hooter. Joanna started.

Harriet swung open the door of the pick-up and jumped out.

'Harriet.' Joanna was smiling by the time she got near, but it didn't touch her dark eyes. She reached for Harriet's shoulders but didn't pull her in close; her kiss was merely a brush on Harriet's cheek. 'Thanks for coming to pick me up.'

'No problem.' Harriet walked round and cleared a space in the passenger side of the cab. A damp, hairy blanket, an empty bucket, a pair of black fingerless woollen gloves . . . 'Sorry it's

20

'a bit of a mess.' She chucked the blanket and the bucket into the back.

'Doesn't matter.' Joanna put her case in the back to join them.

'So, what made you decide to come down so suddenly?' Harriet leant on the driver's side of the truck.

Joanna threw her a bleak look. 'I needed a break,' she said. She opened the passenger door.

'From work?' Didn't they all need a break? Harriet certainly did.

'I just wanted a bit of peace and quiet,' Joanna elaborated, without answering the question, Harriet noted. She climbed into the cab.

Her sister was wearing pristine chocolate-coloured cords, suede ankle boots and a classy jacket Harriet hadn't seen before. London chic, she thought, didn't really go with the pick-up truck. She saw Joanna wrinkle her nose as she fastened her seat belt.

'It's a bit smelly too,' Harriet added as she got in beside her. 'Farms . . . you know.' *City girls*, she thought.

'I know.'

Harriet slammed the door to and Joanna shrank back in alarm. Well. You had to be forceful with pick-up trucks.

She started up the engine, aware of her own muddy jeans and wellies. It was difficult to imagine sometimes that she'd grown up with Joanna, that her sister had ever lived on the farm. Sometimes Joanna seemed so distant that it was hard to accept she was her sister at all. They had played together, yes, sat around the kitchen table together, even compared notes on the relative merits of the boys working on the farm. Once. But it all seemed so long ago. Now they were miles apart

– geographically and in every other way – and sometimes all Harriet could feel was resentment – that Joanna had escaped, that Joanna was free.

'Why didn't you come by car?' she asked.

'Oh . . .' Joanna was staring out of the window. 'Martin needed it. And I didn't know how long I . . .' Her voice tailed off.

Harriet shot her a look. Something was definitely up. Had her sister had a row with Martin? If so, it must have been a bad one. She put the pick-up into reverse, backed out of the parking space and headed away from the station. It had been raining and the tarmac was skiddy. No problem for the Toyota, though – at least with the four-wheel drive switched on. It drank petrol but it was a reliable beast, it clung to the road whatever.

'How's Mother?' Joanna asked.

'You'll see,' Harriet said grimly. She wondered how much they would have in common when Mother was gone.

'So, what's she done this time?'

Harriet kept her attention on the road. 'Well, the latest is that she arranged to have the boiler serviced without telling me and the plumber gave her estimates for a new one, a bathroom and some central heating.'

'Right.'

'I can't watch her every minute, Jo.'

'Of course not.'

'And I spend half the day worrying about who she'll call out next.'

'I know.'

There was a silence in the cab as they both digested this. 'But that wasn't what made me phone you.' Harriet sneaked a glance at her sister as they approached the main road.

22

'What was it then?' Joanna turned to look at her and Harriet noticed for the first time that her eyes were red-rimmed as though she'd been crying.

'She asked me to give her a lift into Abbotsbury yesterday.'

'So?'

Joanna was right. Abbotsbury was only half an hour down the road and obviously Harriet didn't mind – even though she had plenty of things to keep her busy back at the cottage. But . . . 'She was a bit secretive.' Which had made Harriet suspicious.

There was a gap in the traffic and she went for it. 'But I assumed she wanted to look around the art galleries or the Swannery or something. You know Mother.'

'Hmm.'

'Then when I dropped her off in the high street . . .' Harriet changed gear. She could hear her own voice rising alarmingly and cleared her throat to regain control.

'Yes?' Joanna looked worried now.

'She went straight up to some tall guy with a weird beard who was standing outside the art studio. He was wearing a black leather coat and riding boots and carrying a clipboard.' Harriet hadn't known what to do – or say. He seemed to be expecting their mother. All Harriet could think was, what had Mother let herself in for this time?

Beside her, she was aware of her sister's tense frame. She slowed and tucked in behind a VW camper van on the inside lane.

Joanna exhaled. 'A clipboard?' she echoed, as if that was the strangest part.

'And a weird beard,' Harriet confirmed. Because, for her, that was the strangest part.

23

Joanna was looking at her now in a most peculiar way. As if she was thinking that their lives in Dorset were far more eventful than her own.

'He ticked her name off a list when she arrived.' Harriet glanced in her rear-view mirror and indicated right.

Joanna's eyes widened. 'What did you do?'

'Obviously, I went to investigate.' Harriet had parked on double yellow lines and marched right over.

She took the turning. Now that they had left the dual carriageway they were immersed in rural Dorset in seconds.

'And?'

'He said he was an artist.' Harriet didn't add that he had looked her up and down and grinned in a way that made her feel flushed all over. 'And a tutor.'

'I don't get it.' Joanna was shaking her head. 'Is she taking painting classes, is that it? Because that's not so bad. She needs an interest, doesn't she?'

Harriet sighed. 'No, she's not and yes, she does,' she said. She increased her speed. The road was narrow and had few passing places, but Harriet knew every twist and turn as well as she knew her own body – better probably. 'She'd answered an ad, Jo. She thought she was going to be an artist's model for the day. That she'd be painted from all angles by a bunch of students and made to look as glamorous as she'd like to be.'

'Oh.' Harriet could sense her sister taking it in. They both knew that Mother had never really let go of her colonial background and that her dress sense was a touch forties film star to say the least. But that was just the way she was – even when Father was alive. As for the rest . . . Harriet slowed again to take the corner. It was a tight one.

'But why would he want Mother?' Joanna still hadn't got it.

24

'Mother hadn't quite grasped what she was letting herself in for.' Harriet knew her voice was crisp. 'They like to tackle all ages and body shapes.' She glanced across at her sister. 'In a life-drawing class.'

'Oh, God.' Their eyes met. Joanna's expression was one of incredulity. Her mouth twitched.

Harriet frowned. Then something seemed to bubble up inside her and she let it out – a loud snort of laughter. She began to shake and tried to change gear again, forgetting she was already in fourth.

'Poor Mother.' Joanna let out a shriek of laughter. 'You did stop her going in?'

Harriet's lips tightened once more. How long had it been since she'd laughed like that? 'What do you take me for? Of course, I stopped her going in.' Poor Mother indeed – a touch of glamour was very different from all-out nudity.

'It would be awful for her to be an object of ridicule.' Joanna too seemed to have sobered as the implications sunk in. 'She's just lonely,' she said. 'Maybe a hobby would be a good idea?'

'I've thought of that,' Harriet said. She braked and edged closer to the hedgerow as a car appeared from the opposite direction. 'I've suggested everything from a book club to crochet and she's not interested.'

'I'll try and think of something while I'm here. I'll talk to her.'

Oh, yes, she'd sort the whole thing out in seconds, no problem. Harriet was about to make some sarcastic comment to this effect when something stopped her. She bit her lip.

Joanna was staring out of the window. The hills to their left were green and shiny from the rain, the hedgerows damp and overgrown. But it was the expression in her sister's eyes that had silenced her.

25

'How long will you stay?' This emerged more abruptly than Harriet had intended. Most things she said to Joanna seemed to come out that way.

'I'm not sure yet.' Joanna didn't look at her. 'You don't mind, do you? It's not putting you out?'

'No, it's not putting me out. Don't be daft.' Although it was. Everything and everyone that created more work put her out. Why wouldn't it? But still, there was something reassuring about the fact that Joanna was sitting here next to her. A trouble shared, perhaps?

Once again, silence filtered through the cab of the pick-up, broken by the intermittent squeak of the windscreen wipers. It needed new rubbers, probably. Everything in Harriet's life needed new something.

She followed the lane round towards home. One way up, one way down. To the cliff or to the beach. There was a natural simplicity to the landscape; it wasn't pretending to be anything it wasn't. She glanced again at Joanna. She was looking awfully pale. 'Have you left him?' she asked.

Joanna flinched. 'No.' She fidgeted. 'Well, sort of. Yes. No. I don't know yet.'

Clear as a bell. Crikey, thought Harriet again, was she coming back to Mulberry Farm Cottage forever? 'Do you want to talk about it?' She hoped not. Harriet knew nothing about men. She was her sister and they should be able to discuss such things. But Joanna's sad eyes were making her feel out of her depth.

'Not really.' Joanna's mouth wobbled.

Oh, dear. Harriet took the bend too fast. The narrow lane was shady and lush, shrouded by ferns and nettles, the trees in autumnal leaf meeting in the middle to form a golden tunnel.

26

They drove past the pub and the first of the stone cottages. She slowed.

Ahead of them, their neighbour, Owen Matthews, was driving his tractor and there was no room to overtake. Typical. He flashed his hazard lights in greeting. Harriet tapped her fingers on the dashboard. There was a farm gateway just coming up. 'Move over then, you great lummox,' she muttered. What was it about this place she'd grown up in, this place whose hills and valleys were as familiar to her as her own skin . . . ?

'That's Owen,' Joanna said, waving. As if Harriet didn't know.

Harriet waved too, nodded, smiled, absolutely the genial neighbour. And perhaps that was it. Perhaps it was that very familiarity that gnawed away at her sense of well-being. The knowledge that here everyone knew everyone else.

They were crawling along now, inching up the lane between the high banks and stone walls bound with ivy. She was trapped. There was no getting away from Linda at the pub, from Mother, from Owen, from the whole lot of them. Harriet was clamped into their landscape. She belonged, whether she liked it or not – she really had been given no choice. She knew everything about them and they knew everything about her. Well . . . almost. In front of them the tractor trundled along. And there was no escape – at least not for now.

'Perhaps I could help?' Had Joanna read her mind?

She wanted to sound the hooter again; she wanted to get past Owen and his tractor. She wanted to scream. Harriet was suddenly worried that she was losing her mind. 'Help?'

Joanna waved vaguely at the road ahead. The wall was low now; on the other side Harriet could see the stream, lined with reeds and rushes. 'With the cottage,' she said. 'With Mother.'

27

Harriet breathed deeply. 'Maybe.' She knew she sounded grudging. Was she never satisfied? And yet what would Joanna do exactly? She couldn't see her baking bread, making jam, even feeding the hens – not in those boots. And as for Mother . . .

'While I'm around, you could go away – for a weekend or something,' said Joanna.

Harriet braked – much too sharply – as Owen squeezed the tractor into a passing place. At last. She overtook, noticed out of the corner of her eye the way he grinned at Joanna. 'Where?' She blinked at the empty lane ahead. If they kept going, they would pass the country hotel and end up at the sea. In the sea, actually.

'Anywhere.' Joanna laughed, but it was a flat sound. 'The world is your oyster, Harriet.'

Harriet snorted. 'Apart from the fact that we can't afford it, who'd do the fruit and veg and look after the pigs?' Not to mention Mother and the rest of it. She swung right onto the track that led to Mulberry Farm Cottage and Owen's farm. Joanna had always been a dreamer. Harriet was the practical one. Only now, she was going much too fast down the rutted track and she and Joanna were bouncing around in the pick-up like a couple of punk rockers. Only the approaching cattle grid made her slow down.

Joanna gave her a long look.

Harriet fidgeted uncomfortably, controlling the steering wheel with two fingers. 'What?'

'You're scared,' Joanna said.

'Don't be ridiculous.' Harriet turned an abrupt left onto the muddy front driveway and slammed on the brakes with much more force than necessary. How dare she say that? How dare she turn up here and . . . say that.

'Sorry, Harriet.' Joanna looked repentant. 'I thought that you could do with a break, that's all. I know you're not scared. It's just—'

'Come on.' Harriet was out of the pick-up before she could elaborate. And suddenly she didn't have the energy to argue. 'She's waiting to see you. All dressed up like a dog's dinner.'

They exchanged a rare complicit smile.

'OK.' Joanna touched her arm as she came round to her side of the truck. 'But think about it, Harriet, please? It would do you good. And we could manage without you for a few days, don't you think?'

'Mother would love it.' But would her sister be able to keep the tradesmen at bay?

'Then do it.' Joanna's eyes were bright now although the sadness still clung to her mouth. 'Do something. Just for a few days. Get away. Go somewhere.'

Somewhere . . . 'Maybe.' Harriet straightened up. It had stopped raining and the clouds were dispersing. In the distance the sun was low over the grey of the horizon, lighting up the honey-gold stone of Mulberry Farm Cottage, casting afternoon shadows on the green hills where Owen's sheep were grazing. She thought of the world online that she escaped to every evening when the chores were done.

Beyond the hills the sea stretched out, cool and inviting, like a promise. 'Maybe I will,' she said.

CHAPTER 4

Joanna

Dorset

'It's so wonderful to see you, darling.' Their mother was beaming. But even after the two months since Joanna's last visit, Mother looked older, her hair whiter, her skin paper-thin. 'I suppose Martin was too busy to come with you?'

Martin. Joanna avoided Harriet's eye. She knew she'd been evasive. But right now, she didn't want to talk about it, didn't want to think about it either. Was Martin already taking advantage of her absence? Was he with Hilary? She doubted it, if Brian knew about the affair. She shook the thought away. It was so sordid. When she and Martin had first met in the college bar, when they'd become an item only days later, when they'd got married . . . She had never imagined a moment like this could come.

'Yes,' she said. 'He sends his love.'

'And what about your work?' Their mother had hardly touched her food. All her attention was fixed on Joanna and she felt a sudden dart of sympathy for her sister. 'What are you writing at the moment?' Her mother settled back to listen.

Joanna told her a bit about the latest article she was writing for a well-known women's magazine. She'd have to get on with that, the deadline was in two days' time. And then she must get in touch with Toby. Her mother seemed interested and asked lots of questions, nodding and smiling in all the right places. Joanna glanced at Harriet. Mother seemed so on the ball, but that was what was so confusing about it all.

There was nothing actually wrong with their mother — or so Martin had always maintained. Apart, that was, from their father dying seven years ago and Mother not getting over it. Apart, that was, from Mother apparently not being able to cope with loneliness or old age, with losing her looks and her infamous ability to command male attention. And apart from a vague depression that seemed to hang over her, clouding every day. Joanna knew that Harriet had taken her to see their GP several times but Mother could be so rational — just as she was being this evening. Neither would she acknowledge the problem, nor accept any medication that might help. Joanna could understand her mother's reluctance to take pills, but it was as if Mother was determined sometimes to wallow.

'And how are you, Mother?' Joanna reached out to squeeze her hand, which seemed so fragile to the touch.

'Sometimes . . .' she began. And there was a bleak expression in her mother's blue eyes that frightened Joanna.

'Yes?'

'Sometimes, I'm scared of forgetting how to feel,' she said.

'Oh, Mother.' Joanna felt her eyes fill. Something lurched inside her — it was that shift, that sadness that was always now mixed in with the love. She glanced again at Harriet, who was biting her

31

lip. Was it because of losing their father? Was that why Mother craved so much attention? Because it enabled her to go on feeling special? And how come exactly had she forgotten how to feel?

'Come on now, Mother.' Harriet's voice was brisk.

Joanna had noticed recently that this was how her sister dealt with things. She supposed Harriet had to find a way — but was it the right way? Not to acknowledge their mother's unhappiness? To treat her almost like a child?

'Joanna's here now. You know how much you were looking forward to seeing her.'

Nevertheless, Joanna found herself taking her sister's lead. 'And we're going to spend some time together you and I.' She patted her mother's hand. It wasn't easy, this false brightness, this lack of admission of her own life issues. But . . . She might not be the mother of Joanna's childhood — the woman Joanna used to run to with every problem, the woman who could always make things better — but that was even more reason to give something back. Joanna missed that woman, especially at times like this, but she had been gone for years and since then, their relationship had gradually changed, inch by inch their roles had reversed.

She saw a glint of gratitude in her sister's eyes. It was the least she could do to give Harriet a break. Besides which, maybe she could really help make things better. But there were no easy answers. They managed on very little money as it was. Harriet would never leave their mother and Mother could never live alone. And how could they ever move out of Mulberry Farm Cottage? The family had lived there for generations. It was part of their history, their roots.

'How long can you stay?' Her mother's eyes were bright and hopeful now.

Joanna caught Harriet's glance. 'I'm not sure yet, Mother,' she said. She could work from here, of course. But clearly, she'd have to go back to Crouch End sometime and equally clearly, she had to talk to Martin, who had already sent her several texts that she hadn't answered. But not yet.

'Stay as long as you like. Remember, this is still your home.' Her mother leant forwards and Joanna caught the scent of her sweet gardenia perfume. She knew her mother wouldn't judge her for leaving Martin, even without the facts, if that was what she decided to do. Her mother had let so many of her own boundaries slip away to nothing.

'Thanks, Mother.'

'You know you're always welcome.' She paused, a rare forkful of Harriet's beef casserole halfway to her mouth. 'Why, you could even have an office here. We've got the room.'

Harriet raised an eyebrow and Joanna couldn't suppress a grin. Mother's thought processes sometimes worked at lightning speed. 'Well,' she began. Much as she loved Mulberry Farm Cottage and whatever happened with Martin, she knew she wouldn't come back to live here permanently – she'd been independent for too long. Besides, she'd never belonged here – not like Harriet did. Harriet had always been glued to their father's side. And when he died, she'd taken over; it had seemed inevitable – at least at the time. Joanna, after all, had left home long before.

'Or we could convert the loft space.' Their mother was on a roll. 'I was speaking to such a nice man the other day—'

'Who?' Harriet swallowed and coughed. 'What man? When were you talking to him?'

Joanna sneaked another look across at her sister. She couldn't blame her for being uptight. This thing of Mother's had obviously got out of control.

33

'Handy Andy?' Their mother frowned. 'Let me try to recall.' She pressed her fingers to her temple.

Harriet got up abruptly and shoved her chair under the table. 'Don't even think about it, Mother,' she growled. She started clearing away. No one else could make it sound so threatening.

'I'll do it.' Joanna rested her hand on Harriet's arm. It felt stiff with tension. 'You sit down.'

'In that case I'm going upstairs.' Harriet looked uncomfortable. 'There's some, er, work I need to be getting on with.'

'Work?' Joanna raised an eyebrow. She'd been hoping they might sit down together, perhaps have a chat after Mother had gone to bed. But clearly there was no sisterly bonding on the agenda – at least not tonight.

When Joanna went up to her room a few hours later, Harriet was still tap tap tapping on her keyboard, a sliver of light escaping from under the closed door of the study. Joanna almost went in. But Harriet would hate to be interrupted . . . So instead, she went to bed, stayed awake, listened to the grandfather clock chime the midnight hour – the Westminster chimes – and she wondered, had she been right to come here?

When she heard Harriet going to her bedroom a few minutes later, she climbed out of bed, pulled on her bathrobe and went over to the window. There was something about night-time in the country; it was so much more complete somehow. She let her eyes adjust to the darkness, put her forehead against the cool glass for a moment. At this time of night nothing seemed certain anymore.

Joanna slipped out of her room. She knocked gently on her sister's bedroom door. She wanted to say goodnight. 'Harriet?'

'What is it, Jo?' She felt Harriet's sigh, though at least she opened the door.

'Sorry to disturb you.' Now she was here, Joanna wasn't sure what to say. Instinctively, she reached over to stroke her sister's hair. 'I always envied you your thick hair,' she said.

Harriet seemed to flinch away from her touch. 'Going grey,' she muttered.

'You should get some highlights done. Maybe chestnut.' She spoke without thinking. Because how could Harriet afford highlights? It was crass, insensitive of her.

Sure enough, 'And how exactly would I pay for it?' Harriet demanded.

Joanna had a sudden moment of inspiration. 'Shepherds' huts?'

'What?' Harriet sighed.

'A lot of people are doing it,' Joanna told her. 'If they've got a big garden and want to earn some extra money.' She'd read an article about it only the other week.

'We can't—'

Joanna knew what she was going to say. But she had an answer ready – gleaned from the same article. 'There might even be someone who owns a shepherd's hut but doesn't have enough outside space for it. We could advertise.' It was an idea at least.

'We're fine as we are,' Harriet snapped.

Joanna didn't understand her at all. 'But you said—'

'Joanna, please don't interfere.'

She was getting nowhere. 'Goodnight, then.' Joanna returned to her room. It was hopeless. Harriet just seemed so angry. Was it her life that had made her this way? She didn't know. She wasn't even sure how she and Harriet had drifted so

35

far apart in the first place. Perhaps it was because she had never been able to find the real Harriet – though hadn't she looked and looked? – just as she'd never been able to find her sister when they'd played one, two, three, alive back in the days of their childhood. She was elusive then and she was elusive now.

As she passed it, Joanna glanced at the picture as she almost always did. Venice. The bridge. Her first holiday with Martin had been to Venice. It had been full of romance, hopes and dreams. And now? What was left now? She shook her head in despair.

She caught sight of her reflection in the tatty gilt mirror on the wall the moment before she put out the light. Losing their shine, both of them. Was her marriage over? And if so, what should she do now? Where should she go?

She would think about it tomorrow, she decided. One step at a time. She could do it – whatever 'it' turned out to be – with or without Martin. It was a chance to help her family, perhaps to get close to them again. It was a chance to do something. Because the old Joanna must still be in there somewhere, mustn't she? And all Joanna had to do now was find her.

CHAPTER 5

Joanna

Dorset

The following morning, Joanna made breakfast, pouring tea from the same faded and tea-stained yellow pot that she remembered from countless other breakfasts and teatimes at Mulberry Farm Cottage. Coming back here, coming home, was like going back in time, she thought. But very, very different. She chatted to their mother, keeping the subjects light, and persuaded Harriet not to hurry back after she'd done her chores in town.

'What would you like to do this morning, Mother?' she asked.

'We could sort through the things in the loft,' her mother said. Nothing wrong with her memory, then. 'Get it cleared out, just in case . . .'

At this, Harriet hovered frowning in the doorway, one basket of vegetables in each hand. The dark-veined leaves of the cabbages crinkled invitingly and the cauliflowers' creamy hearts

37

were shrouded with pale tissue-green. Joanna hadn't asked her what she would do after she'd made the deliveries. Let Harriet have no one to answer to for once in her life.

'Go, go.' And despite everything, Joanna couldn't help laughing. 'No Handy Andy, I promise.'

Joanna cleared up the kitchen, walked with her mother to the orchard, picked some fruit and made morning coffee at eleven just as her mother liked it. Mother chatted on, slipping easily into reminiscences of when Joanna's father was still alive, of when both girls had been young, and as she spoke, there was a wistful expression on her mother's face that tugged at Joanna's heart. This, she thought, was Harriet's life . . . And she was beginning to understand it better than she ever had before. For Joanna, there was something very special about this time with her mother, but if she had to do it every day, she couldn't quite imagine how frustrating that might feel.

'And now the loft?' her mother asked eagerly.

'And now the loft,' Joanna agreed. 'You stay down here and I'll take a look around, see how much is up there and maybe bring a few bits and pieces down. OK?' Photo albums maybe, she was thinking. Old school projects and exercise books. Come to think of it, she had no idea what was up there.

She settled her mother on the sofa with one of her favourite magazines and made her way upstairs, lugging a paint-spattered stepladder she'd found in the porch along with her. The attic trapdoor was closed and bolted. Probably no one had been up here for years. She could remember her father one time, looking for something, scrabbling about under the dusty rafters and lagging. But mostly, things were kept in the sheds and the barns.

Not that Joanna was looking for office space . . . She thought

38

of her own office back in the house at Crouch End. Would she ever work there again? Would she have a new house, a new work space somewhere? It was difficult to imagine . . . *So, don't think about it.*

She unbolted the hatch, pushed the door open and, summoning all her strength, pulled her weight onto her arms and over the edge of the hatchway. *Ouff.* Like a bag of flour, and about as graceful. She pulled up her knees and manoeuvred into a squat.

God, it was like another world up here. A dark world. And she hadn't brought a torch – how stupid was that? She felt around with her hands, though, found the light switch, flicked it on and miraculously the attic was flooded with light.

Joanna brushed the dust from her jeans. It was chilly too and smelt musty. She wrinkled her nose and shivered as she looked around her. She could see some rolls of old carpeting, a few cardboard boxes, and in the far corner an electric fire. Next to that was an ancient canvas bag, some old tools poking from the top, and a big trunk, though how anyone had got that up here she couldn't imagine. She peered into the other corners. No precious works of art, unfortunately, no Ming vases or anything of that calibre to save the cottage from its own decay. Only cobwebs. And not too much to clear out either.

She made her way over to the boxes; they were mostly full of books. She glanced at the spines – she remembered these astronomy and philosophy books of her father's being in the study, recalled that she'd been quite young the first time she considered the incongruity of a farmer who was also an academic. How had that come about, she wondered now – or was she making a stereotypical assumption? Probably. She knew the farm had been in Father's family for generations, that over

39

the years various owners had sold off land from what had once been a bigger estate. But that was all she knew of the family history.

She had, though, one specific memory of when her uncle and his family were staying with them one summer. She thought back. It was teatime. The adults were talking about the mulberry tree – at least that's what she'd thought at the time. Someone (her father?) looked at the children, told his brother to hush, and that was about the sum of it. Joanna had no clue why she'd even remembered, apart from the fact that she'd sensed she wasn't supposed to be listening and that was always a draw. Was it a secret? Maybe. A certain look had passed between Father and her uncle. There had been some hint of disapproval. And that was all. Something and nothing, she thought now. Would Mother want to look through these books? Maybe.

In one of the moth-eaten boxes she found some carrier bags. The plastic had withered but they were full of that old school stuff of hers and Harriet's she'd been thinking of: paintings done at infant school, collages and crafts, cards they'd sent to Mother and Father, gift tags for Christmas presents they'd made themselves using old Christmas cards and Mother's zig-zaggy scissors, as they used to call them – embroidery scissors, that was. Joanna smiled as she dusted her forefinger lightly over the glitter. Fancy their mother keeping all this old stuff. But she was glad. She'd definitely take these bags downstairs, she decided. They could look back over old times, enjoy it all together.

How safe was the floor? Someone had placed an old door across the beams to act as a walkway but it seemed to sag under her weight as she moved gingerly over towards the trunk. She pulled it away from the eaves and dislodged some of the lagging. The insulation was so thin – it was no wonder the cottage was cold and draughty in winter. What was Harriet thinking? Hadn't she considered applying for a grant to get some decent insulation? The heating bills must be enormous.

Downstairs seemed so far away to Joanna right now. This was other; it didn't seem to belong to their family, to the present, or even to Mulberry Farm Cottage, but to some other time, some other person. Joanna felt the goosebumps travel up her arms. Perhaps part of that other person – their spirit maybe – was here still, watching, waiting?

The trunk was coated in thick dust. Joanna sneezed but the sound was muted, as if it was being absorbed into the beams, the rafters and the meagre insulation. She jiggled the catch of the trunk. It was an old-fashioned metal lock that had rusted and stuck fast. She pulled at it again. The trunk seemed almost empty. But not quite. When she moved it, there was a soft rustle from within. Maybe there was a key somewhere? She ran her fingers along the ledge of wood under the rafters. Nothing – only dirt, dust and splinters.

But Joanna had got the bit between her teeth now. She groped around in the canvas bag of tools until she found a chisel with a flat head. Carefully, she slotted this into the latch. Pushed back for leverage. Twang. It burst open. Not locked then. Just old and stiff.

She eased up the lid, which gave a satisfying moan of relief as if it hadn't been opened for years. The trunk was empty, except for a small bundle of papers tied with a black ribbon. How odd. She pulled it out. Letters? Old letters? She felt a dart of excitement. Old family letters? She hesitated. Should she disturb their resting place? They didn't belong to her. If they

41

were letters, and someone had gone to the trouble of keeping them tied with ribbon and stored in the attic, then they must be personal.

But she was a journalist after all and curiosity won over. This was her family and both writer and recipient were presumably long gone. She took a peek. The top page was covered with a faded but flowing delicate script; a woman's hand, surely? She touched the paper it had been written on. It was so old and brittle, she worried it might crack and crumble into dust between her fingers. There was a date written at the top of the first sheet. *31st October 1912. Oh my God. Who . . . ? Venice.* Venice? Her breath caught.

'Joanna?' Her mother's voice, sounding more tremulous than before, drifted through the house and up into the attic. 'Are you still up there? It's past lunchtime, you know, and—'

Joanna pulled herself to her feet. 'I'm coming down, Mother,' she called. 'Just a minute.'

Picking up one of the flimsy carrier bags, she slipped the letters inside, cushioning them between Harriet's pink tissue-paper pineapple and the long cotton-wool beard of a hand-crafted Father Christmas. She made her way over to the hatch, switched off the light, emerged backwards and climbed back down the stepladder.

About to go downstairs, Joanna hesitated for a moment. She slipped into her bedroom, took the letters carefully out of the bag, gave them a longing look and tucked them under the faded coverlet. She would read them – she couldn't resist – but not now. And for some reason that she didn't understand, she didn't want to share them with anyone – not yet.

Her mother was waiting in the hall, looking anxious, her face a web of lines and memories. 'Lunch first then,' Joanna said. She waggled the carrier bag in her hand. 'And then we'll take a look at this little lot.'

Her mother brightened. 'How wonderful,' she breathed.

Joanna felt quite pleased with herself. Harriet had been gone all morning and she'd managed just fine. She might not have got any work done but at least there were no tradesmen in sight. And she had the feeling that she'd inadvertently unearthed something rather exciting – which would be a good distraction to stop her thinking about Martin. Another family secret perhaps? She couldn't wait to find out.

CHAPTER 6

Harriet

Dorset

Harriet had got home earlier this afternoon to find her mother and Joanna sitting on the sofa surrounded by the paraphernalia of hers and Joanna's schooldays, chatting away like old chums and laughing with hilarity.

'Harriet!' Joanna leapt up. 'Let me make some tea. Did you have a nice time?'

Nice time? Harriet didn't want to be ungrateful. But what did her sister imagine she'd been doing exactly? In point of fact, it was all very well to have a few hours of freedom, but when it was unplanned and you found you had nothing specific to do with it (whilst lots of chores remained un-done at home) then free time wasn't quite as wonderful as it might be in theory. Harriet had, in fact, looked around Bridport, treated herself to a coffee in Bucky Doo Square, decided to skip lunch due to lack of funds, driven down to Burton Bradstock to look at the

44

sea and then come home again. Scintillating stuff, she thought now. But that was hardly her sister's fault.

'I saw the plums in the kitchen,' she remarked, rather than answering Joanna's question. Did Joanna really imagine that one morning of looking after Mother could make up for all the months, all the years . . . ? Harriet took a deep breath and steadied herself. Of course she didn't. Harriet was being unfair and she knew it.

'We picked them earlier.' Joanna looked doubtful now. 'Shouldn't we have?'

Harriet relented. 'No, it's fine. I'll make some jam.'

'Now?' Joanna blinked at her. 'We thought you might want to come and look at these—'

'Later,' said Harriet. There was too much to do, and besides . . .

Jam-making always made her feel more in control. Within thirty minutes, she had supper on the go and then she took a deep breath and started on the jam.

Harriet stirred the fragrant mixture. The truth was, reminiscing with her sister and her mother was not such a good idea. It was likely to be both dangerous and emotional, neither of which she could cope with at this moment in time.

Three sharp taps on the back door made her jump – and drop the wooden spoon into the preserving pan.

'Anyone at home?' Without waiting to be asked, their neighbour, Owen Matthews, stomped in through the porch.

Harriet retrieved the spoon. Why couldn't people let her get on? And she had to get her nerves under control. She had to get everything under control, otherwise . . .

'Come in,' she said. A little clipped perhaps and unnecessary

45

since Owen was already in, already pulling off his muddy boots, which he left by the door, great clodhoppers.

'Afternoon, Harriet.' Owen was a well-built man still, at forty-five or thereabouts, but rounded in the shoulders as if life had dealt him a hefty blow. And it had. He had always made a good living from his farm down the lane. But his wife had left him years ago and according to Mother the Oracle, Owen had never recovered from the loss.

However, today he was – by his standards – dressed up, apart from the muddy boots, in clean, dark blue jeans and a thick navy zipped jacket. Harriet's eyes narrowed. Hoping for a chat with Joanna, no doubt.

'What can I do for you, Owen?' Harriet stirred the plums a touch more vigorously.

They would, she acknowledged, have found it hard to manage without Owen. When Harriet had been looking for a way of making more money, he had helped her do up the sty. Now, he provided them with the weaners at three to four weeks of age and helped her take the pigs to market after they had been fattened up. And he was always available to mend a fuse or put up a shelf if Harriet couldn't manage it – though since they'd lost Father, she had taught herself to be as independent as she could. He'd bought a lot of their land when they'd needed urgent repairs to the house – the far two fields to deal with the woodworm and some re-slating on Big Barn and the nearer small one to get the new wood-burning stove. Father had left some money, but not enough and it hadn't lasted long.

Perhaps that was why Harriet had mixed feelings about Owen. She didn't want to resent him, but she couldn't help herself.

The plums had simmered for long enough. Harriet turned

46

them up to boil, still stirring. Jam needed one hundred per cent attention. She appreciated everything that Owen did for them, but now wasn't a good time.

'Have I come at a bad time?' He began to pace the room. He always seemed too big for any room he was in. He belonged outdoors, she supposed.

'No, no.' Harriet wiped her hands on her apron. It was an old wrap-around pinny of her mother's, stained with plums and torn at the shoulder, but this was Owen, so it hardly mattered. 'But I haven't got any more eggs till tomorrow.' She shoved her hair out of her eyes with the back of her free hand. She must wash it tonight. Mustn't let herself go. Although sometimes that was exactly what she wanted to do.

She thought of the way Joanna had stroked her hair last night. Harriet had always found it hard to accept a compliment. And why Joanna, who had so much, should be envious of her, she had no idea. More to the point, nobody touched her hair. They hadn't since Father, who used to stroke her head before kissing her goodnight, lightly on the temple. She sniffed, thought of that recurring dream that sometimes haunted her waking hours too. Another dangerous and emotional pathway that needed to be avoided at all costs.

Joanna seemed to live in another world. Shepherds' huts? Where had that idea sprung from? The thought of doing more housekeeping, not to mention having to be polite to guests whom she neither knew nor particularly liked, filled Harriet with dread.

Even so, she had lingered outside Hair Magic in Bridport this morning. Fingered the pig money in her pocket. Thought about chestnut highlights.

'I didn't come for eggs.'

47

'Oh?' She sensed Owen behind her, looking over her shoulder into the vat of jam. 'Then, why . . . ?' She swung round to face him, still half focused on the plums. Joanna – of course, Joanna.

'You seem a bit tense, Harriet,' Owen observed. 'I only came by to say hello.'

'To me?' Harriet kept half an eye on the jam, half an eye on Owen.

'To all of you, yes.' He glanced around. Disappointed not to find Joanna here, no doubt.

The steam from the jam was hot on her skin. Harriet drew back.

Owen sniffed appreciatively. 'That smells good, Harriet,' he said. 'Very good.'

'Thanks. I'll save you a jar.' Harriet carefully scraped off the frothy scum as it rose to the surface of the preserving pan. The village shop would take most of the jam, but she'd keep some in store for the café next summer. The liquid was boiling rapidly now; she had to keep stirring to stop the bottom of the pan from burning. This was hot stuff. She thought of the email she wrote last night and suppressed a giggle. What would Mother say if she knew? And Owen? And Joanna?

'Is there anything I can do for you while I'm here?' he asked. 'I noticed a bit of your fencing was down.'

The navy jacket needed darning at the elbows, Harriet noted out of the corner of her eye. She supposed she should offer to mend that for him. She should do something to reciprocate. And although he looked quite smart at the outset, he had brought, she realised, a faint smell of manure into the kitchen that was at odds with the pleasing tartness of her plum jam.

'I can manage, thanks,' she said before she could stop herself.

Fool. Why couldn't she just be nice? He'd probably been up since dawn milking and what have you. Surely the least she could do . . . 'Cup of tea?'

'Now you're talking.' He rubbed his hands together and sat down at the oak table, pitted and pockmarked and as old as the cottage itself probably.

The kitchen had always been the hub of things when Mother had presided over it, the table the centrefold. Mother had kneaded dough on it, Harriet and Joanna had done their homework on it, Father had even dried out the onions on it. It was stained with ink, oil and red mulberry juice, it was battered by Mother's meat pulveriser and scarred by kitchen knives. But it remained as solid as ever.

'But you'll have to make it.' She nodded towards the preserving pan where the jam was really steaming now. 'I've got my hands full, as you can see.'

'Right you are.' Owen immediately jumped up to fill the kettle and Harriet took the saucer from the freezer, spooned on some jam and peered closely.

Come on, come on. The blob of jam went a bit crinkly and she gave it a poke with the spoon. It seemed about right. She glanced across at the work surface. Indulged in a brief fantasy about a contemporary granite counter not mended with brown tape, an in-your-dreams dishwasher that produced warm, dry and shiny plates, ready to stack away in some soft-close, high-rise cupboard. And a woman – a girl – who'd once had the time and the inclination to curl up with a book on the wooden bench under the mulberry tree, listening to the wind in the leaves. Hmph.

She refocused on the jam. Sterilised jam jars, transparent covers, waxed circles, rubber bands, self-adhesive labels . . .

God, but jam-making was a kerfuffle. Nevertheless . . . She wiped her hands on the pinny. She did like it.

Behind her, Owen bustled around making the tea: warming the pot, assembling the cups, even pouring milk into the little blue jug. It was quite comforting, she thought, working together with someone. She and Mother had never had that, not really. Once Father died, Mother had begun to wilt. And that was only the start.

OK. The fifteen minutes' rapid boil time was up. First things first. Plum jam. And tea.

She put on her oven gloves and lifted the preserving pan by its handles. It weighed a ton, but she could never get on with ladles and funnels. She steadied herself and began to pour jam into the first sterilised jar.

'Owen, how lovely . . .' – Mother stood in the doorway dressed in a sky-blue, pleated floral number, holding out her hand in that way she had, for it to be clasped and kissed; clearly, she had finished reminiscing with Joanna – 'to see a man about the house.'

Harriet rolled her eyes.

'Hello, Audrey.' Owen grinned and obligingly took her hand.

He was a nice man. Harriet rested the pan on the stove for a moment, wiped her brow. Which was probably why his wife had treated him so badly, come to think about it. She got a firm hold of the preserving pan and continued to pour into the warmed and sterilised jars. Five, six, seven, eight; she was really getting into her stride. Plus, the pan was getting lighter, of course.

She set to, popping the wax circles onto the top of each jar of jam. Fixing the transparent polythene tops with a rubber

50

band, writing and labelling. Twenty-five jars. Not bad for a couple of hours' work. She scraped the sides of the preserving pan with her wooden spoon, squirted washing-up liquid, eased the sticky pan into the well of the sink and turned on the hot tap. Once it set, jam could be a bugger.

Harriet had been fully preoccupied with her task, but now, snatches of the conversation between Owen and her mother wafted over to her.

'You're always welcome . . .' (Mother).

'Well, if you're sure . . .' (Owen).

'Joanna would adore seeing you . . .' (Mother).

'Never too much trouble to cook for one more . . .' (Mother again).

Harriet stopped scouring. Her mother had just invited Owen to supper, she realised. Tonight. What was she trying to do? Send Harriet to an early grave? That would make two nights running that Harriet had been forced to improvise. She paused for breath. On the counter the neat rows of plum jam smiled at her. Ah, well. Chicken chasseur it was then. With not much chicken and a lot of chasseur (whatever that might be).

She pulled off her pinny. Owen and Mother were still chatting away, and so she slipped outside, taking deep breaths of the earthy autumnal air. The sun was setting – a deep rich red – beyond the hills and casting an amber light over the fields and the sea. There was a chill in the air, but it wasn't unpleasant; it was fresh and invigorating after the heavy sweetness of the jammy kitchen.

She rounded the kitchen garden. Joanna was sitting under the mulberry tree reading. She looked so absorbed and Harriet allowed herself a brief moment of fond affection before she backtracked. She didn't want to get into another conversation about what she should do to her hair, or – heaven forbid – shepherds' huts, let alone what might have happened between her sister and her husband to make Joanna run back home. Supper was in the oven. She'd sneak upstairs, she decided, while the coast was clear. And she would do it, she would finally do it. She would take the plunge. Joanna wasn't the only one who could have a life. *Just watch me*, she thought.

CHAPTER 7

Joanna

Dorset

After various incidents from her childhood had been recounted and relived, such as the time Joanna had written a memorable poem about Colmer's Hill ('the first sign of your writing talent, darling,' said Mother), and when her mother seemed to be tiring of looking through their old school stuff, Joanna had packed it all away again, feeling nostalgic for those simple childhood days. Harriet hadn't seemed interested and now she was busy in the kitchen, so Joanna left her mother to rest, slipped up to her room to fetch the letters from her bedroom and headed outside, intent on sitting under the mulberry tree to read them in peace. There was an autumnal and musty tang in the air, a stillness in the hills of Warren Down tinged with the lightest of late afternoon mists.

It was, she thought, so very different from Crouch End. Joanna almost felt that she was entirely alone in the world as she skirted round the kitchen garden, until the view of the village houses, the church, the town of Bridport and the V-shaped dart of the sea opened up in front of her. She breathed deeply. She'd forgotten how wonderful it could feel. Slowly, she walked past the fusty woodpile stacked up against Big Barn and down the winding path that led to the mulberry tree and the pond.

She looked up into the branches of the tree. It was great for climbing. She had never been able to get as high as Harriet, but she could always get high enough to see the ginger sandstone cliffs. It was a place she'd always loved. When she was a baby, so the story went, Mother used to park the pram near the pond in the shade of the mulberry tree, and Joanna would sleep for hours. 'But not,' her mother had added, 'when the fruit was ripe and might have fallen. Mulberries stain like billy-oh.'

It was true that when the mulberry fruit ripened, it fell to the ground in blood-red heaps, and Joanna and Harriet grew up knowing better than to get the juice on their clothes or they'd never hear the last of it. Sometimes, when the fruit was ripe enough and not too tart, Mother made jam from the mulberries, sometimes Father used it to make wine. And Harriet would look so self-important as she helped him gather the fruit, fetch all the bags and bottles and other paraphernalia ready for the mixing and fermenting. Had Harriet harvested the fruit this year? There was none left on the tree that Joanna could see, but all the rain they'd had would have removed all traces from the lawn and the path.

Wanting perversely to stretch out the delicious and anticipatory moment before she started reading the letters, Joanna stood on the edge of the pond and peered into the murky water. It needed clearing. It was clogged with algae and rotting leaves; the water buttercups and lilies of the summer had wilted and died. Joanna remembered playing boat races with Harriet, poking the floating mulberry leaves with a stick, staring into the pond in the spring as the water flickered in the weak sunlight, searching for the first sight of a skinny tadpole. She remembered picnics, a tartan rug spread out under the tree, Mother's home-made lemonade, the snuffling of the pigs and the bleating of the sheep, the taste of the farmyard summertime in her eyes, on her skin.

She reached out to touch the bark of the mulberry tree. The bark felt dry under her fingertips, but not brittle. And yes, the tree looked stronger and more rugged than ever. Which was reassuring, she found. While the tree was still standing, there was still safety; there had to be. This tree was iconic of her childhood, and it felt good to be here. She tested the wooden bench for dampness with the flat of her hand and sat down. She might clear the pond tomorrow, though in truth she rather liked Mulberry Farm Cottage this way. The general air of being run-down, dilapidated, on the edge of decay, seemed to suit the place, it was part of its charm; it quite liked being wild, she decided.

As she watched, the serrated leaves of the mulberry seemed to shiver in the breeze, and a leaf floated down through the air, to rest on the lawn by the pond. Joanna remembered the time her father had cut the tree back too heavily and they thought it would die. But it hadn't died. *What doesn't kill you makes you stronger.* Would it be like that with Martin? She thought of his unanswered texts. She had put up a barrier, a wall – at least for now. She didn't want to talk until she'd had more time to think, and she certainly didn't want to argue. Someone on the radio last week had said that arguments kept a relationship alive because they showed you still cared. But now she was wondering if the opposite was true. If arguments could simply batter the love out of you.

55

And now, here she was, back at Mulberry Farm Cottage, and she could almost smell the change in the air. Could you go back in order to decide how to go forwards? Mother might not be the mother of her childhood and Harriet was never exactly sisterly . . . But this was still home and this was where she wanted to be for now. Because she felt battered. She felt adrift. Had it happened without her even noticing?

She took the letters out of her bag, looked around to check she wasn't being observed. There was something illicit about the discovery, something thrilling that made her want to keep this to herself. Gently, she untied the black ribbon. She'd find out first what they were all about — who'd written them and if they revealed anything interesting — and then — she sighed — she'd share them with her mother and her sister. But for now, they were for her eyes only.

There were three letters of several pages each, fastened with three separate clips. She unclipped the first pages and began to read, her gaze skating down to the end of the final page to discover the name of the author. *Emmy*, she read, in the lovely looping handwriting. So, she'd been right, it was a woman's hand.

And she'd written it in Venice. It was written again at the bottom of the letter. *From Venice with love*. Inevitably, Martin and that romantic trip came again to mind.

She began reading the first page. *My dearest Rufus, my heart's love.*

Oh my . . . Joanna looked up, away into the distance of the green rolling fields of the Down where the grass was glistening in the late afternoon sun and the sheep were calmly grazing. It was a love letter. From Venice with love, of course. Perhaps they were all love letters . . . She looked down at the pages

56

on her lap. Despite her curiosity, she still felt as if she were intruding. What would this Emmy feel about someone reading her letters to Rufus? But it was so long ago. And Joanna was so curious. She read on.

How I wish you could be with us in this glorious city.

Us? Who were *us*? Joanna wondered.

Father is feeling quite well and his breathing seems easier – the warm air here agrees with him, I believe.

Ah, she was with her father then. Joanna read on.

Today, we visited St Mark's Square, which is very grand, and the architecture is most fine. Ah, my dearest, how I dream of you being here with me on a boat on the Canal Grande passing by the most magnificent of palaces, my hand in yours, you whispering to me the sweetest of words, such as you have whispered to me so many times before.

Joanna let out another small sigh. Emmy certainly missed him, that much was obvious. Who was he? Her lover? Her husband? She looked up once more. The sun was setting and there was now a chill to the early evening air. Over the sea in the V of the hills, the light was red-gold, gilding the rolling tide. And behind the cottage, the tall pine trees marked the beginning of Warren Woods where she and Harriet used to gather bluebells in the spring, bringing them to Mother for her to put into vases, their fragrance filling the cottage with heady summertime.

Did she miss Martin? she asked herself. Not enough perhaps. There was an emotion in this letter that Joanna couldn't help envying. Whoever Rufus was, clearly Emmy had left him at home . . . Here at Mulberry Farm Cottage perhaps? How old was the cottage? It had been built in the 1880s, she thought, though there might have been another building on the site even earlier. So, perhaps Emmy had left him here while she travelled with her sick father on a trip. Drinking the waters or taking the air, or whatever they called it back then. Were they married? She sounded educated and they must have had money to be able to travel. Who was she? A previous resident of Mulberry Farm Cottage? An ancestor of theirs perhaps? Joanna felt a small shiver of excitement.

In the afternoons, she read, going on to the second page, *Father takes a nap and I set off with my board and my easel to the bridge. Oh, how you would smile if you could see me, my dearest.*

The bridge? Joanna frowned. Something nudged at her mind, something she couldn't quite capture. And board and easel? So, Emmy was an artist. Was that why they had gone to Venice? She was going to paint . . . ?

Oh, my. Joanna jumped to her feet. How could she be so dense? Emmy was going to paint a bridge in Venice!

She made her way inside, hoping no one was around. She was in luck. The kitchen was empty, though the meaty fragrance of supper cooking was entwined enticingly with the sweetness of plum jam. Harriet was nowhere to be seen. Joanna took the stairs at a half-run. From the bathroom, she could hear her mother singing 'Diamonds Are a Girl's Best Friend' and from the study came Harriet's tap tap tapping.

She slipped into her bedroom. She pulled the letters out of her bag once more. *Venice.* Her gaze travelled from the letter written in that watery Italian city to the picture on her primrose-wallpapered bedroom wall. It had been there as long as she could remember, so familiar during her childhood that back then she hardly gave it a second glance. But it was beautiful. The wooden bridge lit into gold by the yellow light of early evening formed a perfect arc over the canal. The sun was low in the blue sky and the water was rich with flecks of light and shade.

Joanna had never known the name of the artist – the signature was illegible – though she saw now as she looked closer that it could be 'Emily' and the surname definitely began with an S. She peered at it again. 'Emily' to 'Emmy' wasn't a stretch. And the handwriting had the same graceful slope to it, although the letter was easy to read and the surname of the signature on the painting almost illegible.

She paused, hovering in front of the picture, holding up the letter, comparing the two signatures. They had to be the same hand. And it wasn't a coincidence, because they were both in this house, the letters and the picture, so Emmy must have lived here in Mulberry Farm Cottage, which had been in Joanna's family, the Shepherd family, for generations. The surname on the painting began with an 'S'. She was definitely an ancestor then. But who exactly? Joanna didn't know much about their family tree. Would Harriet have any idea?

Joanna was out of the door in seconds. Unthinking, she burst into the study without knocking.

'Harriet . . .'

Her sister jumped, clicked the minimise button on the PC, but not before Joanna had clocked the picture of some bloke of forty plus smiling into the camera. Well, now . . . The image changed back to Harriet's screensaver – an innocent Austrian landscape scene.

'I wish you wouldn't burst in like that,' Harriet grumbled. 'What's the matter? Is it Mother?'

'No, no. Sorry.' What was Harriet up to? 'I was just wondering . . . have you ever investigated our family tree?'

'What?' Harriet was looking at her as if she were mad.

'Do you know the names of our ancestors? The people who lived here – in the cottage – before us?'

'Well, obviously the grandparents.' Harriet's fingers were tapping on the desk next to the keyboard. Clearly, she was anxious to get on. Alone. 'Father's parents.'

'No, not them. Before that. In the early 1900s.'

'Early 1900s?' Harriet's eyebrows rose. 'Why?'

'Oh . . .' For a moment, Joanna floundered. She still wasn't quite ready to share. 'Research,' she said.

Harriet didn't even question this. 'There are some photos around somewhere.' She waved an arm vaguely towards the old mahogany bookcase. 'I'll have a look after supper, if you want.'

'I could look. Now.'

Harriet's gaze could transmit frostbite. 'I'm busy in here, Joanna,' she snapped. 'Can't you see?'

'OK, sorry.' Joanna backed out. She certainly had seen. 'One thing, though, Het . . .'

Harriet blinked at her. Joanna realised she hadn't used that pet name for . . . well, for ages.

'What?'

'Who painted the bridge?'

'The bridge?'

'The Venetian bridge in my room. The picture.'

'No idea.' Already her fingers were back on the keyboard, her shoulders were hunched, she was focusing all her attention on the Austrian mountains.

Joanna left her to it.

Back in her room, she flicked through the letters. They were written from the cities of Venice, Lisbon and Prague, three long letters, hence the three bundles. Why those three cities? Joanna was intrigued. They were all addressed to *my dearest Rufus, my heart's love*. Emmy didn't hold back.

Joanna returned to the final page of the letter from Venice.

You have asked me why, on this trip, I shall paint so many bridges. An excellent question, my dear. A bridge, it seems to me, is a crossing point, a joining, a connection. Place to place, time to time; the bond that you and I share is just such a joining in my mind and in my heart.

Wow. It must have been quite a relationship. Special. The once in a lifetime kind. Joanna thought of Martin. Had it ever been that way with him? She had thought so – at first. But now, when she looked back on it, she wasn't so sure. She wondered if she'd simply been young, impressionable, more than ready to fall in love and forge a partnership with a man who had made her heart flutter.

Bridges provide a pathway, do they not? A way through. At a certain point, there are choices: to go back, to go forward or to stay still; much as in life. From the bridge there is a broad perspective, a new way of seeing. The bridge rises above the men who built it, the men who walk it, even the water or earth beneath it.

And, my dearest love, at the top of its span there lies a particular moment, still and tangible; a pause in time. It is this moment, this pause, which I should like to paint, to capture. We are in that moment, Rufus. Which pathway is it to be? I know that you, my most dear, my heart's love, will understand. And so I remain, as I write from Venice with love,

Your Emmy

It was powerful stuff. Emmy's letters contained tantalising fragments of a life, and a love; glimpses of an artist and a traveller. An ancestor who had shared Joanna's travelling gene . . . She put the letters down on the bed beside her. She stared at the painting, imagined her – Emmy – with her brushes and paints, all those years ago, trying to capture the water, the bridge, the moment in time . . .

Joanna heard her mother get out of the bath, heard her humming 'Move Over Darling' as she crossed the landing.

61

'I'm out of the bath now, Harriet,' their mother called. 'Is supper ready?'

'Ten minutes,' Harriet called back.

Joanna tucked the letters under the coverlet again and smiled to herself as she reviewed what she had discovered. Emmy was in love with Rufus and so perhaps they had lived together here at Mulberry Farm Cottage which still housed her painting and her letters. Rufus was, then, her husband. Emmy travelled a lot with her father. And everywhere she went she painted bridges. *A crossing point. A spanning point. A pause. A moment.* What had she meant by that exactly?

'I'll lay the table,' she called out to Harriet.

'You'd better lay a place for Owen too. He's on his way.'

'Oh, that's nice.' Joanna had always liked Owen with his friendly manner and directness. You knew where you were with a man like Owen – probably on a farm mucking out a pigsty. She chuckled to herself. Briskly, she walked down the stairs to the kitchen. Tomorrow morning she would phone Toby. And despite everything, she felt a shiver of excitement. It was time to take stock and make some changes. Endings – if this was an ending – could lead to new beginnings. It was only the seed of an idea. But when you had such a seed you had to nurture it. Sometimes, some things were meant to be.

CHAPTER 8

Harriet

Dorset

'Isn't this wonderful?' Their mother's face was still flushed from her bath. She clasped her hands. Harriet dished out more potatoes. She doubted Mother was talking about the chicken chasseur.

'Wonderful,' Owen agreed, tucking in to his second plateful.

Harriet felt sorry for him and gave him the last bit of mash. Mother was right – he must be lonely and he had been good to them. More than that, they should be kind to him because of what he'd been through with his wife. It was just that she found it hard to find the energy required for empathy. Life was too full of making ends meet, paying the latest bill and ensuring that Mother was kept away from tradesmen. It had made Harriet hard, she realised, with a slight sense of shock. But she had never been hard, had she? Not before?

'Sitting here, all together, like a real family.' Mother beamed at Joanna first and then Owen. Harriet, of course, was always there, she thought morosely.

'Pity Martin can't join us,' Harriet heard herself saying dryly. There she went again. Saying things she didn't have to say, spoiling the atmosphere.

Joanna made no comment, though. She just sipped her water and gave a little nod of agreement. What was she really thinking? What had happened with Martin exactly? And why was she suddenly so interested in their ancestors?

'How is Martin?' Owen asked. He was such an innocent – or pretended to be. 'Keeping well, is he?' Obviously, he was trying to find out how the land lay in that direction. Joanna had always been a hit with the boys working on the farm; Harriet less so. Of course, Owen was hardly a boy working on the farm, but it was a similar situation. Some things never changed.

'Not too bad, thanks.' Joanna put down her glass. 'The truth is . . .'

Harriet stared at her. Surely, she wasn't going to spill over the dinner table, with Owen here as well? Why on earth would she do such a thing?

'We're having a bit of a break,' Joanna continued. 'From each other, that is.'

Their mother stared at her younger daughter. She looked confused and upset. Harriet searched her mind for a change of subject. 'I was wondering, Jo . . .' she said.

'Yes?' Joanna looked as if she might cry. Harriet refilled her water glass. Should she open a bottle of wine? They had some tucked away in one of the kitchen cupboards. But that might look as if she was trying to celebrate; alternatively it might bring even more emotions to the dinner table.

'Are you free tomorrow afternoon?' Harriet asked firmly. After all this time emailing, Hector had been very insistent on meeting without delay. And in for a penny, Harriet had thought. She might as well get it over with.

'Tomorrow afternoon?' Joanna blinked. 'Yes, of course. I've got some calls I need to make first and some writing—'

'Oh, Harriet.' Their mother clicked her tongue. 'Joanna has her own work to do, remember. She hasn't come here just to be at your beck and call, you know.'

Harriet stared at her, speechless. Did she really have such little grip on reality, that—

'It's fine.' Joanna patted their mother's hand. 'I want to help. What do you need me to do, Harriet?'

What did she need her to do?

'Just stay here at home.' Harriet waved her hand around breezily. 'I have to go into Bridport to . . .' To do what exactly? How much should she tell them? And then she straightened her back. She didn't have to tell them anything. She could be as private as she liked. 'On a personal matter,' she amended.

Her mother arched her eyebrows and smiled at Joanna. 'How intriguing,' she said. She seemed to have forgotten Martin. She leant forwards as if to investigate further.

'So, what else did you find in the attic, Jo?' Harriet cut her off before Mother could ask any more. This, she thought, was what she had to go through in order to have a life of her own.

'Oh, nothing much.' Joanna toyed with her food. 'A bag of old tools, a roll of carpet, some books.'

'Father's books?' Harriet would like to see them restored to the study.

'Yes. If you give me a hand, Harriet, we can bring them down.' Joanna glanced at Owen and gave him one of those smiles she seemed to have on tap. The ones that had always sent the boys running to do her bidding.

'Just say the word, Joanna,' he responded gallantly. 'Books are heavy things. I'm always happy to help.'

'No need, thank you,' Harriet said.

'How kind of you, thanks so much, Owen,' her sister said at the exact same moment.

Owen looked from one to the other of them in confusion.

Harriet shrugged. It was up to Joanna. If she wanted to be beholden. 'And what else was up there, Jo?' she persevered. She might be imagining it, but Joanna had that secretive look on her face that Harriet remembered so well from childhood, when Joanna had hidden one of Harriet's schoolbooks or played some prank or other.

'A big old trunk,' Joanna said at last. 'God knows how it got up there.'

'Empty?'

'More or less.'

Harriet gave her one of her looks. They'd always been effective in the past, but apparently were no longer, since Joanna just gave her a mysterious smile. Her sister was hiding something, Harriet was sure, but if it was in the attic, how vital could it be? Harriet had far more important things to think about.

Such as what was going to happen tomorrow afternoon . . .

Later, after Owen had gone back home and Joanna and Mother were in bed, Harriet stayed up, reflecting on her momentous decision. What was she thinking? What would they talk about? She must be mad.

Online dating had begun as a game – something to fill the lonely winter evenings. And it had become . . . addictive. Her sessions online were her fix. She needed them, but . . . she was aware that she was never satisfied. Each session became more

66

frenzied – typing out hurried emails, waiting for the replies, putting on her glasses to scrutinise the pictures more closely.

She wandered upstairs and began to get undressed. *Frenzied, but not desperate*, she told herself firmly. And yet each session online left her feeling empty. Because, well, she wasn't getting anywhere, was she? Something kept stopping her. And there was so little time left. Which was why she had decided to muster the courage, seize the moment and possibly even the man.

How had she come to be in this position? She examined her face in the mirror. As usual, she looked tired. Other girls met a special someone almost, it seemed, without trying. What had stopped Harriet? That promise to Father? Fear? Or was it isolation, lack of opportunity, being so damned busy all the time that one year ran into the next, one decade leapfrogged into another, youth had turned into middle age and would soon be stumbling past it? She was thirty-nine years old. Had she left it too late, after all?

She realised that online dating had become commonplace in the last twenty years. But it had never been in the least commonplace for Harriet. She stripped off her clothes and hung them on the back of the bedroom chair as usual. She wouldn't sleep; she was so nervous. Wouldn't anyone be nervous in her position? Anyone who hadn't . . . well, who hadn't . . .

Right from the start she had thought Hector a possibility – if that was even his real name. Harriet sniffed. He was forty-five, so his profile claimed, but she'd spent some time looking at his picture and there was something suspicious about the area between the upper jaw and the earlobe that said facelift to Harriet. Also, she wasn't sure about his eyes.

They'd been emailing for months and so, predictably,

Hector had sounded delighted when after weeks of making lame excuses she had emailed him after her jam-making session to suggest meeting for coffee.

I can't wait, he told her. *Tomorrow would be perfect. Drive to Bridport? I'd drive to the end of the earth to meet you.*

He sounded very keen. Harriet went over to the window and drew back the yellow cotton curtain of her childhood. The night was still, the sky thick and almost moonless, the farmyard below perfectly quiet. It was her favourite time – a time when there were no demands for her to actually do anything; she could just be. From her vantage point she could just see the dark shape of the pig shed at the far end of the cobbled yard, Little Barn with the chicken run behind, and in front of this, the considerable bulk of Big Barn-cum-tea room. In front of it, as her eyes grew accustomed to the darkness, she could make out the misshapen woodpile opposite the old cow shed, and the lines of the ancient blue tractor too – unused for years. She could feel, rather than see, the mulberry tree. She always could. It watched over the cottage, so much a part of the place, so much a part of Harriet. It must, she thought, have seen it all.

It would only be quiet for a few more hours, she thought, glancing at her watch. She pulled it from her wrist and as she did so, a movement outside caught her eye. The moon had edged from its cloud cover and the farmyard was revealed. The veil lifted. She could see all the farm buildings quite clearly, even the cobbles on the yard and a wheelbarrow she'd left by the . . .

Crikey. Harriet froze. A man was standing in the farmyard by the old cow shed. A man wearing an overcoat and glasses. He seemed to be looking up at the house, but he didn't seem to see her. Or had he? *Ye Gods.* And she was naked. *Oh, my giddy aunt* . . . She shrank back to the side of the window, thrust the curtains back into place, peered round to see if she'd imagined it, imagined him.

He wasn't a mirage. She realised that now. It wasn't her imagination. He had been real enough. Even though the moon was still casting its white eerie light. And even though the man was gone.

CHAPTER 9

Joanna

Dorset

Joanna was already feeling as if she had never left home at all.
Supper had been awkward last night — mainly because of her
announcement about Martin, she supposed, but she didn't want
to keep lying to everyone about it and they'd have to know
sooner or later if she didn't go back . . . Mother hadn't mentioned it since — perhaps that was how she coped with the bad
things of life, like the cottage being in such a state of disrepair
and losing their father; perhaps she simply swept them under
the proverbial carpet and pretended they hadn't happened? And
that was a relief, because this morning Joanna had work to do.

She finished the article she was working on, did some editing
and then ran the vacuum cleaner round the sitting room while
Harriet was out collecting eggs and feeding the pigs. Although
Harriet was in a weird mood as usual, there was a sense of
peace here at Mulberry Farm Cottage that Joanna relished.
She hadn't realised how much she had missed being in the

country, away from traffic noise and crowds. It was conducive to writing – maybe even inspirational in its own way. Perhaps, Joanna thought, she'd lived in London for too long. Perhaps, after all, it was time for a change.

As for Mother, she didn't need to be watched all the time; she seemed quite happy reading her magazines and wandering around the orchard. Joanna wondered if her sister was exaggerating about Mother. She wasn't her old self, of course not, but she didn't seem to pose any threat – either to herself or to anyone else come to that.

Straight after lunch, Joanna headed outside to call Toby. The mobile signal was better and she didn't want to be overheard. She edged through the damp and cobwebby porch. Numerous pairs of wellies stood amongst Harriet's gardening tools, piles of old animal blankets, and an assortment of buckets. The shelves along the wall were crammed with baskets and egg boxes, glass jars and clay pots. It was a mess, but a comforting mess. Joanna supposed it was all so familiar to Harriet and Mother that they no longer even registered it.

'Yes, sweetie?' Toby seemed pleased to hear from her. 'What can I do for you?'

'You mentioned some travel brochures. Before . . .' Before she left London, before she came here, before her husband told her he had been seeing another woman. It had only been a couple of days, but it seemed an awfully long time ago already.

'Oh, yes, the travel information job.' There was a pause. 'You said you weren't interested, Jo.'

Ah. Had he offered it to someone else then? 'Things have changed,' she told him. And how. 'I'm very interested now.' She felt guilty, planning to leave when she'd only just got here, but this was her job, this was a way she could help.

71

'OK.' She could hear him tapping on his computer. 'Let me check to see if they're still available.'

She waited.

'Yeah,' he said at last. 'All yours if you fancy it.'

Joanna exhaled. Oh, she fancied it. 'So, can you remind me what the job entails?' It had gone in one ear and out the other. Last time she and Toby had spoken, she had been focusing on work she could do without going away. Now, though . . .

'Galileo want a series,' Toby said. "They're being commissioned for tourist information offices abroad. City travel brochures with a theme. Three now, but they'll probably want more at some point later down the line.'

A theme. Joanna thought fast. 'And definitely still available?'

'I kind of put them to one side,' he admitted. 'I thought it sounded like just your sort of thing, then you said no, so I was going to offer it to Sean, but he's just taken on a big project and can't spare the time . . .' She heard him shuffling some papers.

'I'll do it,' she said.

'The money's not bad,' he added. 'It's some sort of sponsorship thing.'

Thank goodness. She had always tried to help Harriet and Mother out a bit financially but what with their mortgage and her own unstable income, not to mention Harriet's pride, it had never been easy. Now, though . . . 'What sort of theme?' she asked.

'Something that hasn't been done before,' he said. 'A new angle. Walking behind the scenes. Something away from the obvious.'

'So they have no idea what they want?' Same old story, she thought.

Toby chuckled. 'They will when we give it to them, sweetie.

72

I'm telling you, this is a decent commission. Who knows where it could lead?'

But Joanna didn't want to look too far ahead. 'Which cities?' she asked. It was too much to hope. Of course, she didn't want to go away so soon. She'd promised to help out and she would. But on the other hand, Harriet wouldn't want her around all the time; she'd made that clear. And if Jo was bringing in enough money to make a significant contribution . . . it would make sense. This could be her base. Just for a short while. Until she'd decided what to do about Martin.

'Anywhere in Europe,' Toby replied.

'Italy?'

'Perfect.'

Joanna smiled. Italy always was. She thought of Emmy's letters. It was a sign all right, but she could hardly believe her luck. She had googled the three cities and linked them in to the UK. If Emmy and her father had travelled from the UK to Venice, then Lisbon, then Prague, then back to the UK again, the shape of their journey was uncannily like an egg timer, an hourglass, the sands of time . . . 'And Lisbon?'

'Good choice.'

She imagined Toby whisking through his mental index of travel hotspots.

'Berlin?' he suggested hopefully. 'Vienna?'

'Or Prague?' she said.

'Yeah, maybe.' Less enthusiastically now.

Oh, yes. She thought of Emmy. *Definitely Prague.*

'I'll check that for you,' Toby said. 'And the theme?'

That was easy. Emmy had done that part for her. She thought of the bridges, the pause, the moment in time. 'Bridge walks?' she said.

'Bridge walks?' Toby sounded even less enthused at this.

'Past to present,' Joanna went on smoothly. 'A moment in time. A decision. A new way of seeing. A pathway.' She was improvising, because she hadn't yet thought this through.

'Hmm, sounds interesting – possibly.' Clearly, he wasn't convinced.

Joanna was in the kitchen garden now and she watched as Harriet emerged from the porch. She was wearing faded blue jeans, scuffed shoes, an old tweed jacket and a yellow scarf. Bohemian wasn't the half of it. Joanna tutted. 'Hang on a sec, Toby.'

She switched her mobile to mute. 'Want to borrow?' She indicated her own chestnut-coloured leather jacket hanging on the peg. What, she wondered, was Harriet's pathway this afternoon? And could it conceivably have something to do with that man whose image she'd seen on Harriet's computer screen last night?

Harriet hesitated. 'All right then,' she said. 'Thanks.' She took off the tweed number, hung it up and put on Joanna's, carefully, as if it might bite.

'Bye. Have a good time.' She smiled at Harriet's expression and turned her attention back to Toby as she unmuted the phone. 'Sorry about that. My sister.'

'A moment in time?' Toby made a noise halfway between a grunt and a sigh.

'A pause,' Joanna confirmed, remembering Emmy's words.

'I trust you, Jo,' said Toby. 'Don't let me down.'

'Great. And of course I won't.' Joanna crossed her fingers. 'But—'

'I'll make it work, Toby,' she said. 'Don't worry.'

She waved at her mother, who had come to stand in the kitchen doorway. 'Just coming,' she called out to her.

'You sound busy, sweetie,' he said. 'Where are you exactly?'

'Dorset,' she told him. 'A family visit.'

'Right. OK. I'll email you the style and word count notes.'

'Thanks.' Synchronicity, thought Joanna. Sometimes that was what life was all about. Being open to opportunities, catching them at the right moment.

'And just so you know,' Toby added.

'Yes?'

'You need to get online and book a flight pronto.'

'Pronto?'

'Yeah. The first one needs to be done yesterday.'

Joanna was thoughtful as she went back inside. She put the kettle on for tea while her mother sat down at the old kitchen table. Mother might be in denial about Martin, Joanna thought, but she seemed happier now that she had all her chicks back in the nest – for a while at least. And maybe she knew something about the mysterious Emmy?

'Mother, do you know who painted the Venetian picture in my bedroom?' she asked her as she waited for the kettle to boil.

Her mother frowned. 'I don't know, darling,' she said at last, an expression of defeat flitting across her features. 'Is it important?'

'No, not at all.' Joanna warmed the teapot and spooned in the tea. 'I just wondered if it might be one of our ancestors.'

She shook her head. 'I don't think so, no. I can't think of anyone who was an artist.'

Joanna decided to come clean. 'I found some letters in the attic,' she confided.

'Letters?'

'From someone called Emmy?'

Her mother shook her head.

'To someone called Rufus?'

She shook her head again.

Joanna poured the tea. 'Never mind, Ma,' she soothed. 'It's a bit of a mystery. But you know me.'

Her mother smiled. She was on safer ground here. 'You always liked reading Agatha Christie books,' she pronounced triumphantly.

'I did.'

She'd been right. A mysterious family secret was exactly the kind of distraction that Joanna needed to stop her feeling maudlin about the end of her marriage – if it had ended, that was. She would find out the identity of Emmy and Rufus and she would follow Emmy's pathway – at least until she had a clearer pathway of her own.

CHAPTER 10

Harriet

Dorset

'Tell me all about yourself,' he had said.

Harriet had panicked. *All about yourself* was an awful lot. And this experience hadn't been quite what she'd expected. Though what she had been expecting, she couldn't exactly say.

Since Joanna's return, things seemed to be changing. Wasn't she glad that her sister was around? Well, yes, but . . . One moment Joanna was being evasive and secretive, the next thing she was treating supper with their neighbour as some sort of counselling session. Mother was revelling in the attention of her younger daughter and hadn't called a tradesman out for days and Harriet had found herself with a rare commodity known as free time, which she wasn't quite sure what to do with. She'd seen a prowler last night who might or might not be dangerous. And she'd just had her first blind date in the Boat and Barnacle. Life seemed to be becoming very complicated.

She was walking back to the long-stay car park, snug in

Joanna's chestnut-coloured leather jacket. The shops on East Street were closing and the town was quiet. She glanced at her watch. Telling Hector all about herself had taken just one hour and forty-five minutes. What did that say about her life?

It had started well enough. She'd made her way to the Boat and Barnacle, taken a deep breath and pushed open the door, blinking as the comforting fug and fragrance of roasted coffee and chocolate brownies wafted her way. She'd walked confidently across the varnished floorboards towards the counter, still scanning the occupants of the café, and then she'd spotted him.

'Harriet?' And then when she failed to respond: 'You are Harriet?'

She'd nodded dumbly. Where had her confidence gone? Where was her determination? All she could do was wonder why she was here. It was all very well emailing and fantasising and the like. But that was a very different prospect from actually meeting someone.

Hector seemed undeterred. 'What will you have? Coffee? Tea? Glass of wine?'

Harriet felt a spear of panic. For goodness' sake . . . 'Coffee,' she croaked. 'Please.' Did that sound as if she was assuming he'd pay for it? She groped for her purse.

'Oh, no. Allow me.' He held up one hand. Masterful? Or controlling?

She shrugged. Ungrateful? Or indifferent? What a minefield this was. Why would anyone do this awful, scary thing?

A few minutes later they were seated in the upstairs lounge. The walls were painted a deep pomegranate and rich velvet curtains framed the Georgian windows. Someone at the Boat and Barnacle knew about creating atmosphere; the lamps were dim, letting out a warm, golden light that somehow made Harriet feel safe.

78

'Why do it, eh?' he said.

'Exactly what I was thinking.' She tried not to stare at the part of his face where cheek met ear. After all, countless people had facelifts these days.

'Searching for a mate,' Hector said. 'I suppose that's it.'

'Yes.' Harriet tried not to dwell on this.

'Looking for love,' he elaborated, gazing into her eyes.

Harriet didn't respond. She wasn't sure she knew why she was doing online dating. She had joined for a bit of fun and simply got interested in reading profiles and indulging in unthreatening banter with unknown men – something she'd never had the chance to do before. Oh, she knew that she wanted to escape from her life somehow, but the practical part of her also knew that the dating site she was using, Someone Somewhere, was unlikely to provide such an escape – for that, she needed a miracle. She missed her father. Harriet felt the accustomed boot in her stomach that she experienced whenever she thought of him. Like the dream, it never went away.

A waiter appeared with their coffees and what looked like a large brandy for Hector.

'Don't look so worried.'

Was she?

'You know what they say.'

'No.'

'Smile and it might never happen.'

Harriet scowled even more. 'Or it might,' she felt bound to point out.

He beamed. 'Sit back and relax.' Now, he was beginning to sound like her dentist. 'And tell me all about yourself.'

★

79

'Have you done this often?' she had asked him, having told him about the farm (a version of), her childhood (a version of) and her family (she'd have to be crazy . . .).

'I've met a few ladies,' he admitted. His voice wasn't bad, she decided – low and a bit like a mug of night-time Ovaltine. If you closed your eyes . . .

He leant closer. 'How else do you meet people these days?' he asked.

Harriet presumed this was a rhetorical question. She didn't meet anyone. 'I know.'

'But online dating's a bit like a chocolate box,' he elaborated.

'In what way?' Harriet had no idea what he was talking about. How could you tell anyway, if someone was insane? She thought of the mysterious stranger she'd seen in the farmyard last night. Who was he? What was he doing there? What exactly had he wanted? She'd even wondered for one mad moment if there was some connection with Someone Somewhere. People hacked into other people's computers, didn't they? Hector could be a potential stalker for all she knew. The unknown prowler from last night hadn't looked dangerous with that oversized coat and the owlish glasses. But appearances could be deceptive.

'You select the coffee cream.' Hector's eyebrows rose alarmingly. 'And you take a bite.'

Harriet flinched. 'Yes?'

He pushed his empty glass to one side and eyed her appraisingly. 'Then you look at what's left in the box.'

'Oh.' Harriet was beginning to see.

'You look very closely,' he said. 'And then right at the bottom . . .' He took hold of Harriet's hand.

'Yes?' Though she wasn't sure she was ready for physical contact.

80

'You find the hazelnut whirl,' he said.

Harriet wasn't sure she wanted to be a hazelnut whirl. But what did she want?

Hector ordered another double brandy from the waiter. 'Trust me,' he said, 'everyone is economic with the truth on Someone Somewhere.'

Which must be why he hadn't told her he was an alcoholic. 'But you,' he said, 'you're different.'

Was this what she had joined the dating site to hear? Insincere flattery from a stranger? 'How do you know?' she challenged.

He tapped his nose. 'Call it intuition,' he said. 'In fact, Harriet, I really think I could fall in love with you.'

Harriet gulped.

'What do you think about that, Harriet?' Hector was waiting expectantly.

'I think I'd like to be someone else,' she heard herself say.

'Sorry?' He looked baffled.

'Someone unshackled,' she said. 'Someone who might travel the world – if she felt like it. Or even get a proper job,' she added as an afterthought.

'A proper job?' He let go of her hand.

'Someone who doesn't have to look after my mother,' she added. Like Joanna? Was that what she wanted? To be Joanna?

He leant back in his chair. 'You have to care for your mother?' His voice was neutral now.

'I wish I didn't have to,' she confessed. Only she shouldn't really say that, because that would mean . . . and obviously she didn't want . . .

'Can't you pay someone to do that for you?' He waved his hand and Harriet looked round, half expecting a nursing assistant to materialise from behind the pine doorway.

81

What with? Harriet wondered. She shook her head. 'It's complicated,' she said. 'My life is complicated. Everything's complicated.'

He looked up at the big station clock on the wall of the Boat and Barnacle. 'Ah, well,' he said. 'It's rather late. I should be getting along.'

They lingered for only a moment outside. Harriet supposed that if he planned to fall in love with her in the not so distant future then there was a distinct possibility that he would ask her for a second date. He didn't, though.

Now, she pulled the keys of the pick-up from her jacket pocket. She opened the door and almost stumbled as she climbed inside. Well, it was heady stuff. She put the key in the ignition. But also, pure fantasy.

Nevertheless, she felt relieved as she backed the pick-up out of the parking space. She had done it, hadn't she? She had made the effort. She had followed through. And she had hardly thought all afternoon about the problems in her life — the money she didn't have, the cottage that was crumbling around her, the non-existent shepherds' huts, even the prowler from last night. But now she was eager to get home. She couldn't really trust Joanna to look after Mother, and there was supper to prepare.

She drove out of the long stay, turning left and heading for the traffic lights by Bucky Doo Square. What kind of man would have a facelift anyway? And what kind of man drank four brandies in the middle of the afternoon? It might be time, she thought, to turn her attention to contender number two.

CHAPTER 11

Joanna

Venice
A week later

It felt bitter-sweet for Joanna to be back in Venice. She was swept up in the memories of her previous visit – when she and Martin had been so new, so happy, embarking on what they'd thought would be a whole life together. They'd explored the canals by *vaporetto*, they'd walked miles through narrow streets and alleyways, they'd admired the churches, the frescoes, the crumbling buildings. They'd drunk prosecco in tiny bars and watched the sun setting over the Canal Grande. And just before they left, he'd turned to her. 'We'll come back, Jo,' he'd said. 'One day when we're old and grey, we'll come back.'

'Of course, we will,' she'd laughed. And here she was – not old and grey and not with Martin either.

'You're going off again already?' Harriet had said when Joanna had told her sister and her mother about her forth-coming trip a week ago.

83

'I have to, it's my job.'

'A bit like running away, though, isn't it, Jo?'

'No!' Joanna was stung. Of course she hadn't wanted to leave West Dorset so soon after she'd arrived, but Toby had left her with little choice.

At least Mother had been understanding. She had shushed Harriet and said, 'Of course you must go, darling. Joanna has to work, you know, Harriet.'

'And I'll be back in a few days.' How soon she had become sucked into the slipstream of Mulberry Farm Cottage, she thought. Into the feelings of guilt and very different shared responsibilities from the ones she'd shared with Martin.

Harriet had shrugged. 'It makes no difference to me,' she said.

Was that what her sister really felt? Joanna didn't know. Something had happened the day before; Harriet had looked quite nervous when she left the cottage, having borrowed Joanna's leather jacket. But whatever it was, Harriet wasn't going to share.

Joanna had thought – naively as it turned out – that her being at home again would give them a chance to get closer, that maybe after all these years she might discover a softer side to Harriet's character that hadn't been available to her in childhood or when Martin was around. But if there was such a side, Harriet was keeping it well hidden. And it had always been that way. It had always been Harriet and Father, Father and Harriet. Mother in the kitchen and Joanna left out in the cold.

But whatever her sister thought, at least Joanna knew she was doing something to help – in real and practical terms. And she hoped that this project would help her too, because already, Emmy's pathway had inexplicably become her own.

And here she was. Seeing once again the glorious and ornate palaces on the Grand Canal that Emmy had spoken of in her letter. And exploring the bridges . . . Joanna was beginning to understand Emmy's fascination. There were, she had learnt from her research, over four hundred in Venice. They ranged from delicate little fairy bridges over the narrowest of canals to wide, graceful arcs spanning Venice's primary waterway. Like this one.

Joanna spread the city map flat on the table next to her cappuccino and croissant and took out her notebook. She was sitting outside a café in the vibrant labyrinth of sellers, sounds and smells that was the Rialto, near the famous bridge of the same name, planning the route of the first bridge walk. Opposite the café, the bleached red facade of the Hotel Rialto seemed to gaze back at her in placid contentment. But Joanna wasn't running away, she really wasn't. That wouldn't solve anything. She couldn't run away from what was happening to Mulberry Farm Cottage and to her mother. And she couldn't run away from Martin either. Harriet was right in one way. Joanna must face up to things, deal with it all, sort it out. She must decide what to do about her marriage and she must help Harriet deal with Mother. And she would.

But for now . . . She'd spent the last two days scouting around La Serenissima, getting a feel for the territory, drinking in the city's sights and smells, its textures and flavours. Joanna sipped her coffee and licked a flaky croissant crumb from her finger. She'd decided which bridges to include in the walk, and most importantly, where to finish. The end shouldn't just tail off, it should finish with a flourish.

Once again, she pulled Emmy's letter from Venice from her bag.

Many people regard Venice as the most beautiful city in the world, she read, *and it is plain to see why. As we visit the elegant caffès and piazzas, and admire the richly decorated churches and art and sculpture of the Renaissance, it is hard to believe that this place was once made up of mudbanks inhospitable enough to provide a safe haven for refugees fleeing the barbarian destroyers of the Roman Empire.*

Joanna would find out more about that later, before she wrote up the copy, she decided.

But Emmy clearly had more pressing things on her mind. She noted the art and architecture of the buildings, which presumably were in better shape then than they were now after decades of water damage, Joanna thought. But her mind – and heart – was on her Rufus.

I did not begin to live until we met . . . Joanna read. *And now I miss you, more than I would oceans or the sun, more than I will the stars in this velvet Venetian sky.*

What would it be like, Joanna asked herself, *to miss someone that much?*

She looked down at her wedding ring of white twisted gold and her engagement ring, a solitary diamond also set in white gold. Martin had been so self-conscious the day he gave that ring to her – not knowing if he'd done the right thing, or if she'd turn him down. And she had loved that in him. *Oh, Martin.* How things had changed.

Joanna's sight blurred with unshed tears. She refocused on Emmy's letter from Venice. There was so much sadness in the missing. Did that mean . . . ? Was there more to Emmy's relationship with Rufus than met the eye? *What is next for us?* she read. Were Emmy and Rufus considering their next step? Children? Travel? And, *we are all searching for the way.* Did she mean a way forward for her painting perhaps? Joanna could certainly empathise. She too was searching for her way – she had a decision to make that would affect her future dramatically. Could it have been the same for Emmy?

She gazed across the misty water of the canal. The sky was platinum blue; the city existed in a dreamy shimmer. But although it was romantic, it also possessed an unexpected edge. The scent of sweet pizza and pastry dough laced with tomato and oregano, porcini and Italian sausage fought a running battle with stale canal water, while the seductive richness of roasting coffee seemed to sink into the damp grey and white stone.

This morning before breakfast, Joanna had crossed the Lungo at the Lido where she was staying and walked to the seafront. She'd pulled off her shoes and let her feet sink into the pale brown sand, relishing the grainy feel of it against her skin. The sea was flat and vast with a grey-green glint that reminded her of a rare family holiday in Cornwall when she was a girl. Usually, their parents were too busy with the farm to go away, but on this one occasion something had happened; her mother had been upset, though Joanna had no idea why, and her father's younger brother had stepped in for a few days so that they could go away. The resulting holiday had now acquired an almost dream-like quality in her mind.

The beach at the Lido was so deserted at this time in the morning that Joanna had a glimpse of how wonderfully unique Venice must have been for the Venetians – before tourists interrupted their idyll. She'd almost felt she owned it: this shoreline, this silvery day.

She brushed her lips with the napkin and took another sip of coffee. Shifted her position so that her perspective of the Ponte Rialto shifted too. According to Emmy, she must be ready to see things in a different way . . .

Why hadn't Emmy painted this bridge? Joanna wondered.

It was high and masterful with steps of marble and stone and it boasted magnificent views over the palaces and domes lining the Canal Grande and the *vaporetti*, motorboats and gondolas that chugged and wove along the wide waterway. Better still, its stony backside hosted part of San Polo's Rialto market, tiny shops selling glass, linen, scarves and soft, sweet-smelling leather.

Joanna pondered. Which came first, the market or the bridge? According to her research, it was the market traders; the bridge itself had a history of collapse – it had been rebuilt several times. And perhaps it wasn't quite elegant enough for Emmy. Joanna liked to think she was getting to know this possible ancestor of hers and she reckoned Emmy would prefer a quieter and less obvious sort of beauty.

A text pinged in to Joanna's phone and she sighed. It would be Martin. She checked anyway.

Surely you know she means nothing to me? was all it said.

Joanna sighed. And how was that the point? Didn't that even somehow make it worse? She should, though, she thought, at least go back to Crouch End for some of her things – she had been dithering about this ever since she'd left. It would mean seeing Martin, but she couldn't avoid him forever.

But she wouldn't reply to his text, she decided, not yet. She was working – the last thing she needed was to get into another pointless exchange of messages; there'd been enough of those already.

I miss you. I love you. When are you coming back?

Moving on to: *Don't you think you're overreacting, Jo?*

No, actually.

Joanna thought of the day they'd met. She'd been drawn to him from the first moment she saw him in the bar. It had been so easy to chat to him, then later to dance with him, kiss him on the lawn outside the halls that stood thirteen storeys high, looming into the darkness behind them. It had been easy to fall in love with him when she discovered he wasn't quite as confident as he appeared, even easy to marry him, because by then she couldn't imagine any alternative. But now . . .

In her letter from Venice, Emmy had been searching for the real heart of the city and Joanna wanted to do the same. But in the rest of her life, she felt in danger of losing her way. When had she and Martin stopped doing things together? When had they stepped apart? When had he started looking elsewhere?

She gazed into the watery distance. And more to the point, could they come back from this? Did she even want to? They had been together for such a long time that it was hard to visualise a life without him. And yet Joanna still felt the dead pain of betrayal. She had returned to the place where they had been happy. So, was she going forwards or backwards? She wasn't sure.

She frowned, reached for her notebook. *Venice*, she wrote, *is a disorientating city. Unsure of her direction. She and I should get along just fine . . .*

She liked the idea of mingling with all the other people in a city, being as anonymous as she chose. Here in the Rialto, people thronged the streets, milled up the steps of the bridge, jostled in the famous archways in front of the outer balustrades that looked out over the Grand Canal, searching for the right position, the perfect photograph or selfie that would somehow capture the multiplicity in water and stone, the reflections, the light, the romantic, musical soul that was Venice. Everywhere she looked, there were people – and yet Joanna knew no one.

At a table nearby, a couple kissed and she looked away. They didn't notice her, didn't care – and why should they? She turned to a new page in her notebook. Clean pages were full of possibilities. And she smoothed the map out once more, marking with a bold asterisk the place where the bridge walk would begin. Ponte degli Scalzi.

Slowly and carefully, she traced a line on the map, marking the path she would follow. The walk would begin in Santa Croce among the art galleries and bookshops of Dorsoduro. She would conclude, of course, with the bridge Emmy had painted and that Joanna had now identified as Ponte Accademia, the bridge from the painting in her childhood bedroom, with its criss-crossed wooden structure and high wide arch. Emmy's bridge, as she liked to think of it. Where else?

She would follow Emmy's example and avoid the obvious. This – she tapped the map with her fingernail – would be a walk designed to find the real city, or at least part of it. Bridge to bridge to discover the heart.

Joanna folded up the map and put it in her backpack with her notebook and camera. She got to her feet. And now she would take a *vaporetto* to the beginning. She moved towards the bus stop, closer to the bridge, to the water. The silvery blue light this morning made the tall buildings on either side of the canal seem almost surreal, their edges blurred as if they were gently swaying. A gondola crammed with Japanese tourists swept by, the strains of an Italian opera – *Madame Butterfly* or *Tosca* perhaps – momentarily strung through the air. A *vaporetto* chugged towards the station, slowed, screamed into reverse and thumped against the landing stage, making it shiver.

She was close to Emmy's moment of pause, she realised. The contemplation. At least she was getting there. Was that what Emmy had meant in her letter to Rufus? After a few days, perhaps Joanna too would decide which way to go – backwards or forwards. Beginnings, endings . . . Which would it be for her?

CHAPTER 12

Harriet

Dorset

Harriet decided to go for a walk. If she didn't get out of the house, she'd spontaneously combust.

Lucky Joanna, to be in Venice . . . One minute she'd been here, then whoosh, a lift to the railway station and she was off to the airport. Jet-setting around, and being paid for it too. Her sister might be having marital problems but there were compensations. What would it be like, Harriet wondered, to be so free?

This morning, when Harriet went out to collect the eggs, she noticed that another two tiles had come off the roof; they were lying, in pieces, by the front door, like symbols of doom. 'Bugger,' she said.

Mother hadn't wasted any time. While Harriet was doing some digging in the kitchen garden, she must have gone through the *Yellow Pages* because after lunch three different roofers turned up to give them estimates for a new roof.

'And how much just to replace the broken tiles?' Harriet had asked.

'Well, now . . .' Eventually, one of them reluctantly agreed to do the work; the others all shook their heads and told her that there was a 'limit to the number of times you can do repairs, love.' She knew they were right and they'd have to get a new roof eventually, but how could they possibly afford it?

Harriet plucked her jacket from the hook by the door. And not that she had ever been expecting anyone from Someone Somewhere to rescue her exactly . . . But it would be nice to have the choice. Predictably, Hector hadn't got back in touch, despite the fact that he'd thought he was going to fall in love with her. Though Harriet had to admit, she felt more relieved than offended.

She allowed herself to briefly consider the two remaining contenders for her affections. Charles was a research scientist – very commendable. Harriet liked intelligence in a man and it was really no trouble to use a dictionary every time Charles sent her an email; at least she was enlarging her vocabulary, which wouldn't do her any harm since most of the time she was stuck here with no one to talk to all day but Mother.

And then there was Malcolm, a pig farmer in East Devon. Malcolm had obvious pluses – he too had been brought up on a farm, so they were compatible in that respect, and he knew everything there was to know about pigs, which could come in useful. But Harriet was beginning to think of this as a negative point. Malcolm never wrote an email that didn't mention pigs. She really couldn't imagine what sort of a life partner he would be. Or at least she could, which was the problem.

Harriet strode out through the cluttered porch, kicking a moth-eaten blanket to one side. Pausing, she took a deep breath to let the smell of the freshly turned soil in the kitchen garden filter into her senses – all its layers, from the fresh turfy top to the almost foetid underground. That delicious autumn mix of decay and fecundity. She had always loved this time of year. In the lane behind the farmhouse yesterday as the sun was setting, she'd picked a bowlful of luscious blackberries seeping with juice, staining her fingers. Mmm. Sticky soil, wet plants, milky sap, musty leaves; the pigs and the chickens mixing in. Glorious.

Harriet had been flirting with online dating for over a year now, without ever meeting anyone until Hector. *Early days*, she thought. She didn't want to rush into anything. Because although a lot of people were doing it these days, online dating was still a risky way to meet a partner, wasn't it? Compatibility and chemistry could hardly be detected via a text or an email – though the way things were going round here it would be useful to have a man about the place.

She walked down the track, past the tottering woodpile – which reminded her that the logs Owen had delivered yesterday needed sorting and chopping – across the grey cobbled farmyard and beyond the pen where the pigs were snuffling. She glanced back towards the mulberry tree, thought of Joanna sitting under it only a week or so ago, reading something that made her smile that secret smile. Then she climbed over the wooden stile onto the Down.

The truth was that Harriet wasn't even sure she wanted a man. It had been so long and sometimes she was just plain terrified. She shivered, although the air was warm and the sun was creeping out between the clouds. And even if she were to find the right man, what would she do about Mother? It was all very well keeping promises . . . *Look after your mother. She needs*

93

you. Promise me you'll do that . . . But it was so hard to shoulder all the responsibility. Sometimes . . .

Harriet began to walk across the field. This was Owen's field which used to be their field; full of Owen's sheep which used to be their cows — in a manner of speaking anyway. Last night, she had stayed up until she heard the ancient grandfather clock strike midnight. The cottage was still full of furniture from her childhood and Harriet was glad. Memories had a way of creeping into those old chairs and tables, clocks and bookcases like woodworm; you could touch their dusty wooden surfaces and almost be transported back — well, Harriet could anyhow.

The clock reminded her of Joanna and their childhood game, one, two, three, alive. It was hide-and-seek, but with a time limit. The tradition was to start the game at fifteen minutes to the hour, one of you standing by the clock, the other running off to hide. After five minutes the seeker could start looking. The challenge for the person hiding was to remain undiscovered and then reappear by the grandfather clock as if by magic, as it struck the hour (but not before) shouting 'One, two, three, alive' at the top of their voice.

Harriet grinned at the memory. Try as she might, Joanna had never worked out Harriet's favourite hiding place and Harriet had always refused to tell her. A small triumph perhaps, but . . . 'One, two, three, alive,' she murmured. Joanna had always been easy to find — she'd either be in the old cow shed or Big Barn.

The ground underfoot was humped with rabbit burrows and molehills that she knew drove Owen crazy. Well, not crazy. Owen wasn't the sort of man who did crazy. She couldn't imagine him even being angry. Unlike Harriet who felt angry a lot of the time. She unlocked the gate and swung it open. She didn't want to, but . . . Didn't she have good reason?

94

In the distance now, she could see Owen in his tractor and beyond him the church on the hill. She waved, in case he was looking her way. Did he ever get lonely? she wondered. He seemed pretty self-sufficient, but he was always keen to come to the cottage to drink whisky with Mother and he had certainly been getting on well with Joanna when they had him round to supper the other night, laughing and joking – Joanna must bring it out in him because Harriet had never seen him that way before.

The grass on the Down was clipped short by the sheep and shone green-gold in the autumn sunshine. Harriet paused at the next stile and looked ahead, shielding her eyes. Between the hills, the glistening sea yawned out in front of her into that glorious feeling of infinity that always soothed her ruffled senses. Dorset – land of gentle green hills, fields of grass and acid-yellow rape, flocks of placid grazing sheep, where the seasons dictated the organic produce at farm markets and the air was fresh and clean. She complained about this place, but deep down she loved every muddy inch of it.

She had lived in this same landscape for as long as she could remember. There were more camper vans in the car park in summer, Linda had rashly paid someone to repaint the pub bright tangerine, occasionally there was an unfamiliar fishing boat on the beach. Otherwise, it never changed. And despite everything, that was what Harriet craved. Change. Excitement. And not the kind of excitement that involved shepherds' huts or prowlers either.

It was hard to imagine how she could escape from what her life had become. She had spent all summer baking for the café, and when September came, she had breathed a sigh of relief as she turned her attention to the trees in the orchard – to pickling and bottling and making the jam. As for winter . . . Harriet didn't want to think about that. In winter, she felt more enclosed than ever.

She climbed the next stile and walked on. The afternoon sun was mellow, warming her face and her hair, and the breeze had dropped, although there was a faint chill in the air that reminded her again about the blasted logs. Mother had been cold last night. Time to batten down the hatches, chop the wood, light the stove.

Harriet let herself through the final gate, reached the lane and the stream and made her way down past the old fishing boats to the beach of Warren Cove, tucked between the grass-capped sandstone cliffs. She glanced at her watch. Crikey, she'd been gone forty minutes already; she'd best get back before Mother called out another herd of tradesmen.

She hot-footed it back up the lane and over the Down. And was just crossing the last field when she saw it. Or him. Again! She could barely believe it. A thin figure dodging behind Little Barn by the chicken run where a path led past the pond and up to Blackberry Lane. Unmistakably their prowler.

Harriet increased her pace. 'Hey!' she shouted. 'Hey, you!'

She began a loping run, launched herself over the stile and scooted round the back of Little Barn. Her heart was thumping in her chest. She looked around. Nothing. No one. She bent double for a few seconds to recover, then straightened and headed for the path.

She stopped. All was quiet, except for the rustling and squawking of the chickens, the snuffling of the pigs and the distant rumble of the tractor.

Her breath was still coming in short gasps. Her side was aching. But she ran on past the pond and the mulberry tree up to the lane. And she saw him, in the distance, racing down the road towards the village.

'Stay away from here!' she yelled. 'Stay away from us, or I'll ... I'll ...' Damn. She couldn't think of anything. But anyhow, he was gone, out of sight, probably he hadn't even heard her.

Harriet was so angry now she could scream. What right did he have to keep coming here scaring everyone half to death? Who was he? What should she do? What could she do? *Stop shaking for a start*, she told herself. But what in heaven's name was he after? There was no doubt in her mind, she would have to find out.

CHAPTER 13

Nicholas

Cornwall

Nicholas Tresillion was cooking a Thai curry. He relished cooking now that he lived alone, now that he didn't have to adapt the recipe for family members who happened not to like porcini mushrooms, garlic or lashings of hot chilli. He also relished living here in Godrevy where it was wild, bleak and, yes, sometimes lonely. He'd always enjoyed solitude – that feeling of being at one with the sea, the sky, the Cornish cliffs. Everyone needed space sometimes. Time to reflect. Only now he had more space and solitude than he'd bargained for. And even after all this time, the cottage still reminded him of Rachel. Didn't everything?

He had no idea how to get Rachel from under his skin. Perhaps they'd been together too many years. Or perhaps he was just that sort of a man. He went out into the back garden to pick the basil from the greenhouse – the purply Thai basil that tasted of aniseed and hot summer nights.

But it wasn't only their twenty-year-long marriage or Celie, their daughter, nineteen and with a life of her own . . . He clipped the stem of the plant, crushed it into his hand and sniffed deeply. It took him back to those aniseed gobstoppers of his childhood bought from the post office after school. No. It was something more nebulous that held him to Rachel, something more uncertain.

He stomped back through the small garden whose sandy soil refused to sustain anything much other than tamarisk, grasses and sea campion. It felt almost as though he'd failed. Not at marriage, but at prising something out of Rachel, something that he felt was there, inaccessible, and therefore so damned infuriating.

In the kitchen he washed the leaves. Through the window he could see the length of his sea garden and the dry-stone wall that separated it from the field beyond. Beyond that rose the grass-capped dunes and beyond them was the sea – the wild Atlantic coastline that he loved, the cliff, and the lighthouse at Godrevy.

Rachel had been a holiday visitor. Girls like Rachel didn't grow up in Cornwall. They came from Sussex or Surrey; they were elegant, sleek, well polished. They had upper-class accents and had attended private schools, which gave them this terrible confidence, this apparent ability to deal with anything or anyone.

Nicholas put the steak on the chopping board and began to pound it with a wooden mallet. It was from the local butcher and good quality; it gave in gracefully. He sliced it into thin strips and pushed it to one side of the board.

He had been drinking in the Sloop Inn at St Ives when he first saw her. Part of the building dated from the fourteenth century and Nicholas loved the sea-feel of it – the low black treacly beams and flagstone floor, the ancient lanterns, and sketches of the pub's old-timers hanging on the walls. Plus, it did a good pint. He usually sat at one of the long wooden tables in the Public Bar with the local fishermen and artists – a way of keeping in touch with his roots perhaps – but that day, he was relaxing in the Lounge. Outside, only a cobbled forecourt and a narrow road separated the pub from the harbour beach.

Rachel was sitting at the polished mahogany bar talking to an older, Mediterranean-looking man. Her skin had the faintest of olive sheens, her hair was smooth and long, and he almost knew already the scent of her shampoo. Her eyes were clear – green and translucent. She had a look about her; as if she always knew exactly where she was going.

Nicholas dried his hands and started working on the Thai paste. Red, he decided. He remembered thinking, *How do men like that get women like her?* Then another woman joined them and he realised his mistake. She was less complicated-looking than Rachel, and she linked arms with the Mediterranean-looking man in the way a wife does – unthinking; a casual gesture of intimacy.

Rachel got to her feet then – Nicholas realised that she was even taller than he'd guessed – and disappeared off into the other bar. She came back waving a menu. 'It can't be too bad. They've got fresh flowers on the tables.' She glanced down. 'And a half-decent wine list.'

She hadn't bothered to lower her voice and her accent made Nicholas raise an eyebrow. He heated the paste up slowly, adding small amounts of coconut milk, blending it in with a wooden spoon. The pungent scent began to fill his small white-walled kitchen – lemongrass and chilli, ginger and saffron . . .

The only empty table happened to be close to the threesome. Nicholas unfolded his napkin, looked into the middle distance and homed in on the conversation.

'St Ives is sweet,' Rachel was saying. She was the type who would describe an ardent admirer that way, he guessed, thus destroying his manhood forever. 'But who would want to live here?'

'I'd love it,' the other woman said.

Nicholas liked her passion. And over the years, as he'd got to know Rachel's sister better, he had continued to like her, which was why he was still working with her and Giuseppe, why he would never lose touch.

Nicholas swirled the thick paste around in the wok (Rachel had always said he cooked like a drama queen, but then Rachel had said lots of things, including, *I'll always love you, Nicholas*). He added the beef, browning it quickly on a high heat. Some things were best forgotten.

'But it's a bit of a cultural backwater, don't you think?' And Rachel had looked around her and frowned.

The other woman laughed. 'It's charming,' she said. 'And very creative.'

'They're just local artists, though.' Rachel's tone was scathing. But Nicholas could see the hollow inside her collarbone. It was exquisite. He wanted to touch it. He wanted to run his tongue along its curve. 'After a week,' Rachel continued, 'I'd be bored to death.'

And the Mediterranean man seemed to agree with her because he launched into an accolade to Milan – Italian then.

'Of course,' said Rachel, re-crossing her legs. 'The Italians have unquestionable style.'

And so had she, Nicholas couldn't help thinking. So had she.

After the meat had sizzled for a while, he added the rest of the coconut milk. Nicholas had always been fond of St Ives and he hadn't much liked Rachel's tone, so he hadn't been too sorry when the three of them left the pub, leaving him to reflect into what remained of his cod and chips and his beer on what might have been.

But he saw Rachel again the following day, quite unexpectedly, in one of those galleries she had been so disparaging about. He was about to walk straight past, but she was alone and, well, it seemed a bit like fate. What harm could it do?

Nicholas moved away from the stove and began to wipe the mushrooms clean. What harm indeed?

He had stood behind her in the cream-coloured gallery. Light flooded through the front windows, streaking her hair with dark amber. Her body shifted slightly, showing him she was aware of his presence.

'Only a local artist,' he murmured. 'But perhaps he has promise?'

She didn't turn round. Perhaps random people started conversations with her every time she looked at a painting in a gallery. 'Perhaps,' she said doubtfully.

It was an abstract of sea and sky with pleasing shades of blue. 'But you could do better,' he suggested, in a moment of inspiration.

She turned around then. Her eyes were so bright it was almost shocking. 'How do you know I paint?' She folded her arms. 'Who are you?'

Nicholas shrugged. What, had he forgotten who he was?

It had almost seemed like it, he recalled now. He sliced the peppers and tipped them in, their red strips splashing into the curry like blood.

102

'I guessed,' he said. 'So many people who come here do. Or would like to.'

She laughed. 'I suppose so.' Then she narrowed her eyes at him. 'Do I know you?' she asked.

'I saw you yesterday in the pub.' She was stunning, even more so with less make-up on and close up. He couldn't stop staring at her mouth.

'Are you stalking me?' But she was smiling.

'Yeah.' He stuck his hands in his pockets. 'I was hoping you'd join me for a coffee.'

She looked him up and down then – no one but Rachel had ever done that, at least not in such an obvious way; it was male in its arrogance.

Thinking about it now, Nicholas realised that she had picked him up just as much as the other way about, only she hadn't let him know it at the time. He added the mushrooms and threw in the basil. The aniseed fragrance hit the hot spices almost immediately. Nicholas felt his stomach growl. Time to put on the rice.

'OK,' she said. 'Why not?'

He stuck out his hand. 'Nicholas Tresillion.'

'Rachel Pascoe.' She put her hand in his – briefly. 'Are you an artist?'

'I'm not, no.' He led the way out of the gallery. He would take her to the hotel up the road, perched on the water's edge. That would impress her; it impressed everyone, especially on a day like this when the sea was so wild. 'I'm an accountant.' In heels they were the same height, he realised. And he was six two.

He was used to a certain reaction – most people thought numbers were boring. But she gave him that appraising look

103

again. A smile hovered around her mouth. 'Nicholas Tresillion,' she said, as if she were trying it on for size.

And suddenly it was too late to go back. He had sunk without trace.

Perhaps it was appropriate that now, all these years later, he was back in Cornwall, trying to forget her and the life they had shared.

Nicholas dished out the curry and took it over to the table by the window in the sitting room. Celie had visited last weekend and she had picked some late-flowering honeysuckle from the garden, put it in a small vase that she'd bought in a second-hand shop in Penzance. The sweet-smelling honeysuckle was drooping now, but Nicholas was reluctant to throw it away – when it was gone it would feel as if Celie was gone, even more than it did already. She lived in London now; she had a new job and a steady boyfriend; she didn't visit Cornwall often these days. And Nicholas was pleased for her – he was glad that she'd apparently taken the divorce in her stride, that she was happy and independent. Even so . . . he missed her.

The curry was good. He looked out of the window as he ate. It was the end of September and the light had already faded as he cooked, dusk moving into twilight, into darkness now. The church was lit up – its tower and four spires shone golden against the night sky, and this was comforting. Not that Nicholas was religious; but he liked the building and the sense of continuity it had always given him, its four spires a landmark for the village from afar, as if it wanted to remind him where he should be.

He had tried very hard to get over Rachel. He had changed the furniture she'd chosen for the cottage – he'd never liked steel and chrome; it had no depth or memory, it was all surface and reflection; Rachel could keep her minimalism in the flat in Rome. He had sometimes drunk too much and even had a few brief affairs that had left him feeling vaguely ashamed.

He looked out to where the trees in the churchyard were stirring in the wind. How many times had he looked into Rachel's eyes and seen something so distant, so elusive that he longed for it all the more?

Now, sitting here as the sky grew darker still, the moon hanging limpid and almost full in the sky, he wondered if that depth, that elusiveness, was all an illusion. Even something he had projected onto her because he wanted it so much to be that way. Really, she was quite simple in her desires and her dreams.

When he'd finished eating, he took his plate back to the kitchen, rinsed it and put it on the draining board. Outside, his garden had absorbed the darkness. He opened the back door. He could smell the dry sandy earth and the scent of the sea, edgy and compelling in the air. The sky was clear tonight and the stars seemed brighter than usual. If he concentrated hard enough, he could hear the waves in the distance, high tide, crashing onto the rocks. He loved that sound.

There was no doubt about it. He had to focus on getting Rachel out from under his skin. But he needed to find a different way.

When had it been right between them? Not here, but somewhere else. A place they had found together and shared. A special place.

Nicholas found he was gripping the door handle. He didn't seem capable of moving forward from the position he was in right now. What if he went back to when they were happy? Would that do it? His fists clenched. Or would it finish him? Make or break . . . Softly, he closed the door.

He switched on his laptop to check the flights.

Half an hour later he had booked a flight to Fuerteventura. He would go to El Cotillo for a holiday, stay in a house they'd always loved and coveted, which might not be such a bright idea, come to think about it.

Nicholas switched off his laptop. He felt as if he was saying to Rachel, *Look, I can have that dream. It's mine, not yours. Watch me.*

And in the meantime . . . Next month he would be in Venice for work, visiting retailers who stocked their jewellery. There was plenty to do, surely plenty of things to take his mind off Rachel. All he had to do was find them.

CHAPTER 14

Joanna

Venice

With her forefinger, Joanna traced the pattern of a diamond carved into the crumbling marble of the parapet of Ponte degli Scalzi. It was an impressive bridge from which to begin the walk, with a high arch and a far-reaching view down the Grand Canal. Above her, the sky was ice blue, the water a dense olive. It was a mesmerising combination, meeting at the horizon in pale mauve.

Joanna scrutinised the map. 'Take a look at the *palazzo*,' she said into her Dictaphone and took a picture which included the stone balconies of the salmon-pink Hotel Bellini. This was a quiet part of Venice, close to the railway station, the point at which the canal opened out into the wide lagoon. *Into the rest of the world*, she found herself thinking.

Had Emmy wanted the rest of the world? Joanna didn't think so. She seemed only to want her Rufus. And Joanna? What did she want? She continued down the narrow street, past tourist shops selling glass and Venetian masks, cosy cafés and chic boutiques.

Come on, Jo, Martin had written in his latest text. *Come on, Jo . . . Is one little fling enough to end a marriage?*

Just maybe it was.

The next bridge was constructed in wrought iron and crossed the narrow Rio Marin canal, where buildings with black grilles over windows and doors reached down to the water and washing was strung from top-storey window on one side of the street to top-storey window on the other.

I told you – I need time to think things over, she had texted back to him.

Do you want to talk? he asked her.

Joanna considered. She had to go back sometime. But: *Not yet*.

In the distance, the yellow and cherry-red painted buildings drew her along the walkway by the canal. Venice was such a romantic city; already, she had taken so many photos. And then there were the memories. In her situation, why on earth had she come?

Because she was following Emmy's journey. She stopped to make a few notes and mark up the map. So far, so good. *I did not start to live until you and I met*, Emmy had written to Rufus in her letter from Venice. Joanna had thought about that a lot. Realised that she had never felt like that about Martin – and yet still she had married him. 'Oh, Emmy,' she said out loud.

She let her gaze drift from water to sky. The colours of Venice – silver, sharp blue, lilac – glinted in the early afternoon sun. Blue and white boats were moored on the side of the canal and the water lapped gently onto the stone steps like a cat. She heard the distant tolling of a church bell, paused to enjoy the rare moment of tranquillity. It felt as though she had found the true heart of the city at last.

Joanna walked on. If she went back to Martin, she could return to her own home, to the house in Crouch End; she could write at her own desk in her own room; she'd be back in town, close to her friends, back in the life she'd had before, the safe life. She stopped abruptly. But was it a safe life? And did she want it? Did she want to go back?

'Walk into the wide-open square of Campo San Stin,' she told her Dictaphone. The buildings here were painted in shades of terracotta, ginger, ochre and that dark red she loved, the paint-work bleached, faded or peeling, and in the centre of the piazza stood an old well. Pigeons were flying so low that she ducked instinctively. Pigeons, canals, crumbling stone, an atmosphere of faded glamour and decay . . . Venice was undeniably unique.

Another bell tolled, louder this time, and she made her way to the next bridge. She went into the church alongside and made a few notes on the interior – high vaulted ceiling, red and white marble floor and, of course, Titian's *Assunta* over the high altar, 'a must for any art lover,' she added. This was a tourism project after all.

To go back . . .

Outside again, by the bridge, a man was playing a soulful mandolin. Joanna stood there for a moment to listen.

And if she didn't go back?

She could still live in London, of course – they'd have to sell the house, but she'd be able to afford a small flat, maybe get in a lodger to help with the mortgage repayments. She heard the ping of a text message and checked her phone. Martin again.

I still feel the same about you, Jo, the same as I always did. Nothing has to change.

She tucked it back into her pocket. But how exactly had he felt before? Not strongly enough to say no to Hilary, for starters. He had said himself that they'd grown apart and it was true. As for what had happened with Hilary – that had changed everything. Martin had crossed the line. Joanna might be able to forgive, but did she want to? It seemed that Emmy was sending her another message entirely. *This is the way that you should love . . .*

Joanna stopped at the Caffè Dei Frari for coffee. It was like entering another world. The light filtering from sepia lamps over the bar was low and the atmosphere warm. Huge pictures of men in tri-cornered hats and wigs, and women in long, high-waisted dresses sitting on English lawns filled the wall space and part of the ceiling was cut away to reveal the gallery upstairs.

Joanna smiled as she looked round. It was charming. How much of this Venice had existed back in 1912? she wondered. Had Emmy known there was a war approaching, a bloody war that would wipe out over half a generation of young men? Had Rufus fought in that war? Joanna shivered. She felt such a strong connection to Emmy. But who was she? Her mother hadn't heard of her, so maybe she was an ancestor on Joanna's father's side? She would start researching the family tree as soon as she got back, she decided.

Joanna ordered her cappuccino and sat down at the marble-topped table. Some jazzy instrumental music was playing in the background. She decided to phone Mulberry Farm Cottage to see how things were going back home.

Her sister answered after several rings. 'Yes? Hello?' She sounded busy as usual.

'Harriet, it's me. How's everything?'

'Everything?' Harriet's tone was different from usual – more flustered.

Joanna frowned. 'Has something happened?'

She heard Harriet sigh. 'Some bloke's been hanging around the cottage, that's all. I wasn't going to mention it, but . . .'

'What?'

'I've seen him twice now, once in the middle of the night and once in broad daylight, would you believe, hiding behind Big Barn.' She paused for breath.

'Harriet!' Joanna was shocked. 'And you didn't think to tell me this before?' It was so like her sister to keep it to herself.

'I didn't want a fuss,' Harriet said.

'Harriet! But what did you do?'

'When?'

'When you saw him? When he was hiding behind the barn?' Joanna hoped she would have called the police. But knowing Harriet . . .

'I chased him.'

'Harriet!'

'Will you stop saying that, Joanna?' She sounded cross again now which was rather a relief. 'I'm fine.'

She clearly hadn't even considered the consequences. You couldn't just start chasing intruders away. He could have turned around and attacked her, or anything. 'What did he do when you went after him?'

'He ran away. So he can't be dangerous, I suppose.'

She didn't get it. Of course he could be dangerous. 'Harriet—'

'Don't fuss, Joanna,' Harriet growled.

Don't fuss? Don't worry? When her mother and her sister were alone in the middle of nowhere and some nutter was hanging around the place? 'And Mother? How's she?'

'She's fine. We're both fine.' Joanna heard her sigh once more. 'You really don't have to phone every five minutes to check up on us.'

'But—'

'We're perfectly capable of managing. We're used to it.'

'I know you are.' But yet again, Joanna hadn't been there. Guilt streaked down the telephone line and twisted itself in a knot around her.

'So stop worrying,' Harriet said.

Joanna focused on a tub of pink oleander by the door. 'You should inform the police,' she told her sister. 'You need more security, maybe a burglar alarm, a motion detector light or a camera or something. At least a security light. Maybe Owen could come round to check on things after dark. Or—'

'Really, Joanna, don't you think you're overreacting?' Harriet said.

She sounded like Martin. But it would be too late to take preventative measures when they were all dead in their beds. 'No, I don't,' she said firmly. 'But I'll be back the day after tomorrow and we can talk about it then.'

'And as for Mother . . .' Harriet said darkly.

'Yes?'

'It's the tradesmen, Jo.'

'Oh.' So, she'd been at it again. Was it just a need for attention? A form of depression? An addiction? Joanna simply didn't know.

'I had to do something, so I've put a bar on the phone.'

'Really? But it's—'

'Her house too, I know.' Harriet's voice was brisk. 'It's also her phone and I've got no right to treat her like a child.'

Exactly. 'How did she take it?'

'Not well.'

'And have you told her about this man who's been hanging around?'

'No.'

No? Surely she should warn her at least? 'But—'

'And neither should you, Jo.'

'But, Harriet—'

'I have to go.'

Joanna gave up. 'All right, but be careful, Het.'

'Of course.'

Of course . . . 'Bye then.'

Joanna ended the call. She was only just beginning to understand the extent of the problem – and that Harriet was reaching the end of her tether. She felt a pang of regret. It wasn't enough to encourage her sister to go out or take a break from time to time, she realised. And it certainly wasn't enough to sit around looking at old snapshots of the past, reminiscing with Mother. Added to this, there was now a prowler on the loose. There was no doubt in her mind. Joanna had to do something more.

When she'd finished her coffee, she went upstairs, more to take a look around the upper floor of the interesting little café than to use the facilities. The upstairs gallery was laid out like a sixties coffee bar, with wooden benches arranged like islands and lots of scarlet cushions. The smallest room was bizarre. The cistern was low, she had to crouch over it, the window was open and only a blue canopy prevented a full view of people walking alongside the canal, barely a few feet under the window.

She returned downstairs and gathered up her things, leaving some change for her coffee on the table. Of course, she had to try the ice cream at the Millevoglie – otherwise how could she write about it? She decided on strawberry. There was no doubt, Italian ice cream was the best. Beyond the *gelateria* was the geometric and marbled wedding-cake facade of Scuola Grande di San Rocco, all icing and show. She took a picture. Masks were everywhere in Venice. But it was what lay underneath the facade that Joanna most wanted to find.

She asked an Italian passer-by the name of the tree growing next to the Frari building.

He flashed her a dazzling Italian smile. '*Pitosforo.*'

Joanna smiled back at him. 'Can you write it down for me?'

'But of course.' He took the pen from her and wrote in her notebook with a typical Italian flourish. 'Anything else I can help you with, *signorina*?'

Joanna laughed. 'No, *signore*, but *grazie*.'

'*Prego*. You are very welcome, beautiful lady.' His gaze lingered on her face.

Hey, she still had it then: something . . . The Italians were such charmers. But it was good to hear – especially when you'd just found out your husband had been playing around.

She thought of Harriet, of the man she'd seen pictured on her sister's computer screen and the way Harriet had looked when she went out that day. Was her sister doing online dating? Was Harriet, after all these years, looking for a man? Joanna chuckled. She wouldn't blame her sister for wanting someone to share her life with, but she was surprised. Harriet had never shown any interest before. Or had she? What did Joanna really know about her sister's life?

In Campo Santa Margherita, there was a small fish market, the stalls laden with fresh squid, white and speckled pink; the sharp grey fin of a swordfish, a cuttlefish sitting damply in its

114

own black ink; white fleshy scallops and blocks of blood-red tuna. Joanna bought a slice of pizza from a nearby café, sat down for a moment to eat. The bridge walk had gone well so far. She would write it up tomorrow and then walk it again to double-check the details as if she were a tourist who had never been here before.

She was moving into a very different area now. There were more cafés, bookshops and stationers. The people on the streets were younger, many of them students, she supposed, for they were approaching Accademia – and Emmy's bridge.

In the canal, alongside the walkway, was a barge stuffed full of vegetables: a floating market selling shiny red peppers, glossy purple aubergines, courgettes with bright yellow flowers, bulging artichokes, small tight green cabbages. Joanna paused, caught by the reflections in the canal. As her eyes adjusted, she could see not only the shape of the boat, but the buildings opposite, a woman in a fluorescent pink coat and an upside-down man swinging his arms, as he walked along the pavement on the other side of the canal. The more you look, the more you see. The bodies and the buildings ghostly and gliding moved with the water, rippling, it seemed, almost into another reality. Joanna stood still to watch.

When you lost something – and in a way, with Martin, she had – maybe your sense of the surreal became more potent? Maybe you somehow became more open? But who would read these brochures? Who would do a bridge walk in Venice? Who would care what colours the buildings were or what fragrances of rich roasted coffee or sweet tomato and pastry tiptoed out of cafés and bars and onto the walkways by the canal? Who would want to explore what was underneath the facade?

All of a sudden, Accademia Bridge was in front of her.

Joanna climbed the steps to the top. She had reached Emmy's moment of contemplation. There were fabulous views from the wide wooden bridge, out over the busy waterway of the Grand Canal. She stood there, letting it wash over her – the never-ending silvery sky, the broad expanse of the waterway lined with white domes and colourful palaces, a yellow *vaporetto* at the water bus stop below. Lazy jazz music floated up from the musicians playing at the bottom of the bridge and the fragrance of damp wood and fresh coffee filled the air.

And underneath it all?

She looked up to a place beyond the bridge where the sun glimmered on the water, transforming it into golden olive. *Look carefully. Blink and it might be gone.*

Her eyes had become accustomed to reflection, accustomed to light. She felt as if she could see, in a different way, almost for the first time. She blinked.

Deep in the water was a young woman of maybe seventeen. She was wearing a blue dress. She was running, her long fair hair half untied, tumbling down her back and flowing behind her in the watery wind. She was laughing, laughing with delight.

What was she running from? Joanna shielded her eyes. Why was she laughing? There was nothing behind her, just an empty space. And then she realised. The girl was running towards something, or someone. Towards her future perhaps? She was running and laughing and the sun was shining, glinting on the golden ribbon in her hair.

116

CHAPTER 15

Harriet

Dorset

Harriet was chopping wood, but already the axe seemed heavy and the handle slippery in her palms. Owen had sold them a load of logs, at an extremely good price, which he'd already sawn into round sections, and she had accepted the kindness with good grace because, after all, they were in no position to argue. The cheeses and quarter cheeses were ready for chopping, and she couldn't keep putting it off. They wouldn't be able to use the wood till next year, but it still needed to be cut and stacked in the woodpile before winter so it had a chance to season. She sighed and put down the axe. But before she could do that, she had to make some space by taking some of the older seasoned wood inside to the porch.

She began stacking these logs in the barrow, neatly, no gaps, ensuring the bulk of the weight was over the wheel. This was a good job to do when you were anxious or angry, she decided

– it was therapeutic. And Harriet needed therapy because she was angry. And anxious.

She hadn't seen the prowler for a couple of days but the shadow of him still seemed to lurk in the farmyard. Harriet didn't agree with Joanna that she should phone the police – she couldn't face the thought of being interviewed, dealing with Mother as she was being interviewed or of having people wandering around the place. And she always felt guilty when police were around, regardless of whether she'd done anything or not. Besides, what would they find? What could they possibly do? You couldn't arrest shadows. Whoever he was, he had long gone.

The first load was done. Harriet took a deep breath, steadied herself, and lifted the handles, trundling the barrow over the cobbles of the farmyard. Gradually, she picked up speed until the wheel was really rattling. '*One wheel on my wagon,*' she sang to cheer herself up. Hopefully, she'd scared him when she chased him away and presumably the shadow would dematerialise in time. Phew. She broke off for a moment and stretched. The muscles in her back twinged in complaint and then relaxed.

Last night, she'd had the dream again. It began as always with a vague sense of sleep becoming elusive, a tossing and turning, a darkness dimming something Harriet believed in. Harriet was a young girl, seven or eight years old. There were voices, but there was something wrong with the voices. There was something jarring, harsh and chilled.

As always, Harriet was aware of her own footsteps on the stairs. 'Daddy? Daddy?' Her own hand opening the door.

There was a gasp. A scream. A low groan. And then she woke up, as she always did – as if her mind would let her go no further. She didn't know if it was a real memory, a fantasy,

118

an anxiety or what. It was impossible to differentiate between memory and imagination, between dream and reality. She woke – as she always woke – cold, sweaty and shivering, her pillow damp, tears on her face. Not knowing.

In the morning, she'd been dismayed to find water gushing out of their overflow pipe.

'We'll have to phone a plumber, Harriet,' Mother had declared, eyes gleaming.

'Not yet. Let me think.' Harriet had put a hand to her head. 'I'll take a look at the tank in the attic.' A new one would probably cost at least five hundred pounds. Hopefully it was just a faulty ballcock or something. There was no doubt about it – the place was falling to bits, and she wasn't far behind.

'You don't know anything about water tanks, Harriet,' her mother pointed out, quite reasonably. 'We'll have to get a plumber in. I insist.'

'OK, OK.' Harriet didn't have the strength to argue – it was only seven o'clock in the morning. Even so, where was she going to find the money? A bank loan? She'd be lucky. She supposed Joanna might be able to help out, but it probably still wouldn't be enough. In the meantime: 'Buckets,' she said. 'We need buckets.'

In the porch now, she stood next to the barrow and began to unload the split logs. Bending, lifting, stacking; it became a rhythm that was monotonous but soothing. So, of course she was cross . . . She was cross with Joanna for being in Venice, for not being here – just as she was cross with her when she was. She was cross with the prowler for making her anxious, she was cross with Hector for turning out to be a dead loss. She was cross with her mother for no longer being the capable mother of her childhood. And . . . though this was harder for her to admit, she was cross with her father for dying. That was about it.

At least the water tank had been fixed without bankrupting them this morning, but the plumber had warned her the repair wouldn't last forever and Harriet was always waiting for the next thing to fall apart; it was just a question of time.

Hector had finally sent her a short and brisk email, saying how pleasant it had been to meet her. *Pleasant* . . . She lifted the empty barrow and wheeled it back along the cobbles. This time the wheel really bounced. She shoved the barrow back into position and began on the new cheeses. The crosser the better, when you were chopping wood.

But, Hector had continued, *after giving it some thought*, he didn't think they were a *match made in heaven*. Harriet picked up the axe. She couldn't agree more. *Thwack* . . .

Harriet had become practised at reading the wood. The knots could be hard as steel and often needed some serious work with the splitter, so she went first of all for the easier knot-free stuff. She soon got into a rhythm with the axe. Down went the blade into the wood. She loved the crack and the creak as the wood continued to tear apart of its own volition; it was such a satisfying sound. She breathed in, out, steady . . . Once again, she swept the axe down.

The truth was that she didn't mind about Hector, she hadn't been too impressed with him either. It was what he'd said: *I think I'm falling in love with you* . . . For one precious moment, Harriet had forgotten about her problems. She had thought, had hoped . . . But it was utter rubbish. And Harriet was old enough to know better. Of course, she had put him off with her talk of lack of funds and caring for Mother. And good riddance.

Once more, she stretched her back for a moment, rubbing the muscles where the dull ache was beginning to throb. In front of her in the distance beyond the springy green Down, the V of the sea was a dark and glimmering blue-grey. There was a thick pink autumn light on the hills and on the cluster of buildings in the distance that made up the town of Bridport. The afternoon sun was slanting onto the Gothic church on the hill, reflecting from one arched window like rosy quartz torchlight.

Mother was still sulking about only being allowed to use the phone when Harriet was around to monitor the calls. But what did she expect? Joanna had said she shouldn't treat their mother like a child – which was easy for her to say, when she wasn't here looking after Mother full time. Harriet had to find some way of keeping control.

Would Joanna go back to Martin? Had she even left him? And more to the point, for how long did she intend to stick around? Harriet wasn't sure how she felt about her sister being here – her emotions were mixed. The scent of the amber pine resin collecting at the joints and faults in the wood was sweet and heady. Harriet bent and picked up the split log; it was smooth and damp from sap and in a moment of tenderness, she rubbed it against her cheek, drank in the fragrance. It was so uncomplicated in comparison. She loved wood. Loved the smell of it, the feel of it, the warmth of it.

The rumble of Owen's tractor in the lane sounded closer than usual. Next thing, the machine trundled into the farm-yard, scattering bits of straw in its wake. Harriet laid down the axe and put a hand to her brow. Goodness, she was sweating. But it was still warm for late September and this was hot work. There were two warms to be got out of wood, it was said – the chopping and then the burning. She glanced at the piece of wood still in her hand. It wasn't damp just from the sap – she'd even sweated onto that. Heavens. It came to something when you were reduced to mingling bodily fluids with a lump of wood.

'Afternoon, Harriet.' Owen sounded cheerful, as usual. He was wearing his trademark boots and green boiler suit with the sleeves rolled up, displaying forearms that were big, brown and muscled.

'Afternoon, Owen.' She lifted the axe once more. 'What can I do for you?' Had he somehow heard about the prowler? She hoped Joanna hadn't contacted him, but she wouldn't put it past her. Joanna spent years pretending problems at the cottage didn't exist, then she swept in and tried to take over.

Swiftly and smoothly, she split the next log.

Owen took a step back. Very wise. 'Nice action you've got there, Harriet.' He smiled approvingly.

'Thanks.' She hoped he wasn't expecting her to stop what she was doing and offer him a cup of tea.

'But, Harriet, I've told you before . . .'

It was a conspiracy. She looked around for the wood she'd just split into two – one piece was there, the other had disappeared. Why did that keep happening?

'I'd do that chopping for you, you know.' For once his soft, slow, Dorset burr didn't grate on Harriet's nerves. 'I did say.'

'No need.' It was becoming difficult to breathe. Harriet stopped for a moment and wiped her brow once more with the back of her arm. She didn't want to look as though she was trying too hard. 'I can do it perfectly well myself.'

It was hard sometimes, she couldn't deny it. But she liked to be self-sufficient. She preferred not to depend on anyone else for anything. Look what had happened to Mother. She was lost without Father and she'd be even more lost if anything happened to Harriet. It was all very well for Joanna to say she'd look after her and see to the farm, but her sister simply had no idea. Mother would have to go into a nursing home. It would finish her. Harriet couldn't bear that.

She looked down. The missing piece of wood was on the ground right there in front of her; she was going wood-crazy. She needed more room. She began to stack the logs onto the woodpile – plenty of gaps this time to allow the air to circulate and speed up the drying process. Even wood had to breathe.

'It wouldn't be a bother,' Owen said. 'I'd be happy to help out.'

When she didn't reply, he moved back towards the tractor. 'With anything. Anytime.'

Bless him. Harriet paused. He meant well. He was a kind man. She shouldn't be so ungrateful. 'Thanks,' she said. 'I'll remember.' She considered. 'I just wanted to ask you . . .'

'Yes?' He waited.

'If you'd seen anyone hanging around here lately? A man? A stranger?'

Owen frowned. 'Can't say that I have.' He gave Harriet a long look. 'Why? Has someone been bothering you?'

'Oh, no, no.' Harriet didn't want any more fuss. If Joanna had her way, she'd be installing Owen in Big Barn as some sort of security guard. 'You don't have anyone staying with you then?' she asked. 'A friend? A relative? A man?'

He shook his head. 'But like I said, Harriet, if you or your mother, or Joanna, ever need—'

Oh, Joanna . . . 'Yes,' she said. 'I know. Thank you.'

He nodded. Looked out towards the fields as if they could

123

tell him something he needed to know. He seemed to be listening too, but Harriet had no idea to what. All she could hear were the hens and the pigs, the breeze in the trees and a bird chirruping away. 'Well then,' he said.

Harriet smiled. *Well then*.

Owen swung open the door of the tractor. He looked back at Harriet.

She waited.

'I was wondering . . .' His face reddened. He was so awkward.

'Yes?' She smiled again – encouragingly this time.

'If I could call round this evening?'

'This evening?' Harriet had things to do. She wanted to get back online and get her new contenders into some sort of order. But Mother would certainly be glad to see him and it would take her mind off the call barring and the plumber. Would the chilli stretch to three? Another tin of tomatoes would do it, she decided. 'Yes, of course. Come to supper,' she said.

His face lit up. 'That'd be lovely.'

Heavens, he must lead a boring life. 'It's only chilli con carne,' she said. 'Nothing fancy.'

'Right you are.' He beamed.

'And Joanna's not back yet. From Venice.' In case he hadn't realised. Though she would be back tomorrow. Harriet turned her attention back to the woodpile. The first stack was growing. She was getting there.

'Just the three of us then?' he said. Was there a note of disappointment in his voice? She couldn't really tell.

'Just the three of us.'

'Okey dokey. I'll be on my way then.' He climbed back into the cab and started the engine.

In a sudden spurt of energy, Harriet went into whirling dervish mode – high-speed repeated splitting, not pausing between axe strokes, wood flying everywhere. Lovely.

After a few minutes, she stopped. She was utterly drained. Her back was complaining and what she really needed was a hot bath. But she felt good. Better. And that was enough for today. She stuck the axe into one of the remaining cheeses and loaded the rest of the logs onto the woodpile. As for tonight . . . That was something to look forward to – Mother occupied with Owen, giving Harriet a long evening with Someone Somewhere. Bugger Hector. Bugger the prowler. Bugger everything that needed fixing in Mulberry Farm Cottage. There were other things in life. Like the anticipation of what might turn out to be a successful first date. A date that could lead towards a different future. Who knew?

CHAPTER 16

Joanna

Venice

It was Joanna's last day in Venice and she decided to take the *vaporetto* from the Lido down the Grand Canal, past all the palaces to the Piazzale Roma. Emmy had described the palaces in her letter and it was the kind of tour that Emmy and her father would have taken back in their day. The Grand Canal travelled in an S shape between the two islands on which Venice was built. Two islands, but at least four footbridges to join them together.

The sky was a deep and vibrant blue and only the light autumn breeze reminded her that even the Mediterranean summer was slipping away, as they chugged towards the lush greenery of Giardini. The sunlight rippled on the water and the distant buildings had moved into a hazy silhouette. Joanna held her breath. The shimmering city of Venice still seemed not quite real. It was fragile – how could these buildings continue to survive with so much water around them? She could imagine the city becoming some sort of Atlantis, lost under the sea. And yet underneath it all, she'd glimpsed enough of La Serenissima to be sure it was strong.

And she felt strong too — a new kind of strength running through her veins that came, perhaps, from being here alone, from taking the time to come to a decision about her marriage. She put her hands on the rail of the *vaporetto* and braced herself as the side of the boat barged into the floating pontoon that was the disembarkation point for the garden of Venice.

She had thought it would be difficult — coming back here to a romantic city that held so many memories. Joanna looked out into the distance. And she'd had her moments . . . But overall, it hadn't turned out that way. Because this was a reflective city too, and that was what Joanna had done: allowed herself to reflect upon Martin, their marriage and also Emmy — this woman from the past who might or might not be an ancestor of Joanna's, who seemed to have crept inside her head.

She thought of the vision she'd seen — the girl in the blue dress with the golden ribbon in her hair. Had she been only a figment of Joanna's imagination, conjured by the sunlight, the rippling water, the magic of Venice? Perhaps. She'd been there only for seconds, and yet in those seconds she'd seemed so real — Joanna had almost thought she could turn and touch the hem of her dress, hold out a hand to her. And had she ever actually been real . . . ? If so, who was she and to whom or what was she running? She had looked so happy and excited, her eyes bright, her smile warm and wide. Perhaps to her lover then? Perhaps to some young man who had found a way to her heart?

Joanna watched the people getting on and off the boat. Dark-eyed young men in leather jackets, girls in skinny blue jeans and high heels, an old man smoking a pipe, a woman with a poodle in her shopping bag . . . Venice was the perfect place for people-watching. She had come here undecided what to do about her marriage. But Emmy and this magical city had helped her see – the heart of it was long gone, and the sad thing was that she had hardly noticed its passing. Perhaps she should shoulder some of the blame; perhaps there had been a point in time when she could have rescued it and stopped herself and Martin from growing so far apart. But lovers grew apart for a reason – often because they had fallen out of love.

As they veered away from the water bus stop, the driver hooted loudly at a varnished wooden speedboat, a Riva, and received a V sign in return, along with a torrent of abuse. If only she understood more Italian . . . Joanna watched, fascinated. It was a miracle there were so few collisions, what with Italian volatility and all the traffic on the canal. It was a crazy place all right – the dominance of the waterways prevailed, but however mad it got, it seemed the Venetians were adept at finding ways around it.

She moved aside to let an Italian woman – dressed in black coat and boots as if it were the dead of winter – pass by. Plenty of couples fell out of love. It happened. And Martin seemed to have recognised it too – despite all those texts of his desperately trying to hang on to what they had lost.

Joanna craned forwards as they reached the famous Bridge of Sighs. She felt the brush of the breeze on her face as the water bus turned to come in at the next stop. She understood why Emmy had been captivated by these bridges. Bridges provided a path forward or back, a connection, a way of avoiding the troubled waters below.

For Joanna, Venice had been a turning point. *What is next for us?* Emmy had written. So, had it been like that for Emmy too?

They passed the big white dome of Salute and the Gritti Palace, constructed from tiny, narrow bricks. Joanna had been part of a couple with Martin for a long time. But that didn't mean she had lost her independent spirit, or that she couldn't live alone. She usually travelled solo for work and this had never been a problem – in fact, she was rather good at it. It would be nice to have someone to share Venice with, but she would do that with the piece she was writing; she would share it with so many visitors to the city – all being well.

Once again, they arrived at Rialto. Joanna took a few more photos of the famous bridge as they slowed pace. More shabby white palaces, Gothic windows and stone balustrades. Little waterways forking off from the main canal, a gondolier singing lustily, black eyes glittering. With its wonderful, misty sense of Italian tragedy, the city was irresistible. Joanna watched as the sun sent a rope of undulating light onto the water of the canal. The gondolier paused in his singing; the note seemed to hang in the air, in time. Then, as she watched, a cloud feathered across the sun and the light dimmed, the moment was gone.

Joanna knew what she had to do. She took her mobile from her bag and called Martin.

He answered quickly as if he thought she might ring off any second. 'Jo. At last. How are you?'

'Fine. You?'

'Oh . . .' She heard his hesitation. 'Missing you. It's been a long time.'

Had it been so long? Not really. Less than two weeks, she reckoned. Not so long to make a decision that would affect her whole life.

'When are you coming home, Jo?'

She took a deep breath. 'That's why I'm phoning, Martin.

I've thought about it a lot.' She really had. 'And I'm . . . I'm not coming home.'

Silence.

Joanna gazed out at the still canal. This was harder than she'd thought it would be.

'Jo—'

'I've made up my mind. I want us to separate.'

'I can't believe it,' he said. 'But it's still raw. Maybe in a month or two—'

'Martin . . .'

He laughed. 'When your mother and your sister have driven you completely crazy.'

Joanna didn't appreciate his tone. And she liked to think that she was re-establishing a long overdue bond with her mother and sister in Dorset. It was still pretty hard going with Harriet at times, but . . . 'I'm in Venice,' she said. 'But I'll be back at Mulberry Farm Cottage tomorrow.'

'Venice,' he said.

She knew exactly what he was thinking. But that was a long time ago.

'And if you leave me, where will you go?'

'I don't know.' She hadn't got that far, not yet.

'Won't you at least come back to talk about things first, Jo?' he asked. 'There's no need to make any hasty decisions. I was an idiot and I'm sorry. But this is our life together we're talking about. One stupid mistake doesn't mean we have to throw everything away.'

Joanna sighed. 'It's not what you did,' she tried to explain. 'It's how distant we've become, Martin. You said it yourself that day. What happened with Hilary made me see it too. You were right. We never grew closer, we just grew apart.'

'But we can get closer again. Please let me try to make it up to you,' he begged.

'I don't think we can.' Joanna was close to tears now. Why was he making this difficult?

'You'll have to come back to collect some of your stuff at least,' he said and she heard in his voice that he thought he could persuade her to reconsider.

'I know. I will.' She struggled to keep her voice level and her mind clear. 'But I can't come yet. I'm really busy and after this, I'm going to Lisbon.' She thought of what she'd seen in Venice. What would Emmy have in store for her in Lisbon?

He whistled. 'Nice one, Jo. Venice and then Lisbon, you're really getting around.'

Already, their conversation seemed dangerously like old times. 'I'll ring you to fix a date,' she told him.

'All right. But, Jo?'

'Yes?'

'I still love you,' he said. 'So, don't think I'm giving up.'

Joanna ended the call, took a deep breath and let her eyes fix on the mauve horizon. Did Martin still love her? She really didn't think so. And did she still love Martin? No. She'd already acknowledged the truth. She was sad for the end of her marriage, but now it was time to let go. She was stepping forwards, not back. It was time to face up to the challenge of the new.

131

CHAPTER 17

Harriet

Dorset

Joanna was back in Dorset and things had reverted to what was, Harriet supposed, the new normal. Joanna was writing and wafting around the place like a lost spirit and Harriet was doing all the chores while she tried to work out where the next pound was coming from. She was still busy online with Someone Somewhere but she'd given up on Charles and Malcolm and was spending all her energy on a new contender named Jolyon. They hadn't yet met up, but Harriet was resolved not to leave it too long this time. Faint heart never won man.

Over lunch, Joanna informed them that she wasn't going back to Martin – which was hardly a surprise. Harriet couldn't help feeling sorry for her sister, though; it must be hard.

'Oh, I'm so sorry, darling.' Mother's voice filled with tears. Though goodness knows why; Martin had never had much time for her.

'What did he do?' Harriet buttered another crumpet. She

supposed she should watch her weight – given that she was putting herself out there, as it were – but these crumpets were far too good to waste.

'It doesn't matter.'

Harriet raised her eyebrows. She couldn't blame Joanna for not wanting to tell them. It was her business, after all. But perhaps Joanna's life wasn't quite as wonderful as she'd assumed? She reached out her hand and awkwardly patted her sister's hand.

Their mother, though, got to her feet and wrapped Joanna in her arms, rocking her as if she were a baby. 'Poor darling,' she crooned.

After a few moments, Joanna disentangled herself and gave a little shrug. 'Thanks, Mother. But it's for the best.'

Harriet could tell her sister was trying to put on a brave face. There were a few tell-tale signs. For example, she was sure Joanna had been crying again.

'But forgiveness' – their mother gave a knowing look – 'is always important in a marriage, you know.'

Harriet was no expert, but she wasn't so sure. And how would Mother know? What could Father have ever done that would require forgiveness? He'd always adored her.

'It's not about forgiveness,' Joanna said. And Harriet definitely saw her sister blink back a tear.

She decided to be practical. 'So, what will you do?'

'I don't know yet.' Her sister looked lost and Harriet regretted the question immediately.

'It will all work out in the end, you know.' Their mother patted Joanna's hand. A simple gesture, but Harriet could see it made things a little better.

*

Sometimes, thought Harriet later as she went out to the kitchen garden to dig up some potatoes, Mother really seemed almost her old self. Had Harriet made a mistake, what with the call barring and everything? But then . . .

She stopped in her tracks. 'Mother?'

What was she doing, standing there by the mulberry tree? Her mother cut a forlorn figure – her sky-blue dress flaring in the breeze, a lilac cardigan draped over her thin shoulders; she was hardly dressed for a bright but chilly October day.

'Mother?' She moved closer, skirting the pond. Her mother was clutching on to something, holding it close to her breast.

Slowly, she turned around. 'Oh, Harriet. It's you.'

Harriet caught her breath. Her mother was crying; her lined cheeks were wet, her eyes red. What on earth had brought this on? Surely not the news of Joanna and Martin's marriage break-up? 'What is it?' She softened her voice. 'What's wrong?' She took hold of her mother's limp white hand. She could see now that it was a framed photograph Mother was holding. It was the past then, the past that she was mourning.

Her mother sniffed, groped for a tissue in her dress pocket and blew her nose loudly. 'I was thinking back to when . . .' Her voice trailed. 'It was what Joanna said. I was remembering.' She held it out for Harriet to see.

Harriet recognised the framed photograph immediately. It usually sat on the mantelpiece in the living room. 'You and Father,' she said gently. It was a picture of her parents standing in front of the mulberry tree. 'Just look at you both. What a handsome couple.'

Together they examined the photo, almost as if they'd never seen it before. When something was always there in your life, you often stopped looking at it properly, Harriet thought. Her parents did look handsome, but also so young, so innocent. Father's arm was slung over her mother's shoulders, careless, in a way he'd rarely done in real, unphotographed life, so far as Harriet could recall. It was casual, but possessive. He was looking down at his beautiful young wife tenderly. And she was gazing back up at him.

'Was it taken before I was born?' Though Harriet knew the answer to this before she even asked the question. The two of them looked entirely unshackled. She felt a twinge of something that could have been resentment. She had always known he loved her mother, and of course she would never be jealous of that love they shared. But . . . she had never before realised quite how single-minded that love had been. It was embedded in this photo, though – in the way she was looking up at him, in his expression, in the fierceness of his eyes.

Her mother nodded. She reached out to touch the pitted trunk of the mulberry tree. The breeze murmured through the serrated leaves as if the tree might be trying to tell them something. Harriet wouldn't be surprised. The tree seemed so wise. And it had been part of the past, forever watching. There were no longer any children playing amongst its tangled branches, but the mulberry was still here, still serene, still protecting and sheltering them all.

'Your father proposed to me here,' her mother whispered. Her eyes were faraway. 'He said that I was the purest and most beautiful thing that he'd ever seen.'

Harriet felt a lump in her throat. That was just so lovely. 'He worshipped you,' she said.

Her mother's expression changed so abruptly that Harriet was shocked. 'Well, now.' Once again, she seemed to transform back into the mother of Harriet's young years. Capable. Secure. 'You should never put people on a pedestal, Harriet,' she said.

135

But why not? Harriet stared at her. Wouldn't it be wonderful to be cosseted and adored?

Her mother only smiled and patted her arm. 'Further to fall, my darling,' she said. 'Further to fall.'

What did she mean?

They went back inside – Harriet didn't want her to get cold – and Mother replaced the photograph on the mantelpiece with only the faintest of sighs.

Harriet thought about it again, later, as she glanced at the local paper while she was having her afternoon tea. Should she tell Joanna? Best not, she decided, it would only give her something else to fuss about. And having read the phone bill that had just arrived, Harriet decided to keep the call barring in place for now too. They needed to find some money from somewhere . . .

Her attention was caught by an advert in the 'Situations Vacant' column. *Typist required for work at home*, it read. Harriet was pretty sure she'd seen something similar recently on a leaflet put through the door. She didn't want to be a typist – obviously. But with all these bills coming in, winter fast approaching and only Mother's pension and the money she made from produce to live on, things were getting desperate. All the emails she'd been writing lately had made her quite fast on the keyboard and . . .

She rubbed her back, which had not yet fully recovered from all that wood-chopping. It would be refreshingly different from working on the farm, making jam and delivering the veg, not to mention looking after Mother, of course. Joanna had made a contribution, which had eased the financial strain a little, but she was another mouth to feed and besides, Joanna wouldn't be here forever. Another job, a typist's job, might help earn the extra cash they needed to keep afloat.

Joanna came in by the back door and glanced over Harriet's shoulder. 'But you don't have time to do anyone's typing, do you, Het?' she asked mildly.

'I could make time.'

Joanna sat down opposite her. 'Have you seen him again?' she asked.

Harriet frowned. 'Seen who again?'

'You know.' Joanna looked around the room to make sure Mother wasn't within earshot presumably. 'That prowler who was hanging around.'

Ah. 'Not really.' Harriet sipped her tea. 'There's some in the pot,' she told her sister.

'Not really? How can you not really see someone?' Although even as Joanna was saying this, she wore an expression that told Harriet she knew exactly how it could be done.

'I thought I saw him in the village.' Harriet was convinced he was still around – she could sense it. Only yesterday, in the post office, she'd felt a scrutiny on the back of her neck as she was queuing for stamps, whipped round and seen someone disappearing past the open doorway. She was almost sure it was him.

Joanna's eyes widened. 'You don't think he lives here?'

'Well . . .' She'd also seen a man on a bike in the distance a couple of days ago who could have been him. 'He might do.'

'That's it.' Joanna got to her feet. 'I'm going out right now to buy a security light. And I'm going to have a word with Owen. If you see that man around here again, you tell me straightaway, OK, Harriet?'

'OK.' Harriet reached for the phone to ring the number in the ad. 'But there's no need to see Owen – I've already told him.'

Did Joanna look disappointed? Could it be that she recip-rocated their neighbour's feelings? Harriet hadn't seen him since he'd come round for that chilli the other night, but he'd certainly asked a lot of questions about how long Joanna might be staying in the area. Harriet supposed he was impressed by the fact that Joanna was a writer – and a travel writer to boot. Not that Harriet cared a fig. She was more than happy to slope off upstairs, leaving Mother and Owen to their chat and their whisky. Harriet had something much better than that. She had Someone Somewhere . . .

CHAPTER 18

Nicholas

Venice
One month later

Nicholas had finished his meetings and was left with three hours to kill before he must leave for the airport. But, of course, you didn't kill time in Venice, whatever the season, unless you were a cultural blank.

He negotiated the walkway – some wooden planking erected across Piazza San Marco because of the flooding. It was surprising, he thought grimly, that the whole city didn't suffer a similar fate. Progress was slow since everyone was trying to leave the square in single file. It often rained in Venice in October. He should have brought his wellies.

The water gurgled below the planking. Nicholas wasn't sure quite how the city achieved it, but Venice remained impossibly romantic even when the rain had been hammering down and the canals had overflowed onto streets and piazzas. It wasn't raining now, though. The afternoon sun was so warm that a faint mist was rising from the watery pavements and a pink-golden glow was lighting the stone of the crumbling buildings around him.

Nicholas was glad to be here, even though his visits were always fleeting. Isobel and Giuseppe would be pleased – business was good; the jewellery was selling well. And before too long he'd be in El Cotillo. He felt a judder of anticipation. Mixed feelings, though; he still wasn't quite sure whether or not he was a fool to go back there.

He reached to help an elderly lady up onto the walkway. She had braved the puddles in order to get a different perspective on the gloriously gilded facade of the famous cathedral with its decorative spires and painted frescoes and would now have sodden shoes and stockings for the rest of the day, poor dear.

'Thanks, love,' she said, and grinned. British. He should have guessed.

Today, Nicholas had expected to have a late lunch with Fabio, one of his contacts in Venice, and had prepared himself accordingly with an early breakfast of a cappuccino and a small pastry *cornetto* followed by a further fierce espresso during the morning. But Fabio had been called away to deal with some domestic crisis, leaving Nicholas alone in La Serenissima with time on his hands. He'd had lunch already and now he was free – to wander, to do some sightseeing, whatever he chose.

Thankfully, he reached an area that was drier and jumped off the planking. At least his black Italian brogues seemed to have survived the experience. He straightened the jacket of his suit, which was well cut, Italian, naturally, and had been chosen by Rachel who had an eye for such things. In Italy Nicholas wore Italian designer suits, in Cornwall he wore jeans. Sometimes he thought he was so fluid that he'd become two different people – branded by the clothes he wore, the places he lived in.

He glanced up. The sky was misty blue, with a few feathery clouds and that autumnal light that came when the sun was low. He found himself thinking about Christmas. Isobel and Giuseppe had invited him to stay, but there was too much of Rachel in Rome, and besides, they were her family, not his, and family was what Christmas was all about. Celie had already said she'd be with Tom, her boyfriend, visiting his parents in Brighton. It would then be Nicholas's first Christmas without the family since they had become his family. Before that, he'd had his father, and before that . . . There'd never really been a time that he'd been alone.

Back in Cape Cornwall, men like his father didn't take a long Christmas break – they couldn't afford to. His father had never spent Christmas with Nicholas, Rachel and Celie. And only now, with him dead and buried, did Nicholas wonder if he had ever wanted to. Shame on him. He sighed.

'What does your father do?' Rachel had asked him a long time ago, soon after they first met in St Ives.

Nicholas was aware that this was a significant question. He already knew that Rachel's father was 'in banking'. His family background was very different.

'Fish,' he said.

'What?' She looked at him more closely, as if to see if he was joking.

'He's a fisherman. Down the coast, at Cape Cornwall.' No one had ever heard of Priest's Cove, though it was as old as the surrounding hills. Cape Cornwall was the original Land's End, where ocean met ocean and a tall chimney stood like a parody of the old tin mining engine houses on top of the grassy headland.

Nicholas looked back towards the waterlogged square fronted by the imposing basilica and all the famous facades, the canopied coffee bars and porticoes, the regiments of grey and white stone. He admired the shabby grandeur and easy elegance of Venice. But it was all show, wasn't it? It played to the people like a theatre. He walked on. That was what happened, he supposed, when tourism took over and the original city-dwellers slunk backstage and into the wings. They still had their busy streets and canals, their food markets, their sense of community. But that authenticity was kept hidden in the name of survival. And he could sense it, exactly as he had sensed it in Rachel – that quality Venice held of not wanting to be completely known.

Six months after they'd met, Nicholas had taken Rachel to meet his father. Not that he expected her to have anything in common with Robert Tresillion. His father's life was the little stone cottage in which Nicholas had been born, the pub down the lane where he met up with his cronies in the evening to play cribbage. And the sea – mostly the sea. But since his intentions were serious, Nicholas needed Rachel to understand who he was. And this was who he was – at least, who he had been, once upon a time.

He had often wondered what his father had made of her. But he'd never asked him, afraid perhaps that his father would be too honest. She'd sat on the edge of his father's tatty old sofa as if something dangerous inside might drag her down into the rusty springs. And she sipped so cautiously at the strong brown tea – his dad didn't do Earl Grey. She spoke to his father politely but slowly, as if he was in his dotage, instead of fifty-seven years old and still out fishing most days, all seasons, all weathers.

Nicholas had cringed and caught the look in his father's true-blue eyes, but told himself it didn't matter. His father didn't need to understand. Rachel was part of his new life; she didn't need to be part of the old. He loved her, he wanted her, he meant to have her.

After tea, he and Rachel had walked down the narrow winding lane towards the beach, Rachel in her high heels exclaiming every now and then about how steep and stony it was. As they reached the steps that led down to Priest's Cove, she turned to look back, pushing the dark hair out of her eyes. His father's cottage was next to the end of the row of fishermen's dwellings nestling halfway up the green hill; small and compact, with white stone walls, tiny square windows and woodwork needing a lick of paint.

She raised an eyebrow. 'It's hard to believe, Nick,' she said.

He knew what she was saying. He had come from a humble background, yes. But his parents had encouraged him to work hard at school and later, after his mother's death when he was only twelve years old, his father had urged him to consider university. He'd never held him back. Nicholas had no complaints. Only that his mother had given birth to him late in life and had died too young. He was quiet for a moment, remembering the softness of her eyes, the curve of her lips as she gave him that special smile. *My son* . . .

'He's a good man,' he told Rachel.

'Oh, yes, yes, I can see.'

Now, he doubted that she had seen very much at all. Which made him even more of a fool. Because even now he'd rather she was still living with him, still making love with him, still pretending. At least, some days that was what he wished.

He slowed his pace. He came to Venice three or four times a

143

year, but he'd never had so much time to spare. He had never let himself get lost in this city but had never quite found it either, just as he'd never found Rachel.

The other pedestrians were dawdling, gazing into vibrant and seductive Venetian shop windows, pausing to peruse tempting menus in café doorways. Nicholas wasn't sure that he wanted to get lost this afternoon. But he wanted something.

Something . . . He found himself outside the Venice tourist information office and opened the door. Curiosity really. Looking for inspiration.

Inside, it was chilly, white and minimal. He smiled at the woman behind the desk and she shot him an impersonal smile back.

'Just browsing,' he told her, in Italian, before she could ask. She would speak English, of course; everyone did. But . . .

He scanned the postcards in the tourist office. There was the usual stuff: Venice at night, black and white Venice, sepia Venice. He moved on to the brochures, not knowing what he was looking for, waiting for something to catch his eye.

Back at Cape Cornwall, they had walked — he and Rachel — down the slipway at Priest's Cove, past the lobster pots and nets left to dry out in the sun. The Cape jutted out into the sea, its grassy flanks cloaked in wild pink daisies. On a clear day you could look across Whitesand Bay to Sennen Cove and Land's End. Sometimes you could see dolphins, seals or even basking sharks.

'But you're so different.' Rachel had put her hands on his shoulders and laughed. The wind was blowing her hair into her eyes again, but this time she didn't seem to mind. She smelt of jasmine.

He'd always thought that too. But now he knew that he and

144

his father were not so different after all. Nicholas craved the same simplicity in his life. He too was forever pulled to the sea – which was why he had wanted to have a holiday home in Cornwall as soon as he and Rachel could afford it. He'd chosen Godrevy because of his happy teenage memories of staying at his aunt's place in Gwithian, of climbing the dunes, the high towans, of surfing the waves, walking towards the lighthouse on Godrevy Island. His grandmother had grown up there, but she'd fallen in love with a fisherman from Priest's Cove, and the rest was history. For Rachel, of course, it was only a short car journey to the shopping and galleries of St Ives. Which was ideal – for a holiday at least, because he remembered what she'd said about the place that first evening in the Sloop Inn.

The summer after Rachel left him he went to the cottage in Godrevy and never returned to Surrey. The Surrey house was sold, Rachel moved to Rome and Nicholas bought a crash pad in London to make things easier when he was travelling. The rest of the time, he stayed at Godrevy. He sank back into Cornwall with a sigh of relief as if he had never left. Whatever it was, it was in his blood.

In the bookcase of the tourist information office, Nicholas saw something. *A Bridge in Time*. What was that all about? He liked bridges, always had. He flicked it open. *A bridge walk. Explore the bridges of Venice and sightsee as you go. One hour – or take all day.*

Well, why not?

He paid the girl behind the desk and headed for the *vaporetto* stop. It was mid-afternoon but tourist Venice didn't waste shopping time with siestas. The shops, crammed with glittering Venetian masks, Murano glass, leather, scarves and designer clothes, were all open and people still thronged the narrow streets.

There was a queue on the floating pontoon. He joined it and consulted the map to see where he should get off. The author was clear and – he checked the front cover – she had provided a map, historical notes, the lot; it was very comprehensive, much more than a guided walk.

Did he need guiding? Celie told him recently that he'd lost his sense of direction. But Nicholas knew the direction he was heading in – sort of. He looked out to the horizon. There was a band of golden light outlining the blue. He wanted to make enough money from a job that wasn't too stressful and wasn't boring; he enjoyed both travelling and meeting people; he admired Isabel and Giuseppe's jewellery and it had never been a hard sell. And he wanted to spend more time at home. In Cornwall he could live exactly the life he wanted to live – uncomplicated. Friends were always up for a drink and a chat, and he could go to London and see Celie whenever he chose. He enjoyed spending time with Isobel and Giuseppe and their family in Rome, and if he was bored, he'd take a trip somewhere. What was wrong with that for a direction? Plenty of people had a lot less.

But Celie wasn't finished. 'You need to get a grip, Dad,' she'd said. Suddenly she sounded like her mother. 'It's been a year since you guys split. And what's the point of pretending you and Mum were happy?'

He'd stared at her. How had she suddenly got to be so wise? Did she know that her mother had taken a lover? That her father hadn't had what it took to keep her?

His thoughts drifted back again to that day at Cape Cornwall. He had shown Rachel the higgledy-piggledy fishermen's huts built on the ledge above the slipway where his dad kept his gear. His dad's hut was painted turquoise, the colour of

146

the Cornish sea on a sunny summer's day. Beyond the huts, the chimney built on the summit of the Cape stood proud like an omen.

He led her past the brightly painted fishing boats of red, orange and yellow moored at the top of the small beach. The wind was picking up strength, but it was warm in the sun, and he knew exactly where to take her.

'Hang on.' She slipped off her shoes.

That was better. They reached the sheltered grey rock with the scooped-out contours, perfect for sitting in and watching the waves of the Atlantic pounding the Cornish granite. He had often sat here, watching his father heading out to sea, wondering if he would come back this time.

Nicholas touched Rachel's arm. 'Look at those rocks out there.' He pointed to the jagged black rocks ahead, the Brisons, home to the gannets, gulls and cormorants.

'What about them?' She frowned.

'General de Gaulle having a bath,' he said. Once you saw them, the protrusions that formed the belly, the nose and the lips, it was hard to see the cluster of black granite simply as rocks again.

She laughed. 'Can you swim here?' she asked.

'I used to when I was a kid.' He showed her the outcrop he used to dive from into the foaming water. 'It's treacherous, but we did it anyway.' For serious swimming and surfing he and his mates had headed to Sennen Cove, whenever they could get a lift on the back of someone's tractor or pick-up truck. Or to Godrevy; his aunt was always happy for her great-nephew to come and stay.

'I bet it was exciting.' For a moment Rachel looked wistful. She picked up a tiny black stone with a thin white stripe around

147

it, rolled it in her palm. Her nails were perfectly manicured, he noticed. In fact, everything about Rachel was about as perfect as you could get. Nicholas watched the water sheeting into a diamond waterfall off the slipway, listened to the surf crashing onto the boulders. He could close his eyes anytime, anywhere and hear that sound.

Yes, it had been exciting, though he'd never appreciated the landscape so much as a kid. Cape Cornwall was bleak and inhospitable in the winter; it had indeed often seemed like the end of the world to Nicholas and there were times he'd only wanted to get away from it. But he realised now that it was about as Cornish as anywhere. And bloody wonderful.

Rachel had slipped the black pebble into his hand.

His fingers curled around it. 'Will you marry me, Rachel?' he said. Because what else could you say to a perfect woman? He might be young, but he knew what he wanted.

And it might have been the wind. Or it might have been the only time Rachel's eyes had ever filled with tears. 'Yes, Nicholas,' she said. 'I'll marry you.'

The *vaporetto* came to a shuddering halt by the pontoon and Nicholas stepped onto the water bus. Most people were inside – a chilly wind was blowing – but he pulled a scarf out of his bag (Celie called it his Rupert scarf; it was yellow and checked and looked rather dashing, he thought, with his grey pinstriped suit). He wrapped it round his neck. It was invigorating being on deck.

As he watched the palaces wash by, Nicholas thought about what Celie had said. He thought about the kind of life he wanted and what Rachel had wanted. He could smell the musty dampness and stone that was Venice, hear the slow chugging of the engine, the water rolling against the side of the *vaporetto*. He felt his body sway as it picked up the motion of the boat. He held the rail as if to steady himself, looked out again along the horizon, to the point where the ornate buildings met the skyline, spires, domes, campaniles.

Sometimes Nicholas found himself losing sight of what was real. His marriage — which he had always thought to be real enough — had disintegrated and fallen apart. And he had crumbled with it. Just like this city.

Ponte degli Scalzi came into sight — a high, arrogant arch across the Grand Canal. The first bridge. He flicked open the brochure to find the picture of the author. Joanna Shepherd. Classy looking. Early to mid-thirties perhaps. Hair a dark bob that framed an attractive face. Half smiling. Nice eyes. A bit vulnerable looking. But who wasn't vulnerable?

You might be surprised, she had written, *at what you see*. That sounded hopeful. Nicholas wanted to be surprised. Yeah. He almost longed for it.

The Second Bridge

CHAPTER 19

Joanna

Dorset

Joanna had been working in her bedroom at Mulberry Farm Cottage all morning but now she got up, stretched and went to look out of the window at the dusty farmyard and the green hills beyond. She hadn't thought she would stay here so long, but she'd been busy writing up the Venice walk and getting the copy off to Toby prior to publication, finishing some other writing projects, starting her research for Lisbon . . . She hadn't even had time to start investigating her family tree. And somehow, one week had run into the next and then the next until she realised it was a month since she'd come back from Venice. The publisher had required a quick turnaround. By now, she supposed, people might even be reading the brochure, following in her footsteps.

She should, she was aware, be making plans of a more personal nature. Since her announcement to Harriet and her mother, very little had been said on the subject of her marriage.

153

Harriet wasn't the type to invite confidences or emotions and her mother, though sad, had also been accepting. As for Martin . . . apart from the occasional text message, he seemed to have accepted her decision.

Joanna moved away from the window and began collecting up her books from the bed. She'd bought a small desk and office chair from a vintage shop in Bridport, but the desk wasn't big enough for all her stuff; when she was writing and researching she liked to spread.

She thought about that conversation she'd had with Martin when she'd been in Venice, when she had told him that their marriage was over. She'd been surprised by the passion in his voice when he told her he still loved her . . . But even if that were true, it was too little, too late. There was no going back, not now.

She pulled Emmy's letters from the desk drawer where she kept them. She could hear Harriet typing in the study. Joanna went to the door, knocked lightly and went in.

'Hmm?' Harriet was peering at a sheaf of untidy hand-written pages on the desk next to her computer. She'd got that job she'd told Joanna she was going to apply for and it seemed to be taking up rather a lot of her time. 'What's up? Is Mother all right?'

'Last time I saw her she was in the kitchen reading one of her magazines.' Joanna and Harriet had come to an uneasy truce when it came to 'keeping an eye on Mother'. Harriet's call barring was still in force and this made Joanna feel decidedly uncomfortable, but she hadn't forced the issue. Their mother was sometimes vague, sometimes surprisingly sharp and on the ball, but always, there was a sense of affectionate sadness that reminded Joanna just how much Mother had lost when Father died.

'Just need to get to the end of this section, then I'll do lunch,' Harriet said, peering at the manuscript again. 'Half an hour tops.'

'It looks a complete mess.' Joanna still felt that shepherds' huts made more sense and there were plenty of other ways of making money. Perhaps she should phone Martin and push him to put the house on the market?

'It is. But he's offering a good rate, so . . .' Harriet let this hang.

Joanna leant in to take a closer look. Very scientific and totally incomprehensible. 'Didn't Owen say he might be interested in renting the big barn?' she said.

Harriet paused briefly to glare at her. 'Yes.'

'Then . . . ?'

'Then he'd be forever hanging around.' Harriet pulled one of the strangled faces that Joanna remembered from childhood.

She laughed. She would have thought Harriet would welcome the company. And it wasn't as if she used Big Barn for anything much – she could store the fruit in the cellar and the hay in Little Barn or the old sty. She could still do the teas in summer – from the kitchen, with people sitting outside and under the little marquee if it rained. But Harriet preferred problems to solutions. And she valued her privacy – Joanna could understand that.

'I found some letters in the attic, Het.' She dangled Emmy's letters briefly in front of her sister. It wasn't fair not to share, she'd decided. This was Harriet's home – even more than it was Joanna's – and besides, she might know more about the mysterious Emmy than Mother seemed to.

'Oh yes? Anything interesting?' Harriet didn't even stop typing.

155

'Love letters,' Joanna said. 'Written from Venice, Lisbon and Prague.'

'Fascinating,' said Harriet, not taking her fingers from the keyboard.

'Oh, they are.' Joanna held them closer to her breast. If she shared Emmy's letters with Harriet, then her sister might return the compliment and do some sharing of her own. And Joanna wanted that. 'Written by someone, maybe one of our ancestors, called Emmy, to a man called Rufus.'

'Right.' Harriet barely glanced up.

'So, do you want to read them?' She tried for a teasing tone but Harriet just looked cross.

'If I had the time,' she said. 'If I was remotely interested . . .'

Joanna sighed. 'So, you don't know who Emmy is?'

'No idea. Should I?'

'And you haven't found any of those photos of our ancestors you were talking about?'

'Sorry.' Harriet waved her away. 'And now, I really need to get this finished, Jo. All right?'

'All right.'

Joanna returned to her room and put the letters back in the drawer. The trouble with Harriet was that she simply had no imagination.

'I'm going out for a quick walk before lunch,' she called, letting herself out of the cottage before anyone could object. Sometimes, it was so claustrophobic here. So, she really must get her act together and find somewhere else to live.

She headed up the pitted grassy track towards the Beacon. The sky above was a pale grey, and in the distance, the sea glimmered between the lush green hills. But the countryside knew that summer was over and so did Joanna. She couldn't stay here indefinitely. She blew out her cheeks as she climbed, taking deep breaths and pacing herself. So where should she settle?

She'd talked briefly over the past few days to her closest London friends Steph and Lucy, filled them in on what was going on and where she was staying.

'Are you coming back?' Steph had asked.

'Not yet.'

Joanna eased into a deeper breathing pattern, pulling her scarf closer around her neck as she trudged up the hill. Why was Harriet always in such a bad mood anyway? She could at least have shown some interest in Emmy's letters. Was she dating someone she'd met online? If so, it didn't seem to be making her very happy.

She paused to look out over the hills. She hadn't appreciated this landscape as a girl, but now . . . Halfway up the hill, she turned to look back at the rambling stone farmhouse she'd grown up in, with its slate roof and sash windows; at the tall pines outlined against the clear sky, at the mulberry tree beside the pond, the old blue tractor standing forgotten by the barn. She remembered her father driving that tractor, Harriet perched next to him looking smug. Why didn't Harriet sell it on? What use was it just rusting away? The cottage looked older than ever in the autumnal light, the pale gold stone crumbling and flaking in places. Reminding Joanna that nothing lasted forever.

The turf under her feet was peppered with rabbit burrows and sheep droppings. On the hill to the south, Owen's carthorse loped lazily towards the water trough, followed by its gangly foal. She saw that Owen had lit a bonfire in the next field – the smoke was billowing in great grey gusts, mingling with the fusty autumnal air and settling behind the horses like a sea mist.

Joanna pulled out her phone and called Martin. He'd probably be at work, but . . . She breathed in the scent of the smoky
bonfire. It was some distance away but she fancied she could
see the flames leaping into life, feel the heat, hear the crackle
as the dried undergrowth took.

'Jo!' She tried not to hear the hope in his voice.

'Martin, I was just wondering—'

'Yes? Hang on a sec.' She could imagine him going somewhere more private to take the call. And that was another
problem with Mulberry Farm Cottage — there was so little
privacy. If someone phoned, then everybody knew about it.
She smiled. Unless you came up here, that was.

Joanna walked on. A small black-faced sheep bleated at her
approach and ducked away. It was one of Owen's flock. 'I've
been thinking about the house,' she said, when he was back
on the line.

'The house?'

'Well, I have to live somewhere. So . . .'

'You want me to put it on the market. You haven't changed
your mind.'

There was no easy way of saying this. 'We have to, Martin. I
need the money. I need to find somewhere to live.' Then maybe
she could also make more of a contribution to the Mulberry
Cottage Repair Fund, and perhaps Harriet could give up her
typing job at least.

Joanna was at the top of the hill now; she was in better
condition than when she'd first arrived home – she was hardly
out of breath. It was a rewarding climb. The sea spun out in
front of her – a sheet of smooth metallic blue, undulating in
small currents where the breeze caught it.

'Not going so well back in Dorset, is it?' Martin said.

'I never said I was staying here forever.' Joanna walked past the gorse bushes and the wooden beacon and leant on the rail looking out to sea. To the west was the golden roof of the Cap, even higher than the Beacon; beyond, Doghouse Hill and Seatown; to the east, the ribbon of Chesil Beach threaded out of sight towards Portland Bill.

'OK, I get the picture.' There was a pause.

At least he seemed to have accepted how things were, she thought. Joanna took the track which spiralled round and down the cliff, teasing, towards the bay. 'So, will you do it?' she asked him.

'Yeah, I'll do it.'

'Thank you.' Joanna exhaled with relief as she came to the end of the path. She walked on down the road, next to the stream, bordered by brambles, bulrushes and lichen. She walked down the steps to the pebbled beach where the fishing boats were stacked up to one side of the stream. Sat for a moment, on the pebbles, hugging her knees.

Her phone pinged in an email and she instinctively checked it. She must get back, she reminded herself. She'd probably missed lunch, but she should get on with planning the bridge walk in Lisbon; she was leaving in just over a week.

The subject of the email was: *Bridge walk – Venice*. The sender was someone called Nicholas Tresillion. Joanna was intrigued. Someone had done the walk. Someone had written to her about it.

Dear Joanna Shepherd, she read.

I enjoyed your bridge walk in Venice – an ideal place for it, I suppose. And something in particular interested me. You said we might be surprised at what we saw. And let me tell you, I was . . .

159

CHAPTER 20

Harriet

Dorset

Joanna had gone off on one of those long walks of hers – probably annoyed because Harriet wasn't as obsessed with their family history as Joanna seemed to be – and so Harriet and her mother had lunch on their own without her. Quite honestly, the last thing Harriet wanted to think about right now was someone else's love letters – partly because, despite her best efforts, her love life was more or less non-existent.

Joanna still hadn't returned, but Harriet wasn't worried. Mother was taking a nap and it was peaceful here in Little Barn. Harriet was enjoying spending some time with the hens, collecting eggs, murmuring to them softly under her breath.

Non-existent, that was, with the exception of Jolyon. They'd been emailing for a few weeks now but Harriet still hadn't taken the plunge of agreeing to meet him. He was a country and western aficionado, which put her off slightly. There was nothing wrong with country and western music. It wasn't all 'DIVORCE' or, alternatively, 'Stand by Your

Man' – thankfully. But . . . what sort of a man was Jolyon? She wasn't sure. It wasn't your average name, was it? Not that she wanted an average man, not at all. But . . . Harriet's trouble was that she allowed too many 'buts' into her life – she always had.

She heard an engine, but she didn't want to be disturbed by Owen since that was probably who it was. Instead, she went on checking for eggs in the scratchy straw of the nesting boxes. She loved the feel of a freshly laid egg – warm and smooth, coddled in the palm of her hand, slipping reluctantly through her fingers as she placed them one by one in the straw-lined basket she kept for the purpose. Gentle now, they were fragile and new. An egg, she thought, dusting away a pale amber speck of down, was a small miracle.

A door slammed. No doubt Owen was hoping to catch sight of Joanna; he was a much more frequent visitor than he'd ever been before, and like Harriet had said to her sister earlier, it would be even more frequent if they rented him Big Barn. Harriet made a move to go out and speak to him and then stopped. Why should she? Right now, she didn't feel like speaking to anyone. All she wanted was this rare moment of peace.

She placed another egg in the basket. Joanna had her writing while Harriet had . . . this. She stooped as she felt around in the straw and absorbed the animal heat of the barn. It was comforting and safe. Feathery, musty, mealy and . . . yes, delicious. She smiled. She was a farmer's daughter all right; her father's daughter. Above the nesting boxes were the perches where the chickens slept, often huddled together for warmth, feathers fluffed up as the weather grew colder. She stretched. Well, life wouldn't be so bad if it was just moments like this, would it? Or if there was more money in the pot.

She peered through the cobwebby window. No sign of

Owen. In the yard, Clarence the cockerel was strutting around like the bloke he was, his bright feathers ruffled in the wind. King of Little Barn. Harriet brushed away some flaking paintwork. Too many things were flaking around here. She flicked a cobweb out of her hair.

She put down the basket, picked up the broom from where it stood in the corner and began sweeping the floor of the barn. Hens weren't messy creatures, but they liked to scatter. She had noted that they'd perfected an air of what looked like indifference towards Clarence. They didn't care that he was the only one, nor that he was so self-important. It was nothing to them. She chuckled. They knew the universal truth. Eat food, lay eggs, scratch about and sleep in the sun – that was it.

She opened the barn door to deposit the sweepings in the bin by the woodpile and breathed deeply. Owen must have lit a bonfire – the scent of it was warm and toasty in the breeze. And from the other side of the barn she thought she heard a faint whistling: 'Walk on By'. Was that Owen too? She paused. Hang on, the man couldn't be everywhere; she must be imagining it.

She went back for the eggs, opened the door again and reluctantly left the warmth of Little Barn. The harsh light of earlier had become the pinker shade of an autumnal October afternoon.

'Let's make a start then.' The loud nasal voice splintered the peace of the farmyard.

Harriet jumped. Who on earth . . . ? A white lorry was parked by the cottage. And she suddenly became aware of an unfamiliar smell mixing in with the bonfire and the farmyard. It was like hot . . . She sprinted across the yard, her precious basket clutched to her side.

Two youths were sweeping the driveway that led from the lane to the house. It was an ominous sort of sweeping. Two men in

162

white overalls were standing by the front door. Harriet took in the entire scene at a glance. Terry's Tarmac was the name on the lorry. She steadied her breathing. She must stay calm.

'Can I help you?' she enquired icily of one of the men, who looked as if he might be Terry and therefore in charge. Her mind was speeding ahead, though. How *could* she have done it? Mother never ventured into the village these days. Mother didn't own a mobile phone and the call barring on the landline was Mother-proof – Harriet had memorised the code and sworn Joanna to secrecy. It had been a while since the last problem and Harriet had foolishly taken her eye off the ball.

'Tarmac,' the man said. Not hugely articulate then, so probably not the boss. He was eyeing Harriet as if she were some wild animal who had suddenly appeared in the yard.

'Who are you?' Harriet put down the basket so that she could fold her arms in an authoritative manner. Though she knew.

'Terry's. We're laying the tarmac what you asked for, love.' The second man entered the conversation. As she turned to face him, he hitched up his jeans, which was a small relief at least.

Harriet glared at him. This wasn't the time or the place for mentioning grammar, but it still rankled. 'I didn't ask for any tarmac.' She glanced up at the window above. A shadowy figure slipped out of sight. *Mother* . . .

'Yeah, you did. I've got the order sheet.' The second man opened the passenger door of the white lorry and retrieved a clipboard. Maybe he was Terry then.

Harriet barely glanced at it. 'I don't require any tarmac,' she said. 'And I certainly didn't order any.'

As one, the boys stopped sweeping. Maybe they'd learnt to recognise authority when they heard it. They leant on the brooms, dark eyes staring, waiting for instructions.

'We can't hang around, love.' The first man looked her up and down. 'It's hot and it's steaming.'

Harriet stood her ground. 'That doesn't interest me in the least,' she said.

He sighed a world-weary sigh. 'You the house owner then, love?' he asked.

'Yes,' she snapped. Now was not the time for truth.

'And . . . ?' He let his eyes roll towards the house.

'My mother.' Bless her. How could she have? Perhaps she was paying Harriet back for putting the bar on the phone. But there was no money for tarmac. There was no money for anything.

The second man nodded, glanced at his watch. 'All very well,' he said. 'But this lot won't wait.' He pointed towards the lorry. 'It's got to be laid.'

Was it her imagination, or was he trying to tell her something? Harriet forced herself to stay focused.

'Ready to tip, rake and roll.' He raised an eyebrow.

'There was that other job in the village, Terry,' said the other man.

Ah, thought Harriet. They both pored over the clipboard. The boys slouched back towards the lorry.

Terry grunted. He was clearly not a man to be easily placated and there was possibly only one language men like him understood.

'How much do you want?' Harriet asked.

'For the job?'

'No.' Wasn't he listening to what she was telling him? 'We don't want your tarmac,' she repeated. Even if they could afford it, this was a farm, for God's sake. Farms were meant to be stony, scruffy, dusty and peppered with holes. 'How much to go away?' she said. 'I realise you've been called out

164

unnecessarily.' And she would get to the bottom of this – with Mother.

His eyes glinted.

Greed was very unattractive, thought Harriet. Though, of course, she was a realist and everyone needed money. If they didn't, she for one wouldn't be spending her time typing up someone's scruffy and half-illegible scientific manuscript. The man must be desperate; he hadn't even interviewed her, not properly, just a few questions over the phone, taken her address and informed her that the first batch would be delivered as soon as possible.

Terry was on his mobile now. He was humming the same song. Harriet wished they'd all walk on by. Pronto. He broke off to talk to someone. 'Yeah. No, she don't want it.' He looked across at Harriet.

Suddenly, a figure appeared on the brow of the hill, looking down on them like something out of *Wuthering Heights*. Joanna, framed by the dark shimmer of the sea and the green fields, her stripy orange scarf flying, made a dramatic picture. One of Owen's sheep let out a bleat and another replied, the sounds echoing forlornly over the hills.

Harriet watched as Joanna ran down the path towards them like a young girl. Both men were watching her too, and maybe even the boys, who were now standing on the other side of the lorry texting on their mobiles.

Something not particularly pleasant and rarely acknowledged twisted inside Harriet. She pushed it determinedly away. Did she really want a man? Could a man change her life in the way she wanted it to be changed? Probably not.

'What's going on?' Joanna asked as she drew level. She was out of breath; her face was flushed pink from the exercise, her

165

eyes bright. Marital problems seemed to agree with her, Harriet thought uncharitably.

'These men have come to lay some tarmac,' Harriet told her. 'Only we don't want any.'

'No, we don't,' Joanna agreed. A complicit look passed between them.

'So . . .' Harriet began.

'So, clearly there's been an unfortunate misunderstanding.' Joanna smiled sweetly at the men. 'Is that a problem?'

'We've come a hell of a long way for nothing,' Terry complained, not looking at Harriet. 'The stuff's made up and ready to roll, and even if we do have another job to go to—'

'I thought I should give them something.' Heaven knows why she was running this past Joanna anyway. Who was in charge here? Who ran this place single-handed?

'Oh, good idea, Het.' Joanna laughed, she actually laughed. 'How about a nice cup of tea and a piece of cake before you get rid of that stuff somewhere else, boys? Will that do you?'

And not waiting for an answer, she ushered them through the porchway and into the kitchen, clucking like one of the bloody hens. *Boys, indeed.*

'Come through. You must be dying for a cuppa, I know I am.' She beckoned to the boys by the lorry and they pocketed their phones and followed suit.

'Well, since you're asking . . . But it'll have to be a quick one, love . . .' The voices faded.

Harriet stood in the empty farmyard, arms still folded in front of her. Joanna was warm and glowing and good-hearted. As for Harriet – she had a sliver of ice inside her, she must have. Otherwise she would be more charitable in her feelings towards her sister. Wouldn't she?

CHAPTER 21

Joanna

Dorset

Having successfully got rid of the tarmac men, Joanna went up to her room to do another Google search on bridges in Lisbon. *Bridge Deaths: Lisbon accepts blame* . . . That was a bit gruesome. *Spiderman arrested on top of the bridge* . . . Slightly surreal. She was experiencing déjà vu, because she'd been here before – yesterday and the previous day – and she was running out of time. She had read posts from tourists who had been to Lisbon twenty years ago, and a thesis by a student on Portuguese explorers. She had read about Lisbon's best views and quite a few of its hidden secrets. She had to accept it. As far as Emmy's Lisbon bridge was concerned, she was drawing a blank.

There were bridges – two notably modern and famous suspension bridges: the Ponte 25 de Abril which crossed the Tagus, but could only be negotiated on foot once a year if you happened to be running in the city's marathon, and the Vasco da Gama Bridge in the east of the city, named after Portugal's most famous explorer.

Each bridge had an interesting and historical background; each was part of Lisbon's culture. But they weren't historic enough for Emmy. She had gone to Lisbon in 1912 and she had painted a bridge. But that bridge was nowhere to be found.

She would call Toby right now, Joanna decided. She'd been putting it off. But she didn't *have* to follow Emmy's path. There was no earthly reason why some old letters she'd found in the attic should dictate what she wrote about or where she travelled to. Why were they so important? Neither Harriet nor her mother had seemed remotely interested. Even so. How could Joanna explain how Emmy's story drew her, why it seemed so vital to find out what had happened to Emmy and Rufus, let alone her strong feeling that Emmy's letters seemed to be a sign to Joanna to go where Emmy led. Whenever she looked at the painting in her room, whenever she picked up the bundle of Emmy's letters to Rufus, Joanna felt the pull. It was as if the walks, the story, the magic – or whatever it was – was there, waiting to be discovered. She felt that Emmy's direction was her direction too. That there must be a purpose in it all.

And now there was Nicholas Tresillion.

Although Joanna had been about to call Toby, instead, she went to her email inbox and reread the message for the third time. It was always nice to hear from readers; most of them were complimentary and had written to her because something in an article or feature had struck a chord or touched them in some way, though there was always the odd, tricky one complaining about something she'd said.

This, though, was neither.

I've always considered myself a grounded kind of a bloke, he had written. *At any rate, I don't usually see things that aren't there. And life has taught me not to have too many high expectations . . .*

He had added a grimly smiling emoji.

Joanna raised an eyebrow. He'd been disappointed then. In life? In a woman? Most likely a woman, she decided.

But you made me think again, she read.

Which was a positive.

I appreciated the sense of history you included in the walk, the email went on. *It made the place come alive. It gave me a new outlook on a city I've visited many times.*

Why had he visited so many times? Because he loved Venice or because he worked there? Work, she guessed.

So . . . was I looking for something to see?

Joanna chuckled. He had a way of talking to himself at the same time as addressing her, which she quite liked – it showed intelligence at least and a tendency to self-examine that was also refreshing. 'I don't know. Were you?' she heard herself saying.

I think I was, but it still took me by surprise.

Another positive, she thought.

So, my question to you, Joanna Shepherd, is this: were your words an example of what someone might see in the water under the bridge, or did you really see the girl running?

Oh, Joanna had seen her all right.

Because I did. You could have put the picture into my head, I don't know, but I saw every detail of her: a blue dress, a wide smile, the golden ribbon in her hair.

The golden ribbon in her hair . . .

No doubt you'll think I'm crazy. But there's more. Perhaps it was just the moment, but . . . there was something disconcertingly familiar about that girl. So, are you a writer or a magician? I'd be interested to know.

Yours, Nicholas Tresillion

★

Joanna had been slightly apprehensive as to how her Venice bridge walk piece might be received. She'd included plenty of facts – but had it also contained too much fantasy? She'd dithered about what to say and what not to say and eventually she'd left her surreal experience intact in the copy; not the detail, but the outline of her moment of magic . . .

Anyone could write to her and claim they'd seen a girl in a blue dress. It wasn't so strange that he too had experienced a similar moment of illusion as he looked into the sunlit water. But how would he have known about the golden ribbon? Because in the copy she'd sent to Toby, she hadn't mentioned that.

A coincidence perhaps? Joanna frowned. Should she reply to his email? She hadn't decided yet. What did you say to a reader who might have somehow seen inside your head? She didn't have a clue.

She flipped back to her contacts and found Toby. She had a commission to do and she mustn't let herself get distracted by something that might exist only in her imagination. If there were no bridges to walk over in Lisbon, then she wouldn't go there, however much Emmy and her letters were pulling her in that direction. Besides, she'd become wary of her imagination. Martin always said it was overcharged, that she let her writing dictate her life, rather than the other way around, which apparently was the sensible way to do it. Perhaps Martin was right.

'I'm thinking that I'll skip Lisbon,' she said when Toby answered. 'The bridge thing is proving problematic.' To say the least. Lisbon must have been very different in Emmy's day. There had no doubt been some beautiful old bridges for her to paint – that had since fallen down.

Toby let out a deep sigh. 'Joanna . . .'

Here we go, she thought.

'I want Lisbon,' he said. With emphasis. As if it was some guy he'd fallen for. 'It's right on trend. The pitch is done. They're expecting it – intrigued at what you're going to come up with.'

They weren't the only ones. 'But—'

'But you'll have to meet the deadline. OK?'

Well, no. How had she ever considered Toby a pushover?

'I'll do my best,' she said, ending the call.

She spread the map of Lisbon out on the bed. Stared at it, hoping for inspiration. There must be something here, and if she looked hard enough, she would find it. There was always something . . .

Outside, she could hear Harriet talking to the hens. Was Harriet losing control? Joanna wouldn't be surprised after the earlier fiasco with the tarmac and all the other things on her sister's mind. Maybe Harriet was right and Mother was losing it too. Come to think of it, Joanna herself wasn't exactly on the ball.

She should go out and have a word with Harriet. But in the meantime, she mustn't panic. She must focus. And once again, she felt that conviction that Emmy would show her the way.

Joanna got to her feet, retrieved the letters from her desk once more. They felt crisp and fragile, like autumn leaves. Even touching them made her shiver; it was as if she was holding a piece of her past, something that she could link into her future.

Carefully, she sorted through them until she found the one written in Lisbon. She'd read it before, of course, but every time she did so, she seemed to see something new.

My Dearest Rufus . . . I count the days until I shall see your sweet face, until you hold me in your arms . . . I am giddy with thinking of you. How can I bear to be apart from you? I know not.

171

That was love, Joanna thought. To be counting the days, to be giddy with thinking about someone.

As with Venice, Emmy had noted her father's particular historical interest in the city. *It is one of the world's most ancient cities*, she wrote. *Not to mention the point of departure for many famous Portuguese explorers. Indeed, in the fifteenth century, the city was possibly the world's most prosperous trading centre.*

Emmy was her father's daughter, Joanna reflected. His interest in history shone through. She searched in the letter for the reference to Emmy's painting.

I have drawn the ancient bridge, she wrote, *from all angles. I have sat beneath the mulberry trees . . .*

Mulberry trees? That was rather close to home. How had she not noticed that the first time she read the letter? *Mulberry trees?* Once again, Joanna shivered.

She leant closer towards the map, feeling her way, looking for something different, something away from the river, something she had seen before and not registered. And read the street name on which her index finger was resting. Les Amoreiras. Surely . . . ? She turned to her laptop and looked up the Portuguese on Google Translate. *The mulberries.* And there it was. An ancient aqueduct with 165 arches that started on the northern outskirts of the city, in the hills, and ran down the street, alongside the mulberry trees. A bridge. Emmy's second bridge.

Joanna reached for her pen. She had that feeling in her gut. She'd cracked it. Now she just had to go to the old aqueduct, walk it, and write it. She was on her way.

CHAPTER 22

Harriet

Dorset

Later that afternoon, Harriet went out to the kitchen garden to vent some of her frustration on the weeds. Terry's Tarmac indeed. Thanks to Joanna, it had cost no more than the price of a few slices of cake, some tea and a further dent to Harriet's pride. Even so, she would talk to Mother – later, she decided, when she wasn't feeling quite so angry.

After a while, Joanna appeared in the garden, snug inside a thick grey fleece. Her expression suggested that she knew exactly how Harriet was feeling.

'Perhaps we shouldn't have excluded her,' Joanna said. 'After all, it's not as if she can't think for herself, is it? She's not a child.'

'No, she's not.' Which made it even harder. It was all very well for Joanna. Harriet dug into the soil of the herb bed with her trowel. Her sister had no idea. She hadn't seen the half of it yet. She still didn't know how demanding Mother could be.

The metal blade sliced easily through the earth, and Harriet knew instinctively how deep she had to go to get it out. Dandelion. The tip of the white root. What Joanna said made sense — sort of. 'But what else do you suggest we do?' she demanded. They had to stop her somehow, before she bankrupted the place.

Joanna shrugged. 'Talk to her?'

'And you think I haven't?'

'I know you have.' Joanna bent towards her.

Harriet could smell her sister's perfume. She always smelt nice. Probably because she didn't get involved in the messy part of the farm . . .

'But maybe we can talk to her in a different way: as a reasonable and intelligent human being, as a valued part of the family — our family, Het.'

Harriet blinked at her. Didn't she do that? What was Joanna suggesting? She focused on the soil of the kitchen garden once more, waggled the trowel further into the moist earth. 'If you think you can do any better,' she muttered. But inside she was thinking, *didn't she do that?*

'No, I don't think I can do any better.' Joanna rested a hand lightly on Harriet's shoulder. Harriet pretended she couldn't feel it. 'But if we did it together . . .'

Together . . . To her surprise, she felt a tear in the corner of her eye and she blinked it back. It must be the wind — it had picked up during the afternoon.

'I'm only saying . . .' Joanna's voice softened. 'Perhaps we didn't make the right decision about the call barring. You know, as far as Mother's concerned, where there's a will, there's a way.'

She had been kind enough not to mention that the call

barring had been wholly Harriet's idea. 'Or perhaps she's getting worse,' Harriet said.

They looked at each other.

'D'you think so?' Joanna frowned. 'I was thinking that maybe there was an improvement. That she seemed more with it, somehow.'

'Hmm.' Harriet didn't know what to think.

There was only one dandelion left. Harriet pushed in the fork but the root broke near the tip. *Damn.* She exhaled. She could dig the rest of it out but it wasn't the same. It was so much more satisfying when you got the whole thing intact.

Despite this conversation with Joanna, Harriet brought the subject up with her mother the very next morning at breakfast.

'Tell me honestly, Mother,' she said, 'did you get in touch with those men?'

'What men?'

'The tarmac men.' Harriet took deep breaths as she got the bowls and plates out of the kitchen cupboard. Perhaps she should take up yoga? If only she could find the time . . .

'Harriet.' Her mother assumed a majestic expression. 'I don't understand why you always blame me. For every smallest thing . . .'

Smallest thing indeed. Supposing Harriet hadn't come out of Little Barn when she did? Supposing the tarmac had been laid and they'd had to find the money for it? You couldn't exactly return tarmac to the shop.

She sawed through the granary bread with ferocity, thought back again to her conversation with her sister the day before. Joanna had a point; Harriet had to admit that the call barring might have come over as a bit . . . controlling. Even so, she was determined to find out how Mother had contacted them. That way, she might be able to prevent her from doing it again – whether she and Joanna talked to her or not.

Joanna came into the kitchen. 'Morning,' she said breezily. She took a bowl and tipped in some muesli.

'Morning, darling,' their mother replied.

Harriet grunted. 'Someone must have called them out,' she muttered darkly.

'I'm not even allowed to use my own telephone during the day.' Delicately, their mother spooned the last segment of grapefruit into her mouth and dabbed her lips with a tissue. 'So, I really can't imagine why you're accusing me.'

Harriet clicked her tongue. She lifted the toast from the toaster and piled it onto a plate.

Joanna pulled a face at her and helped herself to the first slice. 'Are you going into Bridport this morning, Het?' She was good at changing the subject, but Harriet was determined not to let it drop.

Don't call me Het. She nodded. 'Straight after breakfast.' She had some early leeks and parsnips to deliver to Bloomers; she'd dug them up yesterday afternoon when she'd finished with the weeds. And that wasn't all she had to do in Bridport. Yesterday evening, Harriet had been busy online.

'Can you give me a lift?' Joanna loaded on the butter.

'I suppose so, yes.' Her sister never seemed to put on weight; never got a pimple or greasy skin.

'I need to do some research.'

Oh, research, research. Why did she always have to sound so important? Harriet scraped the butter onto her own toast and was equally frugal with the marmalade. She had no idea why – she didn't suffer from pimples or greasy skin either and

176

she wasn't especially overweight; it was more a case of being lumpy in all the wrong places. 'Fine,' she snapped.

'Thanks.' Joanna looked as if she was about to say more, but changed her mind.

So what if Harriet was in a bad mood? Wouldn't anyone be? And could Joanna really blame her for treating Mother like a child when she behaved like one? She took a swig of tea and reached for the telephone directory. No one wanted to tell her, so she would have to find out.

She flipped through the *Yellow Pages*, looking for Terry's Tarmac. Picked up the phone and punched in the number.

'Yes,' she said, when an efficient-sounding woman answered. 'This is Mulberry Farm Cottage here. Harriet Shepherd speaking.' It was always best to sound brusque and unfriendly, she had found – people wanted to appease you that way.

'Mrs Shepherd? Oh, yes.'

'Ms.'

'Ms Shepherd, sorry. We had you booked in for yesterday.'

Was she imagining the faint note of reproof in the woman's voice? 'Yes, apparently so.' Harriet sighed. 'But I didn't ask you to come in the first place.' She finished her tea and rolled her eyes at Joanna. 'And I have no idea who did.' Like heck.

'Are you sure?'

'Of course I'm sure.' Harriet tried to remain calm. But there was always so much to think of, so much to do. Who could be calm? 'And what I should like to know is, who did contact you?' Out of the corner of her eye, she could see her mother fidgeting. Well, let her fidget, she was not going to wriggle her way out of this one.

'It says Shepherd on here.' The woman's voice became more

clipped and Harriet could hear the shuffling of paperwork. 'And I think we have a letter . . .'

'A letter?' Harriet gave her mother a sharp look. Now they were getting somewhere. 'I see.'

'And then we would phone to make an appointment for Terry to come out and see you, and—'

'Thank you. Thank you very much. But no. Thank you.' Harriet put down the phone. It was pointless to interrogate Mother any further. She would only deny it, and then Harriet would get frustrated and say something she didn't mean. Or say something she did mean but shouldn't say. She got up and grabbed her coat from the hook by the door. She had to get out of here.

'Are you leaving now?' Joanna crammed half a slice of toast into her mouth. 'Is it OK for us both to be out at . . .' She glanced an apology at their mother. 'I mean, what time should we be home for Mother?'

'I'll be back by eleven thirty at the latest.' And Joanna was right. When had they started talking about Mother as if she wasn't there? 'It's up to you. Come back with me or find your own way later. The bus only leaves every two hours these days and it will still only bring you as far as the main road.' She was already halfway out of the door. She knew she sounded bad-tempered and resentful, but she simply couldn't help it. These days it seemed to be her default setting. And right now it was a question of fight or flight.

'But—' their mother began.

'Bye, Mother,' Harriet yelled. 'Leave the breakfast things. I'll clear up later.' She simply couldn't stay here a moment longer listening to her mother denying all knowledge and Joanna appeasing her. Three hours wasn't long to get into

Bridport, do the chores, meet Jolyon for coffee and get back home again, but it would have to do. Besides, it was quite likely that she and Jolyon would hate each other on sight. Or she'd blow it like she had with Hector, by being far too honest.

She crossed the yard and unlocked the pick-up. It wasn't ideal for them both to be out all morning, but hopefully it was safe enough after yesterday's fiasco. And she did understand that Joanna had to work – just as she did. Her sister was scurrying across the yard, still shoving her laptop into an already bulging shoulder bag. 'What's the big hurry?' she was grumbling.

Harriet ignored the question. 'Have you posted any letters for Mother?' she asked instead.

'No.' Joanna gave her that *don't be too hard on her* look again but she ignored that too.

Who else could have done it? Harriet climbed into the driver's seat and put the key in the ignition. In the distance she could see a familiar red tractor trundling across the far field. 'Owen.' She slapped the palm of her hand hard on the steering wheel.

'Owen?'

'Yes.' Harriet put the pick-up into reverse. Honestly, Joanna was so dreamy these days, always a million miles away. Had she always been like that, even as a child? Was that why her sister had always been protected, as if she were living in some bubble-world of her own?

'What about Owen?'

'Owen must have posted the letter to Terry's Tarmac. For Mother.' She spoke slowly and clearly so that even Joanna would understand.

'Oh, I see. Well, in that case, we'll have to talk to him too. Tell him to—'

'Exactly.' Harriet steered the pick-up down the stony, bumpy, un-tarmacked drive. As she turned into the lane a little bit too fast, she almost ran down a cyclist. 'Hellfire!' she shouted.

'Harriet!' Joanna grabbed hold of the dashboard.

For a second, the cyclist seemed to twist towards her, his bike veering from right to left, the expression on his face confused and even a bit scared. Scared? That couldn't be right.

'It's him!' she muttered.

'Him?'

'Yes . . .' As Harriet continued to stare at him, unable for a moment to do anything else, the cyclist almost went down into the ditch, wobbled precariously then righted himself and set off down the lane at a furious pace.

'Who is it, Het?' Joanna was peering down the lane.

'It's the man.' Harriet should go after him. She should drive on, force him to a halt and confront him. Demand to know why he'd been prowling around in the farmyard. But she couldn't move. Her palms were stuck to the steering wheel, her eyes fixed straight in front of her.

'What man?'

'The man who's been hanging around.' Harriet took a deep breath and managed to put the pick-up into gear. So, as she'd thought, he hadn't gone away. Slowly, she accelerated and drove down the lane, in the opposite direction to the one taken by the cyclist. She didn't want to confront him – not now. She had far too much to do this morning and anyway, he'd already disappeared around the corner and out of sight.

'You mean the man who's been stalking you?'

'Well . . .' Joanna did tend to be a bit melodramatic at times.

'Stop the car!' Joanna shouted.

'Don't be ridiculous.' Harriet carried on driving. 'And it's a pick-up truck.'

'But, Harriet . . .'

'What?' *Why had he looked so scared?*

'Don't you think we should call the police?'

'Not really.' Seeing him had only confirmed what Harriet already knew — that he was still around and still watching her. She would have to do something about it, she was aware of that, but not now. An uncertain October sun was inching through the clouds and she had errands to run and a new contender for her affections to meet.

Joanna seemed to give up. She sat back in her seat and muttered something that sounded like, 'Well, it's your funeral.'

Harriet glanced at her watch. Bugger the prowler. He could wait. Bugger the problems that would still be waiting for her when she returned home. Bugger the fact that she was so broke she had become a secretary. There was the distant hope of romance on the horizon. Harriet put her foot down.

181

CHAPTER 23

Nicholas

Cornwall

Something had happened to Nicholas in Venice . . .

He returned home to the cottage at Godrevy, conscious of a
strange dissatisfaction. It was something to do with that bridge
walk. As he'd told Joanna Shepherd, he wasn't given to flights
of the imagination. However . . . He couldn't explain it, but
he knew what he'd seen. It had touched him, moved him in
a way that made him conscious of something missing in his
life. Not Rachel, or Celie, though they were missing too. This
was more a sense of something he'd let go. A part of himself.

The next day he put on a warm fleece and walked to the
headland, looked out at the ocean, watched the wind whipping up the waves in the thick, navy sea. In the distance, the
lighthouse stood white and sturdy on Godrevy Island, silently
watching. Soon, he would be in Cotillo, he thought. And then?

It was one of those late October days when the clouds
moved so fast that it was raining one moment, bright sunshine

182

the next – which rather reflected Nicholas's mood. The surfers were there too; they came in all weathers and all seasons; autumn and winter often brought the best waves. He realised they were holding a surfing competition. On the headland, vans and campers stood in the car park, tents and canopies had been erected, people clustered around the cliff edge using cameras and binoculars to monitor progress. Flags were flying: a red pennant and the black and white Cornish cross.

Nicholas took the path that skirted the car park and led over the dusty boardwalk to the cliff. An Australian commentator cut into the Jack Johnson track that was playing over the loudspeakers, calling for the next surfers to get ready. It took Nicholas way back.

He'd started surfing when he was seven, using a board and wetsuit passed down to him by Jimmy Prisk next door. After that, he did odd jobs for the fishermen whenever he could and saved up enough money to buy his own gear when he was twelve. When his father wanted him to go out fishing, Nicholas only wanted to surf. It had got him into a whole load of trouble.

The surfers in their wetsuits were as sleek as seals. He watched them. Three figures, three boards; he could almost feel the strenuous slog as they made their way back to catch the next set, almost feel their excitement as they waited, assessing each wave's strength and height. He too could almost experience that plunge into the icy water, which seemed like a leap of faith. Then came the best bit, the heady balancing act, as they controlled the board and rode the top of the wave. Before the surge of power as another wave crashed and the tides joined forces to carry the surfer in.

He watched the surfers with a practised eye. He could spot

who would lose balance, who looked confident and sure. A young boy was lying in the damp grass, watching, drinking it in. He wanted it. And if you wanted it that much . . .

Nicholas turned around abruptly. Enough. He made his way back along the boardwalk, over the towans, past the car park and down to the golden beach. In the distance across the bay, the yellow sunlight reflected and glittered on the houses in St Ives.

He had smoked his first cigarette here at fourteen, drunk his first beer, had his first snog with Martha Prisk behind a grey granite stack. Nicholas grinned. He pulled off his trainers and socks, stuffed his socks in his pocket and looped the laces of his trainers round his thumbs. He'd always loved the feel of sand on his bare feet, and some things at least had never changed. The dark rocks rose dramatically from the pale sand peppered with silver and black granite dust.

Nicholas loped over to the sheer cliff face, ran his fingers across the stone. This was a harsh landscape. But it was his land-scape. It was drawn into him, it was part of his foundations; he could no more escape it than get Rachel back. Not that he wanted Rachel back. Rachel belonged in Rome or in leafy Surrey. Leafy Surrey had made Nicholas feel claustrophobic – there were just too many trees. And Nicholas belonged here. He should never have left.

He had stopped surfing. Rachel didn't like it. She didn't think it was responsible behaviour – for a married man, a father. 'It's dangerous, Nicholas,' she said. 'Now that we have Celie . . .'

He'd remonstrated – after all, he'd been doing it for years; he didn't take any risks. But she'd worn him down with her particular brand of emotional blackmail. Why did she mind

184

so much? He'd never understood. Perhaps it didn't fit into the image she'd built of him – the suits and ties, the neatly clipped hair; the businessman, rather than the son of a fisherman from Priest's Cove. Or perhaps she was jealous that there was a part of him she couldn't control?

Whatever, when they were staying at their holiday cottage in Godrevy, Rachel would take out her book on the beach and Nicholas would play with Celie on the sand or take her into the sea to paddle. Not that he didn't want to do those things . . . And when you became a parent, you couldn't do exactly what you'd done before. He knew all that. But . . . he also knew damn well that he should have been stronger with Rachel. When exactly had compromise come to mean sacrifice?

Like his experience in Venice, this made him think.

The sun shone onto the faces of the granite rocks, their bulk creating sharp shadows on the sand at his feet. Once more he looked out to sea. The waves were coming in, swift, insistent, loud. It felt as if they were inside his head.

Was it too late? He was only in his mid-forties, for God's sake, he still kept himself fit enough. She – Joanna Shepherd – had written about a certain moment, a pause in time, and he had responded to that. God knows why. But sometimes rather than question, it was better to accept, to do, to grasp the moment.

He gazed over towards the lighthouse at Godrevy. What had she made of his message? He had no idea why he'd emailed her, only obeyed the strong compulsion to do so. He supposed, though, it was what she'd made him see. Would she write back? He rather hoped so.

Nicholas pulled on his shoes and sprinted back along the sand. He took the steps two at a time. His surfboard would still be at the cottage somewhere – he'd never been able to throw it away. And he still had his winter wetsuit stored in the garage – if it hadn't rotted by now. More to the point, he was going to Fuerteventura and there would be waves.

He had waited so long. And for what? But it was a part of him that he could get back. And if he could get that back, then how much else of the old Nicholas could he get back? At any rate, he was determined to try.

CHAPTER 24

Joanna

Dorset

Harriet dropped her off at Bucky Doo Square and Joanna made her way to Bridport's Local History Centre. She was determined to find out more about Emmy – perhaps if she could discover the family connection between them, then she might understand why Emmy and her letters were getting under her skin.

She had already linked into a couple of promising ancestry sites online, but it was a daunting task and time was against her. It might be a good subject for a feature, though; if she were to continue to delve, by the time she reached the Middle Ages she'd have twenty million relatives, apparently. That would be a lot more than Joanna was bargaining for . . .

Mulberry Farm Cottage had been in Father's family for generations, so clearly, it was the Shepherd line she had to pursue. She'd learnt that the origin of British surnames could be divided into four groups: by trade, by nickname, by place name or by patronymic or matronymic deciders. Emmy clearly fell into the first group. Shepherd. So even back then, her ancestors were into farming. Not Joanna, though – she'd never seen herself living and working in a rural landscape. And not Emmy – like Joanna, she enjoyed travelling; like Joanna, she was drawn to more creative pursuits.

All her mother seemed to know about Joanna's father's parents was that they were called George and Dorothea and were 'very Victorian' in their thinking. It wasn't much, but it was a start, at least. So, Joanna had decided to begin her search by looking for her paternal grandparents' marriage certificate.

She pushed open the door. The History Centre was a treasure trove of local information and history, which included the General Register Office indices for local births and marriages from 1890 to 1945 on microfiche.

She introduced herself to the girl behind the desk and explained what she was looking for.

'Yes, of course. What period are you after?' she asked.

Joanna decided to go back two years from the date of her father's birth. He was the elder of the two sons, so it was logical he might have been born within two years of his parents' marriage. And she'd start with the first quarter. Marriage certificates were invaluable in genealogy, she could see that, since they usually provided both maiden names and fathers' names. Joanna thanked the girl, made herself comfortable and settled down to the task at hand.

It was oddly absorbing. She was hardly aware of time passing by as she trawled through the records looking for her grandfather's name. 'George Shepherd,' she murmured, 'where are you?'

At last she found it. Her eyes were blurred with the effort, her throat dry. But she felt a buzz of achievement. Here was the certificate and here he was. Her grandfather George's father was William Shepherd. Unbelievably, she felt herself choking up. She groped for a tissue from her bag. It was incredible, the sense of history, the sense of connection that she felt, just looking at these family names written so beautifully in ink on old certificates. Joanna could see already how researching your family tree could so easily become addictive. She made notes, quickly, in longhand.

After a few moments, she looked again at what she'd written and leant back in her chair with a sigh. This was a good find. But the important thing for Joanna was, did William have any sisters? Because they would be of the generation she was looking for. Emmy had been a girl in 1912, old enough to be married – or, at least, in love. She had written those letters with such passion, such longing. Joanna thought of the Venetian bridge painting on the wall in her bedroom at the cottage.

Could Emmy be William's sister? It seemed likely. She glanced at her watch. She'd have to go back further to find out, and that would have to wait for another day if she was going to get a lift back with Harriet. She began to pack up her things. She was sure she'd be able to unearth Emmy eventually. And what else would the family tree reveal? Skeletons in the cupboard? Old mysteries to solve? She recalled that odd and secretive look passed between Father and her uncle on that summertime visit long ago. Joanna couldn't wait to find out more.

She just had time to get a quick coffee before she met Harriet in the long-stay car park. Joanna upped her pace. She missed her car. It was hard to be independent in West Dorset without transport. The car she'd shared with Martin, strictly speaking, belonged to him. If she was planning on staying around here, she'd have to think about buying a little runaround of her own. But was she planning to stay around here? After Lisbon, she thought, she'd decide then.

Bridport had changed a lot from the home of her childhood, she found herself thinking as she walked down the road. It had always been a real and working rope-making and market town but although it had kept some of its true character and the street market was livelier than ever, the town now also paid homage to a version of café society. Some of the independent shops had sadly fallen by the wayside. Frosts, for example (which had sold everything from newspapers to cutlery, toys to china figurines), had now become some sort of dismal factory outlet. But others were new and thriving — notably a waste not want not shop that encouraged shoppers to bring in their own containers to cut down single-use plastic, small galleries and interesting craft shops, plus the organic veg shops that bought Harriet's produce from time to time. And despite being under threat, the vintage area continued to flourish.

Joanna escaped into the dim interior of a nearby café, bought a coffee, pulled out her laptop, logged into the café's wi-fi and read the email from Nicholas Tresillion once more. He sounded sincere enough and she hadn't had any other responses to her bridge walk — at least not yet. She'd half expected Toby to tell her it was too oddball; that this wasn't what they wanted at all. But he'd seemed happy enough. It was a bit different, she supposed, and that had been the brief. As for Nicholas Tresillion, she'd write back to him, she decided. He'd taken the trouble to get in contact and he'd had an interesting experience triggered by her own. She was intrigued. She wanted to know more.

She clicked on 'reply'.

Dear Nicholas Tresillion, she wrote. *Did you really see a golden ribbon?*

Which sounded a little peculiar, but . . .

Looking into moving water, seeing reflections, images – that's nothing new, of course. But it's funny, because I saw that golden ribbon too. Did we see the same girl? It doesn't seem likely, but . . .

Joanna didn't expect him to answer that question. It was a coincidence, she supposed. She continued typing.

The odd thing for me was that as I was walking, planning the route, finding out about all those bridges, it seemed more and more to be about me and the direction I was taking in my life.

Joanna frowned. She hadn't meant to write that, it was a bit personal . . . Nevertheless, she continued.

Some people say you have to become lost in a city in order to get to know your way around. So maybe it's like that for people too? We have to lose ourselves a bit in order to discover our true – or new – direction.

She was rambling. She knew she was rambling. Why was she saying all this – and to a total stranger? Because it was easier to talk to a stranger? Because he already thought – no doubt – that she was a bit crazy? Because maybe he was a bit crazy too?

She imagined him reading the email, perhaps while he was having breakfast with his wife and five children, laughing, saying, *Oh my God, the woman has verbal diarrhoea. Never write to a writer. It's the kiss of death.*

Perhaps she wouldn't send it at all. She looked again at the message he'd sent her. *I saw the golden ribbon.* Saved it on draft. She'd send it later tonight – maybe.

Toby had also emailed about the Lisbon brochure to confirm a date for completion of the copy, so she pinged a reply back to him. Thankfully there was nothing new from Martin. Had he done what he'd promised and put the house on the market? Somehow, she doubted it. There was still a big part of her that wished things could have been different for the two of them, that wished it had worked out. They had, as Martin had said, been together so long. But . . . already, she knew that she had taken the first steps, that she was moving away and in a different direction too.

She quickly finished her coffee, shut down her laptop, left the café and made her way to the car park. As she passed the Boat and Barnacle, she glanced in. *Oh, my goodness*. For a moment, she was rooted to the spot. Harriet was sitting at a table near the window, but it was the man she was talking to who held Joanna's attention. He looked very unusual, to say the least.

She saw Harriet glance at her watch and speak to him. They both got to their feet.

Joanna hurried away before they spotted her. The last thing she wanted to do was annoy her sister all over again. She was bad-tempered enough already, what with Terry's Tarmac and their heart-to-heart yesterday – not to mention the fact that they'd seen her prowler in the lane and that Harriet had nearly sent him into the ditch. So, what now? Why, she wondered, was Harriet having coffee with a cowboy?

CHAPTER 25

Harriet

Dorset

'Did you find what you were looking for?' Harriet asked her sister on the way home. She was a bit distracted, still trying to take in the sight that had met her when she entered the Boat and Barnacle earlier this morning. She hadn't been able to miss him. He was very tall. And very, well, different.

Joanna smiled. 'I've made a start,' she said. She gave Harriet a little nudge. 'Did you?'

The first thing she'd noticed was his cowboy hat. Harriet wasn't sure that he looked like the kind of man who could sweep her off her feet and take her away from All This. But then again . . .

He'd also sported a whiskery beard. Bridport was the sort of town where people could be as individual as they wanted to be; its unspoken dress code was casual, unconventional and 'anything goes'. But even here, Jolyon was drawing more than his share of attention.

'Harriet?' he had said.

'Er, Jolyon?'

'Sure thing.' And he'd pulled on the laces of his Stetson. 'Can I call you Hattie?' he'd asked.

Harriet took in the fringed suede jacket – with rhinestones – the red necktie, the buckled belt. She let her gaze run swiftly down past the gun holster – *gun holster?* – to the Cuban-heeled, chiselled-toed cowboy boots. *Oh, Lordy . . .* Did he always dress this way? Or was he heading for a lunchtime fancy dress party? She feared not. 'No,' she'd said. 'I'm afraid you can't.'

'What?' Harriet glanced sharply at Joanna who was still smiling as if at some private joke.

'Oh, nothing,' her sister said.

Once again, the pick-up was practically bouncing along the rutted lane as they approached Warren Down. 'There's Owen.' Harriet braked sharply. He was on the Down, mending one of his fences. He was wearing his usual green boiler suit and a khaki fleece, and looked very ordinary, which came as something of a relief after Jolyon.

Joanna winced and clutched at the dashboard – something she seemed to be doing a lot lately.

'Mind if I stop for a minute and talk to him?'

''Course not.'

Harriet left the pick-up on the side of the lane, by the stream that led down to Warren Cove, swapped her shoes for a pair of green wellies from the back, and made her way across the rather muddy field. The gentle hills of the Down were green from last night's rain and there were glorious views from here along to the Beacon and Golden Cap and right down to the sea. The sheep bleated and scuttled off as Harriet passed by.

Owen seemed preoccupied, however, and didn't look up

until she was only yards away. He jumped, but recovered quickly. 'Harriet! I didn't . . . Well, good morning to you.'

Morning? Could it still only be morning? Harriet looked up at the pale autumnal sky. She checked her watch. It was precisely midday and she could already do with a strong gin and tonic.

'Hello, Owen.' She looked down at his hands as he held the wood steady. Big and square, like the rest of him. 'Sorry to disturb you. But I was wondering . . .'

'Yep?' He rested against the fence, watching her. What was he thinking? She could never really tell. He seemed a simple man, but still waters could be murky. Look at Jolyon . . . He was probably straightforward and normal under that strange attire. She let out a small shudder. But did she want to find out?

'It's about Mother,' Harriet said to Owen. How could she word this exactly? She didn't want to confide in their neighbour – pride, she supposed, and a need to protect her mother from gossip and other people's scrutiny. But neither did she want to sound like a control freak intent on monitoring her mother's every move. It wasn't easy. Especially when she was intent on monitoring her mother's every move.

Owen looked over towards the pick-up truck. His expression changed when he saw Joanna in the passenger seat. He grinned and waved.

Joanna waved back. Harriet sighed.

'So, is there a problem?' Owen asked her.

'No,' she snapped. What was he suggesting? It was simply that she got fed up with every man in the vicinity ogling her sister.

Owen looked confused. 'A problem with your mother?' he clarified.

'Ah, yes. Well . . .' It was tempting, though, to confide in

Owen. He wasn't a gossip and she was pretty sure she could trust him.

But . . . Harriet was too accustomed to keeping her problems to herself. 'Well, no,' she said. 'Only . . . Well, yes.'

Owen didn't seem fazed by her indecision. 'How can I help then, Harriet?'

Best get to the point, Harriet decided. He was making her feel slightly uncomfortable, and they should be getting back for Mother. 'I was wondering, did you post a letter for my mother?' she asked him. It sounded so domestic, so trivial.

'Well, now . . .' Owen scratched his chin.

'To Terry's Tarmac?' Harriet spoke through gritted teeth. She could barely bring herself to utter the words.

'Terry's Tarmac.' He frowned. 'Yes, I do believe I did.'

'OK.' So, what now? Harriet sighed. 'I know this might sound a bit mad to you.'

'Try me.'

She took a deep breath. It had to be done. 'But please could you not post any letters for her in the future?' He was looking at her oddly and she supposed it was a bit of a strange request. 'Or at least run it past me first?'

'Why's that?' he asked.

It was a fair question. 'Mother's not . . .' – she hesitated – 'quite herself at the minute.' Would he trust her on this? Or would he tell Mother what Harriet had asked of him? The two of them were, after all, quite pally.

There was a pause. Then, 'Ah. Right you are.' He touched his nose. 'Mum's the word.'

'Exactly.' She chuckled. The sound quite surprised her.

It obviously surprised Owen too from the look he gave her. And then he grinned as he got the joke.

'Thanks, Owen. I appreciate that.' It wasn't easy to do any of this, that's what no one seemed to understand. But there was something in Owen's manner, almost as if he did understand.

Harriet nodded goodbye and returned to the pick-up. Joanna was looking at her rather strangely too. 'What?' snapped Harriet.

'Nothing.' Joanna held up both hands. And smiled that mysterious smile again.

Harriet shook her head in despair. Sometimes it felt as if the whole world was against her.

Jolyon had asked if he could see her again.

Harriet wasn't sure. 'I don't want to rush into anything,' she'd told him — just so he was clear.

He didn't seem to mind. 'We could meet for an occasional drink,' he suggested. 'A meal out every once in a while. Just as friends?'

Friendship sounded a lot safer to Harriet. And wouldn't it be pleasant to go out for the evening from time to time with no strings attached?

'Perhaps we could, yes.' Harriet was still cautious.

'Shall we give it a go then, ma'am?' he enquired.

Oh, my giddy aunt . . . Harriet tried not to be blinded by his rhinestones. Nobody was perfect. 'All right,' she said. 'You're on.'

CHAPTER 26

Nicholas

El Cotillo

Five days later, Nicholas was in El Cotillo. He looked out of the tiny window of the blue house. The sky was also blue, with that clarity he remembered so well. He decided to walk to the lighthouse.

Memories were deceptive, of course. People remembered what they wanted to, mixed that in with what they'd been told by others, and added a touch of fantasy. Hmm. Fantasy made him think once more of Venice . . . Joanna Shepherd hadn't emailed him back yet. He found himself wondering about her life. Was she married? Where did she live? What was it like to be a travel writer?

Last night, it had been dark when he arrived in the hire car from the airport but he could see there were more buildings in Cotillo – things had changed. But this quirky blue and white stone house still looked the same. He and Rachel first spotted it when walking along the beach with Celie, who was just a toddler then; they'd admired the exotic plants in the walled garden, the slanting blue roofs, the clear bubble of a dome on the top. Like a coffee percolator, Rachel had said. *What would it be like to live there?* Well, now he knew. It was too big for one. Already, he was wandering around in it like a lost soul.

Nicholas left the house and stepped straight into the deep, pale sand of the beach. The sea was royal blue, curling into fronds of white waves, thinning into turquoise where it lay, shallow and inviting, between stacks of volcanic black rocks. The wide expanse of sand was broken up by *corralitos* – smaller, uneven piles of molten lava arranged in a horseshoe, or a seahouse, as Celie called them, where a family (his family) could settle for a day on the beach and be protected from the wind. You could never tell – until you were on top of them – whether the *corralitos* were occupied. Once, he had accidentally come across a couple making love and he'd stumbled away before they saw him, thought about a day in the future when he and Rachel might come here without Celie and simply lie contentedly in each other's arms among the rocks and dunes.

It would never have happened, though.

The sun warmed his skin as he trudged over the fine sand and down to the shore. The sand was compacted here but it still sank under his feet, as if it would pull him in if it could. The silky water of the lagoon shone clear as a diamond. He looked out over the beach which stretched into the distance like a lunar landscape. There were more people – clearly, Cotillo had become something of a tourist destination in the last seventeen years. It wasn't crowded; the beach was too vast for that. But in the distance he could see the new buildings that had sprung up – an ugly brown apartment block with a swimming pool, brash new cafés and bars. El Cotillo was no longer a sleepy fishing village content with itself. Had it lost sight of its true identity? Or simply grown into a new one? He supposed it depended on how you accepted change.

After that single surf at Godrevy five days ago, Nicholas had become aware of his identity seeping back. Cautious at first, the joy, the rush had soon claimed him when he rode his first wave. It turned out to be a bit like riding a bike. You didn't forget. And now he was here to do more.

He walked on. Soon there were fewer people and the landscape grew more desolate – dusty earth, black rock, miles of cratered sand and those shallow rocky bays to swim in. He wouldn't swim, though, not yet. First, the lighthouse.

He had walked alone to the lighthouse on their last day in Cotillo seventeen years ago. Rachel was reading and Celie happily paddling in the lagoon. Nicholas had been restless, though. The lighthouse, rising in the distance, a stick of red and white stripes against the clear sky of this bleak landscape, was a visible goal, a marker; somewhere to aim for, touch, walk back from.

Joanna Shepherd had written about needing to find a sense of direction.

Seventeen years ago when they came here, Nicholas had been thinking about changing direction too. The jewellery business run by Rachel's brother-in-law Giuseppe was doing well and Giuseppe needed someone to find new buyers, take the merchandise to cities in Italy and abroad, deal with the finances, invest in the company so that it could grow. Nicholas could be that person, Giuseppe told him. It was very different from what Nicholas had been doing in Rachel's father's company in Surrey and before that as an accountant in Cornwall. It would mean being away from home a lot. And, at first anyway, a drop in pay.

Nicholas sighed. Like most things in their marriage, this decision had been a battle. Rachel favoured the security of her father's firm. There was Celie to think of, she said (as if he didn't). Didn't she deserve the best? Rachel couldn't understand why Nicholas was even considering it, and since Giuseppe had made the offer, furious unforgiving phone conversations had shot like liquid fire between Rome and Surrey. But Nicholas's working life in Rachel's father's firm sent a knot of tension drilling into him every Monday morning – and it didn't unravel until Friday. He hated it.

Now, Nicholas reached the lighthouse and touched the wall for luck. Even this place had been sanitised: a new car park, the house restored and made into a fishing museum, a café built with a glass wall for protection from the wind. Paths had been forged through the rocky outcrops and down to the shallows with information plaques for tourists. Nicholas supposed it was good to be informed. Little piles of stones had been balanced among the volcanic rock and sand; each visitor making their mark. He liked these – they added a personal touch to the landscape.

Perhaps even back then he had realised he was in danger of losing his sense of self. He thought of his recent revelation in Godrevy. And it hadn't only been the surfing he'd missed. Was it when he moved from Cornwall to Surrey (because Rachel wanted it)? Was it when he joined her father's firm (because she wanted that too)? Or was it when he first felt Rachel's love slip away? Which came first? The lost love or the lost bit of Nicholas Tresillion?

Slowly, he began to walk away from the lighthouse. But, amazingly, those cloudless blue skies back then had melted Rachel. As the days passed, she had become softer again, more

201

caring, somehow. They had thrashed out the subject of the job, mixed it in with swimming in the lagoon, walks over the sand, and eating in the restaurant by the Old Harbour. Nicholas smiled as he remembered . . . The sweetness of those prawns cooked in salt, the soothing curl and fizz of the waves on the pebbled beach, some chilled Doors music playing in the background. Ah . . .

El Cotillo had always reminded him of Cornwall and Godrevy had always reminded him of Cotillo. They shared more than just a lighthouse, more than a surfing beach, more than a desolate landscape. It was, he realised, more about the way they made him feel. Godrevy was all about going back to his roots. But this place – this was about the last time things had been good with Rachel. This place was about change.

Pretty soon he had retraced his steps. He stopped for a coffee in the Azurro bar just back from the shore. From his vantage point on the terrace he had a good view of the beach houses: the Gaudi-esque house with a pear-shaped sculpture on the roof, the white stone building that appeared to have been split in two by a giant axe, the lighthouse back in the distance from which he'd come. To the south, Cotillo was backed by volcanic mountains and a low-level cliff that stretched out to sea like the finger of a pier.

Nicholas sipped his coffee. Who could blame him for coming back? It had been a fabulous holiday. And on that last day, Rachel had walked over to where he was standing by the water's edge and wrapped her arms around him.

'OK,' she whispered.

'OK?' Over her shoulder he had checked automatically on Celie. She was playing in the sand – brown, freckled and healthy.

'I know you're desperate to leave Bannisters,' said Rachel. 'I know you think this job with Giuseppe could work out for us – in the end, I mean.'

'I do.' And God, he had meant it. He felt like he was renewing his marriage vows. *I do, I do* . . .

'So, you should give it a try,' she said. 'Otherwise you'll always wonder.'

'Really?'

'Really.' Her eyes were giving nothing away.

And in that moment, as Nicholas held her, as the wavelets lapped over their feet, he had thought, *This is it, this is my perfect forever moment in this place, and* . . .

And the moment would never come again.

He pushed his coffee cup to one side. That was how it was – with moments, with places, with people . . . They moved, they shifted, they changed.

Abruptly, he got to his feet, left some euros on the table, set off for the village. Who was he kidding? He shouldn't have come back here. Nothing stayed the same. And not all surprises – unlike the one in Venice – were pleasant.

His unease grew as he walked down the road past the white houses with flowering cacti in gardens of water-preserving black picon. 'Jesus,' he muttered. The view down the road was so different from the one he remembered – of winding alleyways, squat blue and white Canarian houses with thick electric cables strung between them. Now, there were more soulless apartment buildings and, worse still, a Corinthian-style hotel that made him recoil in horror. Who had whipped the soul from Cotillo?

Was that why he had come back here? Because Rachel was still in his head, and he had to do something about that in order to move on? Nicholas had to face it. He wasn't stuck in time; he was a moving, living being – a man with a future as well as a past. What he needed were new places, new memories. Would the spirit of El Cotillo survive? Or would it be buried under the weight of a mock Moorish tower block of apartments? He had no idea. But he wasn't about to be buried, he knew that much. His spirit wouldn't be broken.

Nicholas walked past the seat beside the Blue Cow restaurant, once tiled in blue, where the old men used to sit, talk and play cards. Once again, he thought of Venice. He knew it so well and yet on that bridge walk of Joanna Shepherd's, he'd seen things in a different way, just as she'd promised. He had heard her voice in the words he read and somehow felt compelled by it. He leant on the iron railings and looked down over the Old Harbour. A grizzled old fisherman was filleting fish on the beach, the waves were still crashing onto the black volcanic rocks, the blue cow on top of the restaurant was still smiling. Things had changed, yes. But for the first time, Nicholas was glad that he had come back here.

That afternoon, Nicholas returned to the high sandy cliff above the wild surfing beach. He shielded his eyes from the glare of the sun. The volcanic hills sat like huge velvet dinosaurs that had simply folded their limbs and their great creases of skin and sunk down to create the contours of the desert landscape. On the other side, the sea – at once navy, then turquoise, then clear lizard-green – rose in massive rolling waves, before curling, then sparking into spray. It was perfect for the surfers out there, turning and twisting, boogie boarding, tubing the waves.

Nicholas began to unload the car. His body was itching with

anticipation. He undid the straps on the roof rack. The sea was in his blood. That's why he'd never wanted to leave the wild rocky landscape of Cornwall. And he felt it here too – because something vital in the landscape hadn't changed. There was still the sense that it was before man, before time.

He climbed down to the beach, the red surfboard under one arm. On the slope, an installation of mirrors had been planted in formation in the sand. Nicholas wondered what the artist was trying to say about self-image. He moved around the installation, catching glimpses of himself in the mirrors: an arm, a flash of black shorts, a leather sandalled foot, the red surfboard. And in the background – in his background – the sea, the waves, the rocks, the sky. It put him in perspective, he decided. The right perspective.

He moved further down towards the sea, checking out the best break of the waves. He supposed that for some, he had the perfect lifestyle. A cottage in Cornwall – his haven, his roots; a crash pad in London; a life spent travelling around some of the classiest cities in the world. Seeing Celie obviously. And plenty of time to himself. Nicholas spread out his towel. None of that, however, had stopped him feeling lost.

When the waves rose and stretched, they became so thin you could see right through them, like glass; their light underbellies dappled with sand. And as they broke, the spray rose in the wind, streaming in a rainbow behind. Nicholas started to ease his body into his wetsuit, wriggling his arms into the sleeves.

He walked towards the water's edge. The wetsuit and the late afternoon sun were warming his skin. He had changed his mind about the place, he realised, in the short time he'd been back. El Cotillo had altered, but its spirit, miraculously, had stayed the same. He'd just had to search a little deeper to find it. Why should it anyway still be identical to the sleepy fishing village that he remembered? How could it? Why shouldn't it evolve? Didn't everything?

The hazy yellow of the sun spun out over the sea, casting its faintly eerie light over the campo. He half turned. The mountains now had a pinkish glow, the brown earth looked other-worldly and the hair of a blonde woman sitting with her family some twenty metres away had acquired highlights of green.

The sea came to meet him, washing over his feet, pulling him in. It was cool and exhilarating. And now he was ready. He had acknowledged change and he was ready to accept it — for himself too. He stepped forwards with his board, into the waves. There were all sorts of ways, he decided, of moving on.

CHAPTER 27

Harriet

Dorset

Tomorrow, Joanna was leaving for Lisbon, so Harriet and her sister decided that a chat after lunch, just the three of them, was not only required but also long overdue. Mother needed to be told, Harriet would appreciate the moral support, and Joanna was so much more diplomatic than she.

Joanna made tea and they took it into the sitting room where their mother was sitting, staring into space, looking pensive.

'Can we have a word, Ma?' Joanna began. 'We're a bit concerned, about the——'

'Take the tarmac people,' Harriet interjected, before she could stop herself. But resentment had been building, and she hoped there was steel in her eye. 'We know you wrote to them. We just want to know why.'

'Oh.' Their mother looked from one to the other of them in panic.

'It's OK, Ma.' Joanna sat down next to her on the sofa.

'Don't worry.' She held their mother's hand. 'We just want to understand why you would do it, that's all.'

This was 'good cop, bad cop,' Harriet thought. And she always took on the baddie role. 'Although it isn't OK, actually,' she said. The important thing was to be firm; Father would have been firm. She hoped Joanna wasn't thinking about sweeping the whole problem under the carpet. Because Harriet was planning on getting to the bottom of it right now.

Joanna shot her a reproachful look. But, 'Harriet's right,' she said. 'She keeps the books, she's in charge of the finances and, you know, even with your pension, the two of you simply can't afford to have the drive tarmacked.'

Harriet couldn't have put it better herself. 'And even if we could,' she added, to make things clear, 'there are a hundred other things that would take precedence over tarmac.'

Their mother looked up hopefully. 'Such as?'

Harriet didn't trust her an inch. 'Never you mind,' she said.

Joanna got up to pour the tea. 'The thing is, Mother,' she said, 'Harriet doesn't want to tell you what things she's talking about, just in case you call someone round for an estimate.'

This, Harriet thought, was undeniably true.

'She doesn't trust me. Neither of you trust me.' Their mother looked so sad that Harriet had to turn away. She hated to hurt her. And she had promised her father to look after her. Was this the kind of looking after he'd meant her to do? Hardly. She waited for Joanna to deny it.

'You're right, we don't trust you,' her sister agreed.

Harriet blinked at her.

'But we want to,' Joanna added. 'You're our mother. We love and respect you. We want to be able to talk about anything

208

with you, we want to include you in all the household decisions, we want—'

'He noticed things,' their mother announced. 'He knew what had happened. You can think what you like. But he made me feel . . . wanted, appreciated.'

Harriet and Joanna exchanged a look. Harriet didn't know what had happened but she knew Mother wasn't talking about any tradesman.

'He's gone.' Harriet knew her voice was stark. She sniffed. 'And I'm sorry, but you have to find a way to manage without him, Mother.' They were all grieving. But it had been seven years.

Joanna brought over the tray and put a cup of tea in front of her. 'Harriet's right. Everyone suffers losses, Mother.' She gave her shoulder a quick squeeze.

Their mother shot Joanna a dark look. 'I know that. But I've had more than my fair share.'

'Yes.' Joanna's voice was unusually brisk. 'But we lost our father too.'

'I'm not . . .' Mother's voice tailed off. 'Never mind. It doesn't matter.'

'It does matter.' Joanna nodded. 'We understand that. But it's not fair to make it so difficult for Harriet. None of it's her fault and she has so much to worry about as it is.'

Harriet stared at her sister. She'd had no idea that Joanna understood her position so well.

'I know, I know.' Their mother looked contrite. 'And I don't want to be a nuisance, I really don't. It's just that . . . they make me feel . . .' Once again, she seemed unable to go on.

Tradesman therapy, thought Harriet. But her mother looked so vulnerable, so fragile.

Joanna passed their mother the tea.

Mother hung her head, almost as if she were ashamed – which made Harriet feel worse still. She took the cup. 'Thank you, my dear.'

'So, we were wondering . . .' Joanna glanced at Harriet.

She nodded. Let her sister carry on, she was very good at this sort of thing, she should have been a politician.

'Yes, darling?'

'Is it that you're lonely?' Joanna's voice was gentle. Harriet wished she could be like that with Mother. She only seemed capable of being gentle with the hens.

'We only want to help. Is it that you'd like to get out more? See other people? Make new friends?'

Mother shook her head. Was she even listening to Joanna? There was an air of distraction about her, almost as if she was somewhere else entirely. Back in the past perhaps? *Sorry, Father*, Harriet muttered to herself. Would he understand that she was doing her best?

'Is it that you're worried about the state of the cottage?' Joanna persevered. 'All the things that need doing? Harriet's done what she can to keep things going, you know. She can't do much more.'

Once again, Harriet gazed at her sister in surprise. She had been listening. She really understood.

Their mother let out a deep sigh. 'You're right, of course.'

Harriet lost patience. 'Then why do you do it, Mother?' she demanded. 'Why do you keep calling out tradesmen we can't afford? Is it because they're men? Young men?'

'Harriet!'

Harriet didn't need to look at the shocked expression on her sister's face to know she'd gone too far. 'Sorry,' she mumbled.

A tear trailed down their mother's lined cheek, then another. 'I'm sorry too, darling,' she whispered.

'Oh, Mother.' Joanna had already taken her in her arms. She was holding her and stroking her hair, just like she had stroked Harriet's hair when she first came back here from London. 'It's all right,' she was saying. 'Don't worry, Ma.' She looked over at Harriet, her dark eyes sad. She shook her head. *Enough for today*, she seemed to be telling her. And she was right, of course.

Harriet waited a few moments for their mother to come over to her for comfort. But she didn't. Harriet had been too harsh – again. She had thought something and then made the unforgiveable mistake of allowing it to come out of her mouth. When would she learn? She'd made their mother cry and that was unforgiveable. And anyway, why would Mother need Harriet when she had Joanna to comfort her?

Harriet turned and walked away. *Sorry, Father*. There was no getting away from it. She had failed him – again.

Later, Joanna was helping her change the bed linen in Mother's room.

'That didn't go too well, did it?' Harriet hissed. Mother was still in the sitting room but she didn't want her to overhear their conversation.

Joanna whisked off the pillowcase and threw it onto the floor. 'But at least we tried to get through to her.'

'Hmm.'

'I'm certain we made her more aware.'

Maybe she was right. Harriet hoped so.

Joanna took hold of the other end of the sheet and shoved it under the mattress. 'I can't believe you still use sheets and blankets.' She pulled a face. 'Duvets are so much easier. When are you and Mother going to enter the modern world?'

Harriet frowned. 'When we win the lottery,' she snapped.

Joanna's fingertips lingered on their mother's pale pink eiderdown. 'Sorry, it's not great timing – me going away again to Lisbon.'

'It's fine.' Joanna was only going for a few days. And after that . . . ? 'And then?' she asked. 'Will you go back to London?'

'I don't know yet.' She glanced at Harriet. 'I expect you want me out of your hair. I'll find something soon, I promise. Maybe somewhere not quite as far away as London.'

Harriet didn't know whether to be glad or sorry. Joanna did help her out with Mother, she had to admit, and this had given Harriet more free time. The rent and food money was also useful. And . . . well, she'd quite liked having some sisterly companionship – it had made her feel less alone. But Harriet had always known her sister wouldn't be staying here forever. 'No hurry,' she said.

She pulled the eiderdown so that it was taut and neat. Being with Joanna made Harriet miss something – something from her childhood maybe, something she couldn't name or quite catch hold of. Something she didn't want to be reminded of, but which drew her too. She thought back to their old game of hide-and-seek. Joanna could never find her – not once did she come close. Because Harriet had discovered the perfect hiding place and she would never tell. It didn't matter how upset her younger sister got, how much she cried or pleaded to be told. It was Harriet's secret. Her triumph. And Joanna? She was like the innocent part of her childhood – the unknowing, sunshine part. Harriet loved that – and resented it too. Still, she'd miss her when she finally left.

Joanna glanced across at Harriet. 'In that case, I'll stay for a bit longer – if you're sure you don't mind, Het?'

Harriet swallowed. 'I told you, it's fine. It's your home as much as mine.'

'Hardly.' Joanna laughed.

Harriet pounded one of Mother's pillows a little more violently than necessary.

'And while I'm away, you have to promise me to take care.'

'Of Mother?'

'Of yourself.' Joanna pulled a clean pillowcase onto the other pillow. 'And I still think you should inform the police about that prowler of yours.'

'Hmm.' When had he become *her* prowler? she wondered. She arranged the pillows neatly on the bed.

'And what will you be doing while I'm away?' Joanna was smiling that mysterious smile again.

'The chores?' Harriet narrowed her eyes. What was her sister up to?

'Life's too short not to have fun.'

Together they pulled over the vile pink nylon bedspread that their mother adored.

'Fun?' Harriet's antennae were really twitching now.

'All work and no play makes Harriet a dull girl.' Joanna launched herself onto the freshly made bed.

'Jo! What are you—?'

Her sister laughed and Harriet couldn't help grinning back at her. She looked like a kid again. 'So, who is he?'

'What?' To give herself time to think, Harriet began gathering up the dirty sheets.

'Who is he? The guy in the coffee shop?'

'Hmm?'

'You know, the guy in the cowboy outfit.'

Harriet groaned. She'd been spotted. Bugger and hellfire. 'So, you noticed what he was wearing?' she asked Joanna. Pointlessly. How could anyone not?

'Did I notice?' Joanna positively chortled. 'What a look . . .'

'I know.' Harriet began to stagger downstairs with the pile of laundry. 'Shh,' she warned.

Joanna followed her into the kitchen and shut the door. 'And as for that hat . . .'

'I know, Joanna.' How could she make her shut up?

'So, spill, sister. Was he a date?'

'He's just a friend,' Harriet told her firmly.

'But where did you meet him?' There she was, grinning again. Harriet was glad she was providing her with such entertainment.

'I sort of came across him.' Which didn't sound remotely convincing, but Harriet didn't care. Joanna would laugh like a drain if she told her about Someone Somewhere.

'Oh, yes? Unusual get-up.' Joanna leant on the counter. 'I suppose some women might find it sexy.'

Sexy? Harriet hoped that Mother couldn't hear what they were saying. It was bad enough that Joanna had seen her. But now that she had . . . Well, Harriet had to admit it was quite nice to talk to someone about it, to get a second opinion.

She began to load the washing into the machine. 'Sexy?' The thought hadn't occurred to her.

'I only saw his profile,' Joanna admitted. 'But it shows he's interesting, doesn't it?'

'Does it?' Harriet was less sure. It showed he was weird. She wondered what would happen if she carried on seeing him. Would she have to start wearing cowgirl boots with detachable

214

fringes? White calico blouses? Starched petticoats? She gave a little shudder.

'What's his name?' her sister asked.

Harriet scooped in the powder. 'Jolyon.'

Joanna made a noise that sounded suspiciously like stifled laughter.

Harriet glared at her. 'And he is a bit . . .' – she hesitated – 'extreme.'

'In the way he dresses?'

'In his obsession.'

'Oh yeah? With what?'

'Anything country and western, I think. Clothes, music, dancing, the lot.' She set the dial to sixty degrees.

Joanna laughed. 'Oh, God, he hasn't taken you hillbilly boogieing?'

Harriet shot her a look. 'He's asked me to go line dancing,' she said. 'Next week.'

'Wow.' Joanna moved over to the sink to fill the kettle. But her shoulders were still twitching suspiciously. 'Why all the secrecy, though, Het?'

'Oh . . .' Harriet got out the chopping board and inspected the contents of the fridge in readiness for supper. 'I didn't want Mother to start asking questions.' Joanna would understand that, surely? 'I haven't even decided whether or not to go.'

She hoped her sister hadn't seen them holding hands. Well, not holding hands exactly. 'Wichita Lineman' had started playing in the coffee shop and Jolyon had come over a bit emotional. He had taken Harriet's hands, squeezed them hard, said, 'Harriet, I'm so happy to finally meet a woman like you. And I just want to say . . .'

215

Heavens, she thought. He was about to make a declaration. Already.

'Thank you, ma'am. For restoring my faith in the female sex.'

'You're very welcome, Jolyon.' Gently, she'd disengaged herself. Goodness. It was all a bit Miss Ellie and who shot JR.

'I'm glad, Harriet.' Joanna squeezed her arm. 'Who knows where friendship can lead? I'm really pleased for you.'

'Thanks.' Harriet could feel her sister's warmth. And she was quite moved by it. But she wasn't sure she wanted this friendship to lead anywhere. Was she ready to go galloping off into the sunset to La Ponderosa? She didn't think so. Was she so very desperado? She hoped not. Did she want to listen to someone humming 'Rawhide' night and day (it was one of those tunes that got into your head)? Definitely, no, no, no.

Harriet was not at all sure that she wanted to start dating a cowboy.

CHAPTER 28

Joanna

Lisbon

Joanna let her gaze drift over the landscape of northern Lisbon. The air was still warm for the end of October, and the city still had a pinkish, autumnal glow. The ancient grey stone aqueduct – Aqueduto das Aguas Livres – dominated the scene. How could she ever have missed it on the map?

She had taken her first photos of the huge grey arches that appeared to lope over the northern hills on the train from Campolide, and now she was taking some more pictures of the aqueduct and the burnt-orange Portuguese rooftops as she stood by a palm tree in the Rua d'Arcos. The two modern suspension bridges of Vasco de Gama and Ponte 25 de Abril (neither of which were visible from this vantage point) had been built to connect Lisbon with the other side of the River Tagus, and several lanes of traffic flew across them twenty-four hours a day.

Joanna looked into the distance. Whereas the aqueduct, built in 1748, and paid for by the people through a tax on olive oil, meat and wine, was a very different creature indeed. 'Lisbon's "Free Waters",' she said into her Dictaphone, 'named after the water-spring, in Sintra, where it began.'

She checked her notes. The aqueduct ran from the north of the city, through thirty-five arches across the Alcântara valley to the Mãe d'Água reservoir in western Lisbon. Which was exactly where she was heading. Following the ancient waterway on her second bridge walk. Had Emmy done the same thing? *Dearest Rufus, my heart's love, can you taste my lover's tears?* She had written those poignant words in Lisbon. But why tears? Emmy was clearly an emotional woman, but she would soon be going home to him, wouldn't she?

Joanna rested for a moment, leaning against the weathered stone arch. Was it simply that Emmy was finding their parting very hard? Was she very young perhaps? Not sure of his love? Or was there some problem, some added complication that Joanna hadn't yet discovered? She took the Lisbon letter out of her bag and skimmed it again, familiar now with the elegant, looped handwriting of her ancestor. It was mostly in the same vein about love and parting, but: *There will be a way through the mire, the right way, my dearest. We must trust in that*, she read.

Hmm. The 'mire' certainly sounded problematic. Joanna hoped that Emmy and Rufus had found a way through it; their love sounded too special to lose. Joanna felt confident that she too was finding a way through her particular problems, but in her case there was no Rufus around to hold her hand.

She thought of Mulberry Farm Cottage, Mother and Harriet. Could she sense a breakthrough? She ran her fingers across the rough grey stone. Harriet hadn't sounded exactly enamoured of the country and western bloke in the coffee

218

shop, but at least her sister was trying to get a life outside the cottage and Mother – which had to be a good thing. And surely Joanna wasn't imagining the fact that Harriet was being a bit less defensive than usual – she'd opened up to her about Jolyon, after all? Harriet was right, their chat with Mother hadn't worked out quite as they'd hoped, but Joanna had meant what she said – she was convinced they'd got through to her at last.

She consulted her notes and spoke into the machine again. 'The aqueduct has a hundred and nine arches across the valley, the tallest being sixty-six metres high.' And the arches were built to last; the 1755 earthquake that had destroyed so much of the surrounding area had not brought down the stone edifice of the aqueduct. Joanna envied that kind of solidity.

She wanted to include enough information to whet her readers' appetites, but not enough to sound like a guidebook – that's not what her walks were about. Her thoughts returned to her new correspondent, Nicholas Tresillion. He had seemed to get it. She had finally sent the email to him yesterday. And was already quite looking forward to his reply. She slung her rucksack over her shoulder and headed off for the Rua das Amoreiras. She wanted to make these walks more about dis-covery – a subject dear to her heart right now.

Portugal's golden age of discovery was in the late fourteenth and fifteenth century. What was that old rhyme? *In 1492 Columbus sailed the ocean blue* . . . She chuckled. Vasco de Gama had a bridge named after him and wasn't there also someone called Henry the Navigator? Emmy had mentioned the Portu-guese Age of Discovery in her letter – it was one of the reasons her father was so interested in the city. All in all, the city of Lisbon certainly had plenty for the traveller to discover.

Joanna scanned the landscape around her as she walked on.

The red clay roofs and elegant creamy pale terracotta buildings combined with a riotous array of patterned *azulejo* tiles to create the delicious colours of Lisbon. And she loved the hilly and winding cobblestone streets of the Bairro Alto, the old heart of the city, where her hotel was situated and which was crammed with tiny and charming bars, shops and cafés. She had only been here for a day, and yet already she felt thoroughly immersed in the city and confident about this walk to come.

She stopped every minute or two, took photos, made more notes. She wasn't surprised that Emmy had painted this bridge because it truly belonged to another time. But where was the painting? If her ancestor had painted all these bridges, if she was in fact an artist – maybe even a successful one – then where were all the rest of her paintings? Joanna thought of the letters. And most especially, where were the paintings of the aqueduct in Lisbon and the bridge in Prague? Had Emmy sold them?

On this walk, Joanna was instinctively focusing on the old and the new. The ancient decorative tiles, for example, providing original and stunning fascias for garden walls, houses and apartment buildings epitomised the old, while the modern glass-fronted shops and office blocks encapsulated the new. There were so many other compelling contrasts too. The young Portuguese girl in skinny jeans sashaying down the cobbled street past a wizened leather-skinned old woman dressed in black from head to toe. The traditional funiculars that transported walkers up the steep hills to the lookout points, *miradouros*, over the city, while underground, the super-fast Metro provided the transport of the twenty-first century. And not forgetting the new bridges, carrying traffic and people rather than the precious water and nourishment that the old aqueduct had originally brought to the city.

She walked on past houses with faded and peeling paintwork, where vines and climbing bougainvillea had insinuated themselves around wrought-iron gates and latticed balconies. Like Venice, this part of Lisbon wore an air of decay; there was a sense of age resting in the old stone. And yet you could turn a corner and be faced with a massive shopping mall, twin towers like giant liquorice allsorts, people thronging across a busy road. The modern world.

Joanna crossed the road, and turned into Rua das Amoreiras, the road of mulberry trees that had caught her attention when she'd been studying the map, back in Dorset, searching for Emmy's bridge. And to think she had almost given up on her . . . The road was wide, lined with tall buildings painted pink, cream and blue. And as she went further, there in the middle of it, dividing the road into two, was the massive end archway of the aqueduct, *Arco das Amoreiras*, a baroque monument, like a Roman triumphal arch, constructed from ancient grey stone. *Wow*. It was quite something. She stopped and stared; imagined another time – a procession perhaps, an entering of the city.

So much had changed for both men and women when it came to making decisions about life, about love. Some things, though, would always be the same. Emmy's emotions in her letter felt as real to Joanna as if she were experiencing them herself in the here and now. Some things, like love, hadn't changed at all. Was that why she felt compelled to follow in Emmy's footsteps? Because she identified so closely with this ancestor of hers? Or because she knew that Emmy was trying to take her somewhere, show her something that she needed to know?

Somewhere along here, she knew, was the Praça das

Amoreiras, a place of calm and reflection, once housing a silk factory but now an ideal point in the walk's itinerary, she guessed, in which to take a break and have a coffee. She found it easily, and wasn't disappointed. In the centre of the mosaic-cobbled square was a fountain; mulberry trees lined the *praça* and there was a tiny chapel nestled within one of the arches of the aqueduct that framed the square. The square was decorated with *azulejo* tiles and crumbling stone pillars. She sat on one of the stone benches in the sun and looked around. Mulberry trees would always remind her of Dorset and of home.

The sun was skating off the bare branches of the mulberry trees and Joanna had to shield her eyes as she looked up. For a moment she was blinded by the sunlight. She saw two children up in the branches playing. Herself and Harriet. Clear as day. Heard their laughter, their excited voices, their shrieks. It was late summertime. And then it was just Harriet up there shaking the branches so that the fruit fell to the ground like bullets of blood, staining the earth and the grass beneath.

Joanna was on some sort of collision course, she could feel it. Berry stains on their hands, juice streaked across their clothes, their faces. She hardly dared breathe; she couldn't bear for the picture to dissolve. Because these memories were all too few. More often it was Harriet and Father she remembered. Joanna took a swig from her water bottle. Gathering fruit together, in the tractor side by side, closeted in his study with the books. Harriet tiptoeing up the stairs late at night, when Joanna was supposed to be asleep . . .

Which was why . . . Joanna blinked up at the mulberry tree. Damn. The children were gone. Which was why, when he died, she had felt excluded from that small circle of grief. Mother and Harriet. Who could grieve the most? Not Joanna, she was in

London, she didn't even live at home anymore. Nevertheless, he was her father too and she had loved him. As a girl, she had longed to be the one in the tractor, the one by his side carrying the basket to the orchard while he carried the stepladder, the one listening to all his boyhood stories. Only she never was.

And so, Joanna had done other things with her life. She had left the farm and gone to university, made different friends, gone to other places. She had met Martin and she had married him. They had moved to London. Her family didn't want her, so she left them behind. Was that really how it had been?

The mulberry tree was blurring now and Joanna realised that her face was streaked with tears. She brushed them away with the back of her hand. It was ironic, she thought, that back then, she hadn't cried over the death of her father and yet now, she could cry so easily; for others, for herself, for the fact that she had lost him without properly knowing him, without getting close. In the flick of a switch, at thirty-five, she had become an emotional whirlwind.

There were two lovers standing beside the tree now. She was clasped in his embrace and her eyes were closed, her lips slightly parted. She had fair hair and delicate features. She wore a gold chain around her white throat. Joanna had seen her before – running towards her destiny in Venice, running towards her love. Already, she seemed familiar. And the man? His head was bowed, his features blurred, but his hair was red and unruly. Rufus . . . Joanna strained to see him, but the vision had gone, the lovers faded into the branches, twigs and bark of the mulberry tree.

She pulled her notebook out of her bag and began to write; fast, furious. It was Emmy, she knew it. What was she trying to show her? She thought she knew. Emmy was pulling Joanna into her life, into the past, to tell her something about love.

CHAPTER 29

Harriet

Dorset

The dream crept up on Harriet unawares. One moment she was sleeping peacefully, then . . . as always, the voices came.

You should have told me.

You deceived me.

It was such a long time ago.

A gasp. A low-pitched wail.

'Daddy!'

Harriet sat bolt upright, shaking, sweating. What did it mean?

Slowly, she came round, reached for the water by her bedside. Would she ever find out? Did she even want to?

Her father's death had hit Harriet hard; like her mother, she had not been the same since. In the early days and weeks, the grief was overwhelming – he seemed to be there still, watching everything she did. As time went by, this grief settled into a small and hollow part of her. It wasn't always there. Occasionally, she would turn the corner of the lane, humming, expecting to see his blue tractor in a distant field. She would listen for his shout to a man he was working with; for the splash of water into the washbasin that signalled he was in from the fields; for the clatter of his boots in the farmyard. She could tell the time of day from the noises he had made, his presence in the cottage had been so strong. She'd get distracted by one of the hens, the way the sunlight caught her feathers and turned them into gold, or by a particularly red and juicy apple, or a line in a book she was reading under the mulberry tree. She'd smile. And then she'd remember. Father had died from a sudden heart attack and nothing would ever be the same again.

'Have you got anything planned for today, Mother?' Harriet asked at breakfast. She hadn't been quite herself since they'd had that heart-to-heart with Joanna. There hadn't been any more tradesman incidents, but Harriet didn't like this pale, shadowy version of her mother; it worried her.

'I might collect some more apples from the orchard,' she replied. 'Perhaps make a pie?'

Harriet raised her eyebrows. 'Great.' There were plenty of late-fruiters which seemed to keep Mother occupied for hours. As for Harriet . . . She opened the fat envelope that had arrived this morning. It contained the next batch of typing with a note of thanks for the last lot, emailed off to her new employer yesterday. It looked as if, after her morning chores were done, she'd be typing.

Mother was still wandering around the orchard when Harriet took the manuscript upstairs and waggled her fingers into typing mode. She had no idea what this stuff was all about, so that made it tricky – the pages were littered with scientific formulae and itsy-bitsy diagrams. She squinted. But she'd improvised for the last lot and he seemed happy enough, so this time she'd do the same.

She glanced out of the study window. As was so often the case in October, the fields and the Down were vibrant green and swollen with the rain they'd had in the last few days. Her finger paused on the shift key.

Joanna was still in Lisbon and by the time she came back, October would have slipped by. Before they knew it, it would be Christmas. Harriet's typing grew faster as she got into her rhythm – at least Someone Somewhere had been good practice for this, and earning decent money was her priority right now. Harriet's typing might even enable her to buy some Christmas presents . . . Joanna would be here at home presumably, and they'd invite Owen over – they always did.

She frowned at the notes. Her scientist employer had put an asterisk but she couldn't find the corresponding one. What a mess . . . He must be an eccentric, to say the least; after all, most people (even those of her mother's generation) had mastered sufficient technology to manage a computer these days. Not Mother, though; she could barely work the remote control of the television, bless her.

What would Harriet buy her family for Christmas? she wondered. A new nightie for Mother perhaps (something glamorous that would cheer her up), maybe gloves for Owen and a scarf for Joanna? Jolyon was more problematic since their relationship remained uncategorised, and might not even exist by then. A vintage *Bonanza* calendar? What would he buy her? A box set of Hank Williams CDs? A Missy camisole? A Wagon Wheel?

She flicked through the thick sheaf of A4. Some of the pages were crumpled, creased and even stained with what looked like coffee in places. But she wouldn't complain. She'd always been able to decipher her father's handwriting, which had been almost as bad as this; it was a challenge. Harriet looked up at the screen. She'd already done two pages, although she missed her old typewriter — it wasn't quite the same without that satisfying *dring* as the carriage sprang back for a new line. Never mind, she was now, officially, a working woman. She clicked on the spell and grammar check, for a bit of variety really.

She worked on for over an hour, stopping only to answer the phone to the organic veg shop and check on her mother — who was now peeling apples in the kitchen. They had lunch — home-made parsnip soup — and Harriet watched her mother as she ate, silently, staring into space. It was as if she had lost something. Not Father, because she'd lost him years ago, but something else, something inside her perhaps.

'Maybe we could let her have one a month,' Joanna had suggested the night before she went to Lisbon, after Mother had gone to bed, as if they were talking about Walnut Whips rather than painters and decorators and the like. 'Just to provide a quote — you don't have to actually have anything done.'

'Don't be ridiculous,' Harriet had said. 'We mustn't encourage her. She's got to snap out of it.' But would she? It was beginning to look increasingly unlikely.

'Perhaps we should get the doctor out to look at her then,' Joanna had suggested.

Harriet shook her head. 'I don't think doctors count,' she said. 'It's more manual workers, isn't it?'

Joanna had snorted with laughter and then stifled it immediately. 'I meant, to take a look at her . . . problem.'

227

Oh. 'And how would you describe her . . . problem exactly?'

'Sorry, Het.' Joanna had sighed, linked arms with her just like they'd done when they were girls. 'I'm as worried about her as you are. But if she's suffering from depression or anxiety . . .'

'Maybe.' And Harriet had squeezed her hand. She understood. Neither of them knew what to do for the best – because neither of them knew what was wrong.

After lunch, Mother went for a nap and Harriet nipped outside to check on her winter vegetables. The air was cold, but the sun had inched through the clouds and the sky was clearing, leaving the pale yellow afternoon light that she loved. Harriet looked up and over towards the sea. She thought she saw something – a piece of glass maybe? – glinting from behind the fence up on Warren Down. Someone's glasses perhaps? She shielded her eyes and looked up the hill towards the footpath that started back at Warren Cove and ended up at the Beacon. It was a popular round trip – in all seasons.

But she couldn't see anyone. If someone was there, they were hidden from view by a bush or a tree. On purpose? she wondered. Surely not.

Harriet removed some of the old plant debris. She'd do some more mulching tomorrow – she'd prepared a good mulch from the fallen leaves of the mulberry and other fruit trees in the orchard and this helped to prevent frost damage. Frost damage she couldn't afford.

There it was again. Harriet straightened and peered up towards the path once more. Something was up there. Or someone. And they definitely didn't want to be seen. She felt a twinge of unease.

As she left the kitchen garden by the low gate and went into the farmyard, it hit her. Glinting glass. Could someone be up there with a pair of binoculars? That wasn't unheard of – they got a lot of birdwatchers and nature lovers around here – but recent experience had made Harriet more suspicious than usual.

She walked, with what she hoped was a jaunty and carefree air, across the cobbles of the farmyard. Then, as she passed the corner of Big Barn, she ducked behind the wall. *We'll soon see*, she thought grimly.

She edged her way round the back of Big Barn, keeping low, staying out of sight, and skirted the farmyard until she reached the old cow shed. From the other side of the shed she watched. And waited. She just had that feeling – something wasn't right.

A minute later, she saw a movement on the Down, where the glinting had come from. Someone stood up. Even from this distance it was a familiar figure. She narrowed her eyes. It was him – the prowler – spying on them from a distance now, the coward.

He was walking in the opposite direction to the cottage, away from her. What should she do? Harriet was rooted to the spot. On the one hand, she wanted to race up the hill after him, confront him, find out once and for all what he was after. He might insist that he was just a twitcher. But she'd bet anything that his binoculars had been trained on Mulberry Farm Cottage. He had been watching her, she knew it. Spying. And if he was capable of spying, what else might he be capable of? She shivered.

On the other hand, as Joanna kept telling her, confrontation could be dangerous. Supposing he was armed? He might have a knife tucked into his belt, or anything. Supposing – despite

229

appearances – he was strong enough to restrain her? No one else was around. He could probably strangle her with his bare hands.

On the other hand . . . Hang on a minute, Harriet thought, how many hands did she have? How could she let him get away? Again? Because she'd been right all along, her prowler hadn't gone anywhere. And she couldn't live like this – never knowing when he was going to turn up or what he was going to do. So far, he'd just been looking, but what if he was trying to establish their routine, planning something more sinister? And besides, Harriet valued her privacy. No one had the right to spy on them. She wouldn't have it.

She moved. She jumped over the stile and legged it up the Down, which wasn't easy in wellington boots that were stiff with dried mud. Pretty soon she was out of breath, panting, her legs practically buckling under her. But she was gaining on him. And he hadn't seen her – yet.

He turned around. Yes, it was definitely him. And yes, there were the binoculars swinging from his neck, though she couldn't see a dagger.

He stared at Harriet in total disbelief – and who could blame him? – as she stumbled up the path in her ancient blue dungarees and muddy green wellies, her hair no doubt frizzing wildly around her face, missing her footing on the ruts and burrows. Her chest and lungs were aching with the effort. My God. What if she had a heart attack? He wouldn't even need the dagger then.

He ran.

'Come back!' she yelled into the wind. But she had such little breath and voice left by this point that the words seemed to dissolve in the air. 'Wait!' She stopped running – she had to. 'I want to talk to you.' she croaked. 'Come back this minute!'

They had been in this situation before. And once again, it was as if he was frightened of her — which remained very confusing. He accelerated. He was fresh. She had no chance.

All the fight went out of Harriet. All the energy. She bent double and concentrated on breathing. She sank onto the grass and beat the ground with her fists. Bugger it. Her prowler had escaped again.

CHAPTER 30

Joanna

Lisbon

When at last she finished writing, after she'd eaten her sandwiches and the delicious creamy custard *pastel de nata* she'd bought from a nearby café, Joanna left the *praça* and strolled along the road, past steep cobbled side streets that led down towards the river, on her way to the square that held the reservoir of water and signalled the end of the old aqueduct. A warm afternoon light was shining over the tiled buildings and intricately carved wooden doors.

The road opened out at last, into red-rooftop views of Lisbon and the first sighting of the suspension bridge in the distance, spanning the Tagus. *The old and the new*, she thought. Like Joanna and Emmy perhaps. Two moments in time colliding. The reservoir was in a park where strong and ancient trees stood guard, and old men played boules and cards or sat on park benches chatting. There was a Victorian pavilion-style café with a modern, glass conservatory, a large round pond with a fountain, and underneath this, Mãe d'Agua, Mother of Water itself, a building now mainly used for housing art exhibitions.

Joanna began to walk down the concrete steps into the underground reservoir. Inside, the wall of the aqueduct had been turned into a dimly lit grotto. Water dripped, slowly, remorselessly. It was cool and eerie; music was playing, like fingers being run around the rim of a glass bottle, the sound echoing through the stone chambers.

She glanced at the leaflet she'd picked up from the ticket office, as she negotiated the split-level metal walkways. The central tank apparently had the capacity to hold 5,500 cubic metres of water. That was an awful lot. At the top, she peered back down the passage. She made a mental note to find out a bit more about the construction – whether she'd use the information in her brochure, she wasn't sure. But she'd like to know.

Joanna stood for a moment, listening to the music and the sound of the water, breathing in the damp metallic smell. There was something about music and bridges. The drone of traffic, the rush of water, footsteps on a walkway – these were all the music of the bridge, the wind being the main player. The music here, though, was haunting, and she had to fight the sensation that she was drowning. In a tin can; in a submarine. She didn't like it. She headed for the fresh air outside.

As Joanna went into the café for a restorative glass of fresh juice, she heard the ping of an email notification. She gave her order to the waitress and settled herself at a table by the window. She checked her phone. A reply from Nicholas Tresillion. She found herself smiling. That was quick. She opened it.

Dear Joanna Shepherd, she read.

Thanks for replying. I'm sure you get lots of mail about things that

233

you've written (I was wondering, what else have you written?) and that you're very busy. I appreciate it.

Joanna liked the way his mind wandered and the way he allowed these tangential thoughts to spill out. But what else *had* she written? No doubt he was expecting something a bit more worthy than her usual columns and features. A novel?

When she and Martin had first moved to London, that had been Joanna's dream. Martin had supported her then. He'd convinced her that he could earn enough money to keep both of them – for a while, at least. He had given her time and opportunity. He had believed in her, they had been a team.

But it had never happened. Perhaps the problem was that Joanna had never fully believed in herself. Because she'd never finished that novel. There had been a few false starts but the text never seemed good enough, funny enough, clever enough. Features, though, she knew she was good at. She could think up different angles, winkle out truths that others might have missed; she could explore.

The Internet had made the features market more competitive but had also opened up a lot of new avenues. Joanna might be a failed novelist, but at least she made some sort of a living from her writing. She hadn't, though, given up on her dream . . .

I'm writing again, he continued, *(sorry about that if you were hoping to get rid of me!) to say that I know what you mean about directions and getting lost and finding yourself – which is how I interpreted what you wrote, anyway. It's been the same for me. For years you play a certain role; I played a certain role, did what was expected of me. Then the role disappeared and I wasn't sure what was left.*

Joanna paused as the waitress brought her juice. She thanked her and continued reading.

I won't go into details, he went on, *I'm probably saying far too much as it is, but it was as if most of me had disappeared with it. Who had I been before? I could barely remember for a while.*

She sipped her juice. What he was telling her so frankly was sending echoes into her head and her heart. Disconcertingly, she knew exactly what he meant.

In case you're thinking I'm some sort of depressive soul, I should say that I've remembered now — who I was, I mean. Who I am. And it's all good. What I really wrote to ask you is: are you doing another bridge walk in another European city? If so, I'd love to hear about it. In the meantime, it's good to talk to you and sorry for rambling on.

Yours, Nicholas

Joanna read the email through three times. She hadn't quite expected things to get so personal with her mystery correspondent. But she wasn't complaining and, after all, she'd started it. She was intrigued. She wanted to know more about what had happened to him and how he had lost and then found himself again. Behind it all, she thought, there must be a woman.

She pulled her laptop from her bag and tapped out a reply straightaway.

Dear Nicholas,

I'm really glad it's all good, she began. Her fingers flew over the keys. He was easy to write to . . .

It was the right kind of end to the walk through the old and the new, Joanna thought, as she finished her juice. She pressed 'send' straightaway this time and put her laptop away once more. Tracing the path of the ancient waterway through to its original stone, walking out into the square and seeing the new suspension bridge in the far distance, heaving with traffic. The lovers beside the mulberry tree. Even Nicholas's email had seemed a part of it. And it had been a discovery in more ways than she'd expected. As if the past and the present had somehow melded into one. And the future? Had she found any clues about the woman she could be?

CHAPTER 31

Nicholas

Cornwall

The landline rang. Nicholas broke off from studying his computer screen. He'd been unable to concentrate anyway. He was restless. He'd been restless since he got back from El Cotillo; uneasy, certain there was something he should be doing, but not sure what it was.

He picked up the handset. 'Hello?' He was expecting it to be Celie, since it usually was. She worried about him, he knew, and he about her. It was hard not to think of her as his little girl, and perhaps she always would be. The gap she had left in his life was greater than the one Rachel had left. When you were married, he supposed, you didn't always reflect on who kept you locked into it – your wife, or your kids.

But, '*Ciao*, Nico.' It was Giuseppe.

'Hey, how goes it?' Nicholas sat down in the cane chair by the phone, let his body sink into the plump red cushion. Giuseppe's calls were always long ones; this would be a business update, a sort of chilled tele-conference. He stretched out his legs.

'Sales from the new outlets in Venice, they are very encouraging.' Giuseppe never wasted time beating about the bush. He reeled off some figures while Nicholas made the odd note or two, hemmed and hawed, chewed the end of the pen he kept by the phone.

After about five minutes, he heard the word 'expand'.

'Where to?'

They threw some ideas around. Italy was pretty much well covered by stores in Rome, Milan, Venice, Florence and Pisa, plus some smaller outlets that Nicholas didn't visit personally. Barcelona had been a relatively recent successful addition since becoming such a European designer shopping centre; Paris and Nice were also flourishing, as were the various cities they supplied in the UK. Although, much as Nicholas couldn't bring himself to criticise Italian style, the jewellery designed by Rachel's sister Isobel – who undeniably had talent – and handmade by her and Giuseppe was a touch brash for British taste. *It makes a statement* was one of his favourite sales patters. But actually, it was expensive bling – with attitude.

'How about Lisbon?' he heard Giuseppe say. Bloody hell. That was a bit of a coincidence.

He'd received Joanna Shepherd's email but not yet replied. It had swept him away. She'd got pretty personal, understandably after what he'd told her. Nicholas had never written to anyone like that in his entire life and he wasn't sure how an innocent communication could have blossomed into such intensity so fast. Maybe they both needed some counselling . . .

'Lisbon?' he echoed.

238

'It is in our league, do you think?' Giuseppe had picked up some charming English slang. 'They might go for it there, yes?'

Nicholas hesitated. The ball appeared to be in his court. 'I don't see why not. It's—'

'Hang on.'

Nicholas knew that Giuseppe was already online, delving into the jewellery shops, the tourist dens, the department stores of downtown Lisbon. And Nicholas had no idea what he would find. He'd never even visited the city. But he wanted to. He realised now just how much he wanted to. What might she have seen there? he wondered.

When he had first written to Joanna Shepherd, he had thought it would be a one-off. It had been a slightly peculiar and random experience, which no doubt could be explained somehow – by a trick of the imagination or the light perhaps; by coincidence. Reflections in the water indeed. Some sort of Atlantis lost and buried in a Venetian canal? And then he'd seen it too. The woman running – including the golden ribbon that Ms Shepherd had apparently seen but not mentioned in the brochure. How weird was that? He had found the experience both refreshing and fascinating, he had felt a strong urge to tell the author what had happened, to let her know. But now . . .

Giuseppe was analysing out loud the shopping districts of Lisbon. That was his department; he was a good businessman, Nicholas would give him that. Isobel was the creative one, and Nicholas had people skills – although at times he still found this hard to believe; he'd always thought of himself as rather a solitary man.

'It's a popular city obviously – especially with young people,' Giuseppe was saying. 'There's a lot of modern infrastructure, new buildings, hotels . . .'

'Yeah. D'you want me to check it out?' he asked Giuseppe.

'Maybe . . .' He didn't sound sure. And although it was ridiculous, Nicholas wanted to convince him. And yet, what did it matter? If he so wanted to go to Lisbon (did he really? Did he honestly want – or need – to get into this . . . this, whatever it was?), he could go anyway. He didn't have to justify it with a business trip.

'OK,' said Giuseppe. 'Why not? Thanks, Nico.'

And Nicholas felt a twinge of guilt. He'd never thought of himself as a dishonest man.

After the usual exchanges about children and family, Giuseppe rang off and Nicholas read her email once again.

Dear Nicholas, he read.

I'm really glad it's all good.

He smiled.

A similar thing happened to me, you may be surprised to know . . .

She had added a smiley face emoji here.

Are we living parallel lives? I wonder.

'Could be.' Nicholas raised an eyebrow.

I wasn't playing the role of wife exactly, but my husband and I . . . well, we were moving further and further apart.

Nicholas certainly knew how that felt.

I thought and hoped I could do something about that, but it turned out we'd travelled even further away from one another than I'd guessed.

Nicholas nodded. He felt a pang of empathy for Joanna Shepherd.

So that left me without a direction.

Venice, he thought.

I had a decision to make about my marriage which I only made when I got to Venice.

240

Uh-huh, that bridge walk of hers was suddenly making a lot more sense, he thought.

(There's a lot more about Venice that I could say, but that's plenty for now!)

Shame . . .

I have no idea, by the way, why I'm telling you all this. I suppose it's just that you saw the golden ribbon.

The golden ribbon . . . Again, Nicholas smiled.

And yes, I am doing another bridge walk – in Lisbon. I'm there right now. I'll keep you posted . . .

Warm wishes, Joanna

And now he was going to Lisbon too. Nicholas liked the way she wrote, in a stream, as if she were here in the room. And if she were here in the room? They probably wouldn't have a word to say to one another. But he didn't believe that for a moment.

She and her husband had split, he assumed. Just like he and Rachel. They had both been at a crossroads in Venice, both leading separate lives. And now they had both been honest about it, even though they'd never met. So, what? Maybe more people ought to be honest about how they felt instead of constantly pretending everything was fine.

He'd seen what she'd seen. Something that couldn't so easily be explained. Something that must have knocked her sideways. Did he believe in magic? No. He believed in things you could touch and feel and easily understand. Concrete things. But still . . .

He pulled on his fleece, went out of the front door and cut down some foliage from the garden – some holly, some purpley sprigs from the spruce, and some winter jasmine. He sniffed. Tiny white flowers and yet they smelt as heady as

241

summertime. Rachel would have said, *For God's sake, Nick, go to the shop and buy some yellow roses at least*. But sometimes she missed the point, he thought, as he arranged the foliage into a rough sort of bunch.

He crossed the road to the churchyard, entered by the lych-gate and walked down the rough concrete path, alongside the old stone church, over to his aunt's grave, which was tucked into the corner, by the wooden bench under the fig tree. The bench was damp, the fig tree looking a bit bent and battered. But it was a special place for Nicholas.

'Hey,' he said softly, and, ducking under the branches of the fig tree, laid the bunch of greenery on top of the mildewed stone. 'What would you do if you were me? Go back to El Cotillo? Go to Lisbon? Email Joanna Shepherd? Or leave well alone?' When he was young, he'd wanted to be an explorer, wanted to do something different with his life. When you were young you had no fear.

And now?

The wind was whisking through the bare branches of the birch trees around the churchyard; apart from that no other sound could be heard. Not even the birds. In the summer, someone had left a note on the church door asking people to keep it closed so that swallows wouldn't get trapped in the church; they nested up in the beams above the porch.

Ah well. His aunt was as enigmatic in death as she had been in life. She was the older sister, but she had outlived Nicholas's mother by six years – six teenage years for him, and in many ways he felt closer to the woman he'd spent so much time with in summer holidays and suchlike than he did to his own parents. Something about her, some strand of unhappiness, drew him to her. She'd never talked much about her private life. But he

242

kind of knew it hadn't worked out for her exactly how she had hoped it would.

He stuck his hands in the pockets of his jeans. A bit like his own life then.

CHAPTER 32

Joanna

Dorset

Joanna heard the car engine, but didn't think anything of it.
She was back at Mulberry Farm Cottage but still busy thinking
bridges. She'd written the copy for the walk while still in Lisbon,
revised the text on the flight home and sent it to Toby the day
after she got back. The next day, she'd continued researching her
family tree – the Local History Centre had finally revealed the
birth certificate of her grandfather George Shepherd and she now
knew that his father, William Shepherd, was a landowner rather
than a farmer and that he had been married to Edith.

When she'd found the birth certificate, Joanna had wondered
fleetingly if William's wife Edith could be her Emmy, but it
didn't make sense. The names weren't that alike – unless it was
a pet name. But she had a sense that Emmy and Edith weren't
the same woman. What about William's sisters then – if he
had any? If she were to continue searching for Emmy, then
the trail must go on.

244

And now, Joanna was researching Prague. She glanced at Emmy's letter.

As a historian, long fascinated by Charles IV who became King of Bohemia and Emperor of the Holy Roman Empire at the same time – quite a feat, I think you will agree, Rufus – Father is fascinated to learn more about the city in which Charles chose to settle. And I am going to paint his bridge!

The mediaeval Charles Bridge, that was. It would obviously be the focal point of Joanna's walk. She'd seen pictures and it was quite something.

She heard voices downstairs now, but carried on working. And then she heard Harriet calling. 'Jo?'

'Yes?'

Joanna had to admit, she missed the peace and quiet of their house at Crouch End – when Martin was at work and she was writing. That stillness, that knowing you were alone and wouldn't be disturbed. She knew she must look for somewhere else to live, but until she could decide where . . . And besides, something was keeping her here. *There's no hurry*, Harriet had said. Maybe it was Mother and wanting to help Harriet that was keeping her, maybe it was wanting to get closer again to her sister. Maybe it was even Emmy holding her here for now. At any rate, it was easier to research the family tree using Mulberry Farm Cottage as her base. And there was something calming in this landscape of her girlhood that Joanna seemed to need in her life at the moment.

She started to go downstairs but stopped halfway.

He was standing in the hall. 'Martin.'

He turned. 'Hi, Jo.'

He was smiling. Her first thought was that he looked like a stranger. Then he brushed back his fair hair with his hand in a familiar gesture, and she realised he was nervous, unsure of his welcome. She was conscious of Harriet standing in the kitchen doorway, arms folded, most definitely in protective mode, bless her. And Mother in the sitting room, already getting to her feet. 'Is that you, Martin, dear?'

Joanna took a deep breath. 'What are you——?'

'Sorry to turn up unannounced.'

She stemmed her irritation. Why hadn't he phoned at least? But she knew why – Martin liked to take people by surprise. He thought that if you gave them warning, they'd have too much time to get prepared.

'I told you I wasn't giving up,' he said.

Joanna sighed. Mother was hovering in the doorway of the sitting room now. She took a step forwards and Martin bent to kiss her cheek. As he raised his head Joanna would swear he was shooting her a look of triumph.

'How are you?' he asked. He offered a penitent smile.

'Fine.' What should she do with him? Joanna glanced at Harriet, who shrugged.

'Good.' Martin looked from Harriet to Mother to Joanna. 'So, can we talk?'

She took his point. 'Better go out,' she suggested. 'A walk maybe?' It was blowing a gale out there, but at least they'd have some privacy.

She put on her leather jacket, a scarf and the walking boots that she kept in the porch and they went out the back way towards the farmyard and the mulberry tree.

Martin gestured back at the house. 'I can't believe you're still here,' he said.

'Me neither. But I've been away a lot. Why didn't you tell me you were coming?'

He gave her a long look. 'I was afraid you'd avoid seeing me.'

And perhaps she would have. They began to walk up the hill towards the cliff path. It was only the first week of November, but the chill of winter had already set in. 'You're lucky I was here,' she said.

Martin was wearing his brown brogues. He wasn't exactly dressed for a walk in muddy Dorset. 'I've been expecting you to at least come back for your stuff,' he said. 'It's been two months, Jo. And you said you were going to fix a date.'

Two months? It seemed longer. In two months, she'd been to Venice and Lisbon. She'd researched her family tree and she'd done a lot of writing. 'Sorry.' She glanced across at Martin. *You shouldn't skip any steps in your family research*, the girl at the Local History Centre had told her, *you have to be meticulous, otherwise you might miss some vital piece of information*. Was there, she wondered, some vital piece of information about Martin that she had missed? Was that why they had gone so sadly wrong?

'It's OK.' He shrugged. 'But I was waiting . . . .'

'You thought I'd change my mind?' she asked him. The grass underfoot was slick with damp. But although it was breezy, the freshness of the air felt good – on her face, in her lungs.

'I thought you'd at least come back to talk and that I'd have a chance to persuade you,' he admitted.

Joanna thought of her indecision in the beginning; all the times she'd been tempted to go back to London, to collect some of her things, to see Martin. But instead, she'd got caught up with work, with travelling, with finding out about Emmy. And there was a reason for that, she was sure. If she'd gone back, maybe Martin could have persuaded her. But deep inside, she'd known it wasn't the right pathway.

She shoved her hands deep inside her pockets. She should

have brought gloves. 'I'm sorry, Martin,' she said. 'I will have to come back for some stuff.' She should have done it before now; her wardrobe was skimpy to say the least and winter was fast approaching. 'But you should know, I'm not going to change my mind.' She didn't even want to talk about it. It was done.

Martin looked sorrowful. He gazed out towards the Beacon. 'Fifteen years is a long time to throw away, Jo,' he said.

'I know.' And who had thrown it away exactly?

'Things could be different. I could be different. Won't you give me another chance?'

They reached the top of the hill and Joanna looked back as she always did. At Mulberry Farm Cottage – slate tiles, honey stone – snug in the dip between the hills of the Down, surrounded by the barns and the undulating green fields and darker hedgerows, the pine trees standing tall and proud behind and the church in the distance. 'I'm not sure that things could be different,' she said. *Not now.*

'And you're not even willing to try?'

She turned again to face the sea. The cliff here was steep, as if it had been sliced by a knife. Was she willing to try? Joanna almost wished she could say yes. But what point would there be? 'You said you were going to put the house on the market,' she reminded him. 'You know I'll have to find somewhere to live when I leave here.'

Martin frowned. 'I don't get it.' He shoved his hands in his pockets. 'Are we breaking up after all this time because of one small indiscretion?'

'Not really.' Though she'd hardly call it that. Her reply was caught by the wind, tossed towards the waves where it bounced out to sea. The water was olive green today, heavy and rolling.

'What then?'

Joanna began to walk down the cliff path. Martin followed her. She turned towards him, felt the wind whip at her hair. 'Are you still seeing her?'

'No.'

Should she believe him? Did it even matter?

'So, what was it then,' he asked, 'if it wasn't Hilary?'

Below the sandstone cliff ran the strip of beach that led to Warren Cove, tucked out of sight. Beyond that, the cliff rose steeply on the other side, leading to West Bay. 'I told you before. You said it yourself.' She remembered his exact words that first afternoon, before she'd left Crouch End. *We have to face it. Maybe we've just grown apart.*

'Said what?' She heard the irritation in his voice. He would be thinking, *Why did I bother to come here today? Here she is talking in riddles – as usual.*

'That we'd grown apart. Fallen out of love.' They continued to walk down towards the shoreline. That's why Hilary had happened. Why couldn't he see?

'I was trying to explain . . .' He faltered.

'Exactly.' And he had. It had taken Joanna a while to acknowledge it but Martin had been right, she knew that now.

'But, Jo—'

'We're not in love with each other anymore,' she said. 'And we have to accept that.' One of them at least had to be honest.

He grabbed her arm. 'What makes you so sure about how I feel?' he demanded.

She turned to face him. 'How *do* you feel?' she asked.

'I still love you, Jo, whatever I said back then. I never stopped loving you. You're my wife.'

He looked so out of place here in his city brogues and dapper jacket and for a moment her heart went out to him. Something

249

inside her still wanted to believe him. Something inside her wanted to be folded in his arms just like before. But it had taken him a long time to come here and say these things. It had taken him a long time to fight for her – if that's what he was doing now. 'Do you want to make me happy, Martin?' she asked him.

He looked at her warily as if this was a trick question. 'Yes, of course I do.'

They passed the little house on the hill, built so close to the cliff edge that she always feared for its life. She thought of Emmy. 'Have you missed me – every minute of every day?'

There was a look of utter incomprehension on his face now. Joanna almost wanted to laugh.

'It isn't all about love,' Martin said. 'You and I, we're a partnership, a team.'

'We were, yes.' They began to walk through the grassy car park to the road. The place was deserted. But he was wrong. It had everything to do with love.

'D'you know what your trouble is, Joanna?' Martin said.

No, but she was damn sure he was going to tell her. He hadn't changed after all.

'You're a hopeless romantic, an idealist. You go on about love. But love's got nothing to do with the reality of being together, working together, having a life together. That's something else. That's realism and practicality. That's what life's really about.'

Joanna was in front of him as they reached the steps that led down to the cove.

'But, you see, I don't want that,' she said.

'What?' He followed her down the steps and onto the stones, past the tiny stream and the fishing boats battered by wind, storm and sea.

250

'If that's what our life together was all about.' She carried on walking down to the water's edge. 'Then I don't want it. I told you.'

'Ah. But I think I know what the real problem is.' Once again, he was beside her.

'What?' She couldn't believe that he still didn't get it.

'You want a child.' He said it so quietly that his words were almost lost in the rush of the waves, the soft fizz of foamy water over the pebbles.

Joanna folded her arms around her body. They had first talked about it years ago. She had been keen to start a family and he had urged her to wait. 'Do we really want to be tied down, Jo?' he had said. 'It would change everything.'

'Not yet,' she had agreed. She was happy to wait. But 'not yet' had meant 'one day' for Joanna. One day, when she'd made some money or Martin had been promoted or . . . But time had gone by.

She'd had her thirty-fifth birthday earlier this year and over lunch with Lucy – who had three children already – her friend had asked her if her biological clock had 'stopped or what'.

'Huh?' Joanna's mind had been a blank.

'Children, Jo. Aren't you and Martin going to start a family?'

Oh. She considered. Were they? Would they? 'Maybe.' And yet she realised that they hadn't talked about it – not for ages, anyway. And time, well, she supposed it was running out.

Joanna stared across the water. The waves were wild today, the wind taking the spray and lashing it onto the shore. She did want a child. And yes, she did know her biological clock was ticking. But did she want a child with this man? The thought flickered and died.

Martin took her silence for some sort of agreement. 'We could do that, Jo,' he said.

251

Yes, they could. But was that reason enough to stay together? Joanna closed her eyes and felt the breeze on her face, smelt the saltiness of the air. She breathed in deeply. That, she presumed, was his final card. 'I don't think that's the answer, Martin,' she said. No one should have a baby in order to mend a relationship that was already broken.

'Right. I see. That's it then, I suppose. There's just no reasoning with you, is there?' And before Joanna could reply, he had turned around and stomped back up the steps and down the lane. In moments, he was out of sight.

Joanna stayed there at the water's edge for a while until her fingers were numb with cold. And then she walked back over the Down, towards the cottage, knowing even before she got there that his car would be gone.

252

CHAPTER 33

Harriet

Dorset

'Martin didn't stay very long,' Harriet commented to Joanna when she got back.

'No, he didn't.' Joanna gave her a look.

'So, he's not staying for supper then?' She needed to know how many there would be. And she wondered, if Martin and her sister had split up, then why had he come here at all?

'No, he's not staying for supper.'

Harriet's heart went out to her. It can't have been an easy conversation. 'Are you all right, Jo?' Tentatively, she put out a hand.

'Yes, I am.' To Harriet's relief, her sister smiled and some of the anxiety disappeared from her dark eyes. 'You never liked him, did you?' she said.

Had it been that obvious? 'He never liked me.' It was nothing Martin had ever said exactly. More the way he treated her. As if when he came to stay in the country, Harriet was the live-in maid and housekeeper.

Joanna acknowledged this with a small nod. 'I haven't changed my mind,' she said. 'About us splitting up.'

'Right.' Harriet was relieved – her sister deserved far better.

'And you?' Joanna turned, one hand on the banister, about to go upstairs.

'Me?' Harriet hadn't told her about the latest sighting of her prowler. Joanna would only fuss. And besides, she'd had too many other things on her mind.

'How's it going with . . .' Joanna hesitated. 'Jolyon?'

'Ah.' Harriet had half hoped she'd forgotten about Jolyon. 'It never came to anything, actually.' She glanced round to check their mother wasn't listening.

Yesterday, she had told him that it was over almost before it had begun. It had been a difficult conversation.

'But why, Harriet?' he had asked, and for an awful moment she'd thought he was going to cry. Perhaps all country and western people were emotional; it seemed to go with the territory somehow.

'It's not you,' she lied. 'It's just that I'm far too busy to have a relationship at the moment.' She couldn't believe how guilty she felt. She had never meant to hurt him, never meant to lead him on, she supposed. But in a way, she had.

She had gone out with him – to a Cajun dance, which involved a lot of foot stomping and bouncing, but which was surprisingly good fun. And afterwards . . . well, she'd let him kiss her. She hadn't been able to stop him really. She'd had three lager and limes – Harriet wasn't used to drinking – and he'd taken her by surprise. He had brought her home after the dance and gallantly leapt out to open the passenger door for her. She had held out her hand and her cheek at the same time, and he'd lunged. And that's when Harriet knew for certain: she really wasn't attracted to him in the least.

'There's Mother to think of,' she had told Jolyon. 'She takes up so much of my time . . .' Mentally, she'd crossed her fingers. 'And so, I've decided that I simply have to say goodbye.' It wouldn't be so bad if she could stop thinking and speaking in country and western clichés. It had been such a brief relationship – hardly a relationship at all. What on earth had he done to her?

'I'm sorry,' she added, when he said nothing. 'But I don't have time to have a boyfriend.' Which was almost true.

She decided not to tell her sister the details. She wasn't exactly proud of any of it.

'That's a shame, Het,' Joanna said now. 'But you know what they say: plenty more fish in the sea.'

'Yes.' Which was, in fact, the name of another dating website. Not that Harriet needed another dating website. Someone Somewhere had failed her twice, but she was going to give it one last chance. Tomorrow night. And this one sounded much more promising.

Was she being unrealistic to start dating at the age of thirty-nine? Were all the nice ones taken and just the more peculiar ones left on the shelf? 'Same for you, Jo,' she said. 'You'll meet someone else.'

'Maybe.' Joanna grinned. 'But I won't be going out looking – I could do with having a break for a while.'

'What happened with Martin?' Harriet asked her. 'Why did you leave?' It wasn't just that she was curious, though she was. She was so inexperienced. She wanted to know more about what made a relationship tick. And she wanted Joanna to confide in her, she supposed. Over the past weeks she'd liked having someone around to talk to – sometimes, at least.

255

Joanna's expression changed. 'A woman called Hilary happened,' she muttered.

'Oh.' Harriet was surprised. Of course people strayed. But why would any man stray from Joanna?

'But I don't feel bitter about it, Het.' And she managed a smile. 'I should thank her – she opened my eyes to what our marriage had become.'

'Oh,' Harriet said again. She wanted to ask what their marriage had become, but perhaps she should leave that till another day. Perhaps she was learning the art of tact and diplomacy – at last. Instead, she reached out to her sister once more. 'I'm so sorry, Jo.'

It suddenly struck her that she'd been doing that a lot lately. Reaching out to Joanna. No wonder her sister had seemed so vulnerable when she first arrived. No wonder she had wanted to come home to a place where she would feel safe. And what had Harriet done to make her feel better? Not very much actually. Certainly not enough.

Joanna gave a little shrug. 'It's OK. It wasn't, but now it's a lot better. Let's just say it's been one heck of a learning curve.'

She turned to give Harriet a quick hug. Harriet tensed automatically, then felt herself relax into it. She hugged her sister back, surprising Joanna almost as much as herself. 'You know, if you ever want to talk . . .' She let her voice trail.

'Thanks. I know that. You too.'

Harriet watched her sister as she went up the stairs. It hadn't worked out for her and Martin, but some marriages lasted forever, she reminded herself. Because whatever her thoughts about the foolhardiness of looking for a mate, she couldn't help herself. She wanted to experience what Joanna had experienced, at least when her marriage had been good. She wanted someone she could call a companion, hopefully even a friend; if not someone who loved her, then Harriet wanted to meet someone who would look out for her, who would care. She even wanted – God help her – passion.

Joanna would be off again soon – next up she was going to Prague. 'It's nice to have you here, Jo,' Harriet called up the stairs after her. 'Really.'

Joanna turned around at the top of the stairs and gave her a lovely smile. 'It's nice to be here, Het,' she said. 'For the first time in ages . . .' She paused.

'Yes?'

'I feel free.'

CHAPTER 34

Joanna

Dorset

First thing in the morning while Harriet was doing her deliveries, Joanna spent some time with their mother.

'Can you show me how you do your work, darling?' her mother asked. 'On your computer, I mean. I'd be so interested.'

'Of course, Ma.' Joanna was touched.

She brought her laptop down to the sitting room and showed her mother the different documents she was working on.

Mother peered at the screen. 'Fascinating,' she said. 'If only we'd had such a thing when I was a girl.'

'What would you have done, Mother? What would have been your perfect career?' Joanna knew that her mother had married her father when she was only nineteen. After that, the farm was her career – looking after Father and cooking for him and the farmhands, caring for Harriet and Joanna when they came along. That would have been a full-time job in itself.

'Oh, I don't know, darling.' Mother looked out of the

window towards the Down where the hedges had lost a lot of their leaves in the latest autumn gale and the trees were tinged with the reds and yellows of the season. 'But I always felt I wanted to work with people – in an office perhaps?'

Joanna smiled. 'Maybe you would have been a journalist, like me.'

Mother chuckled. 'I don't think I would have been nearly clever enough,' she said. 'All these words . . . You take after your father, you know. If he hadn't been a farmer, he would have been an academic, I'm sure.'

Joanna remembered the books that she and Harriet had heaved down and into the study a few days after she'd found them in the attic. 'I think you're right.'

'But how do you communicate with your editors?' Mother peered closer again as Joanna opened her email and showed her how it worked.

'And then you can look stuff up too.' Joanna illustrated this by opening Google. 'You can find out almost anything.'

'At just the touch of a button. Oh, my.' Mother was transfixed. 'How things have changed, Jo.'

'They certainly have.' Even in Joanna's lifetime. Sometimes even she struggled with technology.

'And do you know . . .' Mother sighed as she sat back in the chair. 'Although there were never so many opportunities when I was a girl, I'm rather glad I never had to worry about all those sorts of things. Life was so much simpler in my day.'

'Yes,' said Joanna. She could see that. 'I suppose it was.'

When Harriet returned at ten thirty, Joanna borrowed the pick-up truck and drove to the Dorset Records Office in Dorchester. After several phone calls, she'd discovered they held microform copies of the census returns from 1841 to 1891 here, so she'd lost no time in making an appointment.

As she drove down the familiar high road, with its panoramic views of the West Dorset countryside and the coast beyond, she thought again about Martin's visit. She had no regrets, but it had left her feeling unsettled. She should go back to London, she decided, if only to go to the house and collect some more of her things. And to make sure he had put the place on the market, of course. Perhaps now, though, he would really accept that it was over between them. She glanced out of the pick-up truck's window as she passed green fields with sheep, cows and horses grazing. The wind had dropped today and there was an icy blue sky above – a promise of the winter approaching. And yes, it really was over.

So where would she live? It was time to think about practicalities, because she couldn't stay at Mulberry Farm Cottage forever. Harriet had made it clear that she was welcome to stay for as long as she needed to – and Joanna was grateful for that, grateful for the warmth she was beginning to feel from her sister. But . . . Dorset? London? She missed Lucy and Steph and her other friends – though plenty of emails continued to wing between them. On the other hand, she'd like to be closer to her family and the tranquil landscape she had once left behind. She couldn't continue living her life in limbo. She must decide.

Joanna parked the truck. She was a bit early, so she checked her emails on her phone before she went inside. Nothing from Nicholas yet. She wondered if she'd given him a bit too much information? There was a WhatsApp message from Toby, though. She opened it:

Good response to your Venice brochure, sweetie, Toby had written. *It's flying off the shelves.*

260

Any complaints? she messaged back, thinking about that first email from Nicholas Tresillion. Surely other people hadn't seen the mirage in the canal too? Surely – *hang on a minute, get a grip on reality, Jo*, she told herself – it hadn't actually been there?

Course not, came the immediate reply. *And Lisbon's ready to go.*

Great.

People in mulberry trees, thought Joanna. *Enough to test the patience and sanity of any walker.*

The census of 1891 – the one she was most interested in, since this would reveal who was living in Mulberry Farm Cottage at the time – proved fascinating. The returns were arranged by parish – Symondsbury, in this case – and district, and households were recorded street by street. But under Warren Farm Lane there were no entries for Mulberry Farm Cottage.

Joanna frowned as she scanned the narrow lines and slanted script, which was so difficult to read in places. What was going on? Was it a mistake perhaps? Where had they got to?

Eventually, she found the householder Edward Shepherd, farmer, with his wife Jane, and – wait for it – three children: William, Mary and Elizabeth. She felt a twist of excitement. William had two sisters. No Emmy – the name she'd been longing to see – but was it possible that one of these two women could be her? They were the right age, and living in the right place.

Later, over lunch with Harriet and Mother, Joanna's head was still buzzing with the past. When they'd cleared up, she went upstairs to get on with some work. But before she could make a start, there was a light knock at the door.

'Yes?'

Harriet came in and dropped a large manilla envelope into Joanna's lap.

'What's this?' she asked as she opened it.

'Photographs mainly.' Harriet peered over her shoulder. 'You said you were looking for old family photos. I found them in the study.'

'Thanks, Het.' Carefully, Joanna pulled them from the envelope. *Wow.* She had spent some time going through the stuff in the study herself and had found nothing but notes about the farm and ancient bills. Harriet had really come up trumps.

Joanna examined the first photo. 'Is this Father?'

'Yes.'

Skinny and fair-haired, wearing short trousers and a shirt, he was standing self-consciously between a stiff, upright couple both wearing black, who were presumably his parents. Joanna thought she must have seen this photo before, years ago, but she couldn't be sure. She put her hand on her sister's arm and thought she felt Harriet tremble.

'I'll leave you to it,' Harriet said. Her expression changed. 'I'm nipping into the village to get a few bits and pieces, OK? I won't be long.'

'OK.' Joanna was happy to examine the past alone. And it was all too easy to drift, to look into the faces and slip into their worlds.

She picked up the photograph. Her father's father, George, looked stern and rather forbidding, just as Mother had said, while Dorothea had a sweet face and a dimpled smile. Joanna touched the images of her paternal grandparents with her fingertip. It meant so much more when you could put a face to a name. It was funny how she'd never bothered before; her grandparents had both died before she was born, and yet now, through Emmy, they seemed so important; they were the landscape she had come from.

She heard the front doorbell go and her mother answer it. She'd call if she needed anything. It was probably Owen coming round for afternoon tea or someone from the village dropping by. Joanna knew she should really be getting prepared for Prague. But . . .

She glanced up at Emmy's Venetian bridge painting. It wasn't a modern affliction, was it – wanting to get away? Emmy had travelled too, though she gave the impression that she wouldn't have minded staying at home with her dearest Rufus, her *heart's love*. Why, Joanna wondered, hadn't he gone with her? Perhaps because her father needed her companionship and help; Rufus would have had to stay behind to look after the farm. This made sense. Emmy's father would have paid for the journey, she supposed. It certainly wasn't uncommon in those days for a daughter – married or not – to travel as a companion to a relative or friend.

Joanna was vaguely aware of the rise and fall of voices from downstairs and the sound of her mother's laughter. Mother was happy and occupied – that was good. It was a shame she didn't have more friends from the village popping by to see her. Joanna started sorting through the photographs. Might Emmy be pictured here somewhere?

Near the bottom of the pile were some older pictures, in sepia, the edges crimped and frayed. One was of a couple – they looked like husband and wife. The man, who wore a flannel blazer and striped trousers, had a thick beard and an unruly head of hair; he was big, smiling and looked like quite a character. Joanna took to him immediately. He seemed rather familiar too – a resemblance to another family member

263

perhaps? She peered closer. He had kind eyes. The woman, though, looked thin and stern. She wore a long dress with lace at the neck, but there was no elegance about her. Her dark hair was scraped from her face and she was glaring at the camera, oblivious to the smiles of the man by her side. They might, Joanna supposed, be William and Edith, her great-grandparents. No way could this woman be Emmy.

Downstairs, she heard a door closing. She'd better go down and check everything was OK – in a minute.

In another photograph, the same man looked more subdued. On this occasion he was wearing a more formal white shirt with stiff collar and necktie and some sort of morning coat. His wife, in a high-waisted dress and wide-brimmed hat, was holding a baby wrapped in a white christening robe. Was this Joanna's grandfather George? At any rate, at least she knew the man and woman were husband and wife and that they'd had a baby. It was progress – of sorts.

'Well, now,' she murmured. The next breakthrough came with the photograph of a boy in a sailor suit and two girls dressed in knee-length dresses with lacy hems, wearing hats over their long curly hair. The boy was clearly the man of the previous photos – already, he had the same hair – and on the back in the faintest of italic scripts, she could just make out: *William, Mary and Elizabeth.* So, she'd been right. The man with the wild hair and kind eyes was her great-grandfather William and these were the two girls, his sisters, the two possible Emmys.

She continued looking through the photos and found another where the girls were a bit older, this time dressed in white ruffled high-necked blouses and long dark skirts. She sat up straighter. How could she tell if one of them was Emmy? Elizabeth was the older and her name was the more similar. In 1913, the year that the Lisbon and Prague letters had been written, she would have been thirty-three. Even if Joanna discounted the figures she'd seen in Venice and Lisbon – because there was no proof that that girl was Emmy, of course – in the letters, Joanna's Emmy sounded younger and more eager, and anyway, Elizabeth didn't look the artistic type. Joanna could imagine her helping on the farm, but not painting bridges somehow.

Mary was taller, but only a year younger than her sister, and in contrast to her brother, she looked very serious. She could be Emmy, but how could the name Mary become Emmy? And how could someone so dour-looking write letters that bubbled over with life, love and a creative spirit? No, it was surely impossible.

Joanna had to concede: as fascinating as these photos were, so far as Emmy was concerned, she had drawn a blank.

She could still hear voices. Whoever it was had been here rather a long time. Joanna felt a twinge of foreboding. And where had Harriet got to? She scrambled to her feet and went down the stairs, taking the photographs with her to show Mother – just in case she could shed any light – aware that she'd let the past take over and forgotten the responsibilities of the present. Whoever was here had come round – she checked her watch – an hour ago, five minutes after Harriet had left the house. A coincidence? Probably not, come to think of it. Oh, dear.

'Mother?' she called.

They were in the kitchen and she could hear her mother giggling like a girl.

A young man with spiky black hair and a T-shirt proclaiming that *Vampires Rule the World* was sitting at the kitchen table, in front of him a mug of tea and a half-eaten slice of Harriet's Dorset apple cake. Her mother, wearing a dress of deep fuchsia and a black mohair wrap, was standing next to him, a glossy brochure in her hand. More brochures littered the tabletop.

'Oh, hello, Joanna, darling,' she said. And then, 'The Rosebud is delightful,' to the young man.

The Rosebud is delightful? It sounded like a secret code to Joanna. 'Hello,' she said pointedly to the man. He didn't look like a salesman, but the brochures looked suspiciously like—

'Cool,' he said. And, 'Conservatories,' to Joanna.

'Conservatories,' she repeated. He had wicked blue eyes. Joanna blinked at him. Would he be safe with Mother?

'This is my daughter Joanna,' her mother said. 'And this is Craig.'

Craig?

'I'm the builder,' he said. 'These are some of the designs I could do for you.'

Ah. Joanna picked up one of the brochures. The Rosebud Room, so named because of the all-inclusive romantic touches. Stained-glass rosebuds, pink-stained wood, Venetian blinds of shell pink. What would Harriet say? She didn't want to think about it. 'We'll let you know,' she said.

'Great.' Craig took another bite of cake. Didn't he have another job to get to? Joanna checked her watch again. Where was Harriet? And more to the point, what would she say when she got home and heard about this? If Rosebud man was still here when she got back, she'd go ballistic.

Her mother had put the kettle on for more tea and she was humming. It sounded suspiciously like 'Gimme Gimme Gimme a Man After Midnight'.

Oh, God, thought Joanna. She'd better get him out of here. Fast.

266

CHAPTER 35

Harriet

Dorset

That evening found Harriet striding down East Street, her hair blowing in the wind. It was dark already but the sky was clear and a half-moon glimmered in the indigo sky. Joanna was about to head off to Prague, so Harriet had decided to take the opportunity to meet her next contender. Third time lucky . . . And she'd decided already that this would be her last. The dating site had been fun, it had taken her out of what she thought of as her rather humdrum existence for a while, it had made her think that she could escape, that she could be someone else. But . . .

She pulled her bag higher onto her shoulder. It was hardly even a bag; just a small black leather purse with a thin shoulder strap. She'd bought it for herself yesterday and felt guilty ever since. She had only ever owned cavernous, practical, no-nonsense bags that would comfortably hold half a kilo of potatoes, a cauliflower and a dozen eggs as well as her purse and a packet of tissues. This black leather purse spoke of a different life. And although she was meant to be browsing for Christmas presents, it had seemed to call out to her. It was the kind of purse that Joanna would own – and it was half price, she saw, as she checked the tag. Cavernous bags were hardly suitable for evening wear. Whereas this . . .

She couldn't escape her life – she had made a promise to her father and she would never break it. But that didn't mean that nothing could change. She touched the purse lightly with her fingertips. It was smooth, soft and blissfully impractical. It was a treat, it made her feel different. Elegant. *The new me*, she thought, with a slight swing of the hips.

She checked her watch. It was seven thirty-two p.m. precisely. She stopped to glance in an estate agents' window, wondered, as she kept doing these days, if Joanna would end up staying in West Dorset. She wouldn't be surprised – and something inside her felt glad. It had been a long time since they were close, but although her sister could still be profoundly irritating, Harriet now realised, after her break-up with Martin, that Joanna's life wasn't perfect either, that she too had her problems, her issues, her fallibilities.

And Joanna had certainly been fallible this afternoon when she'd been so busy looking at old family photographs that she'd entirely failed to notice another tradesman had come to call. Harriet shook her head in despair. She'd only found out about this because she'd slipped into her mother's room earlier this evening to fetch her cardigan and noticed the bed was covered with shiny brochures. Where had they sprung from? She picked one of them up. *The Gardenia Conservatory. Make every day a hothouse.* 'Brimming hellfire,' she'd muttered.

Joanna had come out of her bedroom, looked in and said,

'What's up, Het?' She'd hovered in the doorway – probably poised to make a quick getaway.

'Have you seen these?' Harriet picked up another. 'The Tulip Temple?' *Ye Gods* . . .

Joanna had smiled uncertainly. 'It doesn't hurt to dream,' she said. 'Does it?'

Harriet shook her head. She was entirely missing the point. 'But how did they get here?' she asked. 'Who brought them?' And had Mother committed them to buying a conservatory and simply failed to mention it?

Joanna hesitated. 'There was a builder here this afternoon. But don't worry, I got rid of him.'

Harriet waited.

'Well, to be honest, Het, he was here for a while. I didn't realise who it was downstairs. I assumed it was Owen or someone from the village.'

And she didn't think to check? Harriet clicked her tongue. 'And how exactly did Mother get in touch with a builder?' She felt as if she was fighting a losing battle.

'Ah.' Joanna looked a shade guilty. And took a step back onto the landing. 'That could have been my fault too, I'm afraid.'

'You didn't let her use the phone?'

Joanna grimaced. 'I taught her how to use email.'

'You . . . ?' Words failed her.

'She was interested in my work. She seemed to be enjoying learning about new technology. I wanted to give her a hobby, like we discussed – you know . . .' Already, Joanna was halfway across the landing. 'I didn't really think,' she amended.

No. That was her problem. She never thought. And Mother, it seemed, had turned into someone who was as devious as they came.

'I'm sorry, Het.' She was halfway down the stairs now. 'But maybe she found the builder online.'

'Online . . .' Her mother now had access to every tradesman in the land — virtually. It was hopeless, wasn't it? Why did Harriet bother? She had absolutely no control over this household.

She sighed. And she'd had the dream again last night. *Go back to sleep, little one. By the morning it will have flown away.* Memories like gossamer. Uncatchable. It had been as unsettling as ever.

Seven thirty-five. Harriet didn't want to be early for her date — it was against the rules. She dawdled past the charity shop, pretending an interest in a red teapot complete with turquoise cosy that stood in the window like a reminder of times gone by.

Come to mine, Scott had written in his email. *We can chill out there in comfort.*

Mine . . . It sounded special. In fact, everything about him sounded special.

But Harriet was a realist and it was far too risky to go somewhere private when you didn't know someone from Adam or Jack the Ripper. She thought of her prowler — she hadn't seen him since the binoculars episode, but no doubt he wasn't far away. And she knew Scott even less well than other correspondents from Someone Somewhere. They had only been emailing for a few days. Even meeting, at this stage, was rash. But there was something about this man that seemed different — in a good way.

So . . .

I like comfort, she had written back to him, adding (firmly), *but for a first date I think we should meet somewhere more public.*

It was daring enough to be meeting him in the dark rather

270

than in broad daylight. For heaven's sake. She didn't want to commit dating suicide.

Right, he wrote back. *Cool*.

Indeed.

He had suggested the Vassar Bar at the top of the Bull Hotel. *Go through the ballroom. You can't miss it*.

Harriet walked on. There were still plenty of people wandering up and down the street, going into the pubs, a large group heading into the Thai restaurant over the road. She took a deep breath and entered the Bull Hotel. She checked her watch once more. Seven-forty. Perfect.

She climbed the stairs and walked through the empty ballroom. There was only one man in the bar, so it had to be him. He stood up.

Harriet gulped. Even in the dim light – there was a huge central pear-drop chandelier but it must be on a dimmer switch as it barely shimmered – she could tell that he was absolutely gorgeous. He was tall, lean and rangy. He had long hair tied back in a ponytail – oh, God, just like one of the farm workers they'd had when Harriet was sixteen. Jamie. Harriet shivered at the memory of his brown back and frayed denim jeans. Scott was wearing denim jeans too. And a white linen shirt.

'Hi,' he said in a low and husky voice.

'Hi.' Harriet wondered if she was still breathing.

'Good to meet you, Harriet.' He had restful eyes (blue, she decided, though she couldn't really see in this light) and a welcoming smile.

'And you.' Harriet looked around the small, square room. 'What an amazing place.' She had to distract herself, stop herself from drooling over this apparition. The Vassar Bar had gold brocade curtains at the windows and Persian rugs

271

on the wooden floor. The furniture was antique and ornate, candles burnt on the pitted wooden tables casting a flickering light, and something soulful and jazzy was playing softly in the background. There was a piano in the corner and the bar was long and smooth polished mahogany, backed by stacks of gleaming glasses and bottles of spirits and liqueurs of all shapes and sizes.

'Yeah.' Scott motioned for her to sit down next to him on the red leather Chesterfield in the centre of the room.

Harriet inched her way past the wooden table. How old was he? No more than forty, surely, although fine laughter lines were etched into the soft skin around his eyes. Good sense of humour then, she thought. And maybe a strand or two of distinguished grey in the hair?

'However did you find it?' She had lived all her life a few miles up the road and she hadn't known the bar even existed. Not that she came to the Bull very often – hardly ever, in fact. How would she have the time?

They spent the next hour or so chatting, although it could have been longer, Harriet was so enamoured she even forgot to look at her watch. Anyway, she didn't need to check the time, she had the whole evening off; Owen and Joanna were with Mother (Owen had pretty much jumped at the chance, it had to be said). Harriet was free . . . She looked deep into Scott's eyes. And what a way to enjoy her liberty.

Scott had never been married, he told her, though there had been a few 'special ladies' in his life – which was hardly surprising. Harriet watched him as he sauntered up to the bar, oozing confidence, their two wine glasses held loosely by the stems in one hand.

'I just haven't met the right person,' he said, putting another glass of chilled white wine in front of her. 'I guess I'm too much of a romantic at heart.'

'Me too,' Harriet breathed, although this was a relatively new addition to her persona – it had made a brief appearance in the days of Jamie's supple brown back and then stayed dormant until she walked into the Vassar Bar tonight.

'Truth is, I'm looking for a princess,' he said, leaning closer.

My God, Harriet thought. That was upping the ante. She wasn't sure she would ever be princess material. She eyed the wine warily. She'd had one glass already, and the glasses were so big that each one was practically a jugful.

'Someone to look up to and adore.'

'Really?' Her voice was weak.

'Everyone's so cynical these days.' He twirled the stem of his glass.

She stared, half hypnotised by his long brown fingers, by the pale yellow liquid splashing gently against the sides of the wine glass. 'I suppose they are,' she agreed. And after all, in this world, who could blame them?

'But I can tell you're not cynical in the least,' he assured her.

'Me?' She laughed as if the idea was the funniest thing she'd ever heard.

Scott put his wine down with some force. Harriet felt the vibration. 'Cards on the table,' he said.

'Yes?' Harriet held her breath.

'I'm looking for someone who wants to dream the dream with me,' he said.

'The dream?' She had almost forgotten how to dream. She thought of what Joanna had said about their mother's dreams – Harriet had never seen them as dreams before, never thought about it that way. Of course, there was the dream that she kept having at night – not a nightmare, because her father was in it, so it could never be that. But other dreams . . . She wasn't sure if she had ever even had them. There had only ever been life on the farm, looking after everything, and then the promise she'd made to her father – to keep it all going, to watch over Mother, to be strong. She sighed.

'Someone to love.'

Harriet closed her eyes. Any moment he might propose.

'Is it too much to ask?' he demanded.

I could do it, Harriet wanted to shriek. *I could be that princess, I could live that dream.* But she managed to hold back somehow. Instead, she opened her eyes and sipped her wine. 'Are you a poet?' she asked. 'I write myself occasionally.' Shopping lists mainly, but that was beside the point. Joanna had proved that there was a writing gene in the family and Harriet was damned sure she could do it too – if she only had the time.

'God, you're a perceptive woman.' Scott clasped her hand and Harriet almost passed out in excitement. 'I write lyrics mostly. And I play the guitar, of course.'

Of course . . . Harriet had always wanted to go out with a musician. They would be good at so many things, she felt – understanding, sympathy, rhythm.

'In fact, I got shortlisted for Song for Europe once,' he said modestly.

'Wow.'

'And I sent some stuff to Cat Stevens.'

'Did he—?'

'No, he sent it back. But someone who worked for him said he liked it.'

'Teaser and the Firecat,' she murmured.

'Hmm.'

They seemed to be on the same wavelength and he had started to stroke the base of her thumb absently. Harriet worried that if he didn't stop soon, she was likely to reciprocate by ripping open his shirt.

She just smiled when he went up to the bar to order another two glasses.

'What about you?' he asked on his return.

'Pardon?' Harriet's eyes, which had been half closed in ecstasy, jerked open.

'Have you had much stuff published?'

'Oh, the odd thing here and there.' She waved her hand airily. 'But mostly I write for my own pleasure.'

He nodded appreciatively. 'It's a mistake to allow commercial considerations to intrude on the path of one's vital creativity,' he said. 'Go with the creative flow, that's what I say.'

Harriet couldn't agree more.

And so, half an hour later, when he suggested *coming back to mine* for the second time in their brief acquaintance, she didn't say no. But, 'I must use the . . .' She struggled to her feet, which wasn't easy because of the low height of the Chesterfield, the total state of relaxation and desire that had swept over her and the three large glasses of wine she'd consumed.

The Ladies' Powder Room, as it was called, increased her feeling of the surreal. Harriet stepped back into the past once more, into a land of pink flocked wallpaper, gilt mirrors, Victorian washbasins and scented hand towels. She examined her face in the mirror, dusted more powder on the shiny bits and reapplied Joanna's lipstick. She'd wanted her life to change, hadn't she?

'So?' he asked her when she returned. He put a hand on her

shoulder and the heat of his palm seemed to burn through her thin blouse.

Harriet tried to look casual as though she did this — what? what? — every day of the week. 'The night is yet young,' she said, smothering a giggle.

Scott took her hand. 'You're so right,' he said.

And he led her out of the bar, through the ballroom with the white balustrade and orchestra gallery, and the sash windows of bevelled glass that reached from floor to ceiling. Down the stairs and into the dark, velvet night.

CHAPTER 36

Nicholas

Cornwall

As they strolled along the dunes – almost purple in the dusk of the November afternoon – the sea dark and heavy below them, at last Nicholas began to relax. He had been delighted to hear that Celie was coming for the weekend and had spent all morning since her hurried phone call dusting and vacuuming the cottage until it glowed with the unexpected attention. He wanted everything to be perfect for Celie, wanted to give her every reason he could to visit – often. And to know how much he valued these visits. And her.

He'd even whizzed down to the flower shop to buy sweetly perfumed cream stocks for the guest bedroom and had laid out fresh towels on the bed and soap in the little white washbasin. Rachel would be amazed. Nicholas was amazed at himself.

He tucked Celie's hand into the crook of his arm. The grass was sparse and spiky at this time of year. They were walking past the wetlands and towards the lighthouse, out in the distance, on Godrevy Island. They'd walked here many a time in Celie's childhood. Usually in spring, when the purple thrift grew dense on the cliff, or in summer when the seals could be spotted basking in the bay. Though for Nicholas, Godrevy was special at any time of year.

They paused for a moment. The sun was setting over the sea – a golden-red orb, the sky around it blushed pink and pale blue. Nicholas chuckled.

'What?' She smiled at him.

'Do you remember? That photo we took here?' Rachel and Celie, arms encircled, as though they were cradling the setting sun.

'Yeah.' She laughed. Shot him a bit of a look, though. A sort of *stop living in the past* look. He wasn't. But as you grew older you got a lot of pleasure out of memories.

They walked on, looking down at the black rocks and pale gold sand below. The sharp wind was whipping the tide, sending the spume flying. 'So, how's it going in London?' Nicholas asked her. She'd recently started a new PA job and seemed brighter and happier. In fact, she was positively flushed with it. It couldn't be just the job. It must be love.

Yes, and he remembered that feeling too . . .

She squeezed his arm. 'Work's fine, although one of the project managers is a bit of a pain. He took me out for breakfast last week and . . .'

He let her talk, loving to hear about her new life, enjoying the sound of her voice, her enthusiasm as they climbed up the dunes and along the boardwalk past the clumps of spiny gorse. There weren't many people around today and Nicholas preferred it like that. Cornwall was always more satisfying when

278

the visitors went home, when the weather defeated all but the most hardy, when the place was as bleak as it should be.

Celie paused, as if waiting for him to say something.

'And how's Tom?' he asked. He hadn't quite decided yet, about Tom.

'He's good,' Celie said, and her voice softened, her gaze moving out past the heaving sea into the winter distance of clouds and approaching darkness.

Celie, he realised, had decided about Tom. Celie, for the first time in her life, was serious about a boyfriend. Very serious. He felt a faint sense of loss, of something slipping away. She was still so young.

Up on this cliff the grass was greener and the lighthouse closer, a white beacon on the black rocks of the island. The path was narrower here and they moved into single file. But it was getting chilly. Nicholas began to walk more briskly and felt Celie's steps quicken to match his own. They probably wouldn't walk as far as the lighthouse, he reckoned. As it was, they'd be retracing their steps in the dark, and although he had his torch with him, it would be cold, maybe too cold for Celie, in her thin coat, which was more fashion statement than protection from the elements.

He stuck his hands in the pockets of his warm quilted jacket, tried to make his voice more jolly. Who wanted to visit a grumpy old misery? No way would he become that man. 'I'll come and see you,' he said. 'Take you out to dinner. My treat.' After all, he had a place in London, he just didn't stay there very often. And when he did, he was usually headed for Gatwick or Heathrow the following day.

'That would be nice.' He heard her guarded tone, half lost in the wind. And realised he hadn't encouraged the relationship between Celie and Tom, hadn't welcomed him, hadn't taken much trouble to include him or get to know what made him tick. Perhaps all fathers were the same, he thought. Anxious, possessive, overprotective.

'And you, Dad?' Her voice changed. 'How are you doing?'

'Oh, fine, fine.'

She sighed. 'I mean, really.'

They were higher up now, the cliff steeper, the grass slippy with moisture, the lighthouse seeming to beckon them on.

Sometimes he wondered if Celie really wanted him to be fine. Or if she wanted to despair of him, to say to Tom, *Oh, Dad's lovely, but he's so hopeless. And he'll never get over losing Mum.* But to be fair to Celie, maybe all she wanted was an honest answer.

Nicholas laughed. 'I'm *really* fine,' he said. And it was almost true. He certainly felt more at peace with himself than he had for a while. 'I'm off to Portugal next week. Giuseppe wants to find a new outlet in Lisbon.'

'Right. That sounds great, Dad.'

'Yeah.' Nicholas was really looking forward to it. Because he had a purpose. Not only was he going there to check out the possible traders who might be interested in Insight Jewellery, but he was planning to go on Joanna Shepherd's Lisbon bridge walk. God knows what he was expecting. He would have written back to her by now if it hadn't been for Celie's visit. But he'd do so very soon. He knew what he wanted to say to her – her words about distance had struck a chord. He wanted, for some reason, to tell her about Celie too. And he was eagerly anticipating walk number two.

The path was wider now, the grass grazed short, the lighthouse closer still, the white waves clustering around the rocks

280

at its base. But the afternoon was dimming. 'Shall we head back?' he suggested to Celie. He had a chicken casserole in the oven; he'd light an open fire and some candles. He and Celie would settle down, and things . . . No, of course they wouldn't be as they'd been before. But they would be good, he told himself.

'OK.' She prodded him affectionately. 'But don't change the subject. Are you doing all right on your own? Are you lonely? Have you joined any clubs or anything?'

Nicholas laughed. What did she want him to do – enrol in a ramblers' society or a bridge four? Take up bowling or Pilates? 'You worry too much, my girl.'

'Dad . . .'

'Look.' He took a deep breath. The air was cold on his face. 'You know how devastated I was when your mother left . . .' But sometime after she left, sometime after those tacky one-night stands, that overwhelming sense of loss . . . he had realised that what he missed was not Rachel at all.

Nicholas shook his head and took Celie's arm again as they turned around. 'But that was then,' he said.

No. He missed himself – just like he'd told Joanna Shepherd. But what he also missed was family. It was the sense of belonging to a unit – a damaged unit possibly, but still a unit. He, Rachel and Celie were the Tresillion family. They might argue, or one of them go away without the others, but each of them always returned to the family home. It was a stronghold. When Celie and then Rachel left, Nicholas's sense of family had left with them. He became isolated somehow. That was what had been the hardest, he supposed. Losing his security. His base.

He had tried to explain this in his email to Joanna when he'd

281

told her about losing his role, sensing that she would understand. And now, he tried to explain it to Celie too.

She listened in silence as they trudged back along the cliff, buffeted by the wind, the growing darkness giving his words some surreal quality.

'I know what you mean,' she said at last, not denying it, as he had almost hoped she would. 'The members of the family are all still there. And I know you and Mum both love me. But it's not the same.'

He nodded, not trusting himself to speak. They were back on the purple-brown sand dunes now, the sun had gone down and the sky was edging into night-time.

He listened to the waves as they broke and then drew back from the shore. A long, low *crassshhh* . . . He loved the combination of sea and darkness. It was magical. He put his arm around Celie's shoulders. In that moment he felt as close to her as he ever had. And what really mattered, he knew, was that he hadn't lost her.

They walked down the dunes onto the path, Nicholas shining his torch ahead of them. The light flickered over the grass. He could feel the hesitation.

'I expect you're wondering, why the visit out of the blue?' Celie asked after a few moments.

'Well . . .' He'd kind of assumed she just wanted to see him.

'I wasn't sure how you'd react.' She looked embarrassed, studying first her fingernails, then looking across at him – intently – as they walked towards the cottage. 'And I didn't want to tell you on the phone.'

'How I'd react to what?' His stomach curled. What was the worst thing? She was emigrating to Australia or Thailand? She'd been diagnosed with some dreadful disease? *Jesus* . . .

'I'm pregnant,' she said. She touched her stomach, lightly, with her free hand.

Nicholas stopped walking. 'Pregnant?'

'Yeah.'

What was he supposed to say? Ask her how long? If it was planned? If she was glad?

But he knew she was glad. It was written all over her. She was waiting and it was one of those important moments that he mustn't mess up. He opened his arms and pulled her into a hug.

Celie was glad. So how could he not feel the same?

CHAPTER 37

Harriet

Dorset

Harriet tried to conceal her shock. 'When you said, *come round to mine,*' she said, 'I had no idea . . .'

'I've never been into material things,' said Scott. 'I'm more of a free spirit, an easy come, easy go kind of a guy.' He pulled a key from the pocket of his jeans and unlocked the door.

'Yes, I think I'm beginning to understand.' And she was. It was like a new dawning. A thunderbolt of empathy and a realisation of what she could do. With Scott.

She followed him up the step and into the camper van. She could travel, for a start. Anywhere. Just like Joanna. She was conscious of a sudden dart of loss. She had so rarely been away from West Dorset and the place was undeniably woven into her veins. And then there was her mother – could she leave her? What about the promise she'd made to Father? But Scott turned around to flash her that smile of his and all these thoughts took wings and flew. Perhaps, after all these years, it was Joanna's time to look after Mother.

Scott flicked a switch and a small spotlight was illuminated above her head.

'You've got electricity then,' she said admiringly. 'And everything.'

'Leisure battery.' He bent to light a compact gas fire tucked into the back wall. 'And a gas bottle, of course.'

'Of course.' It all looked very ingenious.

'But mostly I use candles.' He started lighting them one by one, and gradually it came to life. His home. The sweet little gas cooker, the tiny sink, the fridge, the strip of red carpet. And the bed. Harriet gulped. The bed dominated everything. It was covered with a purple tie-dye bedspread and strewn with embroidered Indian cushions – in rich reds and aubergines, bright pinks and ochres.

'It's absolutely charming,' she said. And she meant it. It was such a contrast to the tatty, rambling and run-down Mulberry Farm Cottage. The simplicity of Scott's camper van almost made her ashamed. This was how people should live – in an ideal world. No one needed so much *stuff*.

Scott lit another candle and the scent of incense rose in the air, smoky and sweet.

'Sit down, Harriet,' he said.

She looked around, but there wasn't much choice. She perched gingerly on the edge of the bed. Did he keep it made up (which wouldn't leave much room for manoeuvre in the kitchen space) or had he made the bed up before he came out tonight, fully intending to invite her back here to, to . . . Here her imagination faltered.

'I meditated on your email,' he said. He got a bottle out of the fridge and splashed wine into two glasses.

'No, really,' Harriet said. She shouldn't have any more. Her head was already spinning. She'd have to take a taxi home and she certainly couldn't afford that. Home. Goodness. Home seemed a long, long way away.

'Oh, but I did,' he said, misunderstanding her. 'Technology and spirituality can complement one another beautifully. Like earth and water.' He passed her a glass.

'Yes.' She took it. There was nowhere to put it down so she had a sip or two, just to increase her confidence levels.

'I'm Pisces,' he said. 'The dreamer. And I'm guessing that you . . . ?'

'Taurus.' She didn't want him to get it wrong. 'The bull.'

'Earth and water,' he said. 'There you go.'

Harriet smiled and tried to look as if she understood what he was talking about.

'Earthy.' He regarded her seriously. 'Astute . . . intuitive . . . sensual . . .'

Was she? Harriet adopted an expression that she hoped, somehow, would make her look all four.

Scott flicked a switch and the sound of Indian music filled the camper van and Harriet's ears; a sitar strumming her soul, it felt like.

She exhaled and leant back a little on the bed. It was only inches, but for Harriet it was a mammoth journey. 'How long have you been living here?' she asked him. It was only a car park by the football ground, but it was at least next to the river and only a short walk from the town centre. She tried not to think like an estate agent. The point was that tomorrow, the camper van could be in Cornwall or France . . . or almost anywhere.

'I've been travelling around Somerset and Dorset since Glastonbury,' he said.

Glastonbury – yes, she should have guessed. Harriet wanted to ask him how long he would be staying for, but that sounded needy. She compromised on, 'You travel around a lot then?'

'When I can.' He gazed into her eyes. 'But I believe that the essential journey occurs within.'

Harriet nodded. 'I so agree,' she said. What would Joanna say if she could hear her now? *I so agree, bollocks* . . .

Scott plumped up some cushions and placed them behind her. 'Relax,' he said. 'Would you like me to massage your feet?'

'Er, all right.' Harriet needed something – she was a bag of nerves.

He scooped her legs onto the bed and slipped off the slightly too-small black boots she'd borrowed from Joanna's wardrobe. Harriet hoped they hadn't made her feet sweat. He peeled off her socks one by one without comment. The touch of his hands was perfect. Not too hard, not too soft. He began to rub the balls of each foot. Slowly. Hypnotically. Mmm. She yawned. It was getting harder and harder to remember the all-important first-date questions. He paused to relieve her of her glass, putting it down on a shelf behind him.

'I don't suppose you, er, work, do you, Scott?' she asked.

'When I have to,' he replied. He gave her an enigmatic look. 'Mine is an alternative lifestyle,' he elaborated. 'It wouldn't suit Mr Average.'

No, and he certainly wasn't that. He was about as average as a duck-billed platypus. 'And when you *do* work . . . ?' Harriet wasn't sure why she was even pursuing this subject. The truth was that she wanted to stop thinking. She wanted to lie back and be healed by his touch. She wanted to close her eyes and be transported to heaven. She wanted . . . But she *couldn't* stop thinking. It was ingrained in her psyche – it had been forever. *Thanks, Father*, she thought. 'What do you do?'

'I don't do anything in particular.' He was working on her left ankle. It would never be the same again. 'I just am.'

'Yes, but when—'

'Shh.' His fingers were on her lips now. He was stroking her cheek, her hair. 'It doesn't matter. It's not important.'

'It doesn't matter,' Harriet murmured. What blissful words. With the wine and the music and the candlelight, not to mention the exquisite massage, the tension was at last seeping out of her, bit by bit. 'It's not important.'

Scott was undoing the buttons of her blouse. *It doesn't matter*.

'Nothing matters,' he said. 'Apart from you and me and the moment.'

'The moment.' Why was she repeating everything he said? Didn't she have a mind of her own? Harriet wondered if she was drunk. Not with the wine, but with the sensuality of it all. She had always worried about tomorrow. And this afternoon, and the next hour, minute, second . . . She had never, she realised, lived for the moment.

'In some ways,' Scott was murmuring, as his fingers parted the thin fabric of her blouse and drew it gently from her shoulders. 'You are an innocent woman, Harriet.'

'Oh, I am,' she breathed. Would he guess that she was a virgin? Would it put him off or make him want her more? She couldn't imagine. It was something that she had been embarrassed about for so long. Who was a virgin at thirty-nine years old, for heaven's sake? And she still didn't know how it had happened – or hadn't happened, in her case.

'And I love that about you.' He turned his attention to her breasts. Harriet gasped.

'Really?' She could hardly speak. What had she been missing all these years? Quite a lot, evidently.

'You're beautiful,' he said, sliding a hand under her skirt. 'So, so beautiful.'

And Harriet let out a small sigh of ecstasy. Because this was all so wonderful. And because no one had ever, ever said that to her before . . .

CHAPTER 38

Joanna

Dorset

Joanna folded her black cashmere sweater and added it to the clothes on the bed. It would be cold in Prague. She glanced out of the bedroom window at the cool grey November sky and down at Harriet, who was wandering across the farmyard with a trug of vegetables in her arms. She had a very strange expression on her face – Joanna would have called it dreamy if it had been anyone but Harriet. So, what had happened last night? she wondered.

It was cold here too. The wood-burning stove kept the cottage cosy, but draughts still seemed to seep through the splintered old sash windows and sneak in under warped wooden doors. So much for character . . . How much longer could the place last without a major overhaul and money? Or should Mother and Harriet consider selling up and downsizing?

Joanna watched her sister continuing to waft across the farmyard and chuckled to herself. Harriet had got in very late last night, which was certainly out of character, and she had been very cheerful over breakfast, which was even more so.

'Are you quite all right, dear?' Mother had asked her older daughter when Harriet enquired as to whether anyone would like more toast.

And, 'Yes, thank you, Mother,' Harriet had sweetly replied, which was more unlike her than ever.

'So, where's the pick-up truck?' Joanna had asked her sister, having observed that something was missing from the farmyard.

'Ah.' Harriet smiled. 'I had a drink or two so I had to leave it in the car park in Bridport.'

Joanna raised an eyebrow. *Curiouser and curiouser.*

Harriet got to her feet. 'I'll nip over now and ask Owen if he can give me a lift in to get it,' she said.

Joanna and her mother watched her go.

'She's still got her slippers on,' Mother said after a couple of minutes had passed.

Joanna chuckled. It was too late to go after her. It must have been some hot date. And she might have told Joanna about it too if she hadn't still been annoyed about the builder and the conservatories and the fact that Joanna had foolishly introduced their mother to the world online.

Joanna unzipped her orange suitcase. She was getting rather adept at packing light – and living light, come to that. Since coming to Dorset, she had bought a few clothes, but mostly found it surprisingly liberating that her Crouch End wardrobe had shrunk so drastically. And when she went away, all she needed was one small case that she could lift easily and a foldaway bag that converted into a rucksack for her laptop, books, papers and maps.

Martin had sent her a cool message this morning that was short and to the point.

The house is on the market.

Fine, she had texted back to him.

In many ways it would be a relief to live in her own place again. She was enjoying this time at home and she was getting on better with her sister certainly, but Harriet's moods were still unreliable. Just as Joanna climbed another ladder and imagined she was getting close, she did something foolish like teaching Mother to use the Internet, which annoyed Harriet and sent Joanna slithering down the big snake and back to square one.

She took some clean jeans from the drawer. Her heart was leaning towards coming back to live in the West Country. She'd enjoyed London while she was living there, but now it felt like part of her past, not part of her future. And she was free. She could write the column from anywhere; write all her stuff from anywhere.

Joanna placed Emmy's letter from Prague carefully into the case. Although she had broached the subject of Emmy's letters with Harriet and their mother, she still hadn't told anyone about her distinct sense of following in Emmy's footsteps. Doubtless, they'd think it was bonkers. Neither had she told anyone about her new correspondent, Nicholas Tresillion. Joanna sat down on the bed for a moment to reread his latest email, still open on her laptop.

Dear Joanna, he had written.

I know what you mean about 'distance' and 'growing apart'. As for me, I'm afraid to say that I hardly noticed our growing apart — I must have been living life encased in some sort of fantasy bubble. Until it burst, that is.

Joanna was thoughtful. She could hear the sadness behind his words. *Fantasy bubble . . .* He was putting on a brave face, but he must have been devastated if he'd truly had no idea.

So, what did you decide about your marriage in Venice, may I ask?

She was surprised he hadn't guessed.

I didn't make any decisions, I'm afraid — the decision was thrust upon me. Other than that, yes, perhaps we are leading parallel lives!

'Perhaps we are, though,' she murmured. Anything seemed possible.

What about your family, Joanna?

She smiled. How long did he have?

You and I have entered quite an intense correspondence! (I always wanted a pen pal, by the way). And without the small talk beforehand where we usually find out the details of other people's lives. That golden ribbon has a lot to answer for . . . We've bypassed the surface stuff. Not that I'm complaining — I never was one for surface stuff.

'Me neither,' she murmured.

Do we both have failed marriages behind us? I suspect so.

Ah, so he had realised.

I have a daughter, Celie, whose presence reminds me of the good that came out of it. And I just heard that I'm going to be a grandfather — at forty-three.

Heavens, he must have married young, and his daughter couldn't be much more than a teenager either, thought Joanna.

And to end on another positive note, don't you think that although it can turn out to be frail and fallible, love is also a wonderful thing?

Did she? That was a good question.

I'm looking forward to hearing about Lisbon. I'm going there myself soon, would you believe?

Joanna narrowed her eyes at this. Another coincidence? It seemed so.

293

So, if it's OK by you, I'll look out for that bridge walk of yours while I'm there . . .

He was going to Lisbon. She shivered — and not because of the draught from the window this time. He'd made it sound plausible enough and it was obvious that he travelled around Europe a fair bit. Even so . . .

She added a pair of soft travel slippers to the case — she liked to be comfortable when she was writing, and she had visions of herself padding round the hotel room drinking something hot, spicy and alcoholic, whilst thinking creative thoughts.

Why shouldn't Nicholas Tresillion go to Lisbon? Plenty of people went there all the time. That was why Toby had been so keen on her covering it in the first place. She chose another sweater from the small selection she'd brought with her from Crouch End — a cream cowl neck this time, to go with her chocolate-brown jeans.

She'd be in Prague for several days, which should give her plenty of time to sort out the walk and see some more of the city too. Architecturally, it was supposed to be interesting (though she was aware it had also become a venue for hen and stag weekends) so she might as well take full advantage of the trip.

Nicholas Tresillion certainly didn't come across as a pest. Just a nice sort of man. He seemed genuine, intelligent, sensitive. Although all this was surely too good to be true . . . He'd been through some similar experiences to herself — though he wasn't the only one. And that wasn't all. She smoothed the cowl neck with the palm of her hand, thought once again of what they had both seen in Venice. But what could you tell from an email?

Socks. She stuffed them into the heels of her shoes. Only one pair of boots — the comfortable ones — and she'd be wearing

294

those to the airport. She squeezed her underthings into the corners of the case. Nicholas Tresillion's emails had made her think. He had already mentioned what he'd lost – his role in his family, a big part of himself. And he had said that he had rediscovered who he was, after living in that fantasy bubble.

Joanna too was experiencing a sense of rediscovery. She looked down at the case on the bed. She was rediscovering her freedom, how much satisfaction she could get from being in control of her own life.

What would Nicholas Tresillion see in Lisbon?

Joanna wanted to find out. She opened her laptop.

Dear Nicholas, she wrote.

It's funny you should say that about love. When I was in Lisbon I was thinking about it a lot . . . .

She finished the email and pressed 'send'. She would know soon enough.

There wasn't much space left in her case. She had found a hotel online that was – amazingly – on the pier of the Charles Bridge itself, and she'd asked for a room with a view. She didn't want a long trek into the city centre before she even started researching and planning the walk. She wanted to be there, in the heart of it all, soaking up the mediaeval atmosphere. And she was fizzing with the anticipation of seeing Emmy's third bridge.

Joanna zipped up the case, straightened, and looked across at the painting of Accademia on her bedroom wall. *From Venice with love*, she thought. Where was Emmy's painting of the Charles Bridge? How she would love to know. *Damn it*. She sat on the bed, suddenly swamped with frustration. How she would love to know so many things about this ancestor of hers who was proving so elusive. Joanna simply didn't have enough information to go on. And if she couldn't find out who Emmy was, then how could Joanna find out why she had become so important to her?

She pulled her handwritten copy of the family tree – such as it was – out of the Emmy folder, checked it against the dates on the letters . . . May 1913. June, July . . . She read the names once again. Mary, Elizabeth, George. She didn't see how . . . Could the letters have been written by someone in the next generation up? But that would make her even older, that would make her not the Emmy Joanna had come to know at all. She would guess from the tone of her letters that Emmy was abroad for the first time, writing excitedly to her – older? – lover who she missed more than life itself.

Then it hit her. Lover . . . not husband. Joanna stared into space. How could she have been so stupid? Of course, Emmy wasn't Edith or Mary or Elizabeth – because Emmy didn't live here in Mulberry Farm Cottage. She never had. She had sent the letters here, yes. But not because she lived here, rather because her lover lived here. God . . . *Her lover* . . .

It explained why there was only one painting here – she must have given it to Rufus as a present but kept the others, or sold them maybe. It explained why Emmy hated to be apart from him. Their relationship was not one of stability nor security – at least not when the letters had been written. They weren't married, but they were very definitely in love. It even explained why Emmy had referred to 'finding a way through the mire' and other comments that had made Joanna suspect their relationship might be more complex than she had at first assumed.

Joanna held the letters closer to her breast, sniffed the old, faintly musty scent of the browned, crinkled paper, tried to get her thoughts in order. It would be the person who had received the letters who would have them, to keep, to reread, to hide, not the person who had written them. So . . . She held them away from her once more. Rufus was not Emmy's husband, but her lover, her dearest, her heart's love. And . . . *Oh, my God.* Was Rufus a real name? A pet name? A nickname? Rufus could be anyone.

She looked around the room, her room. It had seen her through her childhood, her adolescence, and now her separation from Martin. And the Venetian bridge painting had always been here on the wall, so familiar that until she'd found the letters, she'd been almost blind to it. The signature on the painting . . . She moved closer. Well, it was definitely an S and then a long squiggle which was slashed across. After finding the letters, she'd assumed it was Emmy Shepherd. But she could see now that what she had thought was a ph was more likely to be a double l, and the first h might not be an h at all . . .

She sat down on the bed again. Rufus had lived here. And he could be older than Emmy – that would work. Once more, she scrutinised the family tree. Could Rufus have been William's father, her great-great-grandfather Edward, whose name had been on the census form as head of the household? Or would he have been too old for Emmy? Or could it have been an uncle perhaps? Or even her great-grandfather William himself? Had he once been in love with Emmy before he married the rather stern-looking Edith? It was possible. It was even possible, she supposed, that he'd met Emmy after his marriage to Edith. Edith, as Joanna had already observed, looked neither well nor happy. Whereas William . . . Joanna began to sift through the photos that Harriet had given her.

Rufus? Didn't that mean . . . ? She was almost certain . . .

She got to her feet, still holding the contents of the Emmy folder, returned to her laptop and looked it up. Rufus. *Latin. Meaning red-haired.* Joanna sat back in her chair. Yes. So . . . Emmy might have called him (whoever he was) Rufus, not because that was his given name, but because . . . he had red hair. She thought of the couple she'd seen under the mulberry tree in Lisbon. Emmy and Rufus – the man with red hair. It was mind-blowingly simple. And he had lived here. He . . . whoever he was.

She stared out of the window. The farmyard was empty now; Harriet was probably in the barn collecting eggs. Joanna traced a pattern on the window with her fingertip. She was no nearer to finding out who Emmy really was – her surname was indecipherable from the signature on the painting and all Joanna had discovered was that it probably wasn't Shepherd. Which meant, unless she had gone on to marry a Shepherd – if Rufus even was a Shepherd – that Emmy wasn't an ancestor of Joanna's at all.

She sighed. It was a disappointment. And she had felt so close to Emmy. But was Rufus an ancestor? This was more than possible, given her new theory. Joanna had all the old photographs that might give her a clue as to Rufus's identity, but how could she recognise red hair from a faded sepia photo? As for the red-headed man she'd seen under the mulberry tree in Lisbon, she hadn't seen his face clearly enough, his features had been little more than a blur.

Still . . . Joanna smiled. She felt more confident than before. She was making decisions. She was on her way to Prague. And things were beginning to fall into place: in this story from the past that had drawn her in; maybe in her own life too.

CHAPTER 39

Nicholas

Lisbon

Nicholas was enjoying Lisbon. And now he had that sense of achievement – the jewellery would be selling in a classy outlet near the Bairro Alto, Giuseppe would be more than pleased – combined with the knowledge that he had the rest of the day to himself. It wasn't hard to decide what to do with it.

He went straight to the local tourist information bureau, nerves chasing their own tails in his stomach. What if her brochure wasn't there? What if they hadn't heard of it? What if it had sold out? And why would he mind so much?

But it was OK. He spotted it straightaway. They'd given it a little show card, and as well as the English version there were translations in Spanish, Portuguese and German. He felt ridiculously pleased for Joanna Shepherd and hoped she'd been well paid for the commission.

On the back was the same photo of the author – strangely familiar, wistful and appealing. Swiftly, Nicholas flipped to the beginning, glanced at the map provided. *We start*, she had written, *at the ancient aqueduct*. As if he hadn't known already . . . *Ancient aqueduct*, he thought, *here I come*.

By the time he arrived at Praça das Amoreiras almost an hour later, Nicholas was immersed in the walk, dipping into his surroundings and Joanna Shepherd's descriptions with equal enthusiasm. He appreciated her mixing of the old and the new sights along the way; in the brochure – and now in his camera – there were some great photos of crumbling villas decorated with the old blue *azulejo* tiles, and the smoky-glass modern office blocks parked right next to them. A sense of exploration – her sense of exploration – seemed to seep through the pages of the brochure into Nicholas's mind. Discovery, excitement, reflection . . . This woman knew how to create an atmosphere.

He got the impression that Joanna was investing the mulberry trees with some significance. Nicholas considered. What did he know about mulberry trees? They bore fruit a bit like a loganberry? That didn't seem particularly earth-shattering or unusual. She didn't mention anything specific, but it was in the subtext on the page; she wrote almost reverentially about the trees that lined this street. *Humming with ancient wisdom* . . . Nicholas stared into the bare, crouching branches. Was he missing something here?

God . . . He came to an abrupt standstill. Slap bang in the middle of the road ahead of him was the Roman triumphal arch she called . . . – he checked the brochure – Arco das Amoreiras. He walked up to touch the old grey stone just as, no doubt, Joanna Shepherd had done before him. Now, this was ancient. How had she felt, he wondered, when she saw this in front of her?

It was often simpler, Nicholas found himself thinking, not to change things. You found a way of living, a pattern – or it found you – and you didn't question, you let life pass by, you assumed the role, just as he'd told Joanna in an earlier email. His life had been that way for a long time – certainly since Celie was born nineteen years ago, when he had slipped into the role of father and ended up embracing it wholeheartedly.

And then something might change the way you saw things. A certain birthday maybe? His fortieth three years ago had certainly felt like some sort of milestone at the time. Nicholas let his hand trail over the crumbling white stone. Your wife might leave you. And then you walked down a road in Lisbon and saw a Roman triumphal arch dating from circa 1750.

He took a left, as directed, and entered the Praça das Amoreiras. There had been bitter-sweet times when he'd unknotted that pattern. The sadness and relief of losing the old; the fear and excitement of the new . . .

All this had happened to Joanna too – she'd told him as much in her emails and he could read it here in the brochure too. He could feel the movement of it in the prose she used. He glanced down at the brochure in his hands – *plunge into the busy street, bite into a heavenly custard tart, wallow in the history* . . .

He looked around him. Yes, and dream in the Praça das Amoreiras. It was, as she had written, still and peaceful and grey.

He sat down where she had, opposite the tiny chapel that nestled between the arches of the aqueduct. What had she seen here and what did he expect to see? Nicholas flung the brochure down on the bench beside him. What was he even doing here, come to that?

His mobile went off, sharply, bringing him back to reality and the present, disturbing the spell.

Rachel. 'Hi.' He had to force himself not to sound resentful. It was typical of her to shatter an illusion without even being aware that she was doing it. And he didn't want to share this place with Rachel, he realised.

'Hello, Nick . . .' Swiftly, she came to the point of the call. 'Celie tells me she's talked to you.'

He tried not to feel sour at this. 'Yes.'

'You were nice to her, weren't you?'

For God's sake. 'She's my daughter. I love her. Of course, I was bloody nice to her.' What sort of a monster did she think he was, anyway?

'You see. That's exactly what I mean.'

Nicholas sighed. 'What?'

'I know you don't like Tom.'

He took a deep, calming breath. What had Celie said? 'Pregnancy doesn't have to mean marriage, Dad, we're not living in the Dark Ages.' No, and marriages didn't have to last forever.

'Rachel, I don't really know him. I hope that he'll look after her even when she doesn't deserve it, I hope he'll support her financially when and if she needs him to, I hope he'll be responsible and loyal and all the rest of it. But I don't *know*—'

'Oh, for goodness' sake.' Her exasperation flew down the phone at him. 'He's a nice boy from a nice family. They're having a child together. And Celie must take her chances in life like any other girl.'

'Well, yes, but she's still so young. I can't help worrying about her, can I?'

'She's not your little girl anymore, Nick.'

He would always worry about her. But Nicholas changed tack. 'And how do you feel, Rachel?'

'About Tom?'

302

'About becoming a granny.'

He heard her intake of breath. Chuckled.

'Do you have to, Nick, really?'

'I can't resist,' he told her.

'Hmm.' She paused and her tone changed. 'You know, you sound different.'

'Different bad or different good?' He stared up into the branches of the mulberry tree that rose above him, shielding him from the pale and misty November sun.

'I don't know.' Her voice tailed off. 'Nick?' She let his name hang.

'Yes?'

'I'm having a get-together. A sort of party. With Celie and Tom and his parents. They're all coming over.'

'Bloody hell,' he said. Some party.

'And I've decided . . . you should be here too. It would give us a chance to discuss this whole thing, *en famille*, as it were.'

'Is that really necessary?' He was surprised. It was Rachel's style, but surely not Celie's. He doubted that she would want her condition and circumstances to be discussed *en famille* or anywhere else for that matter.

'Yes,' said Rachel. There was never any dithering for her. 'Let me give you the date.'

'Go ahead then.' He imagined he could hear her flipping through the pages of her diary. Rachel had always been hot on organisation and this had clearly been arranged a while ago.

'I hope you can get a flight in time.' She told him when it was to be.

'That soon?' He frowned.

'Please say you'll come, Nick.'

He supposed he'd have to go. He still wanted to be involved

303

with his family. Besides, he was due to see Giuseppe, so he could kill two birds. 'OK,' he said. And he could almost see Rachel's smile of satisfaction.

After the call, he went to his inbox to read Joanna Shepherd's email once again.

Dear Nicholas, she had written.

It's funny you should say that about love.

He remembered exactly what he'd said: that although it was frail and fallible, love was still a wonderful thing. *Idiot* . . .

When I was in Lisbon, I was thinking about it a lot — not so much the love in my marriage, but in my childhood, my relationship with my parents (very complicated — my father and I were never close and I felt he was taken away from me before I could make things right between us).

Resolution, Nicholas found himself thinking. It was a human need.

And my relationship with my sister Harriet — also complicated. She stayed at home, I moved away. I have a feeling that both of us consider the grass may be greener on the other side.

Didn't everyone? He thought of his call with Rachel.

You're right about the decision I made in Venice. No, I don't have children. You're lucky to have Celie.

He certainly was.

On to Lisbon. It's a wonderful city. The bridge walk is along the old aqueduct and it takes in both the old and the new; the city is full of both, as you probably know.

He did now. Joanna Shepherd would have no idea that he was already here. There was no hint of concern in her message. She seemed to think it was quite normal for him to be following in her footsteps, walking her walks.

I saw the girl again. She looked very much in love so I now know who she was running to at Ponte Accademia!

304

Ah . . . He put his head to one side. Joanna was a writer, of course. Was that why she seemed to be living in two realities at the same time? Handy that — there was always another world to escape to . . .

It is funny, as you say, that we're writing as we are. But I like it too. I had a French pen friend once, called Didier, and I realise now how much I've missed writing to another human being. You and I are emailing, of course, but hey, the world has moved on.

Very true.

But I haven't answered your question. Yes, I do think love is a wonderful thing. The problem being that it can also bring a lot of pain — don't you think?

Oh yes, it certainly can. Nicholas sat back and closed his eyes, let her words sink into him. In her brochure, Joanna had suggested that her readers might be able to see the past in the mulberry trees. Emotions and relationships too apparently. What did she mean? Past places? Past people? Past moments? He smiled. Maybe she was a bit crazy after all.

After a few moments he opened his eyes again and stared up into the winter branches. Drawn to do what she had done, see what she had seen.

He was instantly mesmerised. Was it the breeze shifting the branches, the winter sunlight edging through . . . or had he kept his eyes closed for too long?

He wanted to write it down, but he didn't want to stop seeing. He would do it this evening, he decided: write it down in another email to Joanna Shepherd, who would no doubt know what to make of it.

In the meantime . . . he stared, seeing and unseeing. Done, undone. He didn't want to miss a thing.

CHAPTER 40

Harriet

Dorset

Harriet drove towards Bridport, barely able to contain her excitement at the thought of seeing Scott again. She took a left at the end of the lane, turned up the volume of the radio. '*Baby love,*' she sang along lustily to the Motown hit. The last two days had passed in a blur. Joanna had gone to Prague, their mother had been quiet ever since the conservatory episode and Harriet had been busy typing up the untidy pages of her scientist employer's manuscript in between her usual chores. Nothing had changed and yet everything was different. She was no longer a virgin. She could hardly believe it and obviously there was nobody she could tell . . . And yet, she wanted to shout it from the rooftops.

She felt something catch and tighten within her. Now she knew what it felt like. Now she knew what it meant. Now there were no secrets. She had hovered on the dizzy edge and then she had jumped right in. Heavens. Did she feel more fulfilled? More well rounded and complete? Not exactly. But at least she had finally thrown off the burden of virginity. She was a woman of the world – at last. She was liberated.

She braked as she spotted Owen's red tractor ahead. He always seemed to be holding up her progress, but even that didn't concern her now. Her worries about money, the cottage and Mother had all faded to insignificance. Even the stalker was no longer a worry – and it had been so long since she'd seen him, she'd begun to hope that she might have scared him away at last. She could still feel Scott's fingers on her thighs. She was still floating.

It had been an intense and exciting experience – but embarrassing too. Harriet had felt gauche and inexperienced – which was exactly what she was. A quick fumble with Jamie in Big Barn didn't really count. She'd always known he fancied Joanna. All the farmhands had fancied Joanna. She was taller, slimmer and had oceans more confidence. Joanna could shake her head and her chestnut hair would swing back into perfect shape, her eyes both smiling and knowing at the same time. She was sexy. Harriet had never known how she did it. She watched her younger sister; she even practised in front of her bedroom mirror. But her own curly hair never swung back into shape – most of the time it didn't have any. And sexy remained as elusive as confidence. It still did.

Getting dressed in front of Scott had been equally embarrassing. He lay there, watching her with lazy eyes, smoking on something sweet and heady that he'd lit as soon as she got out of the bed and that she strongly suspected to be marijuana. Even more embarrassing was the whole virginity thing.

Harriet blushed at the memory.

'Fuck me,' he had said, 'it's your first time.'

307

'Yes,' she'd said – clearly her efforts at disguising her lack of experience had been in vain. 'It's a personal choice.'

This had been true to begin with. Because she'd had her opportunities. After Jamie had come Kevin, who worked in the garage on the main road, but this had never progressed beyond kissing, mainly because she knew her father didn't approve of him. There was Rob, a delivery man, who had taken Harriet out for dinner and tried it on in the back of his car – until she got him to admit that he was married. And Stuart from the end cottage in the lane who had always made his feelings clear. But none had made her pulse race. None had made her throw caution to the wind. The village had remained reasonably devoid of single male talent. And after a while, as you slipped into your thirties and trudged towards your forties, it became harder. More of an issue, somehow, to let go.

She wasn't entirely sure why she had let go with Scott. He was very attractive, yes; dreamy, yes, yes; seductive, yes, yes, yes. But it was more than that. It was as if he represented freedom. That freedom of spirit that Harriet longed for.

Owen was chugging along at ten miles an hour. *Ye Gods . . .* Even their own decrepit blue tractor would go faster than that – if it had some diesel in it. What was wrong with him? Didn't he realise the world was passing him by – or at least, on this occasion, wanted to pass him by? But there was no chance in this narrow lane.

It seemed an age since she had walked on air out of Scott's camper van and into the taxi that had taken her home. It had been a bit awkward the morning after when she'd asked Owen for a lift into Bridport and tried to find a reason why she had left the pick-up in the long-stay car park all night, but thankfully, Owen hadn't asked too many questions. Perhaps her neighbour had his own problems to worry about; there was a sadness in his expression, he seemed to lack his normal *joie de vivre*, so perhaps he was thinking about his lost wife again or mourning yet another of Joanna's absences.

Owen was waving his arm energetically out of the cab window. Waving her on, but pointing to the layby ahead. He wanted her to stop, she realised. *Bugger.* She revved the engine impatiently. *Not now, Owen.* She was on a mission and she didn't have the time or inclination to make polite conversation with her neighbour. But she had little choice. She nodded and raised her hand in acknowledgement. Pulled over behind the tractor.

Harriet switched off the engine and wound down her window. She watched as Owen climbed out of the cab. He was a good man, she reminded herself. And he'd done so much to help them over the years since Father died. She should be nicer to him.

'Hello, Harriet.' Now, he was at her window, giving her a strange sort of look.

'Owen . . .' Harriet couldn't resist tapping her fingers on the steering wheel. 'What can I do for you?'

'Well, now . . .' He leant on the door, his expression serious. 'I wanted a word about tomorrow.'

'Tomorrow?' Harriet's mind was blank. What had she forgotten now?

'I haven't told you yet.' He laughed. Looked at her appraisingly.

It was a nice friendly sound and she found herself smiling back at him. 'Oh, I see. What is it then?'

'You look different . . .' He let the word hang.

'Different?'

He didn't elaborate. Heavens, she thought. Did it show on the outside too?

'I've been thinking,' he said. 'You've cooked me so many suppers in the past. It's way beyond time for me to reciprocate, I reckon.'

'Hmm?' Harriet couldn't quite concentrate. She glanced at her watch. Would Scott still be in the car park? She hoped so. Would he be surprised to see her? Probably not. They'd been so caught up in their passionate encounter that they hadn't exchanged numbers. She'd considered emailing, but an email through Someone Somewhere would surely trivialise the experience. Face to face was better, richer, more romantic by far. She sighed.

Owen was still talking '. . . take you out to dinner,' he said.

Harriet did a double-take. 'All of us?' Mother would love it, of course. Joanna would probably go for it too – if she was back from Prague, that was. But she wasn't due back for a few days yet and Owen had mentioned tomorrow. Harriet was certainly tempted too – going out to dinner was a rare occasion in her life. 'That's really kind.'

'Well, now . . .' He paused.

Harriet thought quickly. 'It's sweet of you to suggest it, Owen, but . . .' What if Scott wanted to arrange something special for the two of them tomorrow night? If Joanna had been around to look after Mother, it would be different. But she wouldn't be. Harriet's brain went into overdrive. However, if Mother was being safely looked after by Owen, it would give her the ideal opportunity to meet up with Scott.

Owen was giving her that funny look again. It was making her feel slightly uncomfortable. 'But?'

'Mother would love to go out for dinner,' Harriet said. 'But I'm afraid Jo won't be around – she's in Prague.' That would

310

be a disappointment, she knew. It was obvious he had a bit of a thing for her sister – didn't everyone? But she didn't want him to postpone it – after all, as he'd pointed out, he did owe her for all those suppers. 'I'd be *so* grateful, though.'

'Would you?' He brightened.

'Absolutely.' It was only one night and they got on well enough. Mother would be so thrilled to be taken out – and by a man. 'It will be a real treat for her.'

'Treat for her?' For some reason, Owen seemed confused.

'Yes. Because there's something I might have to do. Somewhere I might have to be.'

'You mean you . . . ?'

'I'm really sorry but I might not be able to make it.' She flashed him another breezy smile. That was how she was going to be from now on – breezy, not a care in the world; that's what losing her virginity would do for her. 'So, it would be a godsend if you could look after Mother.'

She started up the engine, inched the truck forward. Owen frowned as he took a step backwards. Well, he had offered.

'I'll let you know when I get back from Bridport,' she called out of the window as she drove away. 'And, thanks so much.'

Her nerves were fluttering as she drove into the car park. But, thank goodness, Scott's camper van was still parked over by the river. And the door was open . . . He must be inside.

She parked the pick-up and glanced in the mirror. Everything was intact. She'd plucked her eyebrows and was wearing a generous coating of Joanna's lipstick again – with a hint of blusher and some face powder. She took a deep breath, swung herself out of the cab, dusted down her jeans and sauntered over, trying to look casual.

Although it was quite chilly, Scott was sitting on the steps of his van with a notebook and a guitar resting on his knees. He was wearing a parka jacket and a scarf. His hair was loose today, hanging forward to frame his face. Heavens, he looked so wonderfully creative and absorbed.

'Hi.' She hovered.

He glanced up. Looked blank.

Blank? Surely that wasn't right?

'Oh, hi.' He smiled vaguely as though he couldn't quite place her. After less than three days?

Harriet felt her stomach dip. Inside, something that had grown and blossomed began to shrink and fade.

'I was just passing,' she said. 'I wanted to, er . . . thank you for the other night.'

'Yeah.' Scott struggled to his feet. 'The other night. It was great. You were great.'

But he was looking at her as if she appeared much older in this light.

'I thought maybe we could do it again,' she said. She heard herself stammer. 'That is, go out sometime.'

'Right.' He smiled. 'Sure. Sometime.'

'Like tomorrow,' she persevered. 'Dinner perhaps?'

'I'd like to,' he said.

Harriet waited.

'But I'm moving on. In the morning.'

'Oh.' Her heart sank. Literally. What had she done? What had she been thinking of? Why had she ever imagined . . . ?

'It was cool to meet you and all that,' Scott said. 'We had some good vibes, yeah.' He paused. 'But I'm not into commitment, I guess you realised that.'

Commitment? She had only asked him out for dinner.

312

'Of course, I understand perfectly,' she said, sounding about ninety. Yes, she was beginning to understand – only too well.

'The other night was a groove,' Scott said.

'A groove,' she echoed.

'Yeah.' He gazed at a point beyond her left shoulder. 'It's a beautiful thing – to go with the moment.'

Two days ago she had been beautiful too.

Harriet turned away.

Good vibes? Free love? A groove? What a load of bollocks. She crossed the car park to the pick-up truck. Thirty-nine years old and she wasn't safe to be let out alone. And he had made her think that she was special . . . What an idiot she had been.

The Third Bridge

CHAPTER 41

Joanna

Prague

Eagerly, Joanna pulled back the long muslin curtains at the window. She'd asked for a room with a good outlook at the hotel, U Tri Pstrosu – The Three Ostriches – but she hadn't expected this amazing view. It was perfect.

The long window looked out over the length of the Charles Bridge: wide, expansive, lined with baroque statues, thronged with people – milling over the grey cobbles, browsing through the jewellery and prints on the street sellers' stalls. Behind the bridge rose tall trees and elegant cream buildings with orange-tiled roofs and white chimneys. And at the far end, Joanna could see the old tower and the spires that marked the entrance into Staré Město, the Old Town.

'Karlův Most . . .' She mouthed the words. The language of the Czech Republic felt peculiar and unfamiliar on her tongue. The Charles Bridge joined the Old Town to the Lesser Quarter, which led up the hill to the cathedral and the castle.

She took a step back into the room, looping the curtain to one side so that her view was unhindered. This bridge had seen a lot, as she'd discovered from her research. When Karlův Most was being built, the builders had appealed for wine and eggs to mix with lime to create a strong mortar – and legend had it that one lot of eggs had arrived hard-boiled . . . She smiled. That would be a good anecdote to add to her narrative when she wrote the copy. The bridge had been a thoroughfare, a processional way, a venue of commerce and a place of both celebration and punishment. In 1620 – and she'd made a note of this too – at the Battle of the White Mountain, the Czechs had been defeated by a Catholic army and the severed heads of ten Protestant nobles had been displayed on this very parapet for twelve years. Gruesome . . . Joanna blinked, but thankfully this particular image remained in the past.

These days, the bridge seemed to be more of a meeting point. She reached for her camera, which she'd slung on the bed, opened the window wide and lined up a shot. The cold air rushed into the room. It was a sharp and bright November day, the sky a matt sapphire, the cobbles gleaming. Tailor-made for walking . . .

On her way here, Harriet had given her a lift to the station and Joanna had taken the opportunity of asking her if they happened to have an ancestor with red hair.

'What?' Her sister had stopped at the give way sign and given her another of those uncomprehending looks.

'Take our great-grandfather William, for example,' Joanna went on.

'Take him where?'

Joanna ignored this. 'Did he have red hair?'

'How the heck would I know? I didn't even know we had a great-grandfather called William.'

318

'He could have,' Joanna persevered. 'You're fair and I'm dark.'

'And neither of us are redheads,' Harriet pointed out with irritating logic.

'Someone was,' Joanna said. 'There was a man called Rufus, and I'm sure he was a member of our family.' Although sometimes, she was beginning to doubt his existence herself.

'Why do you want to know?' Harriet had asked. She was still in that same dreamy state she'd been in since her mysterious night on the tiles and she still hadn't said a word about it, though Joanna had tried her best to find out. It must be another man from that dating site she was on, Joanna concluded. And this one seemed to have hit her sister hard.

She decided not to tell Harriet about Emmy and Rufus – she hadn't been interested before and she probably wouldn't be now. Joanna could be secretive too. 'No reason,' she said. 'I'm just curious.'

'Maybe you should ask Mother,' Harriet suggested.

'Maybe.' They exchanged a look of sad understanding. Over the past few days their mother seemed to have grown more insubstantial than ever, and neither of them knew quite what to do about it.

They arrived at Dorchester station and Joanna jumped out of the pick-up and rescued her case from the back. 'Thanks for the lift, Het,' she said.

'No problem.'

'And when I get back, we'll . . .' Her voice trailed. What would they do exactly? Joanna was at a loss as how to find a way through.

Now, Joanna moved away from the hotel room window. Her room had turned out to be a suite, with a sitting

319

room-cum-study and a desk . . . Had they known how she planned to spend her evenings? She let her hand trail over the wood, picked up a sheet of the silky headed notepaper decorated with The Three Ostriches' motif.

Who would she write to as she sat at the antique walnut desk? Nicholas Tresillion? She smiled to herself. What would he find in Lisbon? And then? Would Nicholas follow her to Prague? If he did, how would she feel? Flattered? Or concerned?

She replaced the notepaper on the desk. When she came to think of it, what was the difference between exchanging profiles on an Internet dating site and exchanging profiles by email as she seemed to be doing with Nicholas Tresillion? It seemed that for once in their lives, Joanna and Harriet were on the same page as it were.

As Nicholas had said, their emails had been intense right from the start, and they'd exchanged plenty of personal details too. What did Joanna expect to come of it? Anything? Did she want – or need – a pen friend now that she was all grown up? Did she think he could be a friend – some random man who had read one of her walking brochures and written to her? He seemed to understand what she was going through, yes; he'd had a similar experience, he'd even seen the golden ribbon. But that was hardly enough to catapult them into closeness. On the other hand . . .

She sat down at the desk for a moment. There was more than that. There was a subtext over and above the words he wrote that she was drawn to. He, like her, had broken the pattern of his life and was on a journey of rediscovery. And he had seen something that she had thought only she could see. She opened up her email inbox. He had replied.

Dear Joanna, she read.

Love and pain — ah, don't get me started . . .

Fair point, she thought.

I'm in Lisbon right now. I can see what you mean about the old and the new and you've captured that brilliantly, if I may say, in your walk along the old aqueduct.

'Thank you,' Joanna murmured. So, he was there already. He had done her walk.

I don't have any siblings — I wish I did. Of course, there's sometimes rivalry and jealousy too, but I envy you that special closeness.

Joanna thought once again of Harriet. They had never been as close as she would have liked, but maybe now, slowly and gradually . . . Joanna smiled. Nicholas was right. Having a sibling was very special. She read on.

When there's only one of you, there can be a heavy load of expectation on your shoulders.

My father was a fisherman. He was very down to earth and led a simple, sometimes harsh but also rewarding life. My mother sadly died when I was twelve. Dad encouraged me to study, go to university. And it's true that education gives you more choices, so I'm grateful for that, even though I sometimes wonder how my life would have panned out if I'd become a fisherman too.

Interesting, Joanna thought.

You won't be surprised to hear that I also saw some sort of vision in the mulberry tree in the praça . . . Truly! I didn't see my parents or my daughter, but I did see a man — a man with red, unruly hair. He was a big guy with a big smile and he was opening his arms really wide. He certainly seemed happy to see someone. When I blinked, he was gone, so he must have been a figment of my imagination — what else could he be? I certainly have no idea who he is — do you?

No . . . Red hair? A big smile? Joanna sat back in the chair,

321

her gaze drifting to the middle distance. Could Nicholas Tresillion have seen Rufus? The same man she too had seen with Emmy under the mulberry tree? She thought of the sepia photograph of her ancestor. The description sounded like him too. But again, she knew for a fact she hadn't mentioned the colour of his hair in her copy. She flicked back through her files to check. No. She certainly had not. So, how could Nicholas have seen him? It made no sense. She shivered. It was damned spooky, that's what it was. Obviously a coincidence. And yet . . .

She got up, hefted her work bag onto the chair and started to unpack her papers, books and maps. She must focus on Prague. She hadn't yet decided on the route of the walk – there were several possibilities. The old to the new had emerged as a city theme that would apply to Prague too with its architecture that ranged from the Gothic to the baroque, with mediaeval and art deco thrown in for good measure. But maybe there was something else here, something different? And what, she wondered, had Emmy thought of Prague back in the day?

Joanna gazed out of the window. There was a great view from here too of the arch that led through to the busy shopping street of Mostecká. Certainly, the Charles Bridge would be central to her walk. Images of it were everywhere; she had already seen it displayed in art shops from the taxi on the way to the hotel, printed on T-shirts and, most strikingly, in the dark rich-red hallways of the hotel U Tri Pstrosu itself. Outside her room was an old black and white photographic image dated 1909 – only a few years, Joanna realised, before Emmy would have been here. It showed that same archway leading to the Lesser Town, a horse and cart crossing the bridge, a man in a cap leaning on the parapet, a woman with a wicker basket. And the statues . . . What had Emmy made of the Charles Bridge? And what had she done with her painting?

Love is a fire, a madness, Emmy had written in Prague. *Who are we thinking of? Love may undo us all.*

So, who were they thinking of – and how did this fit in with Joanna's new theory? She took the letter out of her bag, handling it carefully as always, putting it gently down on the desk and smoothing out the old creases with her fingertips.

My dearest, my heart's love. There are so many questions, I know this. To whom do we have a duty, you and I? To ourselves and our happiness? To others? Will you make a choice or are we to be trapped for all time?

How were they trapped? Because they were unable to be together? But why? Joanna frowned. Reading the letter with her new theory in mind changed everything. There was a different tone in the Prague letter. One of sadness, almost desperation. Emmy sounded so much more tortured here and she had quoted from 'Song', a sad poem of parting written by the metaphysical poet John Donne.

It was clear that their relationship had reached some sort of turning point, if choices were to be made.

'Who did you choose, Rufus?'

Joanna had already half guessed the answer. She still felt disappointed that there was no apparent blood connection between herself and Emmy, but despite this, the link between them felt as strong as ever. She still had to find out Emmy's story, and this must be related to the red-haired Rufus's story. Rufus, her ancestor, who had surely lived in Mulberry Farm Cottage. But the questions remained – how was their story linked to Joanna's? Why did she feel she had to find out in order to come to any resolution in her own life? And what did Nicholas Tresillion have to do with any of it?

CHAPTER 42

Nicholas

Rome

After the call from Rachel, Nicholas had changed his booking and gone on to take a direct flight from Lisbon to Rome. He picked up a taxi at the airport. He preferred the city at this time of year – there were fewer tourists and no oppressive heat to deal with. He sat back in the passenger seat as the cab wove in and out of traffic, switching lanes apparently at random, amidst blaring horns and wild gesticulating – how the Italians got their kicks, Nicholas thought.

He had fallen in love with Rome on his second visit to Giuseppe and Isobel's. It had been a gorgeous spring afternoon and the four of them went for a picnic cruise up the River Tiber. That evening, Nicholas had gazed out of their apartment window into the night, over the orange rooftops of Rome, over the statues and the church spires illuminated by the lamp light and the moon, the silvery white domes and the satellite discs, the glorious, heady mix of history and modern technology.

And he realised that he loved the city. Rome had crept up on him and taken hold of his heart.

Nicholas glanced at his watch. At this rate he would only have half an hour for a quick freshen-up at the hotel, before heading to the Hotel Bella Roma where the clan were meeting for Rachel's family 'powwow'. He sighed. And what was the point of that powwow? To prove that, despite divorce, they were still one happy family after all? *Bollocks*.

'Your first visit, yes?' The cab driver veered suddenly into the outside lane, almost taking out a motorcyclist.

Nicholas flinched. 'No. I've been here many times.' *So, don't think you can swindle me . . .*

'It is a beautiful city at any time of year.' The driver braked sharply.

Nicholas closed his eyes — it was often the best way. He knew what would happen tonight. They would have drinks — sundowners, Rachel called them, as if she'd been brought up in Sydney, not Surrey. And then dinner the Italian way: four or five courses punctuated by sorbets and subtle changes of wine, starting with *antipasti* and an artful rosé, ending with some scrummy waist-expanding dessert with sweet white, and espresso and dark chocolate to finish. By which time they would all be suitably re-bonded and Nicholas could return to his hotel, duty done and three pounds heavier.

He opened his eyes again. They were approaching the outskirts of the city.

'You stay here long?'

'Not long.' Just a few days. He'd do the family thing, spend a day with Celie, if she'd have him, maybe dinner with Giuseppe and Isobel, a couple of business meetings. Then he'd go. By that time, Rome would be lying heavy on his shoulders and much as he adored her, he'd be glad to shrug her off – Nicholas knew this from experience.

He thought of Celie being launched into motherhood when she was hardly more than a girl herself. And with what sort of commitment from the father? Nicholas sighed. Bugger all, as far as he could tell.

The cab driver was an expert. He knew all the shortcuts and the one-ways and he wasn't afraid to tackle narrow streets that were more like back alleyways. Nicholas watched the landmarks whizz past: stone fountains, crumbling arches, innocent cherubs . . . The city still impressed him anew every time he came here – it probably always would.

Nicholas let his head fall back against the headrest, thankful for the comfort of the cool leather interior. He heard the ping of an email notification and checked his phone. Joanna Shepherd. Well now. What had she made of his experience in Lisbon? He opened it.

Dear Nicholas, she had written.

And I'm now in Prague . . . Someone should publish our emails as tales from European cities!

Yeah. He laughed out loud and the driver glanced at him in the rear-view mirror.

Thanks for your kind words about my bridge walk in Lisbon. I'm glad you enjoyed it. What took you there? (I don't imagine it was just my bridge walk!) It's a vibrant and interesting city, don't you think?

Nicholas nodded. He'd certainly found it extremely interesting.

In answer to your question, I saw that man too and I think I know who he is – an ancestor of mine.

Nicholas blew out through his teeth. *What?*

I know. It's too weird for words. It's peculiar enough for me to see a vision of one of my ancestors – but why would you see him too?

Why, indeed? Nicholas shook his head.

I'd rather conclude that it's a coincidence, that your man isn't the same as mine. Otherwise I'd have to consider the possibility that my visions are being passed on to all my readers, which is more than weird, I think you'll agree.

Or maybe not to all her readers, Nicholas thought. Maybe only to him? The idea made him chuckle and he saw the driver glance at him once more.

Prague is, of course, another city I'm writing about and the bridge on this occasion is the Charles Bridge. Please don't tell me you're going there too! (Though part of me would be very interested in what you see).

Sadly, Nicholas could think of no good reason why he might go to Prague. He sighed.

Your father sounds like a lovely man. Mine was a farmer, so that's another link between us: one bound to the sea, one to the land. As for me, I'm not sure any longer where I belong.

He caught the restlessness in her words here, and once again an unexpected seriousness. Again, he was touched – that she should open up like this to him, a virtual stranger.

This is my final bridge walk, by the way; I was only commissioned to do three – at least for now. They've been fascinating in some very unexpected ways, but unless they commission more, I've come to the end of the trail.

That was a shame.

Nicholas tucked his phone back in his pocket as the taxi finally pulled up outside Hotel Vittorio. He swung open the door. Already, the chilly November air had begun to smell of end of afternoon – beer and sweet, fizzy prosecco; early dinner preparations with tomatoes, peppers and onions sizzling

327

in a pan, their rich aroma wafting out of an open restaurant window. He could hear the buzz of conversation and an Italian aria being played from a nearby open doorway.

'*Grazie.*' He pulled some euros out of his wallet and paid the guy. He'd earned it.

The driver opened the boot and Nicholas took his small case and loped easily up the white steps leading to the hotel.

He checked in, was given his room key and went upstairs to shower. He'd stayed here before – it was only a three star but had great views over the city. He could have stayed with Giuseppe and Isobel, of course – Celie and Tom would be at Rachel's apartment. But he preferred the anonymity of a hotel. It gave him a place to retreat to – should he require it. And – he grinned to himself – he probably would.

Briefly, he checked out the view – yes, he could see the *giardino* and the lake, as he'd hoped. He threw his jacket on the back of a chair. He was tempted to write back to Joanna Shepherd straightaway but there was no time.

Mentally, he checked his itinerary as he stripped off. Thought about Prague. It felt as if he was on a mission; that he shouldn't give up when the journey wasn't yet over. If it really was a journey at all. What he'd seen in Lisbon had been odd, but perhaps it was just his mind playing tricks on him. And as for the fact that Joanna had identified the figure as being one of her ancestors . . . what was going on there? But what reasonable excuse was there to follow the woman to city after city like a man with no purpose, no life of his own? Giuseppe wouldn't be up for another new location so soon after Lisbon.

The hot water rained down on his body. *Ah. It could, though, be for pleasure* . . .

No. 'Too much, Nico, my boy,' he told himself. *Much too much.*

Swiftly, he lathered his body. He held his face up to the water and closed his eyes for a moment, felt the cleansing warmth on his skin. He rinsed off, stepped out of the shower, and towelled himself dry.

What would happen after Prague? She had said it was the end of the trail, but that felt too quick, much too quick. Should he suggest they meet up somewhere back in England? Was that crazy too? But what possible reason would there be for meeting up? And what if it was a complete disaster?

He pulled a fresh shirt from his bag. What if, face to face, they had nothing to say to each other? He wasn't expecting much, mind – though friendship would be nice. But he didn't think he could stomach another disappointment right now. Perhaps it was better to let it go, to enjoy the dream for what it was – some sort of sad fantasy.

Quickly, he dried off his hair and slapped on some after-shave. They were no longer married, but Rachel was still a beautiful woman. He wanted her to have just the smallest of regrets . . .

Nicholas picked up his wallet and was off, out of the door, down the stairs, to join the crisp and wintery early evening with its ache of anticipation, its delicious fragrances, its bitter-sweet memories of Rome.

In the pale green loggia of Hotel Bella Roma they were already assembled. He saw Celie first – she looked fresh and young in wide white linen trousers and a turquoise shirt, the coral earrings he'd given her for Christmas dangling against her slender neck. Her pregnancy was beginning to show – just. She was talking to her mother and, from the expression on her face, she was a bit fed up. *Oh, joy.* Rachel was doing the shrug that she'd perfected until it had become an art form. She was elegant as always in a black silky number he'd never seen before, her dark hair pinned up high, milky pearls at her throat.

'Nico . . .' Someone held him by the shoulders and pulled him into a bear hug. Giuseppe. 'You are OK, huh?'

'Yeah, yeah. Good to see you.' He'd be better when he got a drink inside him, better still when this was over.

'Nicholas, darling.' Isobel kissed him on both cheeks.

Nicholas found himself a drink and did the rounds of the small group clustered around cane furniture and glass tables. Was it his imagination, or were faces a bit wary, slightly embarrassed about this . . . family affair? *So glad you could make it . . . Lovely to see you . . .*

Tom's parents stood awkwardly on the edge of the group, as if not quite sure what they were doing there. Nicholas made an extra effort to chat to them, to make them feel welcomed, even though he felt almost as much of an outsider as they clearly did.

'I'm so glad you came, Dad.' Celie held him the longest, even when he tried to half push her away so that he could see her eyes. 'Are you all right?' Her dark hair smelt of strawberries.

'Sure, baby.'

She pulled him to one side. 'Trust you to be late.'

'Hey, hang on a—'

She brushed away his protestations. 'I haven't had a chance to talk to you, and Mum wants to do this big announcement thing.'

'Yeah, well . . .' He rolled his eyes. All the world was a stage to Rachel.

'But now it's got so complicated.' Celie looked close to tears.

330

He put his arm around her. 'What is it, sweetheart? What's wrong?'

She shook her head and he followed the direction of her gaze, towards a tall, olive-skinned man dressed in a candy-floss pink shirt and what was clearly an Italian designer suit – charcoal grey with tiny pinstripes. Rachel had long ago taught Nicholas how to recognise such things and now, hell, he had one or two of his own. The guy was looking over at Nicholas too. He was in his mid-forties, Nicholas guessed. A gold signet ring glinted on his little finger as he raised his glass to his lips. He was smiling. *Like a bloody shark*, thought Nicholas.

'That's Eduardo,' Celie whispered. 'The thing is, Dad, I've got to tell you, he—'

'Nick.' As usual Rachel's voice was cool and imperious.

He turned. 'Hi, Rach.' It was easy to keep his tone casual, but close up she looked even better than he remembered. The silky black dress clung to her slender body in all the right places, her long legs were encased in sheer nylon and she was wearing stilettos that probably took her to about six foot two. Not a blemish, not a line – although she too had now turned forty. She certainly wasn't losing her touch.

Celie was tugging at his arm. 'Dad, I just need to—'

'I want you to meet someone, Nick.' Rachel took his other hand. He was aware of her long fingers and manicured nails pressed into his palm. And at the same moment he felt Celie let go and the shadowy presence of someone else now looming on the edge of their little group. 'This is—'

'Eduardo Crispino.' The man in the candy-floss shirt had stepped forward. He spoke in clipped tones. 'Pleased to meet you.' Perfect English. Too perfect to be English, naturally.

'Nicholas Tresillion. Likewise.' He would be Rachel's latest,

331

she usually went for Italians; Celie had clearly been trying to warn him. Nicholas was annoyed – not because this man was as smooth as an oil slick, but because he was here at what was supposed to be a family occasion.

'Excuse me for a moment?' He took Rachel's arm and steered her away from her *amour*. 'Showing off are we, darling?' he said. He had changed his travel plans for this – it was pretty bad form to parade some Italian stud in front of him all evening.

She pouted at him. Fortunately, he didn't fall for that anymore.

'Eduardo had to be here,' she said. 'And so did you.'

'Because . . . ?' His eyes strayed over to Tom and Celie. Tom's arm was protective around Celie's shoulders. Which was good.

'They told you, didn't they?' Rachel's voice was hot in his ear.

'Told me?'

'They're getting married, of course.' Rachel could always make him feel a bit slow on the uptake.

'Oh, right.' Wasn't he pleased? He tried to catch Celie's eye, give her the thumbs up. Well, naturally he was pleased. Marriage meant a certain security, even if it offered no guarantees. It meant they wanted to commit to each other, that Tom would look after his little girl, that the child Celie was bearing would have two (proper?) married parents. 'Great,' he said, sounding unconvincing to his own ears. 'Fantastic.' And Celie would have told him – if Rachel had given her a chance.

Rachel was eyeing him strangely.

'Thank God,' he added for good measure.

Rachel brushed an imaginary problem away with a gesture of

332

her slim arm. 'She thought you would mind about everything,' she said. 'But that's silly, isn't it? I mean, it's been ages.'

'Mind?' He laughed. 'Why should I mind?' Everything in this hotel loggia was beginning to seem slightly other-worldly. The lights were casting a faintly green glow over the cane furniture and cream cushions, the people were moving too slowly, almost drifting over the marble floor. What was Rachel talking about? What had been ages?

'No, no . . . I'm not talking about Celie and Tom.' She dangled her hand in front of his face. 'Honestly, Nick . . .'

He realised that she was wearing a very large diamond. And it was on the third finger of her left hand.

'Ah,' he said. Things were coming into focus.

'It's to be a double wedding. In June.' Rachel looked like the cat that had got the cream.

'A double wedding?' Nicholas let the implications of this sink into his head. Surely, not even Rachel . . .

'My idea.'

'It would be.' He drained his glass.

'Though I must say, our daughter has taken some persuading.' Rachel plucked two glasses of prosecco from the tray of a passing waiter and relieved Nicholas of his empty one.

'Has she now?' Did that mean that Celie had agreed? Nicholas shuddered – although he knew from experience how persuasive Rachel could be. And he saw now why Celie had looked so upset. A double wedding – his daughter and his ex-wife. And Celie didn't want it. Lord Almighty. Only Rachel could have planned this.

She passed him one of the glasses. 'I think it's a divine idea,' she said. 'It's perfect timing, isn't it?'

'If you say so.' He would ask Celie how she felt. If she didn't want it, he was damned if he was going to let it happen. If she did – he downed the wine in one – he'd live with it.

'It'll be wonderful for both of us – me and Celie, I mean.' Rachel sipped her drink a touch more delicately. 'I told her, it will be a real mother and daughter bonding experience.'

Yeah, right. Nicholas glared into the room where they were all getting ready to be seated for the dinner. Where had he been placed? Next to bloody Eduardo? So that they could do some bonding too? He wouldn't be surprised.

Rachel let out a small sigh. 'You are pleased for me, aren't you, Nick?'

Jesus Christ. 'Pleased? I'm delighted,' he said.

Rachel's smile stretched across her face. She raised her glass. 'To Celie and Tom,' she called out to the assembled company. 'And to me and Eduardo, of course.'

What could he do? Nicholas raised his glass with the rest of them. *Fucking delighted*, he thought. *Of course.*

CHAPTER 43

Harriet

Dorset

The following day, Harriet was busy tidying the herb garden. It should have been done before now, but more often than not jobs like this got put on to the next day's list. Looking up from her squatting position, she spotted Owen in the field next door, lashing some fencing.

She got to her feet. 'Hello!' she called. She felt a surge of, well, friendship, she supposed. It had been rather lonely here at the cottage with Joanna away, especially after the debacle with Scott and now that she'd given up on Someone Somewhere. She missed her sister, she realised, with a slight shock. Which wasn't good. She was getting far too used to Joanna being around.

'Afternoon.' He nodded but didn't even smile. He was definitely not being as friendly as usual. Harriet frowned. Had she missed something here?

She walked over. 'Mother says don't be a stranger.' She

335

rubbed some of the soil from her hands. 'She hasn't seen you for a while.' She wouldn't tell him that Mother was also in need of a distraction — that was hardly his problem.

He shot her a fierce look. 'Wouldn't want to be a nuisance,' he growled.

'Don't be daft.' Harriet assessed the situation. Had she done something to annoy him? She cast her mind back. Ah. Two days ago, when she'd been on her way into Bridport to see Scott. Suddenly, she remembered. 'I never came back to you about your dinner invitation,' she said. It had gone clean out of her mind.

He raised an eyebrow. Whacked the fencepost with his mallet.

'I'm so sorry, Owen.' It had been incredibly kind of him. And she hadn't even had the consideration to remember the offer. Also, she recalled, she'd seen it more in the light of enabling her to escape from Mulberry Farm Cottage for the evening, rather than as the gesture of friendship that it had been. Harriet felt deeply ashamed. All she'd been thinking of that day was Scott.

'Doesn't matter.' He drove in another nail. 'It was probably a stupid idea.'

'No . . .' It hadn't been a stupid idea. It had been sweet and generous and Harriet had behaved appallingly. 'I had a lot on my mind,' she confessed. 'There was someone . . .'

He looked up enquiringly, but she couldn't go on. She didn't want to tell him about Scott. She didn't need to tell anyone about Scott. He would be her secret. Scott had given her more than she had realised at first. He had given her an exciting experience, showed her what she was capable of. She might never do it again — she probably never would do it again, because she

336

was done with the Scotts of this world. But it had been worth it. To feel, just for one night, loved, beautiful, cared for.

He was still looking at her. 'It wasn't important.'

But it was. They were neighbours and she had been un-neighbourly. More than that, she had been thoughtless – cruel even. 'Come in for a cup of tea,' Harriet said. He would hold her up, but it was the least she could do.

'I don't want to intrude.' He still hadn't forgiven her then.

'Please,' she said. 'You're not intruding in the least.' She didn't want to ruin their relationship. Apart from anything else, she wasn't sure how they would manage without Owen.

'Well, if you're sure . . .' She was conscious of a shift in his attitude. He straightened and looked right at her. That look made her uncomfortable, she had to admit.

'But first I have to feed the fish,' she said.

'The fish?' His mouth curved into a smile.

'Shan't be a minute.' Harriet stomped towards the pond. It was looking a touch unkempt and wintery. The mulberry tree crouched over it, its branches protective, dark and rugged.

Owen followed her. 'Lovely tree.' Affectionately, he thumped the trunk of the mulberry with the palm of his hand. 'Know how old it is? How long has it been here?'

Harriet shrugged. It had always been here. And the house was Mulberry Farm Cottage. So . . . 'Forever?' she guessed.

Owen laughed – an unexpected boom of a laugh.

Harriet raised an eyebrow. She'd never seen anyone come out of a bad mood so fast. 'It looks pretty ancient to me,' she said. 'And our cottage is certainly old.'

Owen fingered one of the twisty, drooping branches. 'The mulberry tree looks old even when it's young,' he said.

'Oh?' What made him so knowledgeable all of a sudden?

337

Harriet pulled the packet of fish food out of her pocket and sprinkled a bit on the surface of the water. A couple of gold and black fish darted up to swallow and plunge back in. Would there be tadpoles this year? she wondered. Last summer there had been frogs hopping all over the place – one or two of the café's patrons had been terrified. But what did they expect if they came to tea on a farm in the country?

'S'pose it would've been planted around the time your place changed its name,' Owen said. 'That would make sense. 1914, I reckon it was.'

Harriet stared at him. 'What?'

'According to the parish records and maps.' He sounded apologetic.

Harriet attempted to assimilate this information. First Joanna looking up parish registers and census details and the like. And now Owen. Was there something in the air? 'Our cottage had a different name?' She stared at the mulberry tree as if it might be to blame. 'But why would anyone change its name? What was it called?'

'Warren Down Farm Cottage.' Owen spoke in his soft, slow voice. 'You can see it marked next to my place on the old maps up at Bridport museum. Last mention would be around 1913.'

'I had no idea.' Warren Down Farm Cottage? This was logical, but why had no one told her? Why had her father never mentioned it? He must have known. And why change the name just because you'd planted a tree next to the farmyard?

'There's a map dated 1914 as it happens,' Owen continued, patting the trunk of the tree again, 'shows it as Mulberry Farm Cottage. I reckon 1914 must have been about when this old fella was planted then.'

1914 . . . Harriet paced to the other side of the murky pond.

It smelt of rotting weed and damp wood. What was the significance of that date? Something to do with the First World War? A remembrance to someone who'd been killed perhaps? Harriet didn't like it. Suddenly, the tree she'd always loved seemed like an interloper.

'Your dad might not even have known,' Owen added. 'Would have been his granddad who planted it, d'you reckon?'

How the heck was Harriet supposed to know? She and Joanna had only been looking at a picture of their grandparents the other week, when she'd found all those old photos in a drawer, but their grandparents had both died before Harriet was born, so they'd never known them. Her father had certainly never mentioned that his grandfather had planted a mulberry tree or changed the name of the farm. Which was rather strange. She should tell Joanna, she supposed. She was the one doing the jigsaw of the past. Though why she should suddenly be so interested in their heritage, Harriet had no idea, and her sister was being rather secretive. 'Maybe,' she said at last.

She shoved her hands in the pockets of her jacket and paced back again. It didn't seem right that Owen should know such a significant piece of information about their cottage. She felt stupid – and that was a feeling she'd never had around Owen before.

'Easy enough to plant 'em,' Owen went on. The more tense she was becoming, the more relaxed he seemed. 'The traditional method is to saw off a section of the trunk and stick it in the soil. Then Bob's your uncle.'

'Then I suppose that's what he did,' Harriet said, somewhat sharply. But one look at Owen's expression and she relented. Her ignorance was hardly his fault, and she was supposed to be being

339

nice to him. 'It could symbolise someone's death, I suppose,' she said. She looked up into the bare wintery branches, remembered all those times she'd climbed the tree, shaken the branches to make the fruit fall to the ground, watched her mother prepare the jam, helped her father make the wine . . . It was symbolic of her childhood too, symbolic of her entire family.

'How do you mean?' Owen was watching her.

'Someone from the family might have perished in World War One.' This sounded suitably dramatic. And likely. She took a step away. Jo might know who had died in the war; she'd ask her when she got back from Prague.

'And?'

'And the tree could have been planted in their memory.' Although hopefully they weren't standing on anyone's remains.

Owen looked straight at her. 'Or it could be love,' he said.

'Pardon?'

Owen's face blushed as red as the mulberries would themselves in high summer. 'Because of the story of Pyramus and Thisbe, I mean,' he said. 'The tree could be a symbol of unrequited love.'

'Pyramus and . . . ?' Harriet did not count herself uneducated. She had GCSEs and A levels and a wealth of knowledge imparted by her father when she was a child. In fact, she would have said she was a lot better educated than Owen. But she was really struggling here. All she could remember about Pyramus and Thisbe was the story performed by a character called Bottom in *A Midsummer Night's Dream*. 'Shakespeare?' she asked weakly.

'It's a Roman tale originally, I believe,' Owen said. 'Though I've only read Ovid's version.'

Ovid? Harriet stared at him. *Ovid?* 'In Latin?' She knew her

340

mouth was open. She was seeing another side of Owen now. A most unexpected side.

'Aw, no . . .' He kicked some dead leaves up with his big black boots. 'I read it in English.'

'And?' Harriet smiled.

'Pyramus and Thisbe, they were neighbours . . .' He wouldn't meet her gaze. 'And very much in love, by all accounts. Their parents forbade the match, so they could only talk to each other through a crack in the wall.'

'A crack in the wall?' But what did that have to do with mulberry trees?

'They planned to meet by a white mulberry tree.' He might have read her mind. 'Beside a fountain.'

Harriet looked down at the pond. It wasn't a fountain, but it was water, and the nearest you could get to a fountain in this farmyard. Perhaps whoever had planted the tree had known the story after all. So, who had planted it? And why?

'What happened?' she whispered. Why was she whispering? She had no idea. All was quiet in the farmyard, almost unnaturally quiet.

'Thisbe left her house first,' he said. 'With a veil over her head so she wouldn't be recognised.'

As Owen spoke, Harriet realised that a veil of darkness was indeed falling over the farmyard and the hills, and she had to strain to see his features; his face was already in shadow.

'She arrived at the tree. And as she sat alone, in the dim light of evening . . .' Owen went on.

Just like now. Harriet shot him a sharp glance. *Don't milk it*.

'She saw a lioness approaching.'

Like you do, thought Harriet. But she shivered nonetheless. And not only because it was getting cold out here.

341

'The lioness's jaws were bloody from a recent kill,' said Owen. 'She had come to the fountain to slake her thirst.'

Slake? Owen was sounding more like a Roman storyteller every second.

'What did Thisbe do?' Harriet asked.

'What would you do?' Owen countered.

'Run like hell?' Harriet hazarded a guess.

'She did,' Owen said. 'But as she ran' – dramatic pause – 'she dropped her veil and the lioness picked it up in her grisly jaws and tore it to shreds.'

Harriet could see the way this was going.

'Meanwhile, Pyramus, having been delayed' – Owen shifted his weight onto the other foot – 'came to the meeting place.'

'And saw the veil?'

'He did.' Owen let out a deep sigh. A natural storyteller indeed. Yes. The man had considerable hidden depths.

'He cursed and cried and vowed that his blood too would stain the tree.' Owen paused. 'So, he plunged his sword deep into his breast.'

'Crikey,' said Harriet. She'd been right. It was *Romeo and Juliet* all over again. Perhaps that was where Shakespeare had got the idea.

'His blood spurted up onto the white mulberries,' Owen went on. 'And turned them blood red.'

It sounded as if he really believed all this. Harriet gazed at the mulberry tree in the growing darkness, but it was saying nothing. Only the winter breeze slunk through the open branches and dimpled the surface of the pond.

'His blood sank into the earth,' Owen said. 'Until it reached the roots of the tree. The redness would rise through the trunk to the fruit forever more.' He patted the trunk with his hand once again.

'So, what happened to Thisbe?' Harriet asked. As if she couldn't guess.

'She saw Pyramus's dead body lying next to her torn, bloody veil, was consumed with guilt and killed herself with the same sword,' Owen said, 'crying that the berries would forever be a memorial of their joined blood.'

Right. Harriet moved closer. Gently touched the bark of the tree. It felt soft but rough under her fingertips. 'And they are,' she said.

'And they are,' Owen agreed.

Harriet nodded. It was a good story. 'Let's go in for that cup of tea,' she suggested.

She parked Owen in the kitchen with her mother and went upstairs to fetch her mother's shawl for her. 'Just call me the Bearer,' she muttered under her breath.

She located the shawl and was about to go back downstairs when something drew her into her own bedroom. She went over to the window, pulled the curtain aside and looked down on the dark farmyard below, the orchard to the left, and to the right, the soft glint of the pond and the obscure shape of the mulberry tree.

Pyramus and Thisbe, she thought to herself. Her shoulders relaxed and she smiled. Mulberry Farm Cottage. Unrequited love. *Well, I never . . .*

CHAPTER 44

Joanna

Prague

Joanna was in Wenceslas Square, which was actually a massive rectangular boulevard lined with trees. It was home to glossy arcades and the National Museum, to the Wiehl building with its *sgraffito* decoration and to the statue of St Wenceslas himself. The wide streets and perfumeries gave the place a cosmopolitan air. It was her final day in Prague and she was putting the last touches to her bridge walk.

From the square, she walked to the art nouveau Municipal House, Obecní Dům. It was a golden palace – filigree metal-work, sculptured relief, stained glass and glazed copper dome. And inside . . . She stepped through the open doorway, sat down on a leather bench. *A classic cream and gold coffee house*, she wrote in her notebook, illuminated by chandeliers – long tubes of light hanging from brass rods. She ordered coffee, gazed around her at the latte and white relief on the ceiling and walls, the gallery, the spiral staircase, the vibrant

344

stained glass. It was so different from anywhere Joanna had been before.

Afterwards, she walked under the charcoal-grey Powder Tower, originally built in the fifteenth century as a ceremonial entrance to the Old Town, according to her research. Emmy had probably visited all these places, though it was hard to tell – in the Prague letter she was so much more concerned with her emotions. Poor Emmy must have found it difficult to enjoy the sights of Prague, with that sense of sad desperation hanging over her. This was her third letter, and Emmy seemed to be at breaking point.

Joanna continued past tall ornate houses where rococo and baroque facades had been added to the original mediaeval buildings – more total reconstruction than subtle facelift. The sky glittered with cold, and although she was well wrapped up in her jacket, scarf, jeans and boots, Joanna couldn't linger as long as she would have liked. She took a shot of the Black Madonna building – she'd read about it, there was indeed a black Madonna trapped in a gilded cage on the side of the red sandstone – 'A perfect example of Czech Cubism,' she said into her Dictaphone.

It made her think about escape and her thoughts returned again to Nicholas and his emails. Emmy too had written about being trapped, though her meaning was unclear. Joanna shook her head in despair. When would she find out the truth, Emmy's truth? She felt as if she was doing this walk with one foot in the present and one foot in the past.

She ducked inside to admire the graceful curving staircase and the collection of Cubist art. She was pleased with what she'd discovered so far. And what else might she see? Would Emmy be providing her with any more clues? Joanna gave a little shiver. She didn't have much time left in the city. When would she find out?

Once outside again, she found her way into the cobbled Tyn Square, where small cafés were tucked into corners, and a bench under a tree would provide a space for contemplation. But it was too cold for contemplation today. She kept going, wandered past the fountain, a bookshop, a jewellery store selling the famous Bohemian garnets, and into the Botanicus, where she bought some organic soap and body lotion for Harriet and her mother. It struck her that with its maze of little *pruchod* passageways, often leading to a *pavlac* – a secret courtyard – that Prague was rather a secretive city. This, then, could be the key to her theme.

Joanna smiled to herself. She was used to secretive in her family. Mother was secretive – look at the way she contacted tradesmen behind their backs. As for Harriet . . . she'd kept very quiet about this dating site and whoever she'd met just before Joanna came away. Her sister had never been the romantic kind, but now Joanna wondered again, had Harriet ever minded staying at the cottage, looking after Mother? Had she ever yearned for a different life?

And Joanna too was keeping Emmy's secret . . . Soon, she found herself in an alleyway being serenaded by *La bohème*. What now? She stood there, buffeted by the winter breeze and the music, feeling it sweep under her, round her, over her, until it seemed to be coming from inside her. Joanna shook the music from her head, ducked into a dark, woody cloister that smelt of damp and brazil nuts. And there, looming in front of her, was Tyn church, all edgy steeples and spiky belfries. She took more photos. Checked her map. And finally emerged in Staré Město, Old Town Square.

It was massive. An orchestra was playing outside the baroque church of St Nicholas . . . *Nicholas* . . . She moved closer, noted the rococo pink and peach Kinsky Palace and the chisel-roofed Stone Bell House; saw the crowds clustering around the corner of the square by the famous astronomical clock. She exhaled, her breath forming a cloud of steam in the cold air. Everything she had read about Prague was true.

She sat down on one of the benches under the trees. She knew from her research that the square used to be a site for hangings and revolution. And it was this past darkness that intrigued her. *Prague is a city still coloured by its past*, she wrote in her notebook. And yet wasn't everywhere? Wasn't everything, everyone, a product of whatever – or whoever – had gone before?

Joanna decided to make her way back to the hotel – she now knew the exact route of the walk. It would be a secret route. A route that ducked its way around the passageways and alleys, a route that would discover some of the quirkiness of the city – in a tiny white statue of a girl perched on a high town wall, or the ancient sign of a battered red boot carved into a gable to signify a shoemaker's trading place. To explore the darker more edgy side of the city that still lived with the shadow of its past, and to emerge next to the unexpected – be it a courtyard garden, a shopping centre or a Gothic church. A walk that would start and finish on the Charles Bridge.

The light was dimming as she approached the Gateway Tower that led to the bridge, but the street sellers were still there with their prints and their T-shirts, their carvings, their sunglasses and their jewellery. And the musicians were still playing, faster jazz now, to keep them warm perhaps; they were dressed in straw hats, berets, thick coats and baggy trousers, playing the mandolin, the banjo, the double bass, their feet tapping to the beat, still smiling.

Joanna paused. This was a perfect vantage point. She gazed southwards along the Vltava to the bridges receding in the hazy distance, down at the weir stretching diagonally across the river, and the steps leading to Kampa Island, built after the big flood. Up the hill, the castle was already illuminated golden in the half-light. If only she could see Emmy's painting of the bridge . . . How exactly had Emmy painted the Vltava, the river of life?

Joanna looked down once more. The water glimmered platinum in the softly growing darkness, swelling as it flowed under the arches of the bridge, all powerful, a soul-force. It was the water once used for drinking, washing, powering machinery, sewerage and as a route for trade. She had read that it symbolised the spirit of a nation, featuring famously in Smetana's orchestral masterpiece, *My Homeland*. She must listen to that, she thought, when she had returned to England, when she was writing this piece, feeling grey and dreary, trying to recapture the feel.

She leant on the stone parapet and her thoughts floated along with the river. If Emmy had loved Rufus and Rufus lived in Mulberry Farm Cottage, where had Emmy lived? She must have lived in Dorset somewhere. Who was she? Clearly not a servant or a farm worker – not if she painted and went travelling with her father; she must have been a girl of class, a girl who had mixed socially with Rufus, a girl who had met him and fallen in love. If it weren't for the letters, Joanna thought, her gloved hands pressing into the cold stone, she almost wouldn't believe . . .

She turned to face the statue of St John Nepomuk, the only

348

bronze statue now remaining on the bridge. He was rather a cutie. His head was cocked to one side under the famous halo of stars and there was a curious expression on his face, as if he didn't quite understand the mortal world, as if he was on quite another plane. His plinth was made of stone and the brass plates had been polished by everyone touching him – for luck. Joanna stepped forwards and did likewise. The picture on the left showed him with a dog, the one on the right showed him being tied and thrown off the bridge as a martyr in 1393. The halo of stars was said to have appeared when he entered the water. *Splash* . . .

It was hard, Joanna found, to drag herself away from him.

She awoke at dawn. The pale morning light was creeping through the muslin curtain. She got up, walked to the window, swept the curtain aside and looked out at the Charles Bridge. It was deserted. No people. No merchandise. Bare cobbles. Still and statuesque . . .

Quickly, she pulled on jeans, a jumper and her jacket, wound a scarf around her neck and slipped out of the room, down the stairs, through the hotel foyer and outside. Her footsteps on the cobbles of the bridge felt fresh and new as if she were the first person. For a moment, she felt conscious of a thick-walled silence; then the only sound was the soft murmur of the river. She knew without thinking about it where she wanted to go. Was she still asleep, still dreaming? It almost seemed that way in the blurred pink light of dawn as the cold numbed her fingers, her lips, her nose.

She stopped in front of him, but to one side to give him space. There was a look on his face now of sadness and pain. He seemed to be waiting for someone – but no one came. What would he do? What could he do? Joanna waited.

As she watched, he stepped off the brass plinth and looked straight at her. Was he asking her something? Did he want her to carry a message to someone? She couldn't speak, couldn't tear her eyes from his.

He ran to the edge, to the stone parapet of the bridge, fast as a flame. Stepped up, pulling his robe around his thin body in one fluid movement. One last look behind him. He jumped.

Splash . . .

My God. Could she have stopped him? She almost thought that she could. Joanna ran to the parapet, leant over. The river flowed on, like life, the stars spluttered in a firework above the spot where he'd entered the water. And in the Vltava, swirling out towards the weir, carried outwards and away, were a painter's palette and a long hank of bloodied red hair.

CHAPTER 45

Harriet

Dorset

The shopping bags were bumping around in the cab of the pick-up, an orange spilling out here, a grapefruit there, as Harriet negotiated the narrow lane leading into the village of Warren Down. She had just dropped the latest package of typed pages off at Bridport post office to be sent to her employer at the PO box address he'd given her, and now she was on her way home. Joanna wasn't back yet – she had called yesterday to tell Harriet that she'd be staying in London for a few days when she returned from Prague; there were things she had to sort out, people she had to see. Which no doubt included Martin. Harriet pulled a face. She was pretty confident her sister wouldn't have a change of heart and go back to him, but who could tell for sure?

As for Harriet, since Scott, she felt she was getting her life into some sort of order. On the surface, nothing had changed, but she felt more content somehow. She didn't even mind all the typing she was doing; she was quite enjoying deciphering all the strange squiggles on the page, translating her employer's untidy script into something neat and legible. It gave her a sense of achievement and she was earning good money too.

The pick-up bumped over a rut in the lane and a bag of grapes went flying. One eye still on the road, Harriet managed to reach over and shove it back in the bag. Perhaps her life wasn't in perfect order, but . . . She slowed as she approached the blind bend, slammed the bridge of her hand to blast the horn, her usual ritual.

Her hand froze. Ahead of her, in the distance, a man was walking down the lane away from her. He wasn't very tall, he was quite thin and there was a distinctive nervous bounce to his step that she remembered.

Hellfire. Instinctively, she braked. It was him. The prowler. So, he was still around after all. Although he was heading, for once, not towards the cottage – to spy on them or whatever he did to get his kicks – but in the opposite direction, walking down towards the village and the sea.

Harriet's turning was coming up on the right. To the left was a gate that led to one of Owen's fields. Without really considering what she was doing, she veered left instead of right, tight in, hard, so that the truck shuddered, before nestling close into the brambles by the gatepost.

What now?

Jumping down from the cab, Harriet edged towards the road and peered down the lane. She could still see him in the distance. There was no sign of his pushbike today – perhaps he had fallen off it once too often? She smiled grimly. If he were to turn around . . . She glanced behind her to check – he wouldn't be able to see the truck. So. This was her chance.

352

Swiftly, she pulled the key out of the ignition and locked the door. She could leave the pick-up here for ten minutes or so – Owen wouldn't mind. She wouldn't get too close to the man – just in case he turned out to be dangerous after all. She would follow at a distance, see where he went, try to find out a bit more about him.

Harriet set off down the narrow country lane, her legs a little shaky and her heart thumping. She was scared, but excited too. This was different, this was a change. Joanna and Mother wouldn't approve; her sister would certainly tell her she should back off and inform the police. But Harriet was doing no such thing. For once, she was living life in the fast lane.

It had been raining, and the undergrowth by the roadside was sappy and damp; there was a path for walkers, but it was muddy, so she stuck to the lane for now. There was still a light mist of drizzle in the air and the sky was a pale grey, the sun hidden behind the clouds. Harriet kept up her pace. She felt as though she was on the verge of a significant discovery. Did he live around here? He must do, she supposed, since he was walking down the lane with no transport in sight.

When she seemed to be getting a bit close, Harriet slowed slightly. She didn't want to catch up with him – at least not yet, perhaps not ever. But for now, the roles were reversed. She had him in her sights and it gave her a sense of power, of control. The boot was definitely on the other foot.

Abruptly, as if sensing her scrutiny, he turned around to peer behind him. Harriet leapt instinctively into the dense undergrowth on the side of the road. She waited, unmoving, listening to the pulse of her heartbeat, feeling the hairs on the back of her neck bristle to attention. Something damp fell softly onto her head. *Yuck*. She brushed it away. This element

353

of detective work wasn't quite so much fun. Silence. Then the sounds crept in. The drip of rainwater from leaves, the caw of rooks in the woods nearby, a distant tractor engine.

Harriet stepped out into the lane again, dusted bits of damp plant and cobweb from her jeans and hair. There was – *damn it* – no sign of him now. He had disappeared. She almost stamped her foot in frustration. After all that, she had lost him.

She set off down the lane again, at a half-jog this time. She had always assumed that the prowler was a stranger from some neighbouring village; she'd never dreamt he would live here in Warren Down. It was much too close for comfort. She paused for breath. But how could he live here? She always heard – usually through Linda from the pub – when a new resident moved into the village; it was inevitably a matter for speculation and interest. Who were they? Where had they come from? What would they bring to the village? How would they fit in? It was a tight community, and it didn't matter how little you socialised, you would always find out the latest gossip from Linda, or Stace, who ran the village store, whether you were interested or not.

The houses in this section of the lane were set back from the road, fairly large and spaced out, and Harriet knew who lived in every one of them. Still, she looked from right to left as she walked on, half convinced that the prowler would suddenly leap out in front of her brandishing a deadly weapon. She would go past the pub and the village shop, she decided, down to the beach and then give up. But where had he gone? How could he have vanished into thin air?

She was just passing one of the holiday lets, glanced automatically into the window and . . .

There he was. *Ye Gods*. She'd assumed they wouldn't be

occupied at this time of year. She ducked, so that her head was on the same level as the low wall. *Bugger and hellfire.* She stooped still further – she couldn't risk him spotting her now.

'Afternoon, Harriet.'

It was Linda. 'Linda, hi.' Harriet made a pretence of staring down at her shoe while simultaneously shuffling to the end of the wall.

'Is something wrong? Are you OK?' Linda was all concern. 'Have you hurt your back?'

She was safe now, Harriet reckoned, he wouldn't be able to see her from here. 'Oh, I'm fine, thanks.' She straightened. 'Had something in my shoe.' She nodded back at the holiday bungalow. 'Unusual for these to be let out in the winter,' she said.

'Hmm, yes, it's a long let.'

Harriet waited for her to elaborate – Linda always elaborated. Who was he? Did he go into the pub? Did he get many visitors? Why was he here?

But nothing.

'Funny place for anyone to want to come to in November,' Harriet persevered. She shivered dramatically. If anyone knew, Linda would know.

But Linda only winked. 'It takes all sorts, Harriet,' she said.

She could say that again. 'Yes, I suppose.' She cast an appraising look back at the house in question. 'Here on his own, is he?'

'Well, now.' Linda put a hand on her hip in that way she had. 'Some special reason you want to know about him, is there, Harriet?' She winked. 'He's not a bad-looking chap, I'll say that. Bit serious for me, but—'

'No, no. Of course not. No.' Harriet was horrified.

'Right you are.' Linda grinned. 'I'll be seeing you then, love.'

'Yes, see you . . .' What should she do now, Harriet

wondered? Write a note to him and tell him he'd been rumbled? Knock on the door and ask to borrow some sugar? She shivered. She wasn't that brave. She now knew what it felt like to watch someone. But she still didn't know the important thing. She didn't know *why*.

Harriet trudged back up the lane. At least she'd remained undetected – he had no idea that she was on to him. And now she knew where he lived, although that was a mixed blessing. But how could she find out more about him? Stace and her husband Mark owned the holiday lets, but since even Linda didn't seem to know much about the prowler, Harriet doubted that she could succeed where Linda had obviously failed.

She unlocked the truck door and climbed back inside the cab. She couldn't leave it. The man hadn't actually done anything, he hadn't threatened her. But he had invaded their privacy. He had scared her and, in a way, she had felt violated. She knew she'd have to try and find out more – whatever Joanna might say.

Absent-mindedly, she helped herself to a grape before starting up the engine. She could still contact the police, give his address, say, *This man is bothering me* . . . Would they follow it up? Maybe not. But she didn't want to. He was just a nuisance and perhaps . . . Well, perhaps he'd simply taken a fancy to her and taken things a bit far. She smiled. It was possible.

She turned down the lane that led to Mulberry Farm Cottage – or Warren Down Farm Cottage as it used to be known, she thought to herself with a slight shake of the head. Who would have thought?

But she wasn't done with the prowler, not yet. Whatever his motives, he needed to know that he couldn't sneak around spying on people, and sooner or later, Harriet was going to tell him exactly that.

CHAPTER 46

Joanna

London

London. Joanna had lived here for thirteen years and taken it for granted: the bustle, the noise, the buildings, the underground. The people . . .

She had come here straight from Prague; it was something she had to do. Martin had messaged to say they'd had a few viewings on the house and yesterday, someone had come back for a second look. The London market might not be quite what it was, but it wouldn't be long. Soon, the house would be gone and Joanna wanted to see it one last time.

She walked through the hotel foyer. An uncertain winter sunlight filtered through a cloudy sky. She sniffed. In Dorset, the air was fresh, slightly salty and sharp; it smelt of the sea, grass, sheep and sand. In London, the air was more knowing. It smelt of newsprint, doughnuts and smoke, spicy food and dustbins. You could actually smell the cosmopolitan-ness of London. Funny, she'd never really noticed that before.

Joanna put on her London feet, walking briskly away from the impersonal modernity of the hotel. She'd chosen not to stay with Steph or Lucy, though they'd both offered a bed for a few nights. She was looking forward to catching up with them, but she also wanted to be free to get all the other stuff done. And she'd decided to start with the hardest part.

Martin had mentioned in his text that he was currently working from home, so it was more than possible he'd be there at the house. Did that matter? She only wanted to pick up a few things and say goodbye to the house that had been her home. Actually, it was probably a good thing. Despite everything, she wanted to say goodbye to Martin too.

She walked up the steps to Waterloo station and headed for the Northern Line. The journey would take her about forty-five minutes. After that, she had a late afternoon meeting with Toby in Covent Garden and then tonight she was meeting up with Steph. Yes, and when the house was gone, Joanna would have to decide where *she* was going to go.

From Archway, it was a short walk to the bus stop and soon she was on her familiar route, on the number 41 that would take her to Crouch End Broadway. She looked out of the window at all the places she'd looked out at so many times, conscious of the empty bag at her feet, waiting to be filled with the parts of her old life that she didn't want to leave behind.

She got off at the usual stop, walked past the Asian supermarket where she'd always bought her coconut milk, lime leaves and spices. Bundles of coriander, layers of okra, aubergines and chilli peppers were stacked in cartons by the doorway. The dry, husky scent crept towards her as she walked by. Joanna breathed it in. And Martin, she thought. Where would he go? He'd stay in London, she was sure. She couldn't imagine him

358

anywhere else. Joanna, though – she already felt like a visitor here. Already, London had opened its fist and let her go.

As always, it surprised her how quickly she seemed to have left the city behind. Crouch End's Broadway was always stuffed with traffic, but the area had more than its share of green spaces – it was one of the reasons she and Martin had chosen to live here. The city was a rush; it had always made Joanna feel alive. But . . . She let out her breath in a slow sigh. After the rush, you needed a sense of calm. Harriet always said there was no peace in London, but this wasn't quite true. There were four miles of tranquillity down Parkland Walk, for example, a former railway line connecting Finsbury Park to Alexandra Palace where orchids grew beside fig trees and it was possible to find a sense of quiet in the middle of it all.

She'd tried to explain this to Harriet, but her sister wouldn't even try to understand. *Well, of course, I've only ever lived in Dorset,* she'd say. As if it were somehow Joanna's fault. *How would I know anything about the Big City?* Joanna smiled. But she felt that she was beginning to understand her sister – much more than she ever had before.

She turned the corner into the familiar and leafy road with its row of three-storey Victorian houses with black railings and dowdy little squares of front garden. For a moment, she held her breath. Martin had already said that he would buy out their furniture and things they'd accumulated in their years together and Joanna was glad – she wanted to feel free of it. Or at least, of most of it. But now. This could, she knew, be the last time she came back here. And there were so many mixed feelings.

One of their neighbours had planted some purple winter pansies in a window box. Joanna knew the woman by sight – she was tall, with a helmet of dark hair that hid her face from scrutiny. Joanna didn't know her name – not unusual in London, where everyone seemed to be so busy most of the time. This had been appealing after growing up in a Dorset village where everyone knew everyone else's business. Joanna walked briskly on. How she had loved the anonymity of the city. The chance to be among people and yet on her own. The bliss of shutting her front door on the world and knowing that it wouldn't come knocking . . .

And Joanna had needed to be here in town too. As a journalist, this was where the work was and as a freelance writer, it wasn't so easy to get commissions or pitch ideas if you were away from the hub of things. London was where it happened. Joanna might not have been born one, but she had become a city girl. And now? The Internet had changed things. It was so much easier to work from a distance and every piece of information was available online. But she was beginning to think that now, she needed different things that London didn't offer. The landscape of the West Country was drawing her away. She didn't have to come back here.

Still . . . She looked up at the house, her house. And she remembered when they'd first seen it, the moment she'd first fallen in love with its bay-fronted windows, the red brickwork, the stained glass in the front door. It was more solid than the flat they'd shared after university and before they got married; more of a home. But that was then. Her gaze moved to the curtains at the window. Now, it wasn't her house anymore. She'd left the house as well as Martin.

Joanna took a deep breath. She walked up the concrete path to their front door and rang the bell. After a moment she could see the shape of Martin and his pale hair through the glass. He opened the door.

'Jo!' For a moment, the grin she hadn't seen for so long illuminated his face and she remembered what she had loved about him – his enthusiasm, his way of making her laugh, making her feel loved.

'Hello, Martin.' She smiled back at him. 'Sorry not to warn you I was coming.' She had, she realised, done exactly what he'd done when he'd surprised her in Dorset.

'It doesn't matter.' He shook his head, but she saw a flicker of concern in his eyes. Perhaps he was wondering if the place wasn't clean enough or tidy enough? Perhaps it wasn't fair to turn up unannounced.

'I could come back later, get a coffee or something?'

He stood aside. 'No, come in. It's good to see you.' And she saw that he meant it.

'Thanks.' She passed him and walked into the hallway.

'Can I take your coat?'

It was so strange, she thought, when this had been her home. She slipped off her jacket and he hung it on the hook – a wood panel from an old school cloakroom; they'd found it at Bridport street market on a visit to Dorset, the first thing they'd bought together. Joanna's breath caught. This was harder than she'd anticipated.

'Can I . . . ?' She gestured to the kitchen. She wanted to look at every room, as if each one was a friend she was about to lose.

'Sure.' He made a gesture to show that she should go where she wanted to go. 'It's your house too, remember?'

She remembered. The dinners she had cooked, the evenings spent together, the days working in her office upstairs. She remembered all right. And yet she didn't feel like a victim; she knew she had broken free. Martin, though, was still at a loss, she could see that.

361

'I've come to collect a few bits,' she said. 'I'll take them back with me.'

'Did you bring a van or something?' He peered outside as if expecting to see a removal lorry or Harriet's pick-up truck parked in the road.

'No.' She held up the bag. 'I've only got this.' She wasn't taking much. There really wasn't much more that she needed. For some time now she'd been decluttering her life and this was where it had begun.

Martin blinked at her as if she had suddenly become Mary Poppins. 'For all of your stuff?'

'Yes.' She relented. 'If there's anything else, maybe you could send it on later?'

'Sure, yeah, no problem.' Joanna watched him as he closed the front door. She had a sudden vision of what he would look like as he grew older. They would still grow older, just not together.

She stepped into the kitchen. She wanted to get this over with, she didn't want to linger. There were good and bad memories in this house and she wasn't sure she wanted either right now.

Martin followed her. 'Have you got time for a coffee?'

Joanna hesitated. Thought of Toby. She did have time, but it probably wasn't a great idea. 'Sorry, no, not really.'

Martin didn't seem surprised. 'So, how have you been?'

'Fine.' There was a bottle of whisky on the worktop, next to a half-eaten loaf of white bread and a bottle of tomato ketchup. Well, Martin had never been a gourmet. She looked around. Kitchen things could so easily be replaced.

'And have you . . . ?' He hesitated.

She turned around. 'Have I what?'

362

'Found . . . someone else?'

Joanna sighed. 'No, of course not.' As if there might be a replacement husband lurking under a Dorset cliff somewhere. She eyed him more speculatively. 'Are you seeing anyone, Martin?'

He shook his head much more emphatically than necessary. 'Absolutely not,' he said.

'Hilary?' On the kitchen shelf she spotted her favourite honeypot. Martin had never liked it.

'No,' he said.

She picked up the honeypot, examined the golden and brown bee on the lid. 'Can I take this?'

'Of course.'

Joanna wrapped it in some bubble wrap she'd brought with her and placed it carefully in the bag.

'You're an attractive woman,' he said, looking at her as if he'd only just realised. 'I wouldn't blame you for finding someone else.'

'No.' What did he expect her to say? She left the kitchen, went into the sitting room, aware once more of Martin behind her, tracking her movements. His name was still on her passport, her bank details, her will. She must change all that. 'I'm not looking for a man,' she told him. 'But if someone came along . . .'

'It would be your business, yeah, I know.'

She regarded him once more. His hands were in his pockets, he had put on a bit of weight and he needed a shave. She wished that he'd leave her for a minute. This was hard enough already without Martin looking lost and reminding her of everything they'd once shared.

There was a miniature on the wall by the fireplace – a small painting Lucy's husband Bill had done of Alexandra Palace. 'I'd like this,' she said.

'Fine.'

Joanna wrapped this in bubble wrap too. 'I'm going upstairs,' she told him.

Their bedroom – this wouldn't be easy. Joanna took a deep breath. Thankfully, Martin didn't follow her this time. She went through her things methodically, selecting only a special few – the rest could go to a charity shop. She was determined to live her life in a more minimalist way from now on; a freedom from the material leading to an uncluttered mind, that sort of thing.

In the bathroom, she saw a lipstick on the shelf. She picked it up, twisted it until the peachy stick emerged. She was almost sure it belonged to Hilary; she remembered that particular shade. But it was Martin's life. And Joanna wasn't part of it anymore.

By the time she left, half an hour later, her bag was full but not too heavy. He was standing by the door.

'I want a divorce, Martin,' she told him.

He didn't seem surprised.

She would put the wheels in motion. She would make a new will, revert to her maiden name officially – not just for her writing, where she had always been Joanna Shepherd and probably always would be. 'And let me know what happens with the house?'

'Yeah, I will.'

There was a moment, as she stood on the doorstep, when she almost doubted herself, a moment when she looked at him and saw the earlier version of Martin, the man she'd loved. She put a hand on his arm and saw his eyes soften. 'Sorry, Martin,' she said.

'Me too, Jo.' He seemed to understand.

She smelt the familiar fragrance of him – a bit of soap, a hint of oak. For a few seconds she breathed it in. Then she gave a brisk nod and she walked away. No looking back this time.

365

CHAPTER 47

Harriet

Dorset

Harriet had gathered the eggs, fed the pigs and returned the
swill bucket to the food store in the old cow shed. It was cold,
but the hens were still laying, bless them.

She went back inside. 'I'm just nipping into the village,'
she told her mother. They had run out of milk. 'Will you be
all right?'

'Of course I will, Harriet.'

Harriet narrowed her eyes. She didn't like this quiet, pensive
version of her mother and she still wasn't sure that she could
be trusted. She also wanted to pull her mother into her arms
and comfort her. But she didn't do it. Harriet wasn't much
use at comfort, she had always known that. Mother's problem
was that she had allowed herself to become too dependent on
Father. So that when he died . . . when he died . . . The dream
nudged at Harriet's subconscious and she pushed it away. *Not
now. Not ever.* Well, it had taken the life out of Mother too.

'I won't be long,' Harriet said.

'When do you think Joanna will be back?' her mother asked.

Joanna, Joanna. But Mother missed her, of course. Like Harriet, she had got used to Joanna being around. And Joanna was so much better in the giving comfort department.

'I don't know.' Harriet pulled her jacket from the hook by the door. 'In a day or two, I expect.' She wound a scarf around her neck and opened the door. But what would happen when Joanna moved out? When it was just the two of them again, Harriet and Mother and all the tensions that seemed to exist between them? She sighed.

Harriet decided to walk into the village – that way she'd stand a better chance of spotting the prowler. She hadn't decided what to do about him yet. As far as she knew, he hadn't been back to the cottage, but the phone had rung a couple of times and when she'd answered, there'd been only silence on the other end. This could be a coincidence, but Harriet was still uneasy, quite sure that he was still around and on the prowl as it were.

It was a cold but sunny mid-November day; a light frost still sparked the tips of the grass blades and undergrowth, and the sea air was invigorating. Harriet could see Owen's tractor in a far-off field, and in the distance the sea shimmered between the gentle curves of the Down. She thought of that conversation she'd had with Owen by the mulberry tree. She hadn't seen him since, but he'd waved to her from afar a couple of times when he was out in the fields working and she was confident that their relationship had returned to normal. He hadn't mentioned any dinner invitation again, naturally . . . But she only had herself to blame.

Harriet tramped off down the lane. She liked winter days

like this one. They had a special sort of clarity about them and in winter she felt that the villagers could reclaim Warren Down and make it once again their own.

Summer would come soon enough. They needed the summer, they needed the tourists; more and more of the houses were being let out to holidaymakers. By next April, Harriet would again be baking cakes and opening up the café in Big Barn for the walkers. Another cycle, another year. But for the people who lived here all year round, they were still a community. This was still their landscape, their home. Harriet thought of the prowler. And that home had been invaded.

There was no sign of activity when she cautiously passed the house he'd rented. Harriet walked on. In the village, she bought the milk, chatted to Maurice, the delivery man, and spent fifteen minutes passing the time of day with Linda (goodness, if she lived in this street, she'd never get anything done). She was just thinking she should get back home when she spotted him – the prowler – cycling up the lane towards her. What now? How could she avoid him? Abruptly, she ducked back inside the shop, without warning.

Linda, who had been in the middle of describing how her husband Eddie had woken her up in the middle of a nightmare thinking he was being strangled by the new James Bond, stood in the shop doorway and eyed her curiously. 'What's the matter, Harriet?'

'Nothing.' Quickly, Harriet turned away, pretending to inspect the magazines on the rack. 'Just need to get . . .' she mumbled, 'my *Cosmopolitan*.'

Cosmopolitan? What was she thinking? That a one-night stand had made her sixteen again? She stared vacantly at the cover.

'*Cosmopolitan?*' Linda followed her inside, which was good, as her bulky frame hid Harriet from view. 'I would have thought you were more *People's Friend*, dear.'

Harriet was tempted to tell her about Scott and the camper van. That would show her what Harriet was really made of. The sensuality that she had always kept hidden – so well hidden that she hadn't even known about it herself. But she held back. She didn't want the whole village to know.

And there he was. Close up. He swung his legs awkwardly off his bike, almost falling over as he did so. Harriet restrained a chuckle then dodged behind a card stand as he peered into the shop. That was a close thing. It was fortunate that Linda had a generous rear end, otherwise he would have spotted her, for sure. And she didn't want him to spot her, at least not yet. Not until she'd decided what to do about him.

As she came out from behind the stand, now holding a birthday card which proclaimed 'Happy Birthday, Grandson' (that would be news to everybody), she saw him lift a brown paper package from his bike rack. *Hellfire* . . . She had to grip Linda's shoulder for support.

'Harriet, what is it, dear? Are you all right?'

Fortunately, he was out of earshot. But Harriet stared after him. She'd recognise that brown paper package anywhere. Mainly because it had fluorescent blue tape stuck all over it – Harriet had run out of the brown stuff.

'I'm fine.' She stood there and let the full implications dawn. The prowler who had been hanging around Mulberry Farm Cottage was the mystery recipient at a PO box address, the scientist who was employing her as a typist. What did it mean? She took a ragged breath. Harriet was working for the prowler. And the prowler who had been hanging around Mulberry

Farm Cottage was so interested in Harriet that he'd employed her to type out his scientific manuscript. *Hell's bells* . . . It was much more of a tangled web than Harriet had suspected. What now?

CHAPTER 48

Joanna

London

On her way to meet Toby, Joanna stopped for coffee in Covent Garden. Seeing Martin, seeing the house – it hadn't been easy, and she was relieved it was over. *Time to move on*, she thought. *Again*.

When she checked her phone she saw she'd had an email from Nicholas Tresillion. She opened it with anticipation.

Dear Joanna, she read.

It was my work that took me to Lisbon. I approach clients – certain pre-selected outlets – that might be interested in stocking my sister-in-law's jewellery. She and my brother-in-law are based in Rome – which is where I am now, but not for much longer. I'm not here for work, and not specifically to see them, though we have fitted in some meetings too, but for a family get-together organised by my ex-wife Rachel to celebrate our daughter's forthcoming marriage. Ouch . . .

It sounded, thought Joanna, as though Nicholas was still very involved with his ex's family. She supposed that was what

371

it was like when you had children – even grown-up children. It was very different to how she felt about Martin. It was even possible – and she flinched at this thought – that she might never see him again. She read on.

It turns out that Rachel's getting married too – to an Italian guy who is obviously far more her style than I could ever be.

Hmm. Did he feel sad about that? Joanna wasn't sure.

Do I sound bitter?

Ha. She chuckled softly.

I'm not, though a double wedding is a bit insensitive and tasteless, don't you think? Families, eh?

A double wedding . . . Joanna shook her head. Poor Nicholas. That would certainly make it hard for him to celebrate his daughter's special day.

But yes, I did enjoy my visit to Lisbon, and I suppose you're right – the man I saw who looked like your man by the mulberry tree must be a coincidence; one hell of a coincidence, I'd say. Though do you ever get the feeling that all this is being orchestrated in some way?

Funny, that. *Yes*, she thought, *I do.*

I don't want to say more in case you think I'm a complete nutter.

Join the club, thought Joanna.

I'm sorry to hear that your bridge walks have come to an end with Prague, he continued. *And no, sadly I have no plans to visit that city, though out of curiosity alone, I'm very tempted . . . But I would like to hear about Prague and what you saw there.*

Joanna thought about what she'd seen and what she'd thought she'd seen. When she'd finally turned around from staring down into the river that morning, there was John of Nepomuk still there on Charles Bridge, a half-smile on his face. But Joanna remained sure of what she'd seen. Once again, she had gazed down into the Vltava . . . Nothing. But like the other

372

visions, hallucinations, or whatever they were – in Venice, in Lisbon – this one too had dematerialised and slipped away. It was imprinted on Joanna's mind, though. Puzzling out the meaning might help her understand the connection between herself, Emmy and Rufus; she was convinced it was another piece of the puzzle.

And I'd also like us to continue writing – if it's OK with you.

Joanna smiled. It was. She didn't want give up this correspondence – at least not yet. Nicholas Tresillion interested her.

Maybe we could even meet up sometime, if that isn't too presumptuous?

Joanna raised an eyebrow. *Well, now . . .*

I assume you're based in London and I spend some of my time there too. Of course, I quite understand if this is a step too far!

Yours, Nicholas

No, thought Joanna, it wasn't a step too far. Once again, she thought of Harriet and her online dating. It was surprising how much you could find out about someone from emailing alone. She sipped her coffee thoughtfully. Would Nicholas still be in Rome or was he back already?

She made a quick decision. She pulled her laptop out of her bag, logged into the café's wi-fi and typed a rapid reply.

The double wedding idea sounds crass, she began. *I hope for your sake that Celie and your ex have had second thoughts . . .*

She continued to type, the words coming as easily as ever.

I'm not based in London, she wrote. *But I am here right now.*

She looked out of the window of the café. The sky was darkening, though it wasn't even four o'clock.

So, if you happen to be around in the next day or so, if you're flying back from Rome . . .

*

373

'What do you think about the walk pieces?' Joanna asked Toby. 'I mean, really?'

She had been slightly apprehensive about this meeting. Toby hadn't said much about the copy she'd sent him – mostly just suggested bits to develop and bits to leave out. There was no one like Toby for cutting to the quick. But he must have noticed the more surreal stuff. Did he think Joanna was losing her touch?

'All good, sweetie.' Toby bit into his slice of pistachio and honey cake. They were in their usual café in Covent Garden. Outside, the market was as colourful as ever; a juggler was throwing silver skittles into the air and a busker was doing a hearty rendition of 'Stairway to Heaven'. Both had attracted quite a crowd.

'And I like the stuff you're putting in the column these days too,' he added. 'It's more sparky and upbeat.'

Joanna exhaled. That was good. She needed to get as much work as she could.

'You've got the right balance in the walking material,' he went on, pushing the wing of newly bleached hair that flopped over his high forehead further back and out of his eyes. 'Not too preachy, not too much like a tourist guide. Different. But lots of interesting info, yeah.'

'Thanks.' She cut her cake into squares and popped one into her mouth.

'They're fun. Quirky.'

'You think so?' Joanna took a sip of her Earl Grey. That was exactly what she'd been hoping. Although Toby didn't know the full extent, did he? He didn't know about Nicholas Tresillion. Or Emmy. 'So, no complaints?'

'From who?'

'Er . . .' From people who had failed to see a mirage in the Venetian canal, for example? From those who had somehow missed the children playing in the mulberry tree, and not noticed the martyred saint leaping off the Charles Bridge at dawn – though to be fair, this one hadn't been published yet. 'Anyone?' she said.

'On the contrary.' Toby took another large bite. 'The tourist offices love 'em. I told you before. They're flying off the shelves.'

'Great.' Joanna ate another square. The cake had a lovely edge of citrus while the honey had caramelised the pistachios, turning them golden and delicious. She knew Toby well enough to recognise the exaggeration. But she didn't care. Any praise from an editor was sweet.

'You even created a love affair by all accounts,' Toby added.

'What?' How on earth did Toby know about Emmy and Rufus? She stared at him. She hadn't written about them – had she?

'Yeah, this woman was doing the Lisbon walk and she bumped into some guy who happened to be doing it at the same time.'

Joanna blinked at him. *Ah.* 'Really?' She licked the crumbs from her fingers.

'Yeah, she wrote you an email – I need to forward it to you. They're an item now, apparently.'

Joanna shook her head. She was lost for words.

'So maybe we'll do another set? Bridges again, d'you think?' Toby lounged back in his chair.

Joanna wondered what it would be like conjuring up bridge walks when she wasn't following in Emmy's footsteps. It was hard to imagine somehow.

'Where do you fancy?' Toby asked. 'Paris? Barcelona? Rome?'

Nicholas was in Rome. Joanna took another sip of her tea. 'There's the Seine,' she pointed out, rather unnecessarily. But not for much longer, he had said. Was he coming back in the next few days? And what would it be like to meet him? She hoped it wouldn't spoil things. She rather liked the feeling of their words meeting when they did not. Or was she being fanciful again? She supposed she didn't want to be disappointed. She wanted the man who also saw visions in mulberry trees to be a bit special, she supposed. Which was silly.

'Paris in springtime would be perfect.' Toby rubbed his hands together. 'Clichés are only clichés because they work so well and always have. We'll leave Rome as we've already done Venice. But Barcelona would work, then maybe Budapest or Berlin?'

'Sounds great.' Joanna closed her eyes for a moment, suddenly feeling weary.

'Are you sure you're up for it, Jo?'

She snapped her eyes open again. Thought about all the work that needed doing at Mulberry Farm Cottage. Her share of the house in Crouch End wouldn't leave much over by the time she'd found somewhere else to live. 'I'm up for it,' she said.

Toby eyed her seriously. 'No chance of a marital reconciliation then?'

Joanna shook her head. 'The house is on the market. It's definitely over.' She sipped her tea. How many more times would she have to say those words? To Steph, to Lucy, to other friends and colleagues who would all be eager to know.

Toby patted her hand. 'Sorry it didn't work out, sweetie.'

'Thanks.'

376

'But if you've really got the travelling bug . . .' Toby was still regarding her intently.

'Yes?' She was enjoying it. But that didn't mean she didn't also want a home. Somewhere to call a base.

'How about a book?'

'A book?' Joanna finished the last square of cake. She hadn't told Toby about that old dream of hers to write a novel. That dream was covered with dust these days, but she still hoped that one day she might feel like getting out a cleaning rag.

'Yeah, you know, one of those things with pages covered in print that we read before we fall asleep at night.'

'Very funny. What sort of a book?'

Toby sat back in his chair. 'A travel book – with a difference.'

She should have guessed. Toby was a single-minded person. He did like the brochures – he really liked the brochures. But now he was thinking ahead to the next logical step – that with the right kind of travel book they could do even better. Which was appealing. Sort of. 'Set where?' she asked him.

He spread his hands. 'Where do you want to go?'

Was it that simple? The world was a big place. It was incredible, she thought, how the patterns of her days had changed following the catalysts of Martin's adultery and Emmy's letters. And now . . . she was living a completely different life. She laughed.

'What?' Toby grinned back at her.

'Well . . .' Joanna hesitated. She still hadn't told anyone about Emmy. The person she'd most wanted to confide in was Nicholas Tresillion, but it had to be face to face – she couldn't bear it if some almost-stranger laughed at her. And something had made her hold back, not wanting to break the spell . . .

But Toby had read the copy and hadn't flipped out.

377

So, she told him about the Venetian bridge painting and Emmy's letters. 'The first one was written from Venice with love,' she said. 'That's what got me started.' It felt odd to be talking about it, this secret that she'd been hugging to herself for the past weeks and months.

'And you haven't discovered who she was yet?' Toby asked when she'd finished.

'I don't have a clue.' And she was no nearer finding out. 'I don't even know her full name.'

He pushed his empty coffee cup away and signalled to the waitress that he'd like another. 'It would be easy enough to find out, I would've thought.'

'Would it?' Was she missing something here? 'The signature on the painting's almost illegible and she just signs her letters *Emmy*.'

'It's a decent painting, though, you say?' He frowned. 'And she did other stuff. It wasn't a one-off?'

Not a one-off certainly – there were the other bridges for starters. Joanna considered. 'Yes, I think in a small way she was a fairly well-established artist. But she was a woman and—'

'Then get it off the bloody wall and take the thing to Sotheby's,' Toby said.

'Sotheby's? Would they—'

'They're bound to have heard of her.' Toby's coffee arrived and he loaded in some sugar. 'If she has any kind of artistic reputation, they'll know about it, and they'll recognise her style. How many women do you think were painting water-colours of foreign bridges before the First World War?'

'Well . . .' Now that he put it like that . . . He was probably right. Why hadn't this occurred to her? She felt a surge of excitement. 'I'll ring them and make an appointment.'

'Good plan.' Toby stirred his coffee. 'And don't forget about the book idea, Jo. Think of something that's never been done.'

They both laughed. Joanna knew as well as he did that everything had been done – you just had to change the angle.

'Cycling over the Himalayas?' she suggested.

'Jet skiing in the Gobi Desert?'

She grinned. 'I'll think of something.' It wasn't a novel, but she liked the idea; she liked it a lot.

CHAPTER 49

Nicholas

Prague

Nicholas stood at one end of the Charles Bridge gazing at the statues, musicians, street traders and tourists. The Vltava flowed under the bridge like a sheet of molten steel. Funny, he thought, that he'd never been here before.

It was cold. The latest email from Joanna Shepherd had arrived yesterday, and although she couldn't have known he'd be here, she had included an attachment: the text of her latest bridge walk piece. Nicholas felt privileged.

It hasn't been revised or edited yet, she had written, *so it's a bit raw. But it'll give you the flavour.*

And it certainly had.

He had enjoyed a couple of beers at a bar next to his hotel – no, he wasn't staying at The Three Ostriches as Joanna had, though he'd spotted the hotel perched by the side of the bridge's pier, the ostriches painted on a fresco on the wall, muslin curtains billowing.

He hadn't planned to come to Prague at all. Maybe that's what happened when you lost sight of where you were going – you began to travel in tangents, following behind some wacky writer, as if you had no pathway of your own. He shook his head. It wasn't like that, though. In fact, this felt like his pathway – the city had been on his bucket list for a long time.

He'd been at the airport in Rome yesterday, about to go through security, his head full of what had happened. Celie and Tom getting married . . . well, that was good. And then there was Rachel and that smooth-talking Italian. What exactly did Nicholas think about that? He frowned. Why should he care what Rachel chose to do with her life? But was it only him who thought the guy was a bit of a dick with his gold signet ring and flash Italian suit? Or was it plain old-fashioned jealousy? Was his ego hurting, just a little bit? *Be honest, now . . . Yes, damn it*. Did the woman have no taste?

The Old Tower stood in front of him, dour and grey, though the sky was still blue, paling into dusk, the milky winter sun shimmering on the water. Nicholas shielded his eyes from the glare, felt the alcohol lurking behind his sinuses.

He pulled his sunglasses out of his top pocket, put them on and walked past the wooden African carvings on the first stall, past the pen-and-ink pictures of a Prague that was long gone, past the jewellery (could there be a market for their jewellery in Prague? Maybe he'd check out some of the more upmarket places while he was here) and the cheap leather bags. The Charles Bridge was wide and packed with tourists, most of whom seemed to be heading in the opposite direction to Nicholas – a group of Japanese businessmen in shades and natty suits, families with small children and buggies, a pack of guys on a stag do, a huddle of giggling girls, young lovers, old lovers, middle-aged lovers; they swarmed by.

A band of musicians were playing 'Blue Moon'. They were really into it. They were just a group of old guys, baseball caps stuck on their white heads; leaning against the parapet or sitting on fold-up chairs; a saxophonist, a banjo player, a man on the bongos; feet tapping, easy grins on lined, weather-beaten faces.

Evening was drawing in. Nicholas moved over to the parapet and stared into the Vltava, at the diagonal weir where the murky grey water poured down. Into the distance, outlined against the blushing early evening sky, the bridges stretched out into the future, exactly as Joanna Shepherd had promised they would. He smiled.

Everyone else in his family seemed to have their future sewn up. But not Nicholas. He needed a project, he realised. And maybe some time off. Maybe a few months in Fuerteventura exploring some of those remote beaches on the west coast. A retreat from life. From people. Enjoying the rediscovery of his self, remembering what it felt like to be free.

He turned back to face the musicians. They seemed happy enough, this motley crew, playing for their supper; they couldn't make much per hour by the time it was split between the six of them. But he'd hazard a guess that they felt free. He dug a ten-euro note out of his wallet and chucked it in the saxophone case. 'Something,' he called.

Surprisingly, they seemed to understand. The lead singer nodded, spoke to the rest of the band. They struck it up. 'Something'.

At the airport outside the city of Rome yesterday, he'd sent an email to Joanna Shepherd while he had a quick coffee and pastry for breakfast. But when he headed for security, he found that the flight he wanted – back to the UK – had been cancelled due to technical issues, whatever that might mean. Perfect. He groaned. Queues were forming and people were panicking. Should they buy a flight from another airline or wait for it to be sorted out?

Nicholas looked up at the departures board and found himself playing that game he'd played with Celie at airports in the past. *Where would you most like to be going?* And then he saw it. Prague. *Synchronicity*, he thought. When he enquired, it turned out that the flight wasn't full. And so he bought a ticket.

Nicholas turned back to the river. The flow of the water was hypnotic. Maybe tomorrow he'd do a boat trip – Joanna had recommended it. Listen to him – *Joanna this, Joanna that* . . . And where was that guy she'd written about?

The musicians finished the song, looked to him for another request. He shrugged. Ah . . . Here he was standing almost right beside him – St John of Nepomuk, the man who had been flung into the river, thus becoming martyred forever. Head on one side, kind of wistful looking. Nicholas pulled out his phone and read the text once again. According to Joanna, she'd seen St John here taking a running leap into the river at dawn . . . He shook his head. It had given her the shivers apparently – understandably. Still, he'd seen some pretty strange things himself lately. *If you look long enough*, she always said.

He flipped back to her email.

I'm not based in London. But I am here right now, she had written. *So if you happen to be around in the next few days or so, if you're flying back from Rome, I'd be happy to meet for a coffee or a drink. It would be good to put a face to your words.*

By the time he'd read this, his flight to the UK had been

cancelled anyway. If not for that, they might have met face to face by now. He read on.

In answer to your question — yes, I do get the sense that someone is orchestrating things, but I'm surprised you feel that too. To be honest with you, I have been 'led' on these walks by some research that I've been doing. It's a long story and perhaps if we meet, I'll tell you about it.

Interesting, thought Nicholas.

Let me know — I'm only here for another day or so, but if you're not back yet or you're busy, no worries.

Joanna

The crowd had thinned. A few metres away from the statue — which, to Nicholas, appeared firmly rooted — a woman sat painting. She was frowning and biting her lower lip in concentration. Her fair hair was piled on top of her head and fastened with a comb, and she was wearing a long black skirt. Curious, Nicholas drew closer, to see the quality of the work. She was painting with watercolours, mixing shades in an old ceramic dish, and after a few deft strokes she cleaned her brush in a small jar of water. There was something old-fashioned about her appearance and the way she was working. But that wasn't so strange. Prague was an historic city — it had an old feel to it, its architecture and people were steeped in the past.

He wanted to speak to her, to ask her about her painting — she was only a girl really, probably about Celie's age — but something stopped him. The expression on her face of intense concentration, maybe, or some ethereal quality about her. She wasn't beautiful, but there was a paleness in her light blue eyes and a translucence to her skin that made her look . . . different. And something else. *Something* . . . The song echoed in his head and he realised the musicians were playing it again. Something familiar about her, almost as if he'd seen her before.

384

Suddenly she looked at him and smiled. And then he knew. *Bloody hell*. So, it was his pathway too. Half hypnotised, he took a step closer towards her to see the picture. Somewhere inside of him, he knew exactly what he would see. The painting featured St John of Nepomuk of course, with his sad bewildered eyes, the dog sitting at his feet, golden stars clustered around the saint's cocked head, shooting up towards the darkening sky.

CHAPTER 50

Harriet

Dorset

Harriet was lifting the last of her leeks and parsnips before the ground froze, heeling them in a trench she'd dug for the purpose next to the path, so that she could easily lift them when needed. They'd keep for a few months like this; it was a trick she'd learnt from her father.

She was a bit behind this morning, mainly because she'd had to traipse over to Bridport following her sister's phone call yesterday afternoon. Harriet clicked her tongue, put some weight on the fork and gently eased up the next two leeks.

'Can you do me a favour, Het?' Joanna had asked. 'I know you're busy, but . . .' Her voice had trailed off.

'What?' Harriet wasn't much in the mood for doing favours. Since her recent discovery about the prowler she hadn't done any more typing either; she needed to think about what to do next. Actually, she needed to talk to someone. But who? Mother was out of the question, Linda would tell the entire village and Joanna . . . well, Joanna would insist that they inform the police.

'I need you to take down the bridge painting in my room,' Joanna said.

That was probably the last thing Harriet had been expecting.

'Then I need you to pack it – very carefully – and send it to London by courier.'

'By courier?' How much was that going to cost? And why on earth did Joanna want the painting in London? Wasn't she coming back here? Was the painting the only thing she wanted from the cottage? Harriet's mind went into overdrive.

'I'll pay you back in a few days,' her sister assured her. 'When I get back home.'

Ah. That answered at least one of her questions.

'I want you to send it to Sotheby's.' Joanna rattled off the address.

Sotheby's? 'Is it valuable?' If so, it probably wasn't a great idea to send it – even by courier.

'Probably not.'

'Then . . . ?' Harriet was confused.

'I need to find out a bit more about the artist,' Joanna said. 'It's a long story. And I will tell you as soon as I get back.'

'But can't you do it yourself when you get back?' Harriet had enough claims on her time already. Not only did she want to get the vegetables lifted, but she had planned to divide the rhubarb and clear up some of the debris around the kitchen garden in order to evict some of the slugs and snails that had taken up residence there.

'I need to be here,' Joanna explained. 'To go to Sotheby's and talk to them about it. If I come back to Dorset, then I'll have to go back to London, then—'

'Oh, all right.' Harriet couldn't bear to hear any more. 'I'll do it.'

'Tomorrow morning?'

She sighed. 'Tomorrow morning.'

'Thanks, Het.'

Harriet had examined the painting when she took it down from the wall first thing. Some bridge in Venice, a watery canal, shades of blue, grey and silver. Nice but not remarkable. But it obviously meant a lot to Joanna, so she wrapped it with care in plenty of plastic bubbles. *Another mystery*, she thought. Right now, there seemed to be a few too many of them for comfort.

Now, she gently shook the soil from the roots before laying the leeks to one side. She stood up to stretch out her back and looked across the fields towards the sea. Owen was a field away trudging down the track. She waved. He waved back but made no move to change direction. Hmm. Their relationship might have gone back to normal, but he certainly didn't come round quite as much as he used to. Was he fed up with them? Or was it that he stayed away when they didn't have the attraction of Joanna to tempt him here?

Harriet considered. But she had to talk to someone. She set off to intercept him.

'Morning, Harriet.' Owen seemed surprised. 'Everything all right?'

Was everything all right? She really had no idea. 'I wonder if I could talk to you sometime,' she said. 'Sometime soon. Like today?' She didn't take her eyes off him. This mattered. But supposing he didn't want to talk to her? She'd hardly bothered with him up till now unless she needed him to help her with something or to entertain her mother. She realised once again how selfish she had been, how un-neighbourly. But the truth was that she valued him, because who else was there to have a serious conversation with around here?

'A cup of tea and a bacon sandwich at one o'clock?' he suggested. 'At my place?'

Harriet grinned with relief. That gave her time to sort out something for Mother first. 'Okey dokey,' she said. 'See you there.'

Harriet and Owen sat in the kitchen at the pockmarked old table, ate the sandwiches and drank tea from Owen's big white china mugs. Everything about Owen and his farm was oversized, Harriet thought. But also comforting. It was slightly odd that she'd never been here before; Owen had always come to them, so there'd been no reason. Now, though, it was ideal and meant there was no chance of being overheard by Mother.

Harriet told him the story of the prowler and he listened, without speaking, which she appreciated. If he'd interrupted, even once, she might not have been able to continue.

'What do you think I should do?' she asked him at last. 'I don't want to go to the police.'

'But you do want to find out who he is.'

'And what he wants from us,' she agreed.

Owen nodded. He took his time, sipping his tea, looking out through the kitchen window across the fields. 'You could ask him,' he said.

Blindingly simple, or blindingly stupid? Harriet was doubtful.

'And if you think he might pose a threat . . .' – he paused – 'well, I could always come with you. Fact is, I should come with you anyway.'

He'd make a good bodyguard, she thought, he was beefy

enough to intimidate anyone – especially her prowler who wasn't exactly overendowed in the muscular department.

'OK,' she said. She didn't think the prowler would pose a threat. But it would make her feel an awful lot safer with Owen by her side.

'OK?' He seemed surprised.

'You're on.'

CHAPTER 51

Joanna

London

Joanna walked towards Waterloo Bridge. She was on her way to meet Lucy and a couple of other friends for drinks. She had spent the morning revising the copy of the Prague bridge walk in a nearby café and working on another article about the city for a monthly women's magazine travel feature. She had thought about Emmy and she had considered Toby's suggestion. Should she write a travel book? It was very different from writing a novel, but it might be fun.

Nicholas Tresillion had written her a short email telling her that he wouldn't be back in London for a few days, by which time Joanna would be gone. She wasn't sure whether to be glad or sorry. But perhaps it was for the best. He'd write properly in a day or two, he'd said, he had more to tell her. She was intrigued. What could have happened now? She'd read the other email too — the one from the woman who had started dating her boyfriend after meeting him on the Lisbon bridge

391

walk. It was a nice story. Emmy, she thought, was beginning to have a lot to answer for.

It was a strange feeling, being in London and working in coffee bars and hotel rooms as if she were still on location. But tomorrow, she had her appointment with Sotheby's. Hopefully, if Harriet had kept her promise, Emmy's painting would have been delivered and Joanna could hear what they had to say about the woman who wasn't her ancestor but who nevertheless had become very important in her life. And then she could travel back to Dorset.

It would be worth the cost of the courier, she'd persuaded herself. At the very least, the Sotheby's expert would be able to provide her with some information about the painting, if not the artist. And at the very best, he might be able to identify her by name. And with a name . . . Joanna took a deep breath. With a name, she could find out so much more.

In the meantime, she was quite enjoying wandering around some of her old haunts, this Thames riverbank walk being one of them. She loved the architecture that lined the South Bank, the galleries and, of course, the bridges . . . . It was a cool and crisp day, her breath was clouding in the air as she walked, her boots snapping on the wide paving stones. She felt an energy in the air that she was feeding off, a strong sense of purpose. Had Emmy ever visited London? she wondered. And if so, had she painted any of its bridges?

She looked out across the Thames. The river was thick and winter-green and Joanna's fingers were cold inside her leather gloves. A pleasure boat was travelling along the water and she stopped to watch it. A moment ago, the air had been clear, and yet now a fine mist seemed to be descending onto the water, like a fret, one of those sea mists in Dorset that appeared from nowhere.

392

She wrapped her scarf closer around her neck, did up the top button of her jacket. She could taste the vapour in the air; it had settled now over the riverbank too, shrouding the buildings on the Embankment, wrapping moist fingers around the bridges as if it might pluck them from sight. The scene in front of her reminded Joanna of an Impressionist painting: blurs of blue, green and grey, mist and smog and night-time.

She walked on, heading for Westminster. In her head some notes rang out – the Westminster chime that had accompanied her childhood, which were, she'd read, based on a phrase from Handel's aria, '*I know that my Redeemer Liveth*', and which still rang out from the grandfather clock in the hall of Mulberry Farm Cottage. Every time Joanna heard that chime she thought of Harriet, of playing one, two, three, alive, and how she'd felt when she could never, ever find her. She thought of how her sister had sounded on the phone last night – irritated and more than a little uptight. She'd thought they were getting closer, but . . . Perhaps some things never changed.

Westminster, the oldest bridge over the River Thames, was now the link between the Houses of Parliament and the London Eye. Joanna moved closer to the water. Was it her imagination or was it suddenly not as busy as it had been minutes before? It was hard to see through the mist. But surely the buildings had changed too? They appeared simpler, older and dirtier and some of them were belching smoke from chimneys into the already smoggy atmosphere. *My God*. It was hard to breathe. Joanna felt the smog drawing down into her lungs, as if it intended to drain her of all that energy she had felt so recently.

There was a long silence. Broken by a motor and the sound of surging water . . .

Slowly, the fog parted over the Thames to reveal the green sludge of the river. And a boat. She blinked. A small paddle steamer, narrow and long, with tall red, white and black funnels, was forging a path through the water, making headway against the current, the water swirling and swishing around the paddle wheel. It drew closer. Joanna watched. She held her breath. She had seen paddle steamers before, but this one seemed different somehow. And oddly, it was the only craft she could see on the river – the other boats had all disappeared.

Closer still, and now the bridge was revealed too. Joanna looked down into the water. At the front of the paddle steamer, a little apart from the others, stood a young woman. Her dress was white and high-waisted and her hands were clasped. Joanna had seen her before. Before, she had been happy. Now, though, she was crying. She was looking up at Waterloo Bridge and weeping as if her very heart would break. Emmy . . . There was so much pain that it seemed to Joanna that she could feel it too.

> *When thou sigh'st*
> *Thou sigh'st not wind*
> *But sigh'st my soul away*
> *When thou weep'st, unkindly kind,*
> *My life's blood doth decay.*

Emmy had quoted those words to Rufus in the letter she'd written in Prague, and Joanna had recognised the poem. 'Song' by John Donne. She thought of it now. She couldn't help thinking of it now.

394

Sweetest love, I do not go,
For weariness of thee,
Nor in hope the world can show
A fitter love for me;

Joanna stood and watched until the boat disappeared from view. Slowly, as if a veil was being raised, the smog lifted, evaporated; the sun came out from behind a cloud and once more the milky winter landscape stretched out into the distance. The distance of now.

CHAPTER 52

Harriet

Dorset

They walked along the Down towards the village in silence. The chilly sea breeze made Harriet pull her scarf more tightly around her neck. She was nervous. She glanced at Owen, who didn't seem anxious in the least. She felt vaguely reassured. At least after this confrontation, she would know what was going on. It was early afternoon, all the chores had been done and a lamb hotpot was gently simmering in the oven at home, Mother on hand to oversee. They had a couple of hours before the winter light would dim. It was always better, Harriet reminded herself, to know the worst.

'Supper when we get back from the lion's den?' she asked Owen.

His eyes lit up. 'I wouldn't say no.' Harriet felt a spear of guilt – it must be lonely on that farm on his own; it had been too long since she'd asked him over.

Harriet hadn't told her mother where they were off to.

Just, 'If I'm not back by six o'clock, help yourself to supper and then turn the oven right down.' And if she wasn't back by seven – then what? Phone the police?

When Owen paused at the five-bar gate and looked back at the farmland bathed in the pale red light of the November afternoon – the Down that was his life, Harriet supposed; his livelihood, certainly – she saw an expression in his eyes that she recognised.

It was a gleam of affectionate propriety. 'You love it, don't you?' she said. She leant on the gate and tried to see it through his eyes. It wasn't hard.

He didn't pretend not to know what she meant. 'It took a while, though.'

This surprised Harriet. 'Where were you before? You never said.' She remembered Owen and Susan as newly-weds, joining the Warren Down village community. They'd never interested her – she was still in her teenage years and the young farmhands were much more appealing. And she had spent so much time with her father, of course, long hours in his study talking, reading, listening to his stories. Was that why Mother had never loved her as much as she loved Joanna? Had her mother been jealous? Could she have been lonely all that time? The thought was surprising – and painful. Harriet frowned.

'Over to the north-west.' He pointed.

Over the hills and far away, Harriet thought. Scott and his camper van slid into her mind and she pushed them firmly out again. Her chance for a taste of freedom had been and gone, and in reality, it had never been more than a fleeting dream. She was bound to Warren Down and Mulberry Farm Cottage. She knew that now. And as for Scott . . . he hadn't given her freedom, but he had given her something else that she was grateful for. An experience of sensuality. A letting-go. Not to mention a reality check.

'My father had a farm in Marshwood Vale,' Owen went on.

They turned and stood side by side, watching the sea in the distance. The waves rose and curled gently in the breeze, soft and grey; the winter tide was receding. *Tranquillity*, Harriet thought. She almost forgot about where they were going and why. A feeling of peace stole over her like a soft silken sheet.

'You didn't want to take over your father's farm then?' she asked.

That was the way around here, as she knew only too well. The farm got handed down from generation to generation and it was hard to escape – if you wanted to do something else, that was.

Owen opened the gate. 'It was losing too much money.' He shoved his hands into the pockets of his forest-green fleecy jacket. 'My old man didn't want to bring it into the twentieth century, that was his trouble.'

Harriet followed him through. She understood. Her father had often talked about this – farming, how it was in the old days and how it was going to be in the future. Getting bigger, surviving when you were smaller, going organic and making it pay . . . And although he'd wanted more than anything for Harriet to step into his shoes – he'd always considered her capable of doing anything he could do, she knew that – he'd also known it would be hard for her. Above all, he was a realist.

'And you couldn't persuade him to make changes? To bring it up to date?'

He closed the gate behind them and they began to stroll on down the grassy path where Owen's sheep were grazing in the field. It felt slightly odd to be with him like this, thought

398

Harriet, but at the same time, companionable. And this was something that Harriet didn't want to do alone. She needed moral support – someone strong by her side.

'He wouldn't listen. Matter of fact . . .' Owen's firm stride faltered for a moment and Harriet glanced across at him.

'What?'

'I wasn't that interested in farming back then.'

'You?' Harriet laughed. 'You're joking.'

'It's true.' He grinned back at her. 'And look at me now.'

Harriet was intrigued. She shot a sidelong glance at the great beefy man walking beside her – a farmer through and through – and she tried to imagine him as a child. Quiet, probably. And shy. Gentle too, she couldn't imagine him pulling the wings off wasps or shooting catapults at dogs or anything. 'What *were* you interested in?' she asked him.

He seemed embarrassed. His shoulders hunched up a bit, his hands went deeper into his pockets. 'Oh, you know . . .'

'No.'

'Well . . .' He hesitated. 'Reading.' He gave an apologetic bark of a laugh. 'And history.'

'Really?' Harriet gawped at him. A bit like her father then. But she'd always thought of Owen as a man of the soil, not of books. In fact, until he'd come out with all that stuff about the mulberry tree, and she'd realised he'd actually heard of Shakespeare . . . She'd always admired his practicality. But his intelligence? The facts he might have at his fingertips? She'd never thought of him in that way at all. Until recently, she'd never imagined she could talk to him – about anything. She'd always been so ready to palm him off with Mother before heading online to Someone Somewhere. She blushed to think of it. How rude she had been, how unfair.

399

'My father thought I was a bit of a wuss.' Owen shrugged his big shoulders. 'He wouldn't have listened to anything I said about farming, no matter how much I'd read up on it. Too stuck in his ways, he was.' He sighed. 'So, I had to sit back and watch them both crumble in front of me – the farm and my old man.'

Harriet wanted to squeeze his arm to comfort him, but she held back; she didn't really do arm-squeezing, she never had. 'What happened?'

He shot her a look she couldn't interpret. His grey-green eyes were calm, though, like the sea. 'Dad had a stroke. It killed him. And Mum sold the farm and moved into the village.' He took a deep breath. 'A year later she died too – lung cancer, and d'you know what?'

'What?' Harriet whispered. She hadn't expected this when they set off on this mission together.

'She never smoked a cigarette in her whole life.' He shook his head in bewilderment, a bewilderment that Harriet guessed had been there ever since he lost the both of them. What could she say?

They were silent as they passed the holiday chalets and reached the edge of the village. 'I'm sorry,' she said at last.

'It was a long time ago.' He helped her over the stile.

But Harriet was confused. 'So, why . . . if your father had died, I mean, why did you . . . ?'

'Why did I take up farming when I didn't have to?' Owen straightened.

Harriet didn't think she'd ever heard him talk so much – especially not in one go.

'I resisted the idea at first,' he admitted. 'I planned on going to university . . .'

University? Crikey, how could she have got him so wrong?

'Then I met Susan.'

'Ah.' Harriet didn't remember that much about Susan Matthews, only that she was nice enough, if a bit of a gossip. She remembered her mother saying things, though – that Susan was forever putting Owen down, talking over him, telling him what to do. Harriet had always interpreted this as meaning Owen had nothing much to say for himself, that he was dull, boring, spineless even. But perhaps he was just shy – until he got to know people. Perhaps he had met Susan when he was vulnerable and still grieving the death of his parents.

'She was the daughter of a farmer too, you see.'

They had reached the lane. To the right was Warren Cove. And to the left . . . As one, they paused.

'A bit of an irony,' Harriet agreed. She did see. She looked up at the soft grey winter sky.

'I thought of how much the old man had wanted me to go into farming,' Owen said. 'And there was Susan and her dad, him wanting to lend us the money to get started.'

'So you bought Warren Farm.' Timing and circumstances so often dictated people's pathways and decisions. It was a matter of chance. Fate, if you like. Harriet turned towards the village. She had to do this. There was no going back. She straightened her shoulders and jutted her chin.

'It took me a while to make something of it,' he said.

Harriet knew that. She had been a first-hand witness. But he had done it. He had made the farm successful. And whenever times were hard for them at Mulberry Farm Cottage, Owen was there, helping her out, giving advice about the pigs, buying off the land to enable them to survive. 'But you did make something of it,' she said. 'You've done really well.'

401

He began to speak so low that Harriet had to lean forwards to hear the words. 'Only Susan didn't stick around long enough to see it,' he said.

Did he still feel bitter? Did he still love her?

'More fool her,' she said.

They began to walk up the lane. Suddenly Harriet lost her nerve. She stopped. 'Will you come to the door with me?' she asked him.

He laughed. ''Course I will.'

She was consumed with relief. 'Thanks, Owen,' she said. 'You're a real . . .' She hesitated. What was he exactly?

He put an arm around her shoulder and squeezed, like she should have done to him fifteen minutes ago. 'What are friends for?' he asked.

Friends. She grinned back at him as they reached her prowler's front gate. The moment of truth was fast approaching. But, yes, of course. Friends. Owen was right. That was what they were. What they always could have been if she'd ever given him the chance. And it was funny, thought Harriet, that she'd simply never realised this before.

CHAPTER 53

Joanna

London

Joanna felt a buzz of excitement as she made her way to Sotheby's for her appointment. It had been an eventful day already. Martin had texted her earlier to let her know they'd had an offer on the house. It was only just under asking price.

Should we accept? he'd asked.

I think so, she'd replied.

It wasn't the best time of year to be selling; and suddenly she wanted this sense of limbo to be over with. She had said her goodbyes, now it was time to move on.

And I've transferred £5,000 to your account, he had messaged back. *For the furniture and other things. OK?*

That's fine, she replied.

In fact, it was more than fine. She didn't want any of that stuff. She wanted to be free to start again. And as for the five thousand pounds, she knew exactly what she was going to do with it. By this evening there was likely to be a big hole in her bank account where that money had been.

Soon after this, she'd received the promised email from Nicholas Tresillion. She opened it, half hoping he was back in London.

I have a confession to make to you, Joanna, she read.

What now? She bit her lip.

I went to Prague.

Her interest was piqued.

And it wasn't on business either. I was at the airport in Rome and my flight back to the UK was cancelled. I made the decision then and there on a whim. I'm not usually that spontaneous, trust me. I just saw Prague on the departures board and . . .

Joanna smiled. She could identify with that. When something tugged at you that way, it was an impulse that was hard to resist. And maybe her bridge walks were tugging at Nicholas in the same way that Emmy and her letters had been tugging at Joanna. It wasn't easy to explain, but sometimes you simply had to go with it.

Please don't think I'm stalking you, he added.

She chuckled. If he was stalking her, he would have gone there at the same time. As it was, they seemed to always be a few steps away from one another. When she was in Prague, he was in Rome. When she was in London, he was in Prague. And when he came back to London . . . by that time she would have returned to Mulberry Farm Cottage. Would they ever meet? She hoped so.

But I was curious, he continued. *I read your copy of the walk — thank you for that preview, by the way, it meant a lot to me.*

'And what did you see?' Joanna wondered aloud.

What I saw there had nothing to do with death or suicide, and nothing to do with the man with the red hair or St John – though I saw the statue, of course.

I also saw a woman with some paints. An artist. Not from today, but from a long time ago. A woman . . . Well, it's had quite an effect on me to tell you the truth. I'll tell you more when we meet – if we meet. Until then . . .

She stared at the screen. It was impossible. It had to be impossible. But . . . What was going on here? She blinked and read on.

Joanna, I'm fascinated about what you said – that you feel you've been 'led' on these walks by some family research that you're doing. Tell me more!

She wasn't sure that she dared – not now. Nicholas Tresillion had seen the golden ribbon in Venice, he had seen the man with red hair in Lisbon – otherwise known as Rufus – and now he had seen Emmy, he must surely have seen Emmy . . .

I've never had an experience like this before, never seen any visions, and never hallucinated, believe me.

Neither had Joanna. It was as if there was a chink in the wall and somehow she and Nicholas were looking straight through.

Maybe there's something out there that we don't understand? Some guardian angel who looks out for every single one of us?

Maybe. But if so, was Emmy Joanna's guardian angel – or was she Nicholas Tresillion's? Guardian angels didn't look out for two people at the same time, did they?

Sometimes, I almost feel I believe this, though I should tell you that if my ex-wife could hear me now, she'd split her sides laughing.

Yes, well . . . Joanna was beginning to wonder why Nicholas had stayed with Rachel as long as he had.

Is it arrogant of us to think that our reality is all there is?

Perhaps so, she thought. Perhaps their reality was only one

of the truths. Perhaps sometimes those truths collided — like now.

I'll be back in London the day after tomorrow — let me know if you're still around and we could meet for that drink and compare notes.

Yours, Nicholas

But by then, of course, Joanna would be gone.

CHAPTER 54

Harriet

Dorset

Harriet glanced at Owen, who gave her a reassuring nod. She rang the doorbell.

Perhaps he was out. The afternoon seemed to be drawing in already and the temperature was certainly dropping, but Harriet's hands were clammy and the hairs on the back of her neck were standing to attention. Was she making an absolute idiot of herself? Again?

Through the glass, she saw him approaching on the other side of the door. What was there to be afraid of? She glanced again at Owen, whose face was impassive. She took a deep breath.

The second he opened the door and they stood there facing each other, she knew she hadn't been imagining things. He looked shocked. The colour drained from his face, his eyes widened and his grip on the door handle grew tighter. He seemed smaller close up – and not dangerous at all. Even so . . .

'Good afternoon,' Harriet said.

'Er . . . good afternoon,' he stuttered back in reply. He made no move to invite them inside.

Harriet glanced at Owen. If he was surprised by the appearance of Harriet's dangerous prowler, he didn't show it. 'I'm Harriet Shepherd,' she went on smoothly. 'But I think you already know that?'

The prowler nodded dumbly. Harriet felt almost sorry for him.

'And this is Owen Matthews, who owns Warren Farm.'

He nodded again.

'And you are . . . ?' she asked helpfully. She knew why she'd never really been scared of this man, never contacted the police as Joanna had urged her to, why she'd been brave enough to turn the tables stalker-wise. It was because he was more scared than Harriet and perhaps she had always sensed that. She waited.

'Henry Adams,' he said at last in a querulous voice. 'Professor.'

Harriet laughed. Professor, yes, that was how he always signed himself in the brief notes to her that accompanied his manuscripts: *Prof A*. A good joke.

'You can drop the *professor*,' she said, aware that she sounded a bit like a New York cop. 'I assume you know that it's me who's been doing your typing for you?'

'Yes, of course.' He opened the door ever so slightly wider. 'Thank you,' he said. 'You've done a good job. I'm very grateful.'

Harriet glared at him. 'But that's not why we're here.'

'No.' He pushed his glasses further up his nose. 'I didn't imagine it was.'

His eyes were pale blue, she noted, his eyelashes slightly ginger. He seemed so harmless. But now was not the time to soften. She glanced once again at Owen. He looked fierce and unsmiling. She was proud of him, glad he was on her side.

'Is Henry Adams your real name?' she asked.

'Oh, yes.' He regarded her intently through the glasses.

In fact, it was odd, but he was looking at her with some warmth, affection even, she realised. Was it possible that one of her previous theories had been correct after all? That he had happened to spot her in the village and had, well, taken a fancy to her? Harriet felt the heat on her face. It was possible, wasn't it? Part of her was extremely flattered by the idea. He was a bit older than her, yes. He didn't cut the most manly of figures. Even so . . . it was always pleasant to be admired.

'And I *am* a professor,' he reiterated. 'For my sins.'

'Is that right?' Owen's voice was mild enough, but he took a step forwards and for a mad moment Harriet thought he was about to clock him one.

The professor must have been anxious too, because he moved back a fraction. 'Yes, yes.' He was nodding frantically. 'I used to work at Aberystwyth University, but I've retired to, er . . . write a few papers, that sort of thing.'

Harriet narrowed her eyes. 'And does *that sort of thing* include spying on people?'

'Oh, no.' He clutched at the door frame for support. 'That is . . . what do you mean?'

Harriet folded her arms. She might have guessed he wouldn't immediately confess to his transgressions. 'I mean that you've been hanging around our cottage – I've seen you in the lane outside too. Once, you nearly fell off your bike and once you were up on the Down. With binoculars.'

Owen cleared his throat loudly and coughed. Harriet hoped he wasn't finding this amusing.

'A public lane?' the professor murmured. 'And a well-trodden footpath in the country? Surely a soul can do a spot of bird-watching or ride along the lane without—'

'I saw you in our farmyard,' Harriet said. 'Twice. And that's private property – especially in the middle of the night.' She gave Owen a *put that in your pipe* sort of a look.

He raised an eyebrow. She hadn't told him about the night-time bit.

'Ah.' The professor bowed his head. 'I'm so sorry. Truly.'

'You admit it then?' Owen demanded. 'What did you think you were playing at, man?' He stuck his hands in his pockets so forcefully that Harriet wondered if he was trying to stop himself throttling the poor old prof. For the first time she wondered if she'd been right to bring him along after all.

The door opened a touch wider. 'I never meant to frighten you. I never meant you any harm. I only wanted . . . Ah, dear.' He clicked his tongue. 'What a fool I have been.'

'Perhaps,' Owen said, 'it might be an idea if you invited us in and told us what it was you did want, eh?'

Harriet shot him another look. The professor seemed harmless, of course, but was it a good idea to go inside? What if he suddenly pulled a knife or something? But looking at him, she had to admit it didn't seem likely . . . He appeared to have entirely caved in. She felt even more sorry for him than before.

The professor scratched his head. His hair was thin and he had a bald patch in the centre that gave him a monkish appearance. 'Yes,' he said. 'I suppose you're right. What point is there skulking around day after day hoping for the merest glimpse . . .'

Ah. Mentally, Harriet couldn't help preening herself. So, she'd been right. He was just trying to catch sightings of her whenever he could. Poor, sad man.

'Come in, please,' he said.

'And you'll tell us everything?' Owen pressed. He still looked rather hostile and Harriet felt a slight shiver. This was a side of Owen she hadn't seen before.

'Indeed, indeed.' The professor sighed. 'I should have come clean from the start.'

'Yes, you should.'

She and Owen followed the professor into a neat, almost bare sitting room. The chairs were worn and on the desk in the corner were a stack of books and some papers she recognised as the manuscript she'd recently been typing for him.

Suddenly, to her horror, the professor took a step towards her and took both her hands in his. *Oh, heavens*. Was the passion going to be too much for him? Was he going to lose control?

'Steady.' Owen stepped forwards too.

But Harriet was mesmerised by the look on the professor's face. He seemed, well, almost besotted. 'Why me?' she whispered.

From the corner of her eye, she saw Owen shoot her a strange look.

'You?' He smiled.

'Yes, me. Why did you want to follow me, catch glimpses of me?' What was it that had made Harriet – perhaps for only the second time in her life – special?

He squeezed her hands. 'She doesn't go out much, does she?'

Harriet frowned. 'Who?'

'Your mother. Audrey Shepherd.'

The affection couldn't be mistaken now. *Ye Gods*. Suddenly

411

Harriet realised what was going on here. 'It's my mother you're after,' she blurted. 'How dare you!' If he hadn't been holding both her hands, she would have slapped him – although whether it was for wanting her mother or not wanting her, she wasn't quite sure.

She shook her hands free. The only time, she realised, that she had not been second best was with her father. He was the only man who had loved her for herself alone. The dream, never far away, edged into her consciousness. And even that was flawed, damn it. She was tempted to let Owen loose on the man – that would teach him.

It was Owen who worked it out. He put a hand on her shoulder as if to calm her, and only then did Harriet realise how much she was shaking.

'And why would you be wanting to see Audrey, may I ask?' he said. But he looked as if he knew.

The professor gazed deep into Harriet's eyes and smiled. It was, she had to admit, rather an endearing smile.

'Why would I want to see her?' He sighed. 'Because she's my mother,' he said.

CHAPTER 55

Joanna

Dorset

When Joanna got back from London, full of excitement about the painting and what she'd discovered about Emmy, Harriet met her at the door of the cottage. Something was going on. Harriet had texted her earlier to find out when she'd be back and she'd sounded more than a little mysterious.

'Oh, hello, Het,' she said. 'What—?'

'You're late,' Harriet hissed. 'I told you I had something to tell you, someone for you to meet.' She rolled her eyes and jabbed her index finger in the direction of the front sitting room, the best room, the room that was rarely used.

'What's happening?' Joanna could hear the murmur of voices and Mother's laughter. There was a different note to it, a note almost of . . . joy. 'Are you all right, Het?'

'Yes, yes.' Harriet's gaze fell on the painting which Joanna had tucked under her arm. 'Why on earth did you want me to send that to Sotheby's anyway?'

'I'll tell you later.' Why were they still standing on the doorstep? Joanna peered past her sister, trying to see who it was that was so important. 'And I would have got here earlier but the traffic was really heavy.'

'Traffic?' Harriet must be very preoccupied – she hadn't twigged that Joanna hadn't asked her for a lift from the station this time.

It was great having a car again. Especially a two-seater. Harriet would say she was being extravagant when she spotted the MX-5, but it was several years old and Martin still had to give her the money for her half of the car they used to share – he'd said he'd do that as soon as the house sale went through. She'd give Harriet a big chunk of that, she decided, to help with whatever work needed doing on Mulberry Farm Cottage.

If she was going to stay in the West Country, Joanna needed a car. And, ah . . . she was happy to be starting afresh. Flying away from London with the top down and Snow Patrol on high volume had made her feel that anything was possible.

'But did you find out anything? What's it worth?' Harriet's financial antennae were on red alert.

And then she spotted the car. Joanna had tucked it up next to the old blue tractor but it was bright yellow, sleek and curvy and stood out like a canary in a snowstorm. Her sister made a sort of spluttering noise.

Joanna ignored this. 'I didn't take it to get it valued.' Though the man at Sotheby's had suggested it might fetch five hundred pounds at auction. Not a huge amount. Anyway, Joanna knew she could never sell the painting. It would always be worth much more to her than money. 'I wanted to find out the name of the artist,' she told her sister.

It had been easy too; Geoffrey Boothroyd at Sotheby's had

certain records at his disposal and had been most helpful. She now knew that Emmy was Emily Selleck (that indecipherable name could have been almost anything beginning with S). She knew that Emily – or Emmy, as she still preferred to call her – had travelled extensively painting city landscapes – especially bridges – in watercolour, in her teens and early twenties, and that although she had received no formal training, her father – also an artist – had taught her some artistic technique.

She wasn't sure how or when Emmy had met Rufus, but Joanna now had a booklist and a few leads from Geoffrey that should help her find out. And she might also be able to discover more about Rufus's end of the story now that she was back in Dorset.

Harriet was still staring at the Mazda. 'Is that yours?' she said.

'Yes.' Joanna turned around and gave the car a fond smile. As soon as Martin had mentioned the five thousand pounds she knew that what she wanted to do with the money was regain some independence. She'd missed having a car.

Harriet snorted. 'It's a bit flash for West Dorset, isn't it, Jo? However did you—?'

'Martin. And it's an awful lot more useful than half a dining table, half a fridge and some crockery,' Joanna said. She hadn't exactly intended to buy a car that was quite so 'out there' but she'd seen it advertised and she couldn't resist. It seemed to suit the new Joanna, the one who was moving on.

At the magic word 'crockery', Harriet seemed to be reminded of tea. 'Come on then.' She ushered Joanna inside. 'Hurry up. Come and meet him.'

'Him?'

'You'll see.' It sounded like the voice of doom.

415

They entered the front room and there they were. Their mother, Owen, who half rose to his feet when Joanna came in, and the prowler. Harriet's prowler.

Joanna stared at him. Last time she'd seen him, he'd been struggling to stay on his bike after Harriet had almost mown him down with the pick-up. What on earth was he doing here? Carefully, she propped Emmy's painting against the wall.

'Joanna! Darling! Thank goodness you're back!' Her mother launched herself from the sofa and enveloped her in a hug. She was wearing a woollen dress of daffodil yellow and she looked very cheerful and, well, different somehow. 'Does she know?' she asked Harriet in a theatrical whisper.

'Not yet.'

'Know what?' Joanna kissed her mother's papery cheek, mouthed 'hi' to Owen and edged her way round the coffee table, which was loaded with cheese scones, fruit loaf and tiny ham and cucumber and salmon sandwiches. Mmm. High tea. Very reminiscent of the old days . . . Harriet had been busy. 'What's going on?' She kept her gaze averted from the man on the sofa.

There were tears in her mother's eyes. 'Joanna, I'd like you to meet Henry,' she said.

Harriet's prowler got to his feet. He wore old-fashioned glasses, a brown shirt and tie, high-waisted trousers and one of those corduroy jackets with leather patches on the elbows.

Joanna nodded at him. 'Hello, Henry.' He didn't look at all threatening now that he was here on their sofa. So what was this all about? No doubt all would be revealed.

Mother was beaming. 'Your brother,' she said.

'What?' Joanna looked at Harriet, who shrugged back at her. Owen was looking at Harriet too and their mother was

416

still beaming at Henry. Their brother? 'What do you mean?' Her mind was racing. *Brother?* This was going to take some explaining, she thought.

'Yes,' said her mother. 'It's true.' She clasped her hands.

'I see.' Though she didn't. Joanna scrutinised him once more, mentally assessing his age. It must have been before Father then, way before they'd come along. God. This was a turn-up. She exchanged a look of understanding with Harriet. 'So that's why . . . ?'

Harriet shot her a grim smile. 'That's why. And I've been doing his typing too.'

'His typing?' Joanna was flabbergasted. 'So you're the—'

'Professor Henry Adams, yes, that's me.' He was coming over, looking as if he might kiss her. It wasn't easy to take in. He had metamorphosed from prowler to brother in seconds. She looked at Harriet again. A moment of compassion passed unspoken between them.

Joanna and Henry shared an awkward embrace and Henry went to sit down again. Harriet poured the tea and they chatted. Not about why their mother had never told them they had a brother living somewhere in the world, but about today's weather, London, what the weather was likely to be tomorrow, and at the weekend, and eventually, when Joanna was about to scream, about how Henry had found them.

He had, he said, hesitated for years, not wanting to upset the foster parents who had brought him up. 'I was unwilling to rake up old memories.' He pushed his glasses further up his nose. 'They were very good to me. I had a happy childhood. I never wanted for anything.'

Their mother squeezed his hand. 'Very commendable,' she murmured. 'Perfectly understandable.' And how would she explain her part in all this, Joanna wondered, to her son and to her daughters?

'So what changed?' Harriet's arms were folded. She didn't look as if she understood perfectly at all. She just looked angry.

'They died.'

Silence. *Well done, Het*, thought Joanna.

Henry gazed straight at their mother. Joanna wasn't sure which of the two of them looked the most besotted. 'And so, I decided to do it before it was too late,' he said. 'I was determined to find my real, biological mother.'

Another hand squeeze.

'But even then,' he added, 'I shied away from direct contact.'

'We noticed,' Harriet said.

'I didn't know whether you'd want to see me again after all these years.'

Mother nodded sadly. 'How could you know?' she agreed.

'So, you rented a house in the village,' Harriet reminded him.

'Which allowed me to assess the situation,' he said.

'See how the land lay,' their mother added.

'Choose the right time.' He smiled back at her. Mother and son and there was something so similar about their mannerisms that left their relationship in no doubt.

But he had scared Harriet. Joanna looked at her sister and read the wary resentment on her face. Harriet would find it hard to warm to this unknown brother. She would be wondering, what did he want from them? Why was he here? And was he expecting them to fling themselves into his arms? Joanna had seen scenarios like this one played out on *Long Lost Family* and she had always marvelled at the way people could throw themselves into the emotions of the moment so completely, so unquestioningly.

418

'And this is the right time?' she asked.

'The right time never came,' Harriet said bluntly before he could reply. 'Owen and I went round to Henry's yesterday afternoon.'

Joanna blinked at her. 'You knew where he lived?'

'I found out where he lived.'

At least she'd had the sense to ask Owen to go with her. Joanna glanced at their neighbour, who shifted in his seat uncomfortably, as if unsure where he fitted into this family scenario and why exactly he was here.

'Aren't you thrilled?' Mother asked them. 'Aren't you absolutely delighted?'

'Absolutely,' Harriet said, without a trace of emotion.

'Thrilled,' Joanna echoed, faintly cross with herself for not being happier when Mother so clearly was.

'I'm not expecting anything from anyone, you know.' Henry leant forwards, his face earnest. 'I'd totally understand it if you told me to get lost.'

'Oh, Henry . . .' Mother looked as if she might cry. 'As if we would.'

Harriet looked like thunder. 'It was a funny way you went about it, that's for sure,' she said. 'I've spent months thinking we had a prowler.'

'I'm sorry.'

Joanna guessed that this wasn't the first time he'd had to apologise to Harriet; she was rather good at holding grudges. Though in this case she had a point. Henry should have come to see them straightaway, instead of skulking around the place like that.

'It's a bit of a shock,' she told him. 'I think we all need time to get used to the idea.' Having a brother . . . would that be

419

so bad? Hadn't she always wanted a brother when they were young? Perhaps, after all, this man, this brother, could bring something to their lives, something that had been missing. And perhaps they could bring something to his life. And as for Mother . . . she was clearly delighted.

'Of course.' Henry sat up straighter. 'Please don't think I'm going to make a nuisance of myself. I'm perfectly used to being on my own. I'm not trying to edge my way into your lives, your family.'

'But Henry' — Mother's smile was sweet — 'you are family. You always have been family.'

Joanna sipped her tea. The way Henry had said the word 'family' touched her rather. She tried to imagine what it would be like to discover your biological mother and your two sisters after all these years. And she began to warm to him. He had been honest with them, and she could feel the air of confidences settling around them in this room, as though the appearance of Henry had made them closer, more balanced somehow. More of a family? Ridiculous. But she decided to tell them — it shouldn't be a secret any longer.

'I've been opening some family cans of worms too,' she said.

Everyone turned to look at her. 'What cans are those, Jo?' Harriet asked.

'It seems the woman who painted this' — she pointed to the Venice bridge painting which she had propped against the wall — 'was having a love affair with one of our ancestors — back in the early 1900s, just before the war. All I know about him is that his nickname was Rufus and he had red hair. At least,' she sighed, 'I think he had red hair.'

'Oh.' Owen leant closer. 'That painting style looks rather familiar.'

420

'Really?' Harriet picked up the painting and held it aloft for them all to see. They gathered around.

Geoffrey Boothroyd had made a comment about the delicacy of the artist's watercolour technique and Joanna could see what he meant. Emmy had captured that pale yellow evening light that hung in the sky and turned the wood of the bridge to a dull but incredibly subtle filigree of gold. The bridge seemed suspended almost. Timeless.

'Which ancestor?' her mother asked. 'Your father's father George had red hair.'

Joanna stared at her. Her mother seemed to be more present somehow, all of a sudden. She wondered if Mother had been mourning just Father's death these past seven years? Or had she been mourning another loss – an earlier loss, the loss of her baby son – that she had never been able to properly mourn before?

'Did he?' All the photographs of Joanna's grandfather were in black and white, and of course he'd died before she was born. 'It can't be him, though. He was only a child when Emmy wrote the letters.' But if he'd had red hair, then wasn't it more than likely that his father . . . ? 'Maybe his father William had red hair too,' she said aloud.

'William Rufus,' said Harriet.

'What?' Joanna stared at her.

'William Rufus. William the Second, King of England.' Harriet looked smug. 'You went to university, Joanna. Isn't it obvious?'

Well, yes. And suddenly it was. That's why Emmy had called her lover Rufus. Because he was called William and he had red hair. Joanna grinned. 'Brilliant, Het! That's it . . . that's right. Rufus was our great-grandfather William. On Father's side. Also known as Rufus because of his wild red hair.'

421

'But how did you find out about the affair?' their mother asked.

'Ah.' Joanna nipped upstairs to her bedroom to fetch the other letters.

'I tried to tell you before,' she said when she came back down. Though perhaps she hadn't tried as hard as she might. It had, she conceded, been fun to hug the secret of Emmy to herself. She placed the three letters carefully into her mother's lap. 'And then I wanted to find out more about the woman who'd written the letters before I told you all about it. And . . .' It was hard to explain.

Her mother gave her an understanding smile. She knew what it was like to keep a secret.

'But I don't know how they met,' Joanna said. 'She wasn't from Dorset at all, and she certainly wouldn't have lived here in Mulberry Farm Cottage. Rufus – William – was married, and I haven't found any evidence yet that even puts Emmy in Dorset at any time. She could have been here for only a short while, I suppose.'

'Long enough to have her wicked way with Rufus, clearly.' Harriet passed a slice of cake to Henry. 'Mother made it,' she said pointedly to Joanna.

Joanna blinked. That was a turn-up. Surely Mother hadn't baked a cake for years?

'And of course,' Harriet went on, 'this place wasn't called Mulberry Farm Cottage back then.' She looked to Owen for confirmation. 'Was it?'

Owen cleared his throat noisily. 'Er, no, that's right, or so I believe.' He glanced at Harriet. 'Maybe . . .' He let the word hang.

'What?' Joanna was impatient.

Harriet's brow cleared. 'You mean that's how it happened?' She sounded excited. 'That's why he put it there and changed the name?'

'How what happened? Why he put what where?' Honestly, how infuriating they were being, both of them. But Joanna remembered now, the details of the census, the fact that the cottage had been listed under a different name. It hadn't seemed important then. But now . . .

'Pyramus and Thisbe?' Owen said.

'Pyramus and Thisbe,' Harriet agreed. She laughed.

'Pyramus and . . . ?'

'You mean the lovers?' Her new half-brother was smiling too.

'The lovers,' Harriet confirmed.

'And neighbours,' Owen added. 'And I believe I have some evidence at home that might confirm our theory.'

'Really?' Harriet was smiling at Owen. 'Something that you could go and get and bring along to the party?'

'Why not?' He got to his feet.

Joanna looked from one to the other to the other. Did they have to practise at being so infuriating or did it come naturally? It seemed that even after all her detective work they knew more about it than she did. 'Tell me,' she said. 'Before I explode.'

'Wait there for a minute or two.' Owen crossed the room. 'While I go and get it. And then I think you'll see . . .'

CHAPTER 56

Harriet

Dorset

'It's possible that your Emmy lived next door to your ancestor William Rufus for a while,' Owen suggested to Joanna when he returned from his place holding a painting they could only see the back of.

Joanna frowned. 'At your farm, you mean?'

'Yes. I don't know the history of Warren Down Farm and who owned the place back then. Maybe she had a friend or a relative there, or she was working at the farm?'

'Perhaps, yes.' Joanna sounded sceptical. She was trying to see the painting that Owen had brought over but he wasn't having any of that, he was keeping it well hidden. 'And then they ran into one another one day. And . . .'

'Fell in love?' suggested Harriet. In those days she supposed it wasn't so uncommon to have a liaison with a neighbour. There must have been evening get-togethers around the piano or something. And who else did you see back then? There was no online dating after all.'

Owen nodded. 'It would have been difficult to meet – their love was forbidden.'

'Obviously, since Rufus was already married,' Harriet pointed out. Joanna had told her he was twenty-eight at the time most of the letters were written.

'Then they might have likened themselves to Pyramus and Thisbe.' Owen shrugged. 'It's a romantic enough story. Lovers do that sort of thing.'

Harriet raised her eyebrows at him, but he wouldn't look at her.

'Pyramus and . . . ?' Joanna was clearly still confused.

At this point Harriet took it upon herself to explain the story. 'They were neighbours,' she began. Love, misunder-standing and death. Same old, same old. She précised the story about the lovers' arranged meeting by the mulberry tree, the lion, the blood and the miscomprehensions. 'So, in the end they both died. And the berries from the red mulberry tree are meant to symbolise their blood.' She finished with a flourish.

'Ugh.' Their mother shuddered. 'How grisly.'

'So, you think Rufus planted the mulberry tree in memory of Emmy, as a symbol of their love.' At last Joanna seemed to get it. For someone who was supposed to be rather bright, Harriet thought, she could be remarkably dense at times.

'It's possible.' Why else would Warren Down Farm Cottage suddenly become Mulberry Farm Cottage? Why else would he (or anyone) decide to plant a mulberry tree? It seemed way too coincidental – given what they already knew.

'And by way of confirmation . . .' Finally, Owen revealed the painting.

Joanna gasped. It was a painting of another bridge she knew rather well, and clearly it had been painted by Emily Selleck. The watercolours had the same delicate touch, the running and blending of the colours employed the same technique. 'The aqueduct,' she breathed.

This time, it was Harriet and Owen who shared a glance of incomprehension.

'In Lisbon,' Joanna explained. 'She wrote a letter to Rufus from there, she wrote that she was painting a bridge. And I . . .' She didn't go on.

Clear as mud, thought Harriet. 'How did you get hold of it?' she asked Owen.

'Found it in the barn.' He eyed the painting speculatively. 'Cleaned it up a bit. Quite liked it, so I decided to keep it.'

'It's beautiful, isn't it?' Joanna smiled at him and Owen blushed. Harriet felt a twinge of something that might have been irritation.

'If Emmy had lived at your farm for a while, she could easily have given the painting to the family or friends who owned the farm,' Joanna said. She seemed fascinated by the picture. 'So, Rufus had the Venice painting and Emmy's family or friends next door had the Lisbon painting.'

Owen shuffled his feet about. Harriet repressed a sigh. She knew what he was about to say before he said it.

'You're welcome to have the picture, Joanna,' he said. 'Seeing as it means so much to you.'

'Oh, no, I couldn't.'

'Call it an early Christmas present.' He smiled. 'I want you to have it.' He glanced awkwardly at Harriet. 'Really.'

'Really?' Joanna seemed overwhelmed. She got to her feet and hugged him. 'Thanks, Owen. Thank you so much.'

426

Owen didn't know where to put his arms. He glanced helplessly at Harriet. At last, gingerly, he put them around Joanna. *Joanna*. Everyone was always half in love with Joanna . . .

'But why did they break up in the first place?' Joanna asked, still gazing at the painting. 'If they were so much in love? You only have to read her letters . . .' Her voice trailed off.

For heaven's sake . . . 'It was 1913, Jo. He was married. He had a child. People didn't just rush off to the divorce courts in those days.' Harriet clicked her tongue. She could quite understand why her sister had left Martin, but honestly . . . 'It was a matter of duty. Even if they were desperately unhappy, they had to grin and bear it.'

'And his wife wasn't a well woman,' Joanna agreed. 'At least, she looks pretty frail and miserable in the photos.'

'Perhaps she had a lot to put up with,' Harriet remarked.

But she was talking to herself because Joanna had already gone haring from the room. To do some more of her detective work, presumably . . .

427

CHAPTER 57

Harriet

Dorset

'We're having supper alone tonight,' Harriet announced to Joanna a week later. 'Just the three of us. All right?' She'd had enough of paintings and secrets and newly discovered half-brothers. It was about time they heard the full story. And she was going to extract it from Mother if it was the last thing she did.

'OK.'

Ever since she'd come back from London, Joanna had either had her head stuck in some book or other, or she'd been locked online. Harriet had to admit that the story of their great-grandfather and this female watercolourist was intriguing – especially Owen's theory that Mulberry Farm Cottage had been named by William Rufus in memory of Emily Selleck. But on a more personal level, Joanna probably hadn't even noticed that Henry had been here for lunch and supper every day, that he'd been taking Mother out for walks, sitting closeted with her for hours.

428

So . . . 'It's the first opportunity we've had to quiz Mother,' Harriet said now. 'Don't you want to know what happened?'

'When?'

It was as if Joanna was in another world. 'When Mother gave her baby away. When she got pregnant in the first place. Don't you want to know who Henry's father is?'

Harriet had made *coq au vin*; not with one of theirs but with an organic, run-around one from the supermarket.

'Henry would have enjoyed this,' their mother said wistfully.

Harriet raised her eyes heavenwards. *Henry this, Henry that.* Straight in, she decided. 'So, when are you going to tell us, Mother?' she demanded.

Mother finished her mouthful and dabbed her lips with her napkin. 'Tell you what, Harriet?'

'About how Henry came into the world.'

Mother shook her head. 'There's not much to tell,' she said. 'It was a long time before I met your father. And now, it's enough that he's here with us again. That's all I care about.'

Harriet couldn't believe it. She forked up some mashed potato and chicken. How could their mother be so selfish? Couldn't she see that there were others involved? Didn't she think she owed them an explanation? And what about Father – had he known about any of this? 'Fine,' she snapped. 'Don't bother to tell us anything then.'

'Harriet . . .' Joanna was trying to shut her up, but Harriet was in full flow. She couldn't stop now.

She put down her fork. 'I could have left home. I could have gone to university. I could have gone anywhere. But what did I do?' Harriet blinked and was amazed to see a tear fall into the chicken stew. What was the matter with her? 'I stayed here with you. Because you couldn't be left, you couldn't bear to be on your own.' She picked up her fork again and glared at her mother. 'And I've stayed ever since. More fool me.'

'Het . . .' Joanna reached out across the table to put her hand on Harriet's arm, but Harriet didn't want her sympathy and she didn't want to be restrained. She didn't know what she wanted really. All she knew was that she had to let this out.

Their mother, however, was saying nothing. She had stopped eating, though, and her milky blue eyes were glazed. She looked as though she'd slipped back in time.

Harriet felt herself getting second wind. 'And then some bloke turns up out of the blue and he's your son and therefore our half-brother, and we're all supposed to say how wonderful, how amazing, how marvellous for you. When really—'

'No one asked you to stay here with me, Harriet,' their mother said. She put her knife and fork neatly together on the plate and held her head high. Her voice was clear and confident. 'It was your choice.'

She's an old lady, Harriet thought. Her skin might be wrinkled, but she still had the cheekbones. Breeding – she hadn't lost it. And besides, someone had asked Harriet. Her father had asked her and Harriet had always done what he wanted her to do.

The anger inside her deflated as quickly as it had risen. 'I had to stay,' she said quietly. 'Father died.' And they all knew what had happened then. Mother had gone to pieces. She was no longer the capable woman she had once been. She couldn't have coped alone.

'But you've always been entitled to your own life, Het,' Joanna said. 'Able to make your own choices.' She sounded shocked. As if she'd never realised that Harriet had minded, that Harriet had never actually made a choice. 'And Father only died seven years ago. What about before that?'

Harriet wanted to laugh. But she was afraid that if she did, it would sound high and hysterical, out of control. And that she wouldn't be able to stop. 'I promised him. I made a promise to Father.' She remembered the day. The sun was high and filtering through the leaves of the mulberry tree, dappling the water of the pond with light and shade.

Promise me you'll look after your mother, Harriet, he had said. *When I'm gone.*

Joanna too had stopped eating. She put her fork on the plate and pushed it away. 'I'm sure he didn't mean for you not to have your own life,' she said again. But she sounded more uncertain now and Harriet could tell she was thinking about it, that she was only just beginning to understand. Still, Joanna was right. It had been Harriet's fault, in a way. There was no point blaming anyone else. And there had been all those years before Father died – years when she had stayed because she wanted to help him on the farm, years when she had prided herself on being his natural successor.

'Of course he didn't.' Mother sounded sad. 'He didn't intend to imprison you in a place you didn't want to be.'

'I know.' Harriet also knew that her mother had loved him – she always had. And Father had loved her too. But Mother had never been his intellectual equal, he had always made that plain to Harriet, during those long evenings when they'd talked about books and history, philosophy and farming. It had made Harriet feel special – but now she wondered for the first time, had Father been right to do this? Wouldn't it have made her mother feel so terribly excluded?

431

'He thought you loved Mulberry Farm Cottage, Harriet.' Her mother's voice was both sad and confused.

'I did.' She sighed. 'I do.'

'He saw you as following in his footsteps.' Their mother's eyes again grew misty with remembering. 'There you were, always chasing him around the farm like a puppy . . .'

'Thanks very much, Mother,' Harriet snapped. Like a puppy indeed. Her mother had no idea. Harriet and her father had spent a lot of time together, yes, but he'd wanted it that way. He'd always appreciated her company, he had got something from his daughter that he could never get from Mother – and her mother probably knew this too. Mother had been a beautiful woman and they'd no doubt shared some sort of grand passion back in the day, but she'd never been the sort of woman you could talk to about anything serious or deep. Harriet had provided the intelligent companionship her father craved. Hadn't she?

Some of the happiest moments of Harriet's life had been spent in her father's study. She leant back in her chair. Even now, she could close her eyes and smell again the musty old papers and books, the wooden furniture, the sweet heady scent of the tobacco he smoked in his pipe. She could feel the roughness of his tweed jacket with leather buttons beneath her fingertips; feel the smooth wooden floorboards under her bare feet as she padded across from the desk to the bookshelf to lift off some great gold-leafed encyclopaedia for him to consult, his nicotine-stained fingertip moving slowly down the page . . . Harriet sniffed.

'You two were always very close.' Joanna was giving her a funny look. Her elbows were on the table and she was cradling her face in her hands. 'I was so jealous.'

Harriet stared at her. 'You were jealous of me?'

'Of course.' Joanna smiled. 'Aren't sisters always a bit jealous no matter how much they love one another?'

'I suppose.' Harriet felt the shutters over her eyes lifting, the tension around her forehead loosening. It was so simple. That was it. Sisters were always a bit jealous. They could still love one other.

'You did everything with him around the farm,' Joanna said.

But Joanna had always been so charming and well loved. Their mother adored her. Joanna wrote articles that people wanted to read. She went to university and made lots of friends, she got married, lived in London, got paid for travelling all round the world. Men fell in love with her. Harriet thought of Owen. They always had. 'But you've always had a fantastic life,' Harriet said. She stared in front of her, at the half-eaten plates of food on the table. It seemed that they had all lost their appetites.

Joanna raised an eyebrow. 'Being married to Martin wasn't easy,' she said. 'And journalism is hard work and not very lucrative.' She sighed. 'I wanted a baby, but it never seemed the right time. To be honest, Martin wasn't keen. I kept putting it off. And now . . .'

Harriet was struggling to take this in. She hadn't thought. Well, maybe that was her trouble – she never did.

'It's not too late, darling,' their mother put in. 'Trust me. It isn't too late for either of you.'

Harriet was dumbfounded. She had always wanted her sister's life. Now, she wasn't so sure. Her sister . . .

'When I was younger, I was always trying to live up to you, Harriet.' Joanna was still talking. 'I wanted Father to notice me for once. And I longed to get close to you, my special big sister.'

Harriet remained speechless – she had never known. Never known about any of this.

'And I could never even find you.' Joanna let out a sigh. 'You were so good at hiding.'

At that, Harriet smiled across at her sister. Yes, she'd always been good at hiding. But no more. There was no point in hiding anymore. Whatever jealousies there had been in the past between them, she could feel them slipping away. The truth was that Joanna was her sister and she loved her – irritating habits and all. They would be there for one another, because that's what sisters did. A trouble shared . . . 'In the mulberry tree,' she said.

'Sorry?' Then Joanna's brow cleared. 'Of course.' She laughed. 'I should have known.'

'Men are never easy,' their mother added somewhat randomly. 'Your father . . .' She let out an involuntary little gasp.

Goodness knows where it had come from. But Harriet froze, just as she had been about to stack the plates and take them back into the kitchen. She had heard that gasp so many times – in the dream.

She turned to look into her mother's eyes. Her mother was scared. But why should she be scared? 'The way you gasped just then,' Harriet said. 'I remember.'

And suddenly she did. She had seen her mother's eyes widen in fear before and she had heard her gasp. She had seen Father move towards her and she had heard her mother scream. She had blocked it but she had seen it. Back then and again and again in her dream. No. Because he wouldn't, would he? Not Father.

'What?' Mother's expression was steady now, but Harriet could hear the trepidation in her voice. 'What do you remember, Harriet?'

434

'His hands around your throat,' Harriet whispered. *How could you? How could you?*

'Harriet, no.' Joanna spoke in a shocked, hushed tone. 'You don't—'

'Nonsense.' Their mother's lips were a thin line of denial. 'You don't know what you're talking about, Harriet. Your father worshipped the ground I walked on. He adored me. He would never have lifted a finger—'

'I saw it, Mother.' Somehow, Harriet couldn't stop now. It was bunched up inside her and she needed to let it go. She had to, otherwise she'd never be free. But God knows what or who she would smash in the process. 'I saw him. He was almost strangling you. If I hadn't come down the stairs when I did, if I hadn't heard you scream—'

'My God, Harriet, that's enough.' Joanna's face was white. 'Stop it. Now.'

Mother was crying. Tears were trickling down the lines of laughter, of worry, of sadness and loss. *So much in one life*, Harriet thought.

Joanna leant forwards across the table and took their mother's hands in hers. 'Is it true, Mother?' she whispered.

Harriet couldn't move. She needed confirmation. Of course, she hadn't realised back then that her father could have actually killed her mother if she hadn't come down the stairs at that exact moment. *Would he have? Surely not.* But she had blocked it nevertheless. Father had always been her hero; after death, even more so. She had forgotten his flaws and built him up into something much more than he had ever been in reality.

'Why did he do it, Mother?' Harriet asked. 'Why did he do it when he loved you so much?' She could barely speak. She felt as if her entire world was falling apart. The man she had loved more than life itself. The man she had looked up to, worshipped and adored. Was it possible he could have done such a thing?

For a moment, their mother was quiet. Harriet wanted her heart to go out to her, but it stayed, trapped and chilly, inside. She simply didn't know what to think anymore.

'I wrote about it all,' their mother whispered. 'About the baby. About that time in my life.'

'About Henry?' Joanna glanced across at Harriet. She reached out a hand and Harriet clutched at it like a drowning man.

'I wrote about it in my diary,' their mother continued. 'I wanted to tell it how it was. I didn't want it to be hushed up by everyone forever. I wanted my baby to exist, you see.'

'I see,' said Joanna.

'I needed to acknowledge him.' Mother's shoulders sagged. She looked so sad, so weary. It must have been hard work, Harriet thought, to keep pretending. 'I know it was only a diary, but it helped, and I never imagined for a second that—'

'Father would read it,' Joanna said it for her.

Had he been a suspicious man? Harriet had never seen that side of him, but she could picture him now, finding Mother's diary in a drawer, wondering what charming domestic trivialities his wife had been writing about, smiling fondly, opening up the journal . . .

'I had to give my son away.' Their mother was still justifying herself. 'You don't know, you can't imagine what it was like then. I was only seventeen.'

'Who was the father?' Harriet saw Joanna shoot her a warning look but she was beyond caring. This was a time for truth. All of it.

'A friend of my brother's,' Mother told them. 'We'd all gone out for a bit of a lark one summer's day. It was hot and sunny. We were by the lake. We got separated from the others. We went swimming. I'd always liked him. Things, well, things got out of control . . .'

'Did he persuade you to give the baby away?' Joanna sounded sympathetic. She always did. But strangely, Harriet no longer felt bitter about that. She and Joanna – they were different, that was all.

'He never knew about the baby.' Mother hung her head. 'Hardly anyone knew. We were both so young, you see. I wasn't allowed to tell a soul. In those days you went away to visit an aunt before you began to show too much, the baby was taken away from you and then you came back and went on as before. When I came back home, he was courting some other girl.' She sighed.

They were silent. Harriet digested the information, the fact that actually her mother hadn't had a choice either; it had all been decided for her. And after that sort of an experience, how could you simply go on as before?

'But I still don't understand . . .' Joanna spoke slowly. 'If it all happened before you even met Father, then why was he so angry?'

But Harriet knew. Things were different then between men and women. Father had put his young, beautiful wife on a pedestal and she'd brought it toppling down. What had he said to her? *You are the purest, most beautiful thing.* Their mother had made him feel a fool.

'Because I hadn't told him,' their mother admitted. 'How could I? He thought I was pure, innocent, untouched.'

Harriet thought of her father's pride, the pleasure he got from his possessions. But they had to belong to him alone.

437

They had to be new and untouched. He might never have wanted their mother if he'd known.

'That's ridiculous,' Joanna said. 'And completely archaic.'

Harriet had to stop herself from leaping to her father's defence. Old habits died hard. Yes, it was ridiculous and, yes, it was archaic. But Mother should have told him before they were married. She shouldn't have pretended that she was pure and untouched and she certainly should have told him she'd had a child. Even if it meant losing him, she should have told him the truth. She must have been ashamed – perhaps other people had made her feel ashamed. But by not telling him, Father must have felt betrayed on two counts. One, she had lied to him by omission; two, she wasn't what he had always believed her to be. She had deceived him and he'd never forgive her for that. Even so . . . She knew that was no excuse.

Harriet scrutinised her mother, an elderly woman now, half broken by her losses, by the punishments meted out for the consequences of actions taken so recklessly and carelessly, for that one moment of passion and spontaneity. Nevertheless, Mother had depended on their father. And when she lost him too . . . She had still craved the attention he'd bestowed on her. Because once, she had been put on a pedestal and it had proven a very long distance to fall. Had he ever forgiven her for what she had done? Yes, he had done his duty as her husband, but had he still loved her, still turned to her? Not really. He had – to all intents and purposes – turned to Harriet instead. And perhaps that had been part of her mother's punishment too.

'Poor Mother.' Joanna got to her feet and took their mother in her arms. 'Having to pretend for all these years.'

And poor Father, Harriet thought. Losing his trust in the

woman he loved. Nevertheless . . . how could she forgive him for doing such a thing?

'Did he ever . . . ? Was it . . . ?' Harriet couldn't say the words.

'It was only that one time.' Her mother seemed to know what she was thinking.

'And did you regret it?' Harriet whispered. 'Did you regret giving your baby away?'

Their mother lifted her head. 'Every day of my life,' she said. 'I never thought he'd make contact with me like he has. I didn't think I deserved it. He's a gift.'

No wonder, Harriet thought. *No wonder she can't get enough of him now.*

Harriet reached for her mother's hand. No one deserved to be punished for the rest of their life for one mistake made when they were seventeen. 'I'm so sorry, Mother,' she said. And she was – for all of it.

'Do you know how much I love you?' Their mother smiled sadly. 'Both of you?'

'Yes, Mother.' Joanna hugged her.

Harriet nodded.

'And do you forgive me?' she said. 'Do you understand?'

'Of course we do,' said Joanna. She didn't even have to think about it, Harriet knew. 'But Father . . .' She shuddered and Harriet could see how horrified she was at what Mother had told them.

'Harriet?'

The shutters were open. The band was loosening. Harriet wondered if she'd ever have that dream again. There were other memories – happy memories. She might have to work at them but she'd get there in the end. 'Nothing to forgive,' she said. Mother was who she was. Father too.

439

CHAPTER 58

Nicholas

London

While he was in London, Nicholas met up with Celie for lunch at a Greek restaurant in Muswell Hill. She'd sounded pleased to hear from him.

'Do you want me and Tom, or just me?' she'd asked him on the phone when they arranged the date. 'Either's cool.'

'I'm happy either way,' he told her, which wasn't quite true, but . . . .

'I'll come on my own then – Tom's got things to do.'

'Great.' Nicholas grinned. Father and daughter alone time was always special.

He made it in an hour and found the place easily. The decor was cream and terracotta and Celie had said the food was simple and good. Nicholas was relieved – he was a hungry man.

'Dad! Sorry, sorry.' She flung her arms around his neck when she arrived. She was fifteen minutes late, but he didn't mind. He'd wait for hours if he had to.

'Hi, darling.' Reluctantly, he disentangled himself from her embrace. She smelt of orange blossom. 'How are you?'

'Good, thanks.'

And she looked it. She was wearing jeans – presumably with a stretchy waistline – brown boots and a baggy red sweater. Her dark brown hair was tied into a ponytail with a red ribbon – she didn't look old enough to get married, let alone to be a mother.

Now they were at arm's length she was eyeing him critically. 'But you haven't just got back from Italy.' She frowned. 'Where were you? I called your mobile. I even tried calling you at home.'

'Prague.' He felt guilty now for switching his mobile off. He hadn't wanted to be bothered by Giuseppe asking him about business or Rachel talking about weddings. After what he saw on the Charles Bridge in Prague, he'd wanted to take a bit of time out. He had a decision to make. He hadn't thought that Celie might worry.

'Prague? Was it a work thing?' She settled herself in the chair opposite him.

'No.' He wasn't sure he'd be able to explain exactly what sort of a 'thing' it was.

'Why did you go there then?' Celie was good at cross-examination – she must have inherited the genes from her mother, he thought.

'There were some things I had to check out.' Nicholas decided to keep it vague for now. 'And Prague's too interesting to be rushed. The architecture, the history, the Charles Bridge . . .'

'Hmm.' Celie was half listening, half perusing the menu. Which was fine.

Nicholas picked up his own menu. He decided not to tell

her about Joanna Shepherd – not yet, anyway. And he decided not to tell her about what – or who – he'd seen on the bridge either; she'd think he was cracking up. And perhaps he was . . .

On the flight back from Prague he'd thought about Joanna, and about the woman he'd seen on the bridge. There was bound to be a simple explanation – there always was. And the mind could play tricks – especially if you were tired or run-down. Was he tired or run-down? He hadn't thought so. But he had been dashing around here, there and everywhere lately. He had been feeling . . . well, not right. And that's why he'd made the decision he had. He wanted to do something different for a while. And no one else could change your life – not really. Only you.

They chatted about Celie's work and Tom and compared notes about the trip to Rome. Nicholas felt himself slowly relax, his shoulders drop, his guard fall. Relaxation – how the hell had it got to be so difficult? But he had plans now. Plans that could change all that.

They ordered their food. Celie looked flushed and happy and he was glad. But as they waited for it to arrive, she touched his hand across the table. 'I'm sorry now,' she said, 'that I let Mum railroad me into this silly, double wedding idea.'

'Having second thoughts?'

The waitress brought his beer and Celie's mineral water.

'Not about the wedding.' Briefly, she touched her belly, as if protecting her unborn child from the very thought. 'But about us doing the double act. I mean, it kind of dilutes everything, doesn't it?'

'Hmm.' *Too bloody right*, he thought. Rachel hadn't exactly been putting her daughter first when she suggested it.

'And what about you?'

442

'Me?'

'I don't want to upset you, Dad,' she said. 'Obviously.'

'So, you don't want to do it because of me?' Nicholas wasn't sure how honest to be with her. The last thing he wanted to do was spoil her plans, but on the other hand he really wasn't sure he could do it – stand there and watch another man marry his ex-wife. He was no longer tied to Rachel. But it still seemed wrong somehow.

Celie giggled. 'We're talking about eloping,' she said. 'And besides, what's the point of going to Italy to get married? What's wrong with doing it in a register office here in the UK? Lots of people do.'

Nicholas traced a pattern in the condensation on his glass. He liked this kind of beer when it was very, very cold. 'I expect your mother would tell you what's wrong with it,' he observed. If Celie dared tell her.

Celie nodded glumly. 'She already has. She says it'd be a hole in the corner affair rather than a celebration. She says we'd always regret it and our memories would be tainted.'

Nicholas sighed. Typical Rachel. She'd always had a way with words. And why put a spanner in the works when a JCB digger would do? 'Honey.' He squeezed Celie's hand. 'You and Tom should do it how you want to do it. Never mind what your mother wants. Never mind what I want. I just want you to be happy.'

She smiled at him gratefully. Why did parents put so much pressure on their kids? he wondered. Why did they need them to fulfil all their own dreams? He hoped he hadn't done that with Celie.

The waiter brought their food. It looked good. The salad was crisp and green and the olives plump and black. Celie's halloumi was lightly grilled and the hummus was creamy, drizzled with olive oil and accompanied by whole chickpeas, roasted red peppers and pitta bread.

'Then we'll get married here in London.' Celie was decisive. 'But it will be a celebration. That's what we both want. We'll invite all our friends and have a big party.'

'Sounds great.' Nicholas tucked in. As Celie had promised, it was good. 'Let me know when it's to be and I'll come back for it.'

'Back for it?' Celie looked up sharply. 'You will be here to give me away?'

'Of course. I wouldn't miss it for the world.' Give her away? In reality, she'd already gone. And he hadn't so much given her away as stood still and watched her fly. Still, he was glad that his being there mattered so much to her.

'Good. Because it won't be a double wedding – that wouldn't be right and it wouldn't be fair. And Tom agrees with me.' Celie cut a slice of her halloumi and scooped up some shredded lettuce with her fork.

Good for Tom. Nicholas was hugely relieved. 'Thanks, love,' he said.

Celie put her head to one side and regarded him quizzically. 'Where are you going then, Dad? Where will you be coming back from this time?'

The million-dollar question. Because Nicholas planned to take a sabbatical – he was going to phone Giuseppe about it later, but to tell the truth, he'd already decided, and nothing his business partner could say would make him change his mind. He needed this. He planned to take an extended trip, find some new horizons. He wanted to get away – to continue his journey and find that elusive sense of self he'd let go while he was with

Rachel. Rediscovering his joy of surfing had been an important first step. Now he wanted to take some time out. The place had always been special to him – it still was. 'I was thinking of spending a few months in Fuerteventura,' he said. 'You could visit me.' Celie, after all, had loved it when she was a child.

She raised an eyebrow. 'A holiday?'

'A bit more than that.' He'd worked hard. He no longer had a mortgage or any dependents. He could afford it.

Celie was still watching him. 'Not much to do in Fuerteventura, is there, Dad? Won't you be bored?'

Nicholas thought of the deserted beaches along the west coast that he planned to discover and explore, the fishing that he used to do with his father. He thought of surfing. Of sunshine and tranquillity, of rest and recuperation and how long it might take him to decide what to do with the remainder of his life. He might get lonely without a companion to share the experience with, but he wouldn't get bored. 'No, Celie,' he said. 'I really don't think I will.'

CHAPTER 59

Joanna

Dorset
Three weeks later

It was three days before Christmas and Joanna was in the reference library at Dorchester. She'd spent a lot of time here since she'd returned from London, since that revelatory tea party at Mulberry Farm Cottage where she'd gained a brother and found out so much more about Emmy, and then later an awful lot more about her parents' marriage.

It had been hard to take it all in. Joanna frowned. Henry appeared to have had a much better effect on their mother than anything the doctor could have prescribed. Mother had never got over the loss of her baby, Joanna supposed; she had never stopped grieving for her son, never stopped feeling guilt at having given him away. And now here he was, a grown man who'd had a happy childhood, perhaps the best childhood Mother could have given him under the circumstances, and

446

he'd not only forgiven her, but also wanted her to be part of his life. It had changed everything.

But what about Harriet? At least she had finally lifted the call barring from the phone. Her sister obviously felt that Mother didn't need tradesmen any longer and Joanna suspected she was right. Why would she, when she had Henry? But would Harriet feel usurped by their new half-brother? Joanna suspected so.

She settled herself in the chair and picked up the first book she'd selected earlier. It was different for Joanna. Mulberry Farm Cottage was her childhood home, but she had moved on a long time ago and she would be moving out again very soon. As soon as the house in Crouch End was sold, as soon as she had some money to her name and therefore some security, she would buy a small place somewhere to use as a base. And from that base she would travel, go somewhere different, maybe get down to writing that travel book she had discussed with Toby. The sale was going through. It wouldn't be long, she realised, before she could be gone.

Joanna pulled her reading glasses from her bag and took a swig of water. It had been a shock to find out about Father. She felt a small shiver. A shock that she hadn't yet fully come to terms with. It might have been only the once and he might have had some provocation. But even so . . . How little she had known him, how little she had known both of her parents and what had gone on behind the closed doors of her own home. But again, it would be harder, she suspected, for Harriet.

Joanna turned her attention once more to Emmy. Every spare moment she had, she'd been continuing to try to solve this mystery from the past. Although she now knew Emmy's full name, there was little information about her online – Emmy had not been sufficiently well known to be well documented, and now it seemed as if Joanna had to trawl through five books for every skimpy line of information. She could see, though, how genealogists got sucked into their subjects and their lives. She was utterly engrossed in this love story from the past. There was no holding back.

The notes that she'd accumulated were still sparse, although they had filled in a few of the gaps in her knowledge of the life of Emily Selleck, little-known Edwardian artist. She knew that Emmy's father had encouraged her to paint, and that she had probably been influenced by Clara Montalba who had exhibited from 1866 at the Royal Academy and whose reputation was founded on the delicate tones and refined colours she used, combined with her careful composition.

Joanna could see the similarity – in subject matters too, for Clara Montalba had painted scenes from the Grand Canal in Venice and also London Bridge. Joanna knew that Emmy was not prolific, and that she hadn't sought professional recognition. It had come in her lifetime – just – but thanks to an inheritance from her father, she had the means not to have to rely on an income from painting which, for her and other women like her, would never be high.

The more she read, the more convinced Joanna was that Owen's theory was correct. She knew now that Emmy had indeed lived for a while in Dorset, so she surely must have lived at Owen's farm, next door to Rufus; the painting she had left there of the ancient aqueduct was further evidence of that.

And now, thanks to Owen's generosity, Joanna had two of Emmy's paintings in her possession. She had been overwhelmed when he had shown it to them, even more so when he gave it to her, and now it hung next to the painting of

Ponte Accademia in her bedroom at Mulberry Farm Cottage. Even without the signature, the two pictures were unmistakably by the same artist. Emmy had painted the sky behind the high Gothic-shaped viaduct in shades of yellow and pale grey, contrasting with the charcoal notes of the high stone aqueduct itself, rising like some great creature of the deep from a sea of dark green forest and a burnt-orange sun setting low on the horizon.

But Joanna was conscious of a continuing sense of frustration. Something about this story of illicit love wasn't clear; there was something she still wasn't seeing. Her bridge walks and her quest to find out Emmy and Rufus's story were inextricably linked somehow. But what happened to the two lovers? And why did William Rufus plant a mulberry tree to remind him of Emmy, when she hadn't died? She outlived Rufus and survived to the ripe old age of ninety-six. But . . .

Joanna rifled through her notebook to recap. When she was nineteen, Emmy had stayed with an aunt and uncle in Dorset, to help out when her aunt was taken ill. The village itself wasn't mentioned, but apparently, she stayed on while the aunt was convalescing. She was there for at least a whole summer. Presumably that was when she had met her Rufus. The man next door – as in Pyramus and Thisbe, the story that Owen and Harriet had already discussed together, rather intriguingly. Joanna doodled a heart in the margin in black ink. Her *heart's love*.

And this, she supposed, was the family secret, the reason for that surreptitious look between her father and her uncle. The planting of the mulberry tree, the changing of the name of the cottage, the dangerous liaison of the past.

The library was filled with the studious buzz of silence,

punctured only by the sound of a page being turned, the soft whirr of a computer fan, the occasional muffled cough. Joanna could imagine how it had been . . .

A young girl, pretty maybe, with little to do and far from home. Maybe she was painting already? An attractive man, ten years older than her perhaps, with a sickly and difficult wife. Perhaps it started with a chance meeting, a random conversation; perhaps he saw her painting the landscape and stopped to exchange a few words of greeting. Maybe they realised that they had things in common. Maybe they shared a joke. Perhaps he confided in her about the difficulties and tribulations of his marriage. Maybe there was a spark of chemistry?

Joanna leant back in her chair. Then one day . . . perhaps they went for a walk together. They might have shared a love of literature or art? Maybe, it started to rain. Maybe they ran to a nearby hayloft to take shelter. And then . . . Well, at some stage they had become lovers. But he was married. Their love was illicit, dangerous, forbidden. But it was also as strong as life itself – and that had to count for something.

She checked her watch. She'd love a coffee and knew it would give her a much-needed adrenalin boost. But there were two more books she wanted to check out before she returned to the cottage.

After a while, Emmy would have been summoned home. Her father needed her; he intended to travel to Europe and she was to accompany him. It was a great opportunity: she could do lots of painting, spend time with her father, see some of the most spectacular sights in Europe. She would write to Rufus – every day.

But love couldn't survive on letters alone. Decisions had to be made, something had to change. Joanna took the letters out

450

of her bag, turned them over in her hands. These thin pages smelt of the past too – of wood and dust and some old musty perfume. She had read them so many times that their edges had become even more frayed and brittle. Perhaps Rufus too had read them so many times, before he hid them away in the big trunk in the attic, she thought. Why had he kept them? Couldn't he bear to let this last part of her go?

I wonder what you will decide, Emmy had written. Had he told her that he would part from his wife, that he longed to be with Emmy, that he was prepared to leave his family for her? Was he considering it during their separation whilst Emmy was abroad with her father? Was he planning how it could be done? It was all or nothing. Emmy wouldn't be able to come back to Dorset – she would have to stay with her father. There would be no more meetings, no more chance encounters, or secret walks along the Down. They would have to run away together and face the scandal – or give each other up.

Thoughtfully, Joanna put the letter to one side. She only held one part of their story in these letters of Emmy's. She would never know the other side. Even if Emmy had kept Rufus's letters, they would probably have been lost or destroyed and it seemed that Emmy had never married, never had children, so there would have been no one to care what happened to them. And yet, there was an air of bleakness about Emmy's words that told Joanna everything she wanted to know. Emmy had sensed what would happen. She knew her Rufus and the kind of man he was. She knew he would never be able to leave his sick wife for her – his sense of responsibility and duty were too great. She knew that he would give her up. He had to.

And that's what he must have done. This was the last letter Rufus had received from Emmy and hidden away in the trunk.

When she returned from the trip to Prague, he must have told her
– written to her perhaps – that there was no future for them, that
they must part. And she would have accepted it. What else could
she do? She had always known he was married and had a family.
She knew where his duties and responsibilities lay. She'd always
known the risk she was taking – with her heart. Poor Emmy.

Joanna put the letters carefully back in her bag. Emmy had
been born in 1895 and she died in 1991. 1991 . . . It seemed
so, well, recent. But the dates of her paintings spanned only
the period from 1910 to 1914. What did that mean? That after
Rufus left her, she stopped painting? Or that the paintings after
1914 had never been shown?

Sweetest love, I do not go for weariness of thee . . .

There were no further clues in the letters – Joanna had read
and analysed them endlessly, and while they told her plenty
about Emmy's state of mind and love for Rufus, they didn't tell
her about afterwards. Afterwards must have been an unhappy
time for both of them.

Joanna shifted in her seat. And why was it that she had seen
visions on her bridge walks that seemed to echo Emmy's experiences as well as her own? In Venice, Joanna had been looking
for a place to run to, when she had seen Emmy laughing and
running towards her true love, running towards her destiny.
Only, Rufus hadn't turned out to be her destiny at all . . . In
Lisbon it had all been about love: Joanna's love for her family;
Emmy's love for Rufus, the man by her side as she stood under
the mulberry tree. And in Prague, there had been the need to
escape. The knowledge that love could slip through your fingers, that love also meant pain, and even death. Joanna wasn't
sure how she related to that, and yet she was more convinced
than ever that Emmy was telling her something.

452

And then there was Nicholas Tresillion. Joanna stared out of the library window, seeing nothing. She had emailed him again this morning, telling him about her plans to write a travel book. *Perhaps I'll do a rerun of the Edwardian Grand Tour*, she had written, only half seriously. *How it would have been for women like Emmy and how it is for me*.

Or, the travel book might metamorphose into that novel she'd always dreamt of writing. Who knew? She didn't tell Nicholas that the person whose journey she was following was also an artist. He'd seen a woman with some paints, in Prague, he'd said. Could it possibly be Emmy? Joanna shook her head. That was mad. But all of this was mad, wasn't it?

Where did Nicholas fit in? Who was he? Why was it that he'd had visions that uncannily matched her own? She couldn't think – not even here, in a place designed for thinking. There were so many pieces of the puzzle and they were all floating in the air. Every time she clutched at one and pulled it down to earth, another escaped and floated off again into Never Never Land. She simply couldn't grasp the connections. Only that it all belonged to a pattern.

Had she really seen Emmy, or was she a figment of Joanna's imagination? Was it possible that somehow she was getting privileged glimpses of Emmy's life? Of Emmy running towards her destiny? Of Emmy falling in love? Of Emmy in pain? But why Joanna? Because she had found the letters? Because she was following in Emmy's footsteps? Because she was related to William Rufus?

It made no sense.

Joanna turned to the penultimate book, flipped through the references listed in the index. There was nothing important. Nothing new.

She checked her watch again. She'd have to make a move soon. There were still Christmas preparations to be getting on with back at Mulberry Farm Cottage. This would be her last visit to the reference library and the History Centre too. Joanna was pretty sure she had found out everything she could about Emily Selleck. Maybe it was time to put Emmy and Rufus to rest and concentrate on her next project after all.

She turned to the final book. And what did Rufus do next? After his affair with Emmy was over, he had presumably devoted himself to his wife and family, after planting a mulberry tree and renaming his cottage in memory of their love. A special love. The love of a lifetime. But a love that was never meant to be . . . How had he explained that to his family? There were no photos of him at Mulberry Farm Cottage from this period of his life, though there were plenty of his wife and children. Joanna knew she should be more sympathetic to poor old Edith, the wronged wife, who was an ancestor of hers after all, but despite her own experiences of what had happened with Martin and Hilary, Joanna's empathy belonged firmly to Emmy.

She blinked at the pages listed in the index. She felt a rapid shiver running through her – the kind of shiver she always had when she suddenly realised she was on the verge of a breakthrough. Because here was a whole section devoted to Emily Selleck, Edwardian artist. She could hardly believe it. Greedily, Joanna leafed through the pages. As she found the chapter, she froze. She stared at the top of the page. There was a photograph of Emmy – the first, the only one that she had found.

She traced the features with a fingertip. Long, delicate nose, fair hair coiled on top of her head, earnest-looking eyes. *My God* . . .

Joanna really had seen her. Or at least a vision of her. It had been no figment of her imagination. Once, running in a field. Once, leaning back against the trunk of a mulberry tree. And once, in a paddle steamer going up the River Thames. Looking up at London Bridge and crying. Crying as if her heart would break.

She frowned. If her visions echoed Emmy's life, then what did this mean? If there were no photographs of William Rufus after that time, did that mean he'd died? Was that it? But how? In the war maybe?

Joanna checked her watch. She needed to get to the Dorset Local History Centre to study the microfiche one last time. She still didn't know what was happening here. But she knew she couldn't rest until she found out.

CHAPTER 60

Harriet

Dorset

It was Christmas Eve and Harriet was in Big Barn, unearthing the trestle table in readiness for a Christmas lunch that would include Owen, who had nowhere else to go, of course, and Harriet's new half-brother. From the doorway, she could see her mother and Henry wandering through the orchard. Mother was well wrapped up in a big old fur coat and scarf, her hand tucked into the arm of her prodigal son. In the past weeks, Harriet had watched them get closer and closer. They were walking slowly, heads bent together, still catching up on the major parts of their lives they'd spent apart, she guessed. Harriet was beginning to realise that, like it or not, Henry was now a permanent fixture in their lives.

They were like two peas, Harriet thought. She shifted a stack of chairs that were in the way and started to drag out the trestle. They had enough chairs and tables to accommodate an army; they needed them for the café which would be opening again

456

in a few months. She paused – it was too heavy for her to do it alone. And she watched the way the two of them walked. They shared the same physicality. Henry wasn't frail – he was still only in his fifties after all – and, she chuckled, she knew from chasing him down the lane that he wasn't unfit. But they had the same slender frame and similar gestures too.

'You're needed,' she told the trestle table as she stood, hands on hips, assessing it. Christmas. She'd made the pudding two weeks ago – according to tradition, she'd steamed three bowls in her mother's ancient steamer: one for Christmas, one for Easter and the other for any old high day or holiday. She'd made the cake a few days ago – it was called 'last-minute Christmas cake', which was particularly apt this year, and given it the usual seed and nut glaze rather than the more traditional marzipan and royal icing. She'd collected the turkey this morning, a woodland free-range bird reared by one of Owen's contacts in North Dorset, wrapped the presents and, together with Joanna, had collected the greenery and decorated the tree.

'It seems like a real Christmas again this year,' her sister had said. And although she was rather enjoying having a moan about all the extra work, Harriet had to agree.

She glanced again at Mother and Henry in the orchard as they walked towards her. How much did she mind the togetherness? She wasn't sure. Mother had changed. But arguably for the better. She seemed much happier. And she'd started baking again, helping in the house, showing an interest in the domestic side of things. Perhaps she would even help Harriet in the café in the spring. Perhaps Harriet wouldn't struggle to do it all alone – as she usually did.

It was hard to mind. The trestle table could do with a good clean and polish. Harriet scraped at a particularly stubborn stain with her fingernail. Her mother seemed restored almost by Henry. She dusted away a cobweb. As if part of Mother's life had been returned to her. Harriet tried to imagine what it would feel like – for a child you thought you had lost forever to suddenly appear once again when you'd lost all hope. It must be amazing. It was as if through Henry, Mother had at last found peace. To Harriet's surprise, she blinked away a tear. What was happening to her? There were always, she supposed, so many mixed emotions at Christmas.

Harriet took a scouring cloth and dunked it in the bucket of water she had brought with her for the purpose. She began to scrub the table. Christmas was also a time when funds were at a traditional low, and this year was no exception. Joanna's contributions had helped no end, but there were now two extra mouths to feed and apart from the odd bottle of wine, Henry hadn't made any offers she couldn't refuse. It seemed harder than ever to keep warm in the cottage with all the draughts and lack of insulation. They needed new windows as well as a new roof, and the back door had warped alarmingly in the last few weeks.

Yesterday, Owen had brought round some big terracotta pots and urns to put outside Big Barn and the cottage, ready for the summer's fun and games, as he put it.

'They're lovely.' Harriet had trailed her fingers along the rough terracotta. 'How much do I owe you?'

'Don't be daft.' He hefted them into place as if they weighed nothing. 'They were part of a job lot.'

'Thanks, Owen.'

He straightened. 'I was thinking maybe geraniums.'

'Good idea.' It would give the café more of a continental feel and geraniums would last until October if they were lucky.

Kept in the old greenhouse, they'd survive year after year. Harriet sighed. But would she?

'I'll bring some potting compost round later.' He was watching her appraisingly as if he might say more.

'All right. Thanks, Owen.' She waited, but he just grinned and walked away. What, she wondered, had he been thinking? It had been kind of him to give that painting to Joanna, but she hoped he wasn't holding out any hope that her wayward sister might be harbouring any romantic ideas about him – it seemed most unlikely. After all, Joanna lived in another world most of the time. It had proved to be an interesting world – all that stuff about their ancestor and the girl next door had been quite the revelation – but it wasn't rooted in the reality of life as Harriet knew it.

Mother and Henry were in the farmyard now, chatting and laughing. They shared the same sense of humour too; they seemed to have quickly become inseparable. He was still staying in the holiday let. But how long would it be until he wanted to move in here? Harriet shook her head. He was nice enough, this new brother of theirs. But he'd move in over her dead body. Since Father died, this had been an all-female household, and she planned to keep it that way. Father . . .

Harriet was still trying to come to terms with what she had learnt about her parents' marriage, and more to the point, what she had learnt about her beloved father. In a way, she had always known and so it was something of a relief to let it emerge fully into her consciousness. Her father had been far from perfect – worse, he had been violent towards her mother, the woman he was supposed to care for and love. Even though it had been only the once, even though he had been shocked and disappointed at what he must have seen as her deception, it was still hard to forgive.

And yet Harriet knew she had to forgive him. He meant too much to her and the man she'd known and loved had been a gentle one. Could that man and the man she'd seen with his hands around her mother's throat be one and the same? Something had stopped her seeing it; her love for him had made it impossible for her to consciously acknowledge. But now, she must accept it; she must see him as he truly was, flaws and all.

As for her mother . . . she'd made mistakes too, and been punished for them. Father had consciously excluded Harriet's mother from so much of his life; Harriet supposed he'd never properly forgiven her. But he had still asked Harriet to look after her. He had still cared enough to do that. Harriet pulled the trestle table further out into the barn. What her father had done was very wrong. Nevertheless . . . Harriet sighed. How could she stop loving him?

'Anything I can do to help?'

Harriet realised that her mother had now gone into the cottage and that Henry was standing in the doorway of Big Barn watching her, a look of compassion on his face. How much had Mother told him? Everything, she supposed.

'Oh, thanks.' There was so much, Harriet thought, to get used to. 'Care to give me a hand with this trestle?' she asked. It was a two-man job and no one else was around.

They struggled outside with it and to her surprise, Henry grasped the hand brush from the bucket of cleaning things and started brushing down the legs and the underside of dust, cobwebs and grit that had accumulated in the winter months, since it had been put away. She'd never taken him for a practical man, but then again, what did she know about him, really? She'd hardly spoken to him without Mother being around – until now.

'I never apologised properly,' he said, as they stood regarding one another on either side of the table. 'For allowing you to think you were being followed by some stalker. I really am so sorry, Harriet.'

'That's OK.' Though he had already apologised – several times. But those prowler days seemed far away now. As did the days of dating online. Harriet didn't regret her time on Someone Somewhere and, most especially, she didn't regret meeting Scott. He had definitely changed her life. She had seen what was possible and she had seen what she had, what she was. She supposed she was feeling, if not exactly contented, then at least more accepting of her lot. And besides, for some reason, she didn't feel so lonely anymore.

'And about the typing . . .'

'Yes?' Harriet had been wondering about this. 'Why did you employ me to do that?' After all, she sent the pages back to a PO box; it hadn't involved any personal contact that could have enabled him to get closer to their family.

'When I came here and looked around' – he gestured to the farmyard, the old blue tractor, the hen coop, the barns – 'it all seemed a bit . . .' He hesitated.

'Tired?' Harriet could see it through his eyes. It was tired, she could accept that. Geraniums in Owen's terracotta pots would help, but what they really needed was—

'I wanted to help out a bit financially,' he admitted. 'Without you realising.'

'I see.' Owen kept telling her she was too proud to accept help. *You're not Superwoman*, he'd told her. Little did he know.

461

'And your typing was great,' Henry said, beaming at her. 'Really great.'

'Thanks.' Harriet didn't need to hear any more. She hadn't even got that job by virtue of her typing skills or interview technique. She'd simply been her mother's daughter. 'I'll make us some tea,' she said.

'Lovely.' He smiled. 'But before you do . . .'

What now? The moving-in speech? Already? Harriet eyed him warily.

'Audrey – our mother . . .' He blinked.

'Yes?'

'Well, she's been telling me that things haven't been too easy here.' He put his hands together to form a pyramid, as though this was a problem that could be solved using the correct mathematical equation.

Harriet tried not to feel resentful. He was family now. 'You could say that,' she hedged.

He gazed at her intently. 'I'd like to help if I can,' he said.

'Really?' It would take a lot more than moving a trestle table to do that.

He nodded. 'You see, I've got a fair bit of cash I don't know what to do with,' he said.

Harriet blinked. She wasn't sure she had ever heard anyone say anything like that before.

'I'd love to, er, invest in Mulberry Farm Cottage.' He seemed embarrassed. 'Bring it a bit more up to date. Make things more comfortable.'

'Would you?' Immediately, Harriet was suspicious. What was his game? Was this how he was planning to inveigle his way in? 'And why would you want to do that?'

He shrugged. 'I suppose I'd like our mother to have a good

462

standard of living,' he said. 'Not that I'm suggesting there's anything wrong—'

'I know.' Now wasn't the time for pride. Owen was right.

'I wouldn't expect anything in return,' he assured her. 'I don't need anything. The cottage would remain yours, naturally.'

Harriet wasn't sure what to say to that.

'And you,' he said.

'Me?'

'I'd like to do something to help you.'

Harriet glared at him. Did she look as though she needed his help? 'Why?' she snapped.

'Because you're my sister.'

Yet again, Harriet felt her eyes fill. Angrily, she turned away. All this emotion – she wasn't used to it, and she didn't seem able to deal with it somehow.

Joanna was in the kitchen. The sharp scent of tomatoes, mixed with sweet basil and oregano, filled the air.

Harriet stared at her. 'What are you doing?'

'Making spaghetti Bolognese. For supper.'

'You're making supper?' Harriet looked around the kitchen. She was ready to complain about the amount of washing-up that needed to be done but Joanna appeared to have only used one pan. What was wrong with everyone today? Why were they all being so helpful?

'Anyone would think I can't cook,' Joanna grumbled. 'Or that I don't help out around here.'

Hmm. Well, she had been a touch distracted lately. Harriet checked the living room to ensure that Mother was out of earshot. All clear.

463

'Henry wants to invest in the cottage,' she told Joanna.

'How much?' Her sister continued stirring the sizzling contents of the pan.

'He didn't say,' Harriet admitted. Though it was bound to be a decent amount. She filled the kettle and switched it on. 'Tea?'

'Hmm. Mother reckons he's loaded,' Joanna went on. She slurped a bit of Bolognese sauce from the wooden spoon. 'Ouch.' Fanned her mouth with her hand. 'He's had all sorts of stuff published; he's quite famous in the academic world.'

'Really?' Harriet looked out of the window to where Henry was still struggling with the trestle table.

'And apparently he's had money left to him too. Quite a bit. So he retired early.'

'Hmm.' Lucky old Henry. 'He'll want to move in,' she said gloomily.

'Mother wants him to.'

Harriet spun round to face her. 'What? You mean you've discussed it?' Without her?

Joanna waved the wooden spoon at her. 'And you know what that means, Het?'

'No more privacy?' She splashed in some water to warm the teapot. Took cups and saucers from the ancient dresser and put them on a tray. 'A stranger in our midst? A male stranger to boot?'

Joanna clicked her tongue – a very irritating habit. 'It means, sweet sister of mine, that you're free.'

'Free?' Had she lost her marbles?

Joanna dropped the wooden spoon. Harriet watched, mesmerised, as it sank slowly into the Bolognese sauce like the *Titanic*. 'No more slaving over a hot stove for the café . . .' She turned and grasped Harriet's hands in hers. 'No more growing

464

veg as if your life depended on it. No more having to stay at home to look after Mother.'

'But . . .'

'No more fattening up the pigs for Owen, collecting the eggs from the henhouse, picking the plums from the orchard.'

'But . . .' She'd never seen Joanna so cheerful. At least, not for a long time.

'No pickling and bottling.' Her sister was laughing now, half dancing round the kitchen, dragging Harriet with her. Clearly, she'd gone completely bonkers. 'No more making jam,' she sang. 'No more produce to take to market. No more blackberry picking. You're free!'

'But . . .' It was too much to take in. Didn't Harriet like to do all those things? Wasn't that her life? Still, she laughed. She couldn't help it. Joanna was making her feel like a child again.

'You could go anywhere.' Joanna stopped dancing. She squeezed Harriet's hands more tightly. Her dark eyes were gleaming.

'So . . .'

'So, you could move out of here. You could do some travelling. Or some studying maybe. You could do anything. Anything you wanted.'

Anything she wanted? In a daze, she watched Joanna turn her attention back to the spag Bol. In a daze she made the tea, set two cups aside for Joanna and Mother, poured the milk into a jug and took the tray out to Big Barn.

Anything she wanted? She was thirty-nine years old. She had lived here all her life. What on earth would she do?

CHAPTER 61

Harriet

Dorset

It was Christmas Day. Owen, Henry, Mother, Joanna and Harriet were sitting around the Christmas tree she and Joanna had decorated together and after two glasses of fizz, Harriet was feeling mellow. The vegetables were in the oven, the turkey was resting (finally she knew how it felt) and most of the presents had been exchanged. Joanna had bought her a silk dress in deep purple (*when I am an old woman I shall wear purple*, thought Harriet) which was quite simply the most beautiful dress she had ever seen; Mother had bought her a black cashmere pashmina and Henry had shyly offered an expensive bath and beauty set, the like of which had never graced Harriet's bathroom before.

Harriet had given out home-made candles and chutneys, woollen sweaters for Mother and Joanna, and thick leather gloves for Owen. The baubles of the Christmas tree reflected the white Christmas lights and the greenery she and Joanna had

466

gathered from the lane smelt green and earthy. Joanna had balanced precariously on the frosty bank of grass and stretched up to cut the sprays of holly with the brightest red berries, while Harriet held her around the waist for balance. They had both ended up with sore pricked fingers but it had been worth it. She couldn't remember the last time she had laughed so much. And when she opened her sister's present, her eyes filled and she was lost for words.

She caught Joanna's eye. 'Perhaps you should put it on, Het,' her sister said.

'Oh, it's far too glamorous.' But Harriet eyed it with longing.

'I agree with Joanna.' Owen eyed Harriet steadily. 'Why not put it on? It's very warm in here. And it is Christmas Day.'

'Well . . .' She couldn't deny that. Harriet couldn't help noticing that Owen was looking rather dapper. He was wearing a blue shirt that brought out the blue of his eyes and instead of his usual jeans, pale dove-grey trousers and polished soft-leather shoes. In fact, he looked so different from usual she couldn't keep her eyes off him. He'd probably made the effort for Joanna. Had her sister noticed? Harriet wasn't sure that she had.

'And you also have your pashmina to keep you warm,' her mother added.

'Thanks, Mother.' Harriet held the wool against her cheek. 'So soft,' she said. 'But what about the lunch?'

'I'll do the greasy bits.' Joanna laughed. 'And isn't that why someone invented aprons?'

So, Harriet went upstairs to change. She held the dress up in front of her and felt its delicate folds shiver against her legs. It was delicious. She would try it on at least and then . . .

She slipped the purple silk dress over her shoulders, wriggled

467

a bit and regarded herself in the mirror. It fitted her perfectly. It flowed. The dress lent her a sort of sophistication – something Joanna possessed that she'd always envied. Was it so easy then? Was it simply a matter of a new dress?

Harriet was a bit surprised that there had been no gift from Owen – especially after he'd made the grand gesture of giving Joanna that painting. Of course, he was just a neighbour, but he had become a friend and she fully recognised that now. She had started to enjoy their conversations instead of trying to avoid him or palm him off with Mother and perhaps that was why she was feeling a lot less lonely these days. Still . . . Owen had given Mother a lovely hamper of food and wine – which was both practical but also a great treat – so she supposed the gift had been meant for them both, to thank them for the meals they'd cooked for him, no doubt. But there had been nothing personal and this put a shadow on the day somehow.

Harriet went back downstairs, feeling more than a little self-conscious. Joanna and Owen were in the kitchen whispering about something. Harriet frowned. More secrets? Now that she could do without.

'Wow.' Joanna voiced approval. 'Het, you look gorgeous. Give us a twirl.'

Embarrassed, Harriet let out a laugh that turned into a cough and then back into a laugh again. She clearly hadn't gained an iota of poise or sophistication after all.

Owen was staring at her. 'You look beautiful,' he murmured.

Oh, honestly . . .

'And this is for you.' He handed her a small package wrapped in silver paper.

As Harriet took it, she was half aware of Joanna scuttling

468

out of the room. 'Just got to . . .' The rest of the sentence was muffled and indistinct.

'Thank you.' So, he hadn't forgotten her after all. Harriet untied the clumsily wrapped package, opened the lilac-coloured box. For some reason it was becoming difficult to breathe. On a nest of white netting lay a gold locket and chain, the front of it bevelled and engraved with . . .

She took it out. It settled into her palm, heavy and satisfying. 'It's lovely.' It was more than lovely. It was too much. Much too much.

'There're no pictures in it,' he said. 'Yet. That's for you to decide.'

It opened with a click between her fingers. There was room for two pictures, one on either side of the locket. She shut it again, traced the engraving with her fingertip. Of course. She smiled. 'It's a mulberry tree.'

He smiled back at her. 'Do you like it?'

Like it? She closed her fingers around it, reached up to kiss his cheek. He smelt different too – of crisp male cologne, of lemon and spice. 'I love it.'

And she took his hand and pressed the locket into his palm, turning so that he could fasten it in place around her neck.

Later, much later, after they had eaten and drunk much more than they probably should, after Christmas telly and charades, after Mother had fallen asleep twice and then woken up again with a start to find them all still laughing and chatting, as if they'd always got on like a house on fire, it was time for the day to end.

'I'd best be getting back,' Owen said.

'Lucky you only live next door,' Joanna teased.

Harriet looked at her watch. It was past midnight and she thought it had been the best Christmas Day ever. Since her father's death she'd imagined that no Christmas could ever be the same without him. But now . . .

Owen was standing beside her and she got to her feet, feeling awkward once again.

'I'll see you out,' she said.

He nodded.

She took off the paper hat that she'd only just realised she was still wearing, wrapped herself in her new pashmina and at the last minute threw her waterproof winter parka on top. Owen smiled. But Harriet didn't want the evening to end quite yet and she sensed that Owen felt the same.

Sure enough, he drew her arm through his and without speaking, slowly, they strolled down to the mulberry tree and the pond.

The farmyard was almost silent and the moon was almost full, but not quite, Harriet realised, not quite. As they moved apart, she fingered the locket around her neck. 'This is so special, Owen,' she said. She wanted to thank him again, but right at this moment she didn't have the words.

He gave her a look. 'The locket?' he asked. 'Or the night?'

'Both.' She couldn't repress a small shiver.

He moved closer. 'I suppose you know that it's a love token,' he said.

Love? Harriet didn't know what to say. *Love?* 'The locket or the night?' she asked.

He seemed very serious now. 'Both.'

Harriet gazed down. The moonlight was shining on the surface of the pond. An occasional arrow of gold wove through the water – the fish weren't sleeping either. Above Owen and Harriet the overhanging boughs of the mulberry tree hung: dense, heavy and waiting. *Love?* But what about Joanna? Harriet realised that she'd been completely wrong about Joanna – in oh, so many ways.

'Owen, I thought—'

'I'd give up the farm,' he said. 'If you wanted to start afresh someplace else.'

'You'd give up the farm?' Harriet hugged her arms around her chest. But he belonged here, didn't he?

'It's only a place,' he said. 'Not so important in the scheme of things.'

Harriet shook her head. It was important. It was part of what made him who he was. She'd railed against Warren Down and Mulberry Farm Cottage and the life she'd had here for so long that it had become a habit. But now that she had the choice, now that she could leave if she wanted to, she found that . . .

'No,' she said.

'No?'

'No.' She didn't want to lose any of it. Which was confusing, very confusing. But the truth was – just as her father had always known, she guessed – that Harriet belonged to this place too. She always had and she always would, despite everything she had now discovered. Yes, in the past, she'd been given no choice. But now that she had a choice, there was no place she'd rather be. Simple. This place was as familiar to her as her own skin. Because it was her skin; it was part of her.

'If you won't have me,' he said. 'I'll be going somewhere else anyhow. I won't be sticking around any longer.'

'Oh.' Harriet tried to imagine Warren Down without Owen. And failed. And as he stood there in front of her, she became

471

aware of something she'd never noticed before. Or maybe she had noticed, but had dismissed it.

He was a big man, of course, six feet two inches in his socks. And bulky. Inside the cottage he had always looked too big for their kitchen. He was ungainly, she had thought. A typical farmer. But she'd been wrong. He was no more a typical farmer than her father had been. What was a typical farmer anyway? She thought of what Owen had said to her about the mulberry tree and Shakespeare, what she now knew of his background. Outside, working in the fields, tending the pigs and the sheep, chopping wood, he was different. He was rooted to the land, she realised, sure of his ground, part of this landscape, his landscape. Not ungainly at all.

It was a revelation. He was a revelation. She hadn't really seen him before. He was solid, that's what he was. Her gaze took in the broad shoulders, the brown weathered skin. Every male inch of him. His body was so substantial. So real. And . . .

She reached out to touch his arm. He hadn't bothered to put on a coat. The blue shirt was soft, but his arm was hard, the flesh firm, the muscles taut. It was a body you could depend on. She moved closer. Under the lemon and spice cologne, she thought she could smell the scent of farmyards, rich, grassy and sweet. She breathed deeply. It was a body you could lean against, lean into. And he wouldn't give way. She put her hands on his chest. Pushed gently.

'What?' He was watching her, smiling.

'You're immovable.'

'Don't you believe it.' He took her hands in his. 'You move me. You always have.'

'But love . . .' she said. She rested her head against his shoulder. It felt good, felt as if that was where it should be,

472

where it should stay. She thought of the others – Jamie and the disasters that had followed when she was young. She thought of the long years of getting older and crosser. She thought of the Someone Somewhere dating site, the men she had met, and she thought of Scott. Mmm. But not *mmm* because of Scott, just *mmm* at the thought of lovemaking. The kind where love was the most important thing.

And all the time, Owen was there. Here. Solid, reliable, trustworthy. A rock. But she hadn't seen.

'Love,' he said decisively. With his fingers he tipped back her chin so that she was looking straight at him.

'For how long?' she whispered. Their lips were very close. And in a moment, he might kiss her. This was doing something with her life, she realised. This was what it was all about.

'Forever,' he said.

That was a long, long time. 'I never knew,' she said. But in a funny sort of way, she had.

CHAPTER 62

Joanna

New Year's Eve

Joanna was enjoying the drive. Although it was still cold, the sky was an edgy winter blue and the sun hazy in the sky. She was wearing a warm coat and scarf, so she put the soft top down on the Mazda, and her music on shuffle. She checked her mirror, indicated, moved into the fast lane.

'*Born to be wild . . .*' she sang. Well, not wild perhaps, but at least free. Free to do what she wanted – within reason; free of guilt at leaving Mother and Harriet behind in Dorset – thanks to Henry who was more than happy to take over where she and Harriet left off. But Mother seemed to have regained the joy in her days – the losses she'd been mourning: of a son she'd never known, of a husband who had never fully forgiven her earlier transgressions, of the attention that could make her forget just how much she had given up . . . Tradesmen therapy indeed. Joanna chuckled. All seemed to have faded in the light of that son having come back into her life.

Joanna thought back to what she had discovered in the Dorset History Centre just before Christmas. She'd had a hunch – well, it was more than a hunch. She kept seeing that face, those tears – Emmy in the paddle steamer travelling up the Thames and looking up towards Waterloo Bridge. And she remembered the dark family secret. Supposing it wasn't the liaison between Emmy and Rufus that was the secret? Supposing it was something else?

She'd asked the research assistant at the Centre if she could see the microfiches for local newspaper records and she handed over the card that had been given to her on her first visit. Emmy's last known painting dated from 1913 – a year before war broke out. Would Rufus have gone to war? Could that explain why there were no photographs of him with his wife and children after those early ones when the children were young?

Maybe, but she wasn't so sure. Joanna inserted the first microfiche into the machine. She had another theory. She'd assumed he had ended the relationship because of Emmy's bleak last letter and the decision she'd implied Rufus was about to make. But . . . supposing he'd regretted that decision; bitterly regretted it? Supposing he couldn't imagine life without her? Or . . . And this had made her stop in her tracks and stare unseeing at the screen. Supposing Emmy had been the one who made the decision – knowing that she couldn't take her lover away from his wife and family and live with herself afterwards? Supposing Emmy had broken it off?

> *Sweetest love I do not go*
> *For weariness of thee,*
> *Nor in hope the world can show*
> *A fitter love for me . . .*

This made perfect sense and somehow Joanna knew she was right. Emmy had ended it. Rufus was heartbroken and planted the mulberry tree in memory of their love. He'd even changed the name of the cottage he lived in. But it wasn't enough, was it? The truth was, he couldn't go on without her.

Three hours later Joanna found what she was looking for. *Local landowner at the centre of scandal and mystery*, she read. It was him. *William Shepherd*. Rufus. She scanned the column. And yes, it had been as she'd imagined, exactly as she had seen.

A shiver ran down her back. John of Nepomuk. He had replayed it for her. But how could she have seen? Unless she was there – in that time. Or they were here – in her time. Or time . . . well, or time didn't run on in quite the way she'd always thought. It was all so confusing. She thought of the sands of time, the shape of Emmy's journey, that hourglass that she had first noticed when she'd had the idea of following in Emmy's footsteps for the bridge walks. Was that a coincidence too? Or was it a touch of magic?

Joanna took the microfiches back to the research assistant. She was ready now. Ready to visit Emmy's grave. For some reason, she'd been directed along this path. Fate or some spirit guide or a force she didn't understand . . . Someone had brought her to this point. The least she could do was visit the place where Emmy had lived, lay flowers on her gravestone.

And that was where she was heading now.

Because Joanna knew what had happened to Rufus. And she knew that what she'd seen in London – Emmy sobbing her heart out as she travelled up the River Thames in a paddle steamer – had been Emmy's pilgrimage to mourn her dead lover. In fact, Joanna knew the whole story. She had, in some way, been shown it all – in Venice, Lisbon and Prague. The only things that she didn't understand were why and how. Joanna was, though, a descendant of William Rufus. And she was certain that this meant she had a part to play. Perhaps because Emmy didn't want their love to die?

Joanna hummed and sang along to her playlist as the winter countryside, the honey and thatch of Devon flashed past. She thought of Harriet and Owen and smiled. She'd seen them outside in the moonlight on Christmas night standing under the mulberry tree, his arm around her sister as if he meant never to let her go, Harriet's head resting on his shoulder as if she was quite happy about that. It was about time.

Joanna had always guessed that Owen was in love with her sister – why else would he have done so much to help their family? He was a kind man but what he had done was way over the call of a dutiful neighbour. Harriet, though – sometimes her sister couldn't see what was right in front of her.

Things were beginning to assume a twist of synchronicity that was pleasing. Joanna eased the MX-5 back into the middle lane. It seemed pretty safe to assume that at some point in the future, Henry would be moving into Mulberry Farm Cottage and Harriet would be moving next door. Sorted.

The music changed. The Cure. Ah, now this would be on Joanna's Desert Island Discs. 'Just Like Heaven'. She accelerated – the Cure always got her that way. Joanna hadn't yet decided where she was going to make her base. It needed to be somewhere tranquil where she had the space to think and she needed to be able to get to London and airports too. It might be Dorset. Somehow, Joanna knew that she and Harriet would become even closer now. So much had been laid bare over the past few weeks, so much resolved between them. They'd

477

probably always clash. Neither of them had had personality transplants. But beneath the clashes would be understanding, sisterhood, love.

She let her shoulders relax. She even understood a bit more about her relationship with her father now. Joanna must have reminded him of his wife – often somewhere else in her head, always hard to pin down. Whereas Harriet . . . Harriet was serious and loyal and would follow him to the end of the earth, no questions asked. Harriet, his older daughter, belonged to him completely. She would never let him down. She never had.

There was a high mist now on the hills – one of those shimmering, winter mists that made the landscape seem almost other-worldly. As she drove, Joanna noted the way the light was creeping under the mist, seeping and spreading over the hilltops in front of her, turning the grey into silver as if with the touch of a magic wand. She could understand why artists liked to come here to paint and maybe Emmy had been inspired by living here too? The quality of the light was unique.

The song ended on a wistful note. But Joanna felt hopeful. What would she find when she reached her destination? Just a gravestone, or something more besides? It felt like a pilgrimage. In the bag on the passenger seat beside her she had Emmy's letters tucked into a small metal box. She had thought carefully about this, and decided that she wanted Emmy to be reunited with them at last. Emmy had brought so much to Joanna's life – not only a new way of seeing; she had helped Joanna discover the part of herself she had lost. In the end, she supposed, you might find the magic anywhere. A place or a person might light the blue touchpaper that turned to a flame. That's how it seemed. But perhaps, all the time, the spark of the magic was inside you. Just waiting for the moment.

478

There were banks of rough granite and dry-stone walls visible now, as the landscape changed again. She could see open fields too and a wind farm on a distant hill. She drove on towards them. Maybe she'd never find out more about Emmy, maybe this truly was the end of the journey. But in some ways, despite the winter air that was cool on her face, despite the fact that this year was soon to end, Joanna's journey felt more like a beginning.

A couple of hours later – including a break for a sandwich for lunch – and she was there.

She found the village easily and spotted the pretty weathered stone church with four spires which stood next to the church hall. She parked the Mazda, got out and walked through the black, wooden gate. There were graves to both sides of the path, a few scrappy winter wild flowers sprinkled in the long grass and undergrowth. Where to begin? The wind was sighing through the trees and Joanna was conscious of a feeling of desolation that made her shiver.

There was a little porch with hydrangea bushes guarding the entrance of the church and a small bench. A notice on the old wooden door cautioned people to shut it in order to prevent swallows getting trapped in the church. And up in the beams above the porch she thought she could see where they were nesting. Back in the graveyard, she peered at the names on the gravestones, some of them barely legible. But no Emily Selleck.

It took her ten minutes to find Emmy's gravestone, which was half hidden, tucked in the corner round the side of the church. She ducked under the tree beside it, ran her fingers over the headstone, tracing out the lettering . . . *Emily Selleck 1895–1991, kind and beloved, may she sleep in peace*. Who were her beloved, Joanna wondered? Did they know anything of Emmy's story? She hadn't married – Selleck was her maiden name. But she must have had family and friends here in this village where she'd lived most of her life. There were flowers on her grave, wilting now and past their best. Someone had laid them. So perhaps after all, Emmy had descendants of her own.

She cleared her throat. 'I want you to know,' she said, 'that Rufus kept your letters.' She tucked the little box gently under the gravestone, where the gravel and the worn grass seemed to be making a hollow for it. She pushed the gravel closer around it so that it was nestling and secure. 'And he planted a tree for you – a mulberry tree. You know what that means . . .' She would know, wouldn't she? 'And he renamed the cottage where he lived. For you. He cared' – her voice broke – 'very much, Emmy.'

Joanna was relieved the place was deserted. She took a step back. That was it then. But . . . she was conscious of a feeling of anti-climax. As if once again she was missing something. As if there must be more.

CHAPTER 63

Nicholas

Cornwall

Nothing had changed at Godrevy. Nicholas wandered from room to room, cleared up a few clothes he'd tossed on the bed in his hurry to be gone, washed up a solitary coffee cup, got some meat out of the freezer for later.

Giuseppe had been surprisingly compliant about him taking some time out. 'I can do the travelling around for a while, Nico,' he said. 'You deserve a break.' The words *after all you've been through* hovered unsaid in the air.

'Cheers.' Nicholas almost said at this point, *What if I choose not to come back?* But he didn't say it – why cause unnecessary anxiety? Why not take each day at a time? And he knew he would come back to Godrevy – the landscape he loved.

In the garden, he performed the usual ritual. Walked to the end and looked out over the dunes. Checked on the flowers and shrubs, mostly dormant at this time of year. He picked a few bits and pieces of yellow winter jasmine, fern and white

Christmas rose and formed them into a rough bunch. He'd neglected her of late.

He went back through the cottage and out into the front. Would his aunt approve of his new plan? He thought so. They'd always been close and he'd spent so much of his time here when he was young . . . He was the one who had sorted out her things after she died; he still had a trunk of papers, letters, photographs, that sort of thing. And one of her paintings, of course. Nicholas valued all her memories.

He crossed the road to the church. There was a jaunty-looking sports car parked outside, which was unusual. Nicholas looked around; someone visiting the church, he supposed. It meant a lot to him to live so close to his aunt's grave – he'd miss that while he was gone.

She'd had a sad life, Aunt Emily. She'd never married. She'd told him once that there was a man – her heart's love, she called him, but he was married and therefore unavailable. 'He killed himself, Nicholas, my dear,' she'd told him one day when Nicholas had asked about him. She said it, quite starkly, almost matter-of-factly, as if over the years she'd managed to anaesthetise herself against the pain.

But Nicholas knew that this wasn't the case – he could see it still lingering in her eyes.

'He jumped into the River Thames. From Waterloo Bridge. He couldn't imagine a life where the two of us weren't together, you see.'

Nicholas thought of his aunt's last painting. She'd painted the Charles Bridge in Prague and it was one of the reasons why Prague had long been on his bucket list. The statue in the foreground was St John of Nepomuk with his sad, bewildered eyes, the dog sitting at his feet, golden stars clustered around the saint's cocked head, shooting up towards the darkening sky.

The painting hung in his bedroom here at Godrevy on the white wall. A stark reminder, he thought, of what could happen when you fell in love. But it didn't always have to be like that, did it? Sometimes there could be a happy ending.

It was a strange coincidence that Joanna Shepherd should have written about the Charles Bridge, even stranger that he should see a vision of his aunt with her paints and easel sitting by the bridge that day, painting the exact picture that now hung on his wall. But why not? Aunt Emily had been on his mind. He wasn't sure even now if her creativity had burnt itself out so young, or if the death of this man that she loved had made it impossible for her to go on, impossible for her to pick up a paintbrush ever again. Whatever, it was a bloody waste. Love affair? It must have been something special.

As he walked through the church gates, he saw a woman leaving the graveyard, walking down the path towards him. Tall, slim, well dressed, a stranger; he glanced at her briefly and nodded hello, only half seeing her, concentrating on his aunt and the job in hand.

At the grave, he laid down the flowers. But beside the headstone was another offering – a sprig from a tree, in leaf. He wasn't sure what kind of tree. He picked it up. Touched the glossy leaves. Remembered Lisbon. Of course. A mulberry tree. Some kind of knowledge hung, almost tangible, in the air.

There was a small metal box tucked beside the gravestone too. Nicholas frowned. He opened it. Inside, were some letters tied with black ribbon. He took one and read the first few lines. The letter had been written from Venice.

Nicholas glanced back towards the road. The woman was

483

leaning on the car. She looked deep in thought. She looked . . .
Bloody hell.

'Hey!' he shouted.

She glanced up, questioning.

Nicholas couldn't believe it. But suddenly, everything was slotting into place. 'Hang on there a minute.'

He ran towards her, quickly, before she could open the car door, before she could drive away. He was still holding the small bundle of letters in his hand. 'Joanna?'

She was going nowhere. She seemed to be waiting. 'Yes?' she said.

She looked down at the letters he held. She frowned and then he saw the understanding appear on her face. Her eyes were the colour of horse chestnuts in the autumn. Her smile was the best thing he'd ever seen.

'Nicholas?' she said. 'Nicholas Tresillion?'

'Yes,' he said. He took a step closer. 'The very same.'

ACKNOWLEDGEMENTS

Thanks as always to the wonderful team at Quercus who make it happen over and over. First and foremost, Stefanie Bierwerth, a superb editor who always understands what I'm trying to do and helps me do it better. Always encouraging, always constructive, always right . . . Special thanks this time to Milly Reid who is the most brilliant publicist. I'd also like to thank Jon Butler, Rachel Neely, Laura McKerrell and everyone else at Quercus who has worked on this book.

Thanks to my agent, Laura Longrigg of MBA, for her friendship, her experienced eye and unflinching support – I am very fortunate to have her on my side. Thanks also to Louisa Pritchard of Louisa Pritchard Associates for her work with MBA and markets and publishers overseas. And to Lorraine Green for a sensitive and incredibly helpful copy-edit.

This book has been evolving for a long time (twelve years!). Because of that, not all my research and travelling was done in the past year or so and so I have sadly lost track of some of my sources. It also means that sincere and grateful thanks are due to Teresa Chris of the Teresa Chris Literary Agency for believing in the original story all those years ago.

All of the characters are entirely fictitious and any mistakes in my research are, as always, my own. I have taken a few liberties with the geography of West Dorset, especially Bridport and Eype, but the places are mostly true to reality, although some names have been changed. It's many years since I first visited and fell in love with West Dorset but it's a landscape that remains as inspirational for me as ever.

Thanks to my family for their love and support. You are the best. Thank you, Grey, for Nicholas Tresillion, Harriet's pick-up truck, El Cotillo and surfing, which all feature in this novel. I love you for finding Harriet funny and for not minding too much when I spend so long in another world . . .

Thanks to friends and fellow writers for their unflagging support and friendship. There are so many of you and you are all brilliant but this time I'm singling out Wendy Tomlins, June Tate, Laura James, Darren Northeast and Linda Hill for an extra-big thank you. Thanks to Alan Fish for helping me (way back in the day) with the description of Harriet chopping wood. To John at Abbotsbury for a version of himself, and to Jackie Harvey for the Wasp – her bright yellow MX-5 (ah, those happy memories of tutoring writing groups in West Sussex!).

Thanks also to writers in the groups I meet with now – in the RNA, in Andalusia at Finca el Cerrillo on my writing holiday (ah, bliss . . .) and in the Dorset Writers' Network (thanks for your support and the workshops) – and most especially a big thank you to fellow Dorset writers Maria Donovan and Gail Aldwin in my writing group. Maria gave up a lot of her time to give me extra feedback on this novel and I very much appreciate that.

Thanks to all the writers who I love reading (too many to mention!) for being fabulous authors. To the libraries who have supported my books and who are so vital in our communities in very many ways. And to all the dedicated and enthusiastic bloggers and reviewers who have read and reviewed my books – where would we authors be without you?

And finally, thanks to the readers – you're the most important, after all . . .

Rosanna Ley

Rosannaley.com
@RosannaLey
@RosannaLeyNovels